MW00830708

FRIENDS INDEED

IN THIS SERIES BY DAVID WEBER

The Star Kingdom:
A Beautiful Friendship
Fire Season, with Jane Lindskold
Treecat Wars, with Jane Lindskold
A New Clan, with Jane Lindskold
Friends Indeed, with Jane Lindskold

Honor Harrington:
On Basilisk Station
The Honor of the Queen
The Short Victorious War
Field of Dishonor
Flag in Exile
Honor Among Enemies
In Enemy Hands
Echoes of Honor
Ashes of Victory
War of Honor
At All Costs
Mission of Honor
A Rising Thunder
Uncompromising Honor

Crown of Slaves:
Crown of Slaves, with Eric Flint
Torch of Freedom, with Eric Flint
Cauldron of Ghosts, with Eric Flint
To End in Fire, with Eric Flint

The Saganami Island:
The Shadow of Saganami
Storm from the Shadows
Shadow of Freedom
Shadow of Victory

Expanded Honor: *Toll of Honor*

Manticore Ascendant:
A Call to Duty, with Timothy Zahn
A Call to Arms, with Timothy Zahn & Thomas Pope
A Call to Vengeance, with Timothy Zahn & Thomas Pope
A Call to Insurrection, with Timothy Zahn & Thomas Pope

Worlds of Honor, edited by David Weber:
More than Honor
Worlds of Honor
Changer of Worlds
The Service of the Sword
In Fire Forged
Beginnings
What Price Victory?

House of Steel: The Honorverse Companion, with BuNine

For a complete listing of Baen titles by David Weber, and to purchase any of these titles in e-book form, please go to www.baen.com.

FRIENDS INDEED

A Star Kingdom Novel

DAVID WEBER & JANE LINDSKOLD

BAEN

FRIENDS INDEED

This is a work of fiction. All the characters and events portrayed in this book are fictional, and any resemblance to real people or incidents is purely coincidental.

Copyright © 2025 by Words of Weber, Inc. & Obsidian Tiger, Inc.

All rights reserved, including the right to reproduce this book or portions thereof in any form.

A Baen Books Original

Baen Publishing Enterprises
P.O. Box 1403
Riverdale, NY 10471
www.baen.com

ISBN: 978-1-6680-7245-5

Cover art by Bob Eggleton

First printing, March 2025

Distributed by Simon & Schuster
1230 Avenue of the Americas
New York, NY 10020

Library of Congress Cataloging-in-Publication Data

Names: Weber, David, 1952– author. | Lindskold, Jane M., author.
Title: Friends indeed / David Weber, Jane Lindskold.
Description: Riverdale, NY : Baen, 2025. | Series: The star kingdom ; 5 |
    Audience term: Teenagers | Summary: Stephanie Harrington, now almost 17,
    is the treecats' greatest champion, and with talk of them being sapient,
    she is aware they and the whole planet Sphinx may be caught up in a
    great conspiracy.
Identifiers: LCCN 2024050622 (print) | LCCN 2024050623 (ebook) | ISBN
    9781668072455 (hardcover) | ISBN 9781964856018 (ebook)
Subjects: CYAC: Science fiction. | Human-animal communication—Fiction. |
    Human-animal relationships—Fiction. | Space colonies—Fiction. | LCGFT:
    Science fiction. | Novels.
Classification: LCC PZ7.W38747 Fr 2025 (print) | LCC PZ7.W38747 (ebook) |
    DDC [Fic]—dc23
LC record available at https://lccn.loc.gov/2024050622
LC ebook record available at https://lccn.loc.gov/2024050623

10   9   8   7   6   5   4   3   2   1

Printed in the United States of America

AUTHORS' NOTE

The Star Kingdom novels and the world of Stephanie Harrington are part of a much larger literary universe. The Honorverse, as it's come to be called, consists (so far) of well over twenty-five novels and seven anthologies of shorter fiction. Most of those other works occur chronologically long after Stephanie Harrington's time, although she makes cameos in several of them as a historical figure and the direct ancestor of Honor Stephanie Harrington, the central character from which the Honorverse takes its name.

The collaborative novels of the "Manticore Ascendant" series, by David, Tom Pope, and Tim Zahn, are set very shortly after Stephanie's day. Most of the rest occur several centuries later and have no direct bearing on the Star Kingdom series. Readers who have read those other novels will find the stories about Stephanie and her friends filling in a lot of essential foundation on how the relationship between humans and treecats ultimately evolves, but for the most part, no one needs to read them to appreciate and enjoy the Star Kingdom books.

There are, however, short stories in some of the anthologies which are contemporary to or even predate Stephanie's adventures, including two novellas by David which form quite a bit of *A Beautiful Friendship* and *A New Clan*. There are others which provide additional background, of which the characters in the novels are aware that readers who haven't read the short stories may miss. So, we thought it would be a good idea to provide a list of all the short stories which precede or take place simultaneously with the Star Kingdom novels.

They are:

"A Beautiful Friendship," set in 1518 PD,
    included in *More Than Honor* (1998)

"Honorverse Tech Bu9," set in 1519 PD,
    included in *Free Stories 2011*

"The Stray," set in 1520 PD,
    included in *Worlds of Honor* (1999)

"Deception on Gryphon," set in 1520 PD,
    included in *What Price Victory?* (2023)

"Heart of Stone," set in 1522 PD,
    included in *Give Me LibertyCon* (2020)

We hope that those of our readers who look up the stories we've listed above will enjoy some of the other stories in those anthologies, of course. We're happy and gratified that you've come with us this far in Stephanie's adventures, but we'd like to think we might have tempted you into poking a little further into the rest of the Honorverse, as well.

Happy reading!

FRIENDS INDEED

PROLOGUE

"I MUST SAY THIS IS . . . AN UNEXPECTED SURPRISE,"
Duncan Harrington said as the well-dressed man stepped
into his office. Then he smiled. "On the other hand, I
don't suppose it could *be* a surprise if I'd been expecting
it, now could it?"

"No, I suppose not," the other man said as he crossed
the comfortably cluttered office. Duncan stood, extending
his hand across his desk, then waved to the comfortable chair in front of it. The visitor seated himself and
looked around.

"I swear, Duncan, you've added at least two more
layers since the last time I was here. What *is* it about
you and hard copy books? Photons pack an awful lot
tighter—and neater—than this."

He waved one hand, indicating the old-fashioned,
over-packed bookshelves, and Duncan chuckled.

"Look, I'll admit e-books are a lot more convenient.
Like you say, they pack tighter, and you can find things

in them a lot faster, for that matter. But that's sort of the point. I enjoy the hunt and the thrill of the chase as much as I enjoy pulling down my prey at the end of the safari. Besides, some of these"—it was his turn to wave at the bookshelves—"are so old I probably couldn't find them in an electronic format even if I tried!"

"Well, I'm afraid you'll have to put them into storage for a while," the other man said in a more serious tone, and Duncan straightened in his own chair.

"I will?" He cocked his head. "Why would that be, Abner?"

"Because something needs looking into, and you're the best man for the job, for several reasons. I know it'll be inconvenient, but we've come up with a pretty fair cover—who you are and what you do for a living helped a lot there. And besides," he smiled, "I think you'll enjoy the trip."

"What trip?"

"The one to visit your cousin Richard in Manticore."

"Excuse me?" Duncan blinked, but his guest only looked at him with that same smile.

"I thought the decision had been made to let that part of the line go," Duncan said after a moment. "And, to be honest, I still think that's the right choice in his case. For that matter, if we were ever going to tell him, we should've done it before he and Marjorie left Meyerdahl."

"I didn't say we were sending you to *recruit* him, Duncan." The other man shook his head. "The truth is, the selection committee agreed with your recommendation at the time, and we haven't changed our minds since. It's a pity, since he's at least as smart as you are, but there's not much question you were right about how he'd have reacted if the Alignment approached him."

"I'm relieved to hear that," Duncan said. "Believe me, nobody could have wished he'd been a more...receptive candidate more than I did, but he never could have accepted such an enormous breach of the Beowulf Code. That was his mother in him, I'm afraid. Aunt Gabriella was downright fanatical about that."

"And it didn't help that the selection group had bypassed his father, either." The other man nodded. "Your evaluation weighed in the decision, Duncan, but it wasn't the decisive factor. The assessors agreed completely with you."

"Then why am I going to visit him?" Duncan asked dryly. "I'm assuming the Powers That Be can come up with a reasonable pretext, but clearing it with the University won't be a trivial challenge. You do realize that, don't you? They're not real crazy about letting their department chairs go haring off across the galaxy just to visit family."

"It won't be a problem with the University," the other man assured him. "I'm meeting with Chancellor Atwell after you and I are finished—officially, this is just me dropping in on an old friend on my way to my appointment with him—but that's for the public record. The truth is, we've already planted the seed, and Atwell's ready to grab the proposal and run with it as soon as we officially drop the credit."

"So the Foundation's fronting for this?"

"In a manner of speaking." Abner Portnoy sat on the Board of Directors of the Prometheus Foundation, whose charter to constantly push the bounds of human knowledge was an excellent cover for his real purpose in life. "For that matter, I didn't even have to concoct a pretext to get the rest of the directors on board. It's more a matter of answering a help-wanted ad or sending a rescue mission than anything else, but this has the potential to completely reorder our understanding of how brains and communication work."

"I know you like your little mysteries, Abner, but could you sort of come to the point?" Duncan shook his head. "You know I'll accept my marching orders, whatever they are, when you finally get around to telling me about them. But I do have a lecture coming up in about forty-five minutes, so if you could see your way to explaining what those orders are, I'd appreciate it."

"Darn, Duncan—you're no fun at all!" Portnoy chuckled, then raised his hands in surrender as Duncan cocked a fist and shook it in his direction. "No need for violence!" he said, lowering his hands, and his expression was far more serious than it had been. "The truth is, your Cousin Stephanie's the real reason for the trip."

"These 'treecats' of hers?" Duncan's dark eyes narrowed. "Is that what this is really about?"

"Of course it is." Portnoy leaned back, crossed his legs, and shrugged. "Your family does seem to produce a lot of overachievers, even for an alpha line, doesn't it? Discoverer of a previously unknown tool-using species when she was only eleven. God save the galaxy from what she'll be doing by the time she's thirty!"

"The last time I saw Stephanie, she was about nine or ten T-years old," Duncan said. "Still, I can't say I was astonished by her accomplishments, especially—I might add, with all due modesty—with me as an example." He buffed his nails on his sweater and blew on them, then grinned. "What's that old saying about the apple not falling far from the tree?"

"She does seem to be a credit to her genotype...even *with* you as 'an example,'" Portnoy observed. "Has she written you about her new friends?"

"Like I just said, the last time I saw her she was about ten. I wouldn't be at all surprised if she's pretty much forgotten about me by now. But, in answer to your question, no, she hasn't. On the other hand, I've had several letters from Richard, and he's clearly excited about them. We don't write as much as we probably should, given the transit time; it's not like there are any direct trade routes between here and Sphinx, so the mail service isn't exactly reliable. But I've got at least a couple of megabytes from him about their physiology, their apparent habitat requirements, and their diet. In that respect, I'm probably better informed than anyone else on Meyerdahl, although at this remove that's not saying all that much."

"What's he told you about their social organization? Or about their intelligence?" Portnoy asked a bit more intently.

"Not as much. In fact, not much at all beyond the fact that he clearly thinks they *are* sapients." Duncan frowned. "The truth is, he's been . . . I don't know. He seems almost *guarded*, if that's not a silly verb, when he talks about that side of them."

"It's probably exactly the right verb, actually," Portnoy said in a much more serious tone. "Have you been keeping up on the literature about them?"

"*What* literature?" Duncan raised both hands. "There's been a certain degree of speculation, but Manticore's over two hundred and sixty light-years from here, Abner, and we don't have any direct academic links or partnerships with the Star Kingdom, you know. Essentially, what I've seen backs up Richard's belief that they are, indeed, tool-users with a sophisticated social organization that—in my opinion, judging from what I've seen at this range—clearly moves them into the category of true sapients. I can't begin to tell you where they'd place on the scale, given the third- and fourth-hand reports I've seen, but I wouldn't be at all surprised if they're in the running to be named Sphinx's native sapient species. Which, I'm sure, would have all sorts of repercussions." He grimaced. "Richard's mentioned Barstool in a couple of his letters. To be honest, I figured that was probably the reason he's not waxing more fulsome even to me.

Keeping them under the radar until their supporters are in a better position to *prove* their sapiency is exactly the way his mind would work."

"And you never wanted to go out and see for yourself, firsthand?" Portnoy asked.

"Of course I did! But unless the University was ready to grant me at least a two and a half T-year sabbatical—or some magical sponsor turned up to underwrite a grant to fund a University-sponsored research trip—there was no way to justify it."

"Well, it happens the Prometheus Foundation is prepared to underwrite that very grant," Portnoy told him.

"Why?" Duncan's eyes narrowed. "What, exactly, does this have to do with understanding brain function or modes of communication? My impression from the literature is that they don't *have* a 'mode of communication.' In fact, that's undoubtedly the biggest single bar against accepting their full sapiency. They don't have a spoken language, they don't use sign language, and there's no real evidence of any olfactory mode of communication, either. Which," he made a small throwing away gesture, "seems very odd to me, given what little I've seen about their social sophistication. You don't get that kind of organization and task sharing without some way of communicating at least basic concepts with your fellows."

"Exactly. Look, we don't have any sources or members in Manticore. To be brutally honest, the 'Star Kingdom' is at the ass end of nowhere, as far as the galaxy at large is concerned. But that doesn't mean we don't hear things, and one of the things we're hearing is that they may be telepathic."

"Telepathic," Duncan repeated carefully, then snorted. "And how long have we been chasing that particular grail without ever once scientifically demonstrating that it's even possible?"

"A long time," Portnoy conceded. "And I don't blame you for feeling a little skeptical. For that matter, you're not the only one who thinks it's a long shot. But if it is possible, and if we can figure out how to replicate it in humans, it could be a game changer, Duncan. Think what we could do with that kind of advantage!"

Duncan leaned back, looking at him, and despite his doubts, he had to admit Portnoy had a point. But still—

"Can I ask just who we're hearing this from?" he said after a moment.

"The most interesting thing, in a lot of ways, is that it's obvious from your reaction that we're *not* hearing it from your cousin. That may be significant, given what you said about Richard's worries about Barstool and the Amphors. Of course, it may also mean there's nothing to it, which is why he hasn't mentioned it. But at least one report from the first wave of xeno-biologists and anthropologists suggests the possibility as the best hypothesis to explain the degree of communication you were just talking about when they don't have a way to communicate that we can detect."

"And that report would be from whom, exactly?" Duncan shook his head. "I'm pretty sure somebody here in the Department would've heard something about it if there were any kind of supporting evidence."

"Probably not, since it was from one of Radzinsky's graduate assistants."

"The Radford Center Radzinsky?" Duncan raised both eyebrows.

"I see you've heard of the lady."

"Of course I have. We travel in the same academic circles, unfortunately."

"Not a huge fan, I take it?"

"You take it correctly," Duncan said flatly. "You know how I feel about the flaws in the sentience scale, and despite her reputation—which, admittedly, is huge—Cleonora

Radzinsky is about as humano-chauvinist as anyone you're ever likely to meet. I haven't seen anything she may have published about it, but let me guess. 'They have no complex means of communication, and therefore cannot be considered truly sapient.' That about right?"

"I see you have *indeed* heard of the lady." Portnoy nodded. "That's almost exactly what she said. And, having said it, how do you think a graduate assistant of hers who seriously postulated that they do, indeed, have a 'complex means of communication' would fare in the ranks of academia?"

"I believe the appropriate term would be 'crash and burn.'" Duncan shook his head. "If there's a woman in the galaxy who's more protective of her reputation, *I've* never heard of her. Another reason I'm not a fan."

"And that's why the assistant's report hasn't been officially circulated anywhere. But a copy of it floated across our horizon a few months ago, shortly after they got home from Sphinx. It was a deep dive into the Radford Center's files looking for something else entirely, and it didn't mean a whole lot to the team that actually stumbled across it. In fact, it didn't mean anything to us until someone on the strategy board happened across it in a summary of the data we'd acquired." Portnoy shrugged. "Sheer serendipity, really."

"Sounds like it," Duncan agreed. "And they really think it's worth looking into as a serious possibility?"

"You know the Alignment." Portnoy shrugged again. "We're probably the galaxy's biggest knowledge sponge. And I figure it probably popped a flag on one of the genome board's search filters. They're always looking for blue-sky possibilities that might give us an edge, and it's not like they're all that concerned about Beowulf finding out they're looking at nonhuman gene donors."

"No, I suppose not," Duncan said thoughtfully. "But you said something about finding a pretext to send me?"

"Didn't even have to look very hard," Portnoy assured him. "The Star Kingdom's asking for more help."

"They are?" Duncan looked at him for a moment, then snorted. "Of course they are. If Richard's right and they see even the remotest possibility of Sphinx turning into a second Barstool, they absolutely have to dot every I and cross every T, don't they? And that's completely on top of the legitimate interest any xenologist worth his salt would feel!"

"Exactly. And since their scientific establishment's not exactly cutting edge—it's not bad at all, considering their circumstances, but they're definitely not a heart world—they're trolling for xeno-anthropologists to help evaluate the treecats. And they're offering some very attractive on-site incentives. Including first publication of anything really interesting that turns up. Reading between the lines, I'd say there's a lot of interest in determining just how intelligent the treecats are and not necessarily on the part of people who wish the little beasties well. It looks to me as if the Star Kingdom's government knows that and they'd love to have as many neutral third parties as possible involved in evaluating the treecats' intelligence or lack thereof, if only to cover their ass when they finally rule one way or the other. The stipends they can offer aren't very high, but they're paying for transportation and defraying virtually all of the researchers' on-site expenses. That's the help-wanted ad I was talking about. We don't want to waste the time sending letters back and forth to get them to pick up your shipfare, though, so—"

"So the way this would work," Duncan interrupted, "is that the Foundation's getting involved proactively because of its mandate, since this is only the twelfth tool-using and at least potentially sentient species we've ever encountered. Obviously we need to find out everything we can about it! And, of course, responding to Manticore's need for assistance ties into the philanthropic side of its mandate. The University's getting involved because the Foundation's willing to pick up the tab for a twenty-one-T-month roundtrip voyage and essentially fund the entire effort. And I'm getting sent along because the fact that I'm the vice chair of the Xeno-Anthropology Department *and* the kid who discovered them is my first cousin—once removed, anyway—makes me the logical person to head the expedition. Which expedition will, hopefully, bring fresh prestige to the University. And, even if it doesn't, the University gets brownie points for trying to help out a poorer-than-dirt star nation that's still coping with the aftereffects of a plague that damn near wiped it out. That's about it?"

"That's about it," Portnoy agreed with a nod. "Except, of course, for the bit you left out."

"That would be the bit where anything I find out about how their telepathy actually works—assuming such a thing really exists—gets shared with the Alignment first."

"And probably never gets shared with anyone else at all, assuming the genome board decides there's really a possibility of modding it into the human genotype," Portnoy said much more seriously.

"Yeah, I can see that," Duncan acknowledged.

"And it does get you out there to visit your cousins," Portnoy pointed out. "That's a plus, too, I think!"

"That's true." Duncan nodded and smiled. "I *miss* Richard, dammit. And Marjorie never did get me the recipe for her Singapore Noodles." He rubbed his chin for a moment. "Should I assume I'll be traveling solo? Aside from whoever the University sends along, at least?"

"The intelligence directorate will probably want to send at least one of its specialists along to ride shotgun," Portnoy said.

"Really? That's necessary?" Duncan's distaste was obvious, and Portnoy shrugged.

"If it turns out there's anything to this whole theory, then the geneticists are going to want treecats, or at least their genetic material, Duncan. Frankly, what they'll really need are live treecats, because it's sort of difficult to demonstrate and evaluate telepathy between living brains when you don't have a living brain to communicate with. It's not likely anyone in the Star Kingdom will sign off on removing any live treecats from Sphinx, though. So it would seem to be a good idea to send along someone with the ... expertise to arrange a treecat extraction if that seems indicated. And, like you say, it's a ten-plus-T-month trip from Meyerdahl to Sphinx, so it makes sense to send the specialist in question on the same ship."

"I suppose," Duncan said.

His distaste didn't abate, however; not that Portnoy was surprised. Like all of the Mesan Alignment's members, Duncan Harrington was fiercely devoted to the concept of humanity's genetic uplift. And equally fiercely opposed to the Beowulf Biosciences Code's prohibition on anything that even hinted at genetically engineered "supermen." Most of them would admit that prohibition had actually made sense immediately after Old Earth's Final War and the horrors of the genetic weapons—and the genetic "super soldiers"—the belligerents had deployed. But that had been over six centuries ago, and what had made sense then was a useless, stultifying relic of the dead past. The potential for improving the basic human genome was mind-staggering. Someone like Duncan—a member of one of the Alignment's alpha lines; Portnoy himself was only a beta line—was an example of what the Alignment's geneticists had already accomplished: smarter, longer-lived, resistant to a host of diseases that had plagued humanity for thousands upon thousands of years, stronger and physically tougher than even the standard Meyerdahl package....It was a long list, and the Harrington Line was scarcely the only alpha line to come out of Meyerdahl. The basic Meyerdahl genetic modifications had been a huge step in that direction, one that had been "grandfathered in" from well before the Final War, and they'd provided an ideal testbed—and concealment—for the Alignment's further improvements.

But the galaxy at large, and especially Beowulf and the Solarian League, the arbiters of interstellar medicine, would never have allowed that sort of planned, targeted improvement. It was anathema to them, which was what had forced the Alignment underground. Forced it to conceal its purpose, conduct its mission—wage its holy war, in many ways—covertly, always in hiding.

That grated on a lot, probably the majority, of the Alignment's members, and that had led to a...division of opinions within it. The vast majority of the Alignment was located on the planet Mesa, where concealment was fairly simple, and worked solely within Mesan family lines. A few of those lines had spread off-world from simple emigration, although those cases were vanishingly rare.

But another portion of the Alignment had very quietly dedicated itself to a far broader and more audacious goal. It might be forced to conceal its actions even from its fellows on Mesa, but its purpose was the genetic uplift of society as a *whole*, and it had been quietly but deliberately extending its efforts to other planets for two or three generations now. Given the galaxy-wide acceptance of the Beowulf Code it was forced to keep its activities very, *very* clandestine, but it was steadily expanding its reach, with more and more of its members achieving positions of influence from which to shape opinion and awareness against the day its mission could become public.

Duncan Harrington was one of those influencers, and Portnoy knew how much Duncan hated the need for secrecy. He *understood* it, but he didn't like it one bit. He'd hated having to recommend against telling his own cousin, someone who'd grown up more as his younger brother than "just" a cousin, the truth, but he understood that the Alignment had to pick and choose the conservators of its mission carefully. There were seldom more than one or two fully informed members in any given line—outside the Mesa System, at least—in any generation, and sometimes, when there were no suitable candidates for the mission, it simply had to let that branch of the genome go completely, as in Richard Harrington's case.

It was just as well that he was unaware of certain other harsh realities, however, Portnoy thought now, looking at his friend. Like the fact that if revealing their branch of the Alignment's existence to a potential recruit turned out to be a mistake, it had to be rectified. He would have reacted poorly to that knowledge.

Yet that was okay, Portnoy reflected. Thinking about things like that was one of his jobs, not Duncan's. On the other hand, Duncan understood the need for the Alignment to consider every possible advantage in its mission, cast the widest possible net as it considered ways in which the genome might be improved. And he understood that required research and that sometimes *clandestine* research had to embrace clandestine means to achieve its ends. So in the end, he'd... accommodate the necessary "specialist," and Portnoy was glad, because he'd known Duncan Harrington since boyhood. Duncan was too good a man—too good a friend—to be burdened with those sorts of decisions, so Abner Portnoy would make certain he wasn't.

"Hopefully, there won't be even a ripple, Duncan," he told his friend now. "So go. Have fun! Spend some time with Richard, hug Marjorie for me, and see what that precocious young cousin of yours has been up to. I know you've missed them, so make the most of it, okay? And this way, the entire trip's on the Alignment's tab!"

"THIS COULD HAVE FAR-REACHING CONSEQUENCES,"
George Lebedyenko, known on social occasions as the
Earl of Adair Hollow, said, tipping back in his office chair
as he watched the smart wall. "From what I've read of
the preliminary coverage, the treecats' actions are central
to the prosecution's entire case. And so far, everything
Karl's said bears that out."

"I agree it's getting the 'cats plenty of coverage,"
Gwendolyn Adair said. "I don't know how much it's
going to move the needle on the question of their intelligence, though."

"Oh, come on, Gwen!" Adair Hollow snorted. "I know
the defense is doing its damnedest to downplay the 'cats'
intelligence to undercut their evidentiary value, but I think
that's going to shoot him in the foot before it's all over.
And you and I have seen the evidence from the Foundation. There's no question that they're a sapient, tool-using

species! And you've seen even more of Stephanie and Lionheart than I have."

"And *I'm* not the one arguing with you," Gwendolyn pointed out just a bit acerbically. "For that matter, I'm pretty sure we both know where the...counternarrative is coming from."

"Angelique," Adair Hollow said in a disgusted tone.

"Not openly, and not all by herself, but almost certainly," Gwendolyn agreed. "You'd think somebody as wealthy as *dear* Countess Frampton would figure she already has enough money, but she's way too invested in those Sphinx land futures to go down without a fight. And the fact that she's not openly campaigning against the treecats worries me."

"I know." Adair Hollow ran his fingers through his dark hair. "And let's face it, she's better at the political stuff than you and I are. That's why she's not 'openly' campaigning. Keeping her hands—and skirts—clean for Parliament and the newsies."

"And disconnecting the nonpartisan, purely scientific debate from anything sordid, like profit," Gwendolyn pointed out to her cousin.

"There shouldn't *be* any debate," Adair Hollow said stubbornly, returning to his original point. "From what Karl's said, the 'cats saved *both* their lives this time!"

"Of course they did. But as Doctor Mulvaney pointed out last night, we have to be 'careful' about assigning 'full sapience' to them."

The irony in Gwendolyn's tone could have turned Jason Bay into a desert, Adair Hollow thought, and with reason. Clifford Mulvaney had an enviable reputation as a xeno-biologist, and Idoya Vásquez, the Star Kingdom's interior minister, had imported him from Sigma Draconis as a consultant. At first, despite a certain professional caution, he'd looked like one of the treecats' greater boosters, but he'd backtracked. To be more precise, he'd begun warning against "prematurely assuming" a greater degree of intelligence on the six-limbed arboreals' part once their lack of any discernible language became apparent. His appearance on Alana Martínez's "Did You Know?" podcast the night before had underscored that point yet again.

"I couldn't believe he was comparing them to 'service animals,'" the earl said disgustedly.

"Fair's fair, George," Gwendolyn replied. "He didn't actually compare them to service animals. He simply said that to date, aside from the very simple tools and artifacts we've seen out of them, they haven't really done anything in relation to humans that service animals haven't also done for millennia. And in a lot of ways, he has a point. For that matter, some of the arguments we've been putting forward in favor of treecats in public places are being construed that way, and you know it."

"But service animals do things because they've been *trained* to," Adair Hollow shot back. "They don't do them *spontaneously*, without ever having been taught to."

"I agree." Gwendolyn nodded. "And it was at best a poorly chosen analogy, since it can be interpreted as suggesting the treecats are no more intelligent than, say, a German Shepherd! But—"

"Hold that thought." Adair Hollow raised one hand. "We're back."

Gwendolyn's green eyes moved back to the smart wall as the holding pattern disappeared to show them the courtroom once again.

"Ms. Harrington," Stephen Ford began, "or would you prefer to be addressed as 'Probationary Ranger' Harrington?"

Ford, the defense attorney for Erina "Stormy" Wether,

looked precisely like central casting's version of the "promising young attorney": well-groomed, not flashy, but somehow completely fake. He spoke to the sixteen-year-old in the tone of voice some adults reserved when they were pretending to treat people they still thought of as "kids" as adults. Stephanie Harrington hoped this was just because she was short for her age. She knew her fine-boned build made her look younger.

She squared her shoulders, but kept her hands neatly folded in her lap, so she wouldn't give into the temptation to play with her hair. Over the last year, she'd been working on growing it out. Today her mom had helped her pull the curly brown locks back into a neat little ponytail that tickled her neck. It also reminded Stephanie acutely of the treecat who wasn't there, but instead waited in the chamber reserved for pets.

"Ms. Harrington is fine," Stephanie said. She was actually very proud of her rank, especially since the position had been created specifically for her, but the way Ford said it, "probationary ranger" sounded more as if she'd done something wrong and was "on probation," rather than what the term actually meant, which was that in defiance of a policy against interns, and especially *junior* interns, Stephanie was officially enrolled as the most junior member of the Sphinx Forest Service.

"Ms. Harrington," Ford continued with a meaningless smile, "you were present in court for the testimony of Ranger Karl Zivonik of the Sphinx Forest Service. Would you confirm whether you agree with the accuracy of his testimony regarding how the two of you came to be in the area where Gill Votano was concealing evidence of valuable mineral resources?"

Stephanie hated how Ford's wording made Gill sound like the criminal, rather than the victim. Nevertheless, she kept her voice level as she replied. "Yes, I do agree."

"Very well. Rather than go over those details, I'd like to move to the point where your specific actions have a marked impact on the evidence against my client."

Ford paused for dramatic effect, drawing his right index finger over his right eyebrow with what, based on how many times Stephanie had seen him do it, was clearly his trademark gesture. Stephanie waited for him to continue with a patience she didn't feel. She wanted her part in this trial to be over, to go back to sitting on the bench next to Karl. Even better, she'd like to collect Lionheart from where he'd been exiled with Survivor in an area reserved for "pets"—if he'd been classed as a "service animal" he'd have been allowed to accompany her, but *of course* he hadn't been granted *that* status—then leave this stuffy courtroom behind for good.

"After learning of the apparent suicide of Gill Votano," Ford continued, "you and Karl Zivonik decided to take an air car ride out in the direction you thought Votano had intended to bring you for a tour that very day. You were upset?"

"Some," Stephanie said honestly. "We didn't know Gill very well, but we did like him, and he'd seemed very enthusiastic about our planned outing. It didn't seem to fit that he'd killed himself, but apparently, he had."

In the months since Gill's death, Stephanie and Karl had worked hard on how to present why they had been in the right place to get the evidence that proved Gill had been murdered while keeping the role Lionheart and Survivor had played in the investigation out of the picture. It wasn't easy since, from the start, Lionheart and Survivor had been deeply involved.

The treecats' sensitivity to emotional landscapes had alerted Stephanie and Karl that there was more to Gill's invitation than the geology field tour he'd ostensibly offered. The treecats also had been the ones who had noticed—likely because they picked up Gill's scent—the concealed crevice which contained the evidence as to why someone might want Gill dead. And it had been the treecats who had alerted their humans to the presence of someone else in the area, which had definitely been crucial to the case's resolution. Finally, the treecats had saved Karl and Stephanie's lives, without which action, there would be no trial today.

"So, you decided on a memorial outing," Ford prompted. "Very touching. Ranger Zivonik has already related how you two came to the place where you noticed a slab of rock where it shouldn't be, and how you decided to move it, thereby finding a concealed crevice. Very impressive."

Stephanie inclined her head slightly, as if acknowledging praise, though she suspected the opposite was intended. When he'd been on the witness stand, Karl had done a magnificent job explaining how the pair had spent a lot of time outdoors, not only in their work, but in hobby activities like hunting. This meant that even in an unfamiliar environment they were inclined to notice what didn't fit. Stephen Ford had been reprimanded by the bench for grandstanding when he'd tried to discredit their testimony by stressing the unlikelihood that their skills would have translated from Sphinx's forests to Gryphon's rocky wastes. After all, how or why they'd ended up in the right place wasn't germane to the case at hand.

"I must say, Sphinx certainly is a challenging environment," Ford continued. "Not only are even you young rangers so keen of eye that you can spot a stone out of place, but you can apparently scent a nearly odorless gas before it knocks you out. Ranger Zivonik has admitted he did not hear or smell the gas. However, Ms. Harrington, you did so with sufficient time to switch your uni-link to record both audio and visual images. Please tell us in your own words what happened."

Stephanie was ready for this question.

"We'd gone back into the crevice and seen the mineral formations. We made some images, and were walking back when, I'm not really sure...I heard something, or maybe Lionheart started acting edgy."

"Lionheart?" Ford cut in. "That's your pet treecat, correct?"

Stephanie fought an urge to roll her eyes. "Yes. Lionheart is a treecat."

"And so when your treekitty got nervous, you—"

"Tree*cat*," Stephanie corrected icily. "*Cattus arbor habitans* if you prefer. That's the currently agreed upon nomenclature."

Ford gave a showman's laugh. "Oh, I don't prefer it, really. Quite a mouthful for such little beasts. Please go on."

Although Stephanie wanted to snap at him, she suddenly realized that the defense attorney wasn't being nearly as stupid as he seemed. Although it was unlikely Stormy would get off on the charge of first-degree murder, she *had* been careful about covering her tracks. This had given the defense the opportunity to portray her as a pathetic and frail old woman who had perhaps been incapable of judging her own actions. Stormy herself had been playing the role to the full, sitting slumped in one corner rarely reacting to anything said. If she did react, she did so inappropriately, seeming to care more about having her teacup full than that she was on trial for her life.

If any of those testifying against Stormy could be made to seem unreliable—especially Jorge Prakel, whose testimony was key to proving that Stormy's actions were premeditated—the defense might be able to get the charge reduced, or even dismissed. If that happened, then the case against Stormy Wether would move to the secondary charges, which included the attempted murder of Stephanie and Karl. Since they'd only escaped death by poisonous insect sting because of the intervention of Lionheart and Survivor, anything that could make what had happened on that stony outcrop in Gryphon's outback seem open to different interpretations would be gravy from the defense's point of view.

So, I need to respond without making the treecats seem dumb or, worse, letting on how smart they are. Okay... time to do a little offensive myself.

Stephanie narrowed her large brown eyes in her best serious and intent expression, then asked, "Why Karl and I were there doesn't really matter, does it? What matters is that I turned on my uni-link to record both audio and visual. The images aren't the best, but they're good enough to show that when Karl and I went down after being gassed, the person who picked us up, moved us, then set us up to—"

Stephen Ford held up one hand.

"What the images apparently show is not germane to my question. Thank you, Ms. Harrington, that will be enough."

He glanced at his notes, apparently decided against the wisdom of keeping Stephanie on the stand any longer than necessary, and asked her to step down. She did so, restraining an urge to hurry to where Karl Zivonik sat, tall, dark, and reassuring. Instead, she held her head high and walked with a measured tread to her seat.

In the lull before Ford called his next witness there was the usual murmur from the press gallery as they speculated on the significance of each stage of the trial. As Stephanie took her seat, she glanced up to see if she could judge what impact her own small contribution might have had. To her surprise and delight, she recognized a familiar face, large-nosed and unmistakable: José "Nosey" Jones, the owner of and sole reporter for the popular *Sphinx Oracle*.

She nudged Karl and said in a soft voice, "Nosey's here!"

Karl grinned, his gray eyes sparkling. "Wondered when you'd notice. He's been up there all day."

A short while later when a recess was called for lunch, Stephanie looked up into the press gallery and gave Nosey a little finger wave. Nosey beamed and pointed to his uni-link. A moment later, a message came up on both her screen and Karl's.

"How about lunch? I'd love a chance to catch up," Nosey suggested. "You've been gone nearly eight months. Messages just aren't the same."

"That would be great," Stephanie replied. "I really want to get away from the courthouse."

"Me, too," Karl added. "I realize the defense has to show willing, but this morning was absolutely no fun."

"Then meet me outside the west exit?" Nosey suggested. "I'm staying at the Blue Basil, which is in easy walking distance. I'll com an order for food in advance. If we take the side entrance into the hotel, then the treecats shouldn't attract too much attention."

"Great!" Stephanie texted back.

After collecting Lionheart and Survivor, Stephanie and Karl met up with Nosey. Nosey's long, lanky build testified to his birth off-Sphinx, but here on Manticore, he could do without a counter-grav unit. His pale blue eyes were thoughtful and sensitive, and nicely contrasted with his reddish-brown complexion. He was somewhat older than Karl, in his twenties. Initially, Nosey and especially his articles in his *Sphinx Oracle,* had more irritated Stephanie than otherwise, but she'd come to appreciate that he cared about Sphinx as much as she did.

"What brings you here?" Karl said, shaking hands with the other man.

"Why do you think I'm here?" Nosey's lips curved in

an impish smile. "I'm here to provide firsthand coverage of the testimony of Sphinx's own heroic rangers. Trust the two of you to get into trouble, even on holiday on another planet!"

"I wish we hadn't," Stephanie said. "I don't mean I regret stepping in, but it would have been a lot more fun to explore a new planet without having a murder investigation mixed in."

"I get you," Nosey said, giving Stephanie a friendly pat on the shoulder that was in no way condescending. "But you two aren't the type to let something go just because you're not on duty. We're all proud of you back home. That's one of the reasons I decided to make the trip and provide an on-the-scene report. Another reason is that I am solidly sick of snow and ice. C'mon, we can walk to the hotel from here. It's great to be out of doors."

As he led the way toward his hotel, Nosey continued chattering.

"Back home, people can follow coverage of the murder trial in the Manticoran press, sure, but they're not going to know the background of the people involved. Stephen Ford, the attorney for the defense, is a great example. He wants to go into politics in a big way. Rumor is, that's why he took this case, even though Ms. Wether isn't likely to get off. Even if Ford fails completely, he's already gotten lots of publicity, as well as support for his claim that he's all for the underdog. Voters love that sort of thing. If Ford gets the charges against Wether reduced, that will work out even better for him."

"Yeah, we heard a few rumors about Ford's ambition," Karl said.

Stephanie nodded agreement, but was too distracted to comment. As Nosey talked, she was picking up some curious vibes. Underlying Nosey's genuine enthusiasm for his topic was a sense of mingled apprehension and excitement. Stephanie had found, since her adoption by Lionheart, that what her mom called her "people sense" had improved markedly. She suspected most of that was simply the fact that she was almost six T-years older and that she'd become much more comfortable with people in general. There were times when she suspected it might be more than that, though. She'd become certain the tree-cats were empaths—that they could literally *feel* another's emotions—and sometimes she suspected that might be leaking over to her. Yet every time she tried to narrow it down, all she got was a frustrating mental tickle she couldn't be at all certain wasn't simply her own imagination. One thing she *did* know, though, was that she'd learned to use Lionheart as an emotional barometer as she'd become more and more adept at reading his body language. At the moment, as he rode in his accustomed place, his rearmost set of feet resting on a reinforced panel in her tunic, his mid-limb hand-feet on her shoulder, his head was cocked with an almost speculative air as he gazed at Nosey.

Nosey's hiding something, Stephanie decided, *but Lionheart doesn't seem worried. If anything, he seems amused! I wonder if there'll be celery for lunch or something.*

She glanced over at Karl and could tell he also suspected Nosey planned to surprise them with something based on Survivor's reaction. Over the last year, they'd had plenty of opportunities to compare how well they could "read" their treecats. Stephanie was definitely better at it, although whether that was because she'd known Lionheart longer and had more practice, or for some other reason, they really didn't have enough information to figure out.

There's still so much we don't know about treecat and human interactions, Stephanie thought. *But, as the pool of adoptees grows, we're getting more and more information.*

Eventually, we can stop generalizing from too small a sample set.

When they reached the Blue Basil, the three Sphinxians slipped in a side door, then took the stairs to the third floor. Once there, Nosey palm-coded open the door to his hotel room, and sniffed the air with ostentatious satisfaction. "The food beat us here. I remembered you both liked pizza, so I ordered several combinations, as well as salad, and dessert. I ordered sushi for the treecats, but extra for the humans, if the 'cats decide to share."

This little bit of business had taken them into the hotel suite proper. The food was indeed waiting, spread out temptingly on a long, low table in front of a comfortable-looking sofa. Presiding over the banquet, managing to look both smug and shy at the same time, was none other than Trudy Franchitti. Trudy got to her feet as they came in, a welcoming smile brightening her undeniably lovely face.

Not too many years ago, if Stephanie had been asked to name her least favorite human on Sphinx, Trudy Franchitti would have likely topped the list. Not quite a year older than Stephanie, Trudy had been her rival on the Twin Forks hang gliding team—that is until she'd dropped out at the prompting of her then-beau, Stan Chang. But Trudy had changed a lot in the last year. She still had the curves that had made Stephanie feel like an underdeveloped kid, the big violet-blue eyes, and the shining dark hair, but Trudy no longer went out of her way to hide her intelligence and how deeply she cared about the well-being of Sphinx's wildlife.

Trudy had always been interested in the wild creatures of Sphinx. In fact, her numerous wild-captured "pets" had been one of the sources of contention between her and Stephanie. However, when the recent severe fire season had put those pets at risk, Trudy had actually stood up to her domineering father, and insisted on getting them treated at Richard Harrington's vet clinic. Soon after, she'd started volunteering with Wild and Free, an animal rescue and rehabilitation group. By the time Stephanie had left for Gryphon, she'd actually been starting to like Trudy. Still, that didn't mean she wasn't shocked to find Trudy sitting here in Nosey's hotel room, or that the slightly open closet door showed what had to be one of Trudy's outfits hanging in the closet.

With the air of one making a wordless declaration, Nosey went over to Trudy and gave her a kiss, right on the lips. Then he motioned to the two chairs set to one side of the coffee table.

"We'll sit on the sofa. You two take the chairs."

Trudy indicated the space between the chairs. "I spread a couple of towels there so Lionheart and Survivor could be as messy as they need to be. I hope you don't mind, but when we ordered lunch, I did ask for a few sticks of celery, along with the salads."

Stephanie managed to swallow all the questions burbling up in her throat and say, "No, I don't mind. Very kind of you to think of them."

Karl, normally the less outspoken member of their team, helped himself to a slice of pizza with mushrooms and sausage, then asked the burning question, "So...How long have you two been dating?"

Trudy actually blushed, which surprised Stephanie, since it had been a pretty open secret that Trudy and Stan had long gotten past holding hands.

But then, romance and sex aren't the same thing, are they? Even if they get mixed up together all the time.

Nosey grinned happily and reached to squeeze Trudy's hand with the hand that wasn't holding a slice of pepperoni and pink olive pizza.

"A few months now. I mean, since we decided to date just each other. We started spending time together further back, when I wanted to do a feature story on Wild and Free for my Nose for News column in the *Oracle*. I'd met Trudy at your sixteenth birthday party, Stephanie, and we'd chatted there, so she offered to be my guide around the facility. We got to talking and—"

"And it was just so easy to talk to him," Trudy cut in, giving Nosey a melting look. "At first, we mostly talked about animals, and the impact of fires on habitats, and stuff like that, but I was still really messed up over Stan's death. For a while after Stan died, I tried not to think about what had happened, concentrated on my PT, all that. But there was too much to just keep stomping down, not just the sorrow—we'd dated for a long time, and Stan hadn't always been such a jerk—but the anger, too. He'd put us at risk, and... Oh! It's stupid, but I couldn't help but feel like Stan had gotten off easy. If it hadn't been for Karl showing up right after the accident, I might have been dead, too. I had a lot of pain, especially during rehab. But thanks to some great doctors, all my scars were inside. Even after my body was mostly healed, and I was supposed to be 'all better,' those emotional scars were still there. Not just still there, worse than ever."

"I understood some of what she was feeling," Nosey continued, motioning for Trudy to take a bite of her pizza. "I mean, I'd had my own experience healing from bad injuries not that long before. My injuries were also connected with fear and resentment, and..." He gave an eloquent shrug. "We talked a lot about how we felt. One thing led to another, and, well, here we are!"

"That's terrific," Stephanie said and meant it. "I'm really glad for both of you. I guess your families must be pretty pleased, too."

Nosey laughed. "My sister is thrilled. She loves Trudy to bits. My mother can hardly believe I have a serious girlfriend. She'd decided I was married to my job."

Trudy laughed with him. "His family is great. I was so nervous when I met his sister—she's the only one of his sibs who lives in the Star Kingdom—but..."

The long, involved anecdote that followed was back-dropped by the demolition of several pizzas, large salads, then slices of a rich, multi-layered cream cake. Stephanie out-ate everyone else, but not even Karl teased her. It was only after the talk had turned to the trial, which Trudy had been watching on the vid, since she couldn't sit with Nosey in the press box, that Stephanie realized Trudy had neatly dodged how the Franchittis felt about their daughter's new boyfriend.

Didn't Nosey call out Jordan Franchitti in at least one of his columns? Something about how the Franchittis weren't helping one of their tenants whose home had been seriously damaged during the fires? Stephanie thought. *But they must not mind the relationship. I mean, Trudy's here, with Nosey, staying in his room.*

But thinking about what Trudy hadn't said, she definitely wondered.

<*I am surprised,*> Climbs Quickly said around a glow of amusement. <*I would not have expected Needs to Know and Walks in Shadow to mate.*>

<*Nor would I,*> Keen Eyes replied with an answering flicker of laughter.

The two People lay stretched comfortably along the backs of their two-legs' sitting things, nibbling the pieces of spicy, bright-tasting food their bondmates offered them from time to time.

<*Still,*> Keen Eyes continued more soberly, <*I think this may be very good for both of them.*>

<*I think it has* already *been good for both of them,*> Climbs Quickly agreed. <*His heart is far lighter than the*

last time I tasted him. And the shadows through which she walks seem lighter, somehow, when she is with him.>

Keen Eyes radiated agreement, and Climbs Quickly thought back to his first meeting with Walks in Shadow and how much the young female two-leg had changed since then. Once again, he wished Death Fang's Bane were able to taste other two-legs' mind-glows, because all *she* had felt where Walks in Shadow was concerned in those early days of their bond had been frustration and anger. Climbs Quickly still had no idea what had shadowed the other two-leg's life, but he knew the pain of it had shaped Walks in Shadow's life as the cold, powerful winds of the high peaks twisted and blighted the trees that grew there. And the things that had so angered Death Fang's Bane had grown out of that pain, out of the defenses Walks in Shadow erected about it.

And they are too mind-blind to recognize even that much about one another, he thought pityingly, for far from the first time.

<And yet is that not a part of their courage?> Keen Eyes asked, following his thought. *<The courage to continue, day after day, and to reach out to one another despite their mind-blindness? I do not think one of the People could do that.>*

<That is a very good observation,> Climbs Quickly said approvingly. *<And I hope Walks in Shadow's courage will carry her still farther from the shadows. There was a time when I would not have believed she and Death Fang's Bane could ever become true friends, yet they have. And now, with Needs to Know, I think perhaps she is ready to take yet another step.>*

2

"STEPHANIE! KARL!"

Stephanie looked up when the deep voice called her name, then smiled as Oswald Morrow crossed the Sweet Onion's lobby toward them. Her smile was a bit restrained, although it wasn't because of anything Morrow had ever done. In fact, he was one of the most helpful and open-minded people she'd ever met where the treecats were concerned. But something about him put Lionheart ever so slightly on edge. Whatever it was, it clearly hadn't set off her companion's "Danger!" alert, but the trace of wariness—that was the only word she could think of—she sensed from Lionheart whenever Oswald was around bothered her. At the same time, she reminded herself conscientiously, despite her enormous faith in the treecat's judgment, Lionheart *was* a treecat, whose understanding of humanity was probably at least as incomplete as humanity's understanding of his species.

Well, maybe not that *incomplete,* she thought dryly as Oswald reached her, Karl, and her parents.

"Richard, Marjorie." He held out his hand, shaking each of the elder Harringtons' hands in turn, and then shook his head at the younger members of the party.

"I've been watching you on HD," he said. "Sounds like your furry friends came through for you two again."

He smiled at Lionheart and Survivor, riding on Stephanie's and Karl's shoulders. The Sweet Onion had become one of the Harringtons' favorite dining spots, and not just because of how good its Old Earth Italian cuisine was. Salvatori Jackson, the owner, had made both treecats welcome, and highchairs were already waiting at what had become the Harringtons' usual table.

"Will you join us?" her father asked.

"No, sorry. Joan and I are dining with friends, and I'm waiting for the rest of them to arrive. But am I going to see you guys at the Foundation next week?"

"We're planning on it," Stephanie replied. "The Earl's invited us to address the members after the trial finally ends."

"I know he's really front and center on looking out for the 'cats," Morrow said in a more serious tone. "For that matter, the entire Foundation's backing them. There's still so much uncertainty about them, though."

"Tell me about it!" Stephanie rolled her eyes.

The Adair Foundation was dedicated to the preservation of the Star Kingdom's native environment, which was always a ticklish proposition when humanity turned up and started changing things. Part of that was both inevitable and deliberate. Humanity *had* to make some changes to make an alien planet its home, and at least over the centuries, Homo sapiens had learned a lot about how to terraform planets with minimum damage to those planets' existing ecosystems. Unfortunately, they'd learned a lot of that by making mistakes on *other* planets, and some of those mistakes had been spectacular. And some, like what had happened to the Amphors, had also been not simply deliberate but among the human race's most shameful acts, in Stephanie's opinion.

She would have been happier if she'd been able to believe that sort of action was behind her species now, but humans were still humans and probably always would be, as the current murder trial illustrated. That was the main reason she and her friends were so protective of the treecats. But even the best-intentioned human populations could unintentionally wreak havoc on the environments of the planets they'd colonized, and that was what the Adair Foundation was dedicated to preventing.

Stephanie approved of the Foundation. Highly.

"Well, you should have pretty good attendance," Morrow said. "It's the quarterly meeting of the Board, after all."

"We're all looking forward to it," Richard said. "I could wish we hadn't been brought to Landing by a murder trial, of course."

"I know." Morrow nodded sympathetically. "But from everything I've heard, your young people did us all proud again. Although"—he transferred his attention back to Stephanie and Karl and shook an admonishing finger— "I wish you two could manage to live just slightly *less* traumatic lives for, oh, a few T-months or so."

"We're working on it—honest!" Stephanie said with a grin.

"Well, work harder!" Morrow laughed, then looked across the lobby. "And there's Joan! Maybe we'll run into each other at the Foundation."

He waved and headed off to meet his wife, and Stephanie smiled after him for a moment before she and Karl followed her parents into the side dining room.

✧　　✧　　✧

"I ran into the Harringtons in the Sweet Onion last night," Morrow said, and grimaced. "Yet another eating establishment letting the little beasties in."

"That's partly George's doing," Gwendolyn Adair replied, then shook her head. "Most of them are already legally required to allow service animals. Unfortunately, young Stephanie's been visible enough to make the leap from that to treecats a relatively short one for most people. And that may actually not be a bad thing, you know. George has had the Foundation leaning on the Restaurant and Hoteliers Association to let them in ever since Karl and Stephanie were at the University, and he has enough influence he'd have gotten them in anyway, one way or another. At least this way they're still in the category of service *animals*. Which, by the way, pisses him off. But it's going to spread, especially on Sphinx, whatever we do, so there's no point trying to stop it now."

"Wonderful." Morrow sipped moodily at his drink, then crossed to the ninetieth-floor window and stood gazing down on the streets of Landing. "Countess Frampton's not happy about this steady erosion of her position, you know."

"Of course I know," Gwendolyn said with a snappishness she wouldn't have let her noble cousin see. "But like I just said"—she gave him a pointed glance—"there's not a lot we can do about that, and at least we've got Mulvaney on board to help push the 'really smart animals' narrative. That was a good catch on your part, by the way."

Morrow nodded with a slight smile. It was his research that had unearthed the fact that one reason Clifford Mulvaney had accepted the invitation to the Star Kingdom was the spate of bad investments which had ruined him financially back home. He'd come primarily to get away from his creditors, without ever expecting he might find a way to actually help deal with them . . . until Gwendolyn and Countess Frampton suggested the possibility ever so subtly and through properly deniable intermediaries. He might not have *liked* the idea of selling his enviable reputation to bolster the anti-treecat effort, but he'd been more than desperate enough to do it anyway.

"I'm afraid that even with Mulvaney we're fighting a losing battle on that front, too, though," Gwendolyn continued sourly. "If Stephanie was just a bit less effective as their spokeswoman, it would help a lot. But the damned girl's 'cute as a button'—that's dear Cousin George's revolting simile, by the way—and smarter than she has any right to be. And then there's the damned treecats themselves." She sipped from her own glass. "Just between you and me, I'm coming to the conclusion that they really are empaths."

"You are?" Morrow looked over his shoulder at her with a quick frown. "I don't like the sound of that. And I thought you'd decided they weren't?"

"What I said—and what Mulvaney said—was that there wasn't any proof they are, and there still isn't. Proof, I mean." Gwendolyn scowled. "I've watched Lionheart's body language, though, both in person and in recorded video, and it's different when I'm around. I think he's picking up on something."

"Like what, specifically?"

"Presumably the fact that I'm not really a great admirer of his species," Gwendolyn said in a poison-dry tone. "It's fairly easy to fool George and the other directors—aside from Jefferson, of course—and I'm confident sweet little Stephanie and Karl haven't figured out we're actually working for the other side. But the furry little troublemaker's obviously twigged to something none of the others can see."

"Well, that's unfortunate." Morrow shook his head.

"Maybe," Gwendolyn replied. "But I think it's also proof that however sensitive they may be to emotions, they can't read actual thoughts. For that matter, it's probably another indication that any kind of meaningful communication between humans and treecats isn't right around the corner." Morrow cocked an eyebrow, and she shrugged. "If he could actually read my thoughts—and understand them—he'd be a lot more than just...edgy around me. And if he were able to communicate clearly to Stephanie, she'd be more skittish around me, too. Assuming she didn't just shoot me."

"That's something," he conceded.

"But we can't count on Stephanie's not beginning to wonder just what it is about me—and probably you, Ozzie—that Lionheart's apparently picking up. She trusts him, trusts his judgment. If I had to guess, I'd say she's putting it down to the fact that they only ever interact with us directly here on Manticore, in the 'big city,' outside his comfort zone back on Sphinx. But eventually, she'll get past that."

"And then?"

"She's still technically a minor, so usually I wouldn't be that worried. But she's got too many friends in too many places, and she's too damned smart." Gwendolyn shook her head. "We need to move on this, Ozzie."

"How?" Morrow asked, his tone a bit wary, and she grimaced.

"George is still wavering, but I think he's inclined to support Hidalgo. I'm getting behind that and pushing as discreetly as I can, because that's probably the best position we'll have if the rest of it goes south on us. Angelique won't like it, but with a little political finesse, we could steer the reservations away from the areas her options cover."

Morrow nodded. Doctor Gary Hidalgo, one of the xeno-anthropologists who'd followed the Whitaker expedition to study the treecats, had come down strongly in favor of their sapience. He'd been unwilling to offer any guesstimates about where the 'cats placed on the sentience scale, although he'd acknowledged that their lack of any spoken form of communication argued for the lower third of the scale. He'd also pointed out, however, that despite that they clearly had significant social organization and were both competent and innovative in the use of their Paleolithic tools. He'd said as much in his report to the Interior Ministry, and also argued that the Star Kingdom had a moral responsibility to minimize the cultural con-tamination the treecats had already suffered and *prevent* any future contamination, which suggested setting aside reservations for them where they could continue their development without human intervention.

Cleonora Radzinsky, on the other hand, had strongly disputed Hidalgo's conclusions about treecat intelligence. She pointed out that even Old Earth dolphins, who rated only a point-six-five on the sentience scale, used complex verbal communication, which treecats manifestly did not. Russell Darrolyn had supported her strongly, which had been even more telling. Although Radzinsky was regarded as one of the human-settled galaxy's foremost specialists in non-human intelligence, Darrolyn's specialization was communication studies.

"I'd prefer Radzinsky's and Darrolyn's interpretation, if we can't just have them classified as animals and be done with it," Gwendolyn continued. "At best, though, we're probably going to find Stephanie and her friends pushing for protected species status for them. And if that happens, it's only a short step from that point to having Hidalgo's reservations as our best fallback. It's not a good one, but if we get to that point, it may be the only one we have. That's one reason I've been positioning Mulvaney to support it if and when the time comes."

"The Countess *really* won't like that," Morrow said. "She already doesn't want anything that supports the notion that they're a truly intelligent species at all. I think she's afraid *any* step in that direction—any official, legal step, at least—will open a door that can only swing wider as time passes. And unless I miss my guess, she'll see the notion of 'reservations' as exactly that: a concession to their intelligence. And that could be a bad thing for all of us."

Gwendolyn looked a question at him, and he shrugged.

"Look, I know I'm the cutout between you and her for most of this, and I'm generally okay with that. The farther apart—officially—we can keep you and her, the less likely your cousin is to figure out what's going on, and that's what they call a Good Thing. But it also means I'm the one more directly exposed to her unhappiness, and I can tell you that if she gets sufficiently unhappy, moderation's likely to go out the window. She won't care where the chips go as long as the tree gets cut down."

"Meaning what?"

"Meaning that if she decides we can't get the job done she's likely to get more directly involved herself. And outside political cajolery, she doesn't do subtle very well. If she starts flailing around, looking for somebody more 'effective' than you and me, she's likely to stub a toe, possibly in spectacular fashion."

"Spectacular enough to splash on us, you mean?"

"It could happen." Morrow nodded, his expression unhappy, and Gwendolyn's frown deepened.

So far, aside from the muggers she'd hired to attack Stephanie and Lionheart on their first visit to Manticore—which, she admitted, had not turned out to be one of her better ideas—nothing she'd done about the treecats was technically illegal, and she was confident her links to the muggers were deeply enough buried no one would ever find them. But if an official investigatory eye were to be focused upon her, an embarrassing number of her *other* activities—the sort that carried prison sentences—might intrude into the light. Which didn't even consider the impact it would have on her lucrative position as Cousin George's right hand woman. For that matter, a forensic audit of the Foundation could have unhappy consequences.

"What was that word you used earlier?" she asked. "'Unfortunate,' I think you said. Just how close do you think she might be to getting more...proactive?"

"For now, she's willing to go on playing the long game," Morrow said. "It's not like she ever really expected anything else. But I think she senses the way the wind is setting, and if she decides the long game is also the *losing* game, all bets are off. I just don't know where that point's likely to come."

"So what we really need is a way to convince her that it's not—not a losing strategy, I mean."

"Excuse me, but isn't that what we've been trying to do all along?" he observed a bit acidly.

"Of course it is. But so far, we've been looking at ways to, um, *mitigate* the problem, let's say. How to deal with the *consequences* of the treecats' existence."

"'Consequences,'" Morrow repeated slowly, and she nodded.

"Maybe we should consider something that looks beyond that. Sort of a Muriel Ubel sort of solution."

Something cold seemed to settle briefly in Oswald Morrow's stomach, but Gwendolyn only smiled at him, and her green eyes were bright.

"That might be—probably is—worth considering for some point in the future," he said after a moment. "It's not exactly something I've spent a lot of thought on, though. Or anything I think we want to be rushing into, for that matter."

"Oh, trust me—I'm not going anywhere near a final solution to the treecat problem unless I'm confident it'll work and that no one could trace it back to you or me," she assured him. "But it's definitely something we need to be thinking about, Ozzie. If it turns out we need it, we don't want to be trying to put the pieces together on the fly. That's how mistakes get made."

"So for now we stick with the existing strategies?"

"Such as they are," Gwendolyn agreed a bit sourly. Then she brightened. "Speaking of which, I have a meeting tomorrow that may give us a little more leverage, at least where the reservation strategy is involved."

❖   ❖   ❖

"Mr. Jones! Thank you for accepting my invitation," Gwendolyn said, standing to offer her hand as her assistant ushered her long, lanky—and generally unprepossessing—guest into her office.

"How could I resist?" Nosey replied with a broad smile, and Gwendolyn revised her initial impression upward. It was a most engaging and infectious smile, the sort that was undoubtedly useful to someone with journalistic pretensions.

"Oh?" She cocked an eyebrow at him, and he shrugged.

"I've been a fan of the Adair Foundation for a long time, Ms. Adair. And my friends Stephanie and Karl have told me how helpful you've been to them. Even putting all of that aside, though, it's my opinion that the story of the treecats can only grow going forward, especially back home on Sphinx. So anything the assistant director of the Adair Foundation—the most influential environmental preservation organization in the entire Star Kingdom—might have to say on the subject is obviously worth hearing."

"Really?" Gwendolyn waved him into a chair and seated herself behind her desk once more. "That's a very flattering description of the Foundation, but we're scarcely alone in our concern for the environment. There's the Donaldson Group, and Stephen Atkinson's organization. And, truth to tell, Interior Minister Vasquez is fully on board."

"I know." Nosey nodded and settled into the indicated armchair. "There's more than one voice speaking up, but Adair *is* the most influential—and best funded—of the lot."

"That's probably true," Gwendolyn acknowledged gravely, leaning back in her own chair. "Still, it's not as if anyone in an official position is about to sign off on any 'slash and burn' approaches to exploiting Manticore or Sphinx. Or even Gryphon! To be honest, that's not really what we're concerned about."

"You're concerned about private enterprise," he said, and it was her turn to nod.

"Exactly!" she replied, putting approval for his ability to see where she was headed into her tone. "That horrible business you were involved in with Lyric Orgeson was bad enough, but then there was Muriel Ubel." She shuddered.

"You're right, Orgeson was pretty bad." Nosey grimaced. "I guess I'd feel that way about anybody who had me beaten up and threatened to have me killed, but I was hardly the only person she was ready to hurt. On the other hand, she was mainly interested in stealing the recipe for baka bakari." He grimaced again. "Somehow, I doubt a drug cartel's likely to do as much damage as Ubel did!"

"No, it's not. But it does rather tie into what most concerns the Foundation as a future threat not just to the treecats, but to any number of other species of flora and fauna that we don't know anything more about—yet—than we knew about treecats before Stephanie encountered Lionheart the first time or about the possibility of baka bakari before Glynis Bonaventure started researching Sphinx's fungi. There's no way of telling what sort of other possibilities we're going to discover, and I'm less concerned—the Foundation is less concerned—about what official agencies might do than we are about private citizens and private entities who recognize those possibilities when they arise. Not all of our citizens are as mindful of the wilderness as Stephanie and her parents—or *you*, judging from your articles, especially about the treecats. What Ubel did after her research went south and got loose was probably worse than the vast majority of other citizens of the Star Kingdom are likely to do. Very few of them would commit mass murder to cover up their mistakes or even their deliberate destruction of habitat! On the other hand, how many of them would have as much to lose as she did if anyone found out about what they'd done? Don't fool yourself. There are plenty of people out there who are willing to exploit our planets however destructively they have to to accomplish whatever goals they may have."

"I suppose that's true," Nosey said. "No, I *know* it's true. If Orgeson had been able to produce the baka bakari she wanted by clearcutting entire hectares of Sphinx, she would've done it. And she wouldn't have cared what she had to do to protect herself if anyone found out and objected to it."

"Precisely." Gwendolyn let her chair come upright. "That's why the Foundation's pursuing a multipronged policy. We're very active in public education, which is one reason we'll be providing private funding for the Forestry Service's Explorers and other leadership programs, and that's only one of the educational initiatives we're backing. At the same time, our staff is in consultation with Ms. Vasquez and her analysts at Interior, as well as private analysts and environmentalists, to develop public policy as proactively as we can. We'd really prefer to have solutions we can offer even before the Star Kingdom at large becomes aware there's a problem that needs solving."

"That makes a lot of sense," Nosey agreed.

"We're looking at quite a lot of potential, long-term issues," she told him. "For example, very few people are aware that it looks as if the hexapuma population is in significant decline."

"Really?" Nosey blinked in surprise.

"It's still hypothetical at the moment, but the research and the number of sightings both suggest that populations are shrinking. Some of that's inevitable, given their territoriality and how large their ranges are. There are seldom as many apex predators as the general public assumes there must be, and something the size of a hexapuma needs a lot of prey animals. Which means that too often human homesteading and other activities encroach on their ranges. And, unfortunately for hexapumas, their territorial nature produces extraordinarily aggressive and dangerous behavior when that happens. That, in turn, results in a steady trickle of dead hexapumas killed in legitimate self-defense, which doesn't even consider the number killed proactively to protect livestock...or by 'big-game hunters' right here in the Star Kingdom who want a hexapuma head in their trophy room."

She grimaced and tipped her chair back again.

"Like I say, it's hypothetical right now—no one has sufficiently hard numbers to know what's really happening out in the bush. But we do know that when an apex predator's removed from its habitat it sets off a trophic cascade that can be catastrophic."

"A...trophic cascade?" Nosey repeated, and she frowned.

"Essentially, the loss of an apex predator sets off a chain of effects that move down through lower levels of the food chain, frequently with disastrous consequences. That happened a lot back on Old Earth, and on some of the older colony planets, as well. If you eliminate something like the Old Terran wolves that preyed on elk, for example, the elk herds explode in numbers and overgraze their habitat until they destroy it and literally starve. That's bad enough for them, but the destruction has a catastrophic 'ripple' effect on everything *else* that lives in that habitat, and that doesn't consider the fact that the predators help keep the herd healthy by culling the old, the infirm, and the sick. Without that, disease spreads much more easily, especially in a herd that's already weakened by starvation and the loss of habitat. The best 'solution' they could come up with in many instances back on Old Earth was to replace the natural predators with human hunters to keep the elk population under control. Eventually, they reintroduced predators into many of the wilderness areas from which they'd been eliminated, but the damage was often extreme before they could accomplish that."

"And you think the loss of the hexapumas could do that to *Sphinx*?"

"I'm sure the notion that something as dangerous as a hexapuma needs to be 'protected' seems ... odd, especially to someone who has to worry about being eaten by one of them!" Gwendolyn chuckled. "And it's not as if we've had time for the sort of long-term studies that could produce hard numbers to prove that's happening. But it's the sort of potential problem we try to look ahead for, because once the disaster's already happened, it's hard to undo it. We think it's a lot smarter to keep it from happening in the first place, if we can."

"Well, I certainly agree with that!" Nosey said. "And if you can throw any of those 'hypothetical' analyses my way, I think there are some people on Sphinx who probably need to be thinking about the same sort of problems."

"Which is exactly why I wanted to have this talk with you," Gwendolyn said. "Oh, not specifically about the hexapumas. Like I say, that's a long-term problem that may never actually arise. But just as we're supporting the Explorers, we're always looking for additional educational opportunities. From your coverage of the treecats, both before and after the Orgeson incident, you seem like a logical avenue for us to pursue. It's obvious you care deeply about them, and no close friend of Stephanie's or Karl's is going to do anything to harm them."

"You can absolutely count on that," Nosey said firmly. "I hadn't realized how smart they really are until all of us got caught up in that baka bakari mess."

"Really?" Gwendolyn asked as casually as she could.

"Before the three of us—and the Schardt-Cordovas and the rest of Stephanie's friends—got involved with stopping Orgeson, I'd thought of the treecats as adorable, really smart animals. In fact, I was worried—still am, really—about how the 'aren't they adorable' quotient could lead to situations in which they need to be protected from human exploitation. To be honest, I was worried about what people like Stephanie might be doing that was actually detrimental to 'their' treecats, but she and Karl—and Jessica, and Cordelia—set me straight at least on that. The thing is, the 'cats are even smarter than I'd thought they were, and they aren't really 'pets' at all. It's more like a . . . partnership."

"I know some people, including Clifford Mulvaney, are comparing them to service animals," Gwendolyn said, and Nosey shook his head a bit impatiently.

"I know they are, but that's not what I'm talking about. Steph and the others haven't *trained* their friends to do the things they do. They do them because they're so darned *smart*. Doctor Mulvaney's right that they don't have any way to actually communicate with us, but I'm convinced that if they did, they'd have a lot more to say than, say, an Old Terran dolphin or one of the Beowulf gremlins."

"You'd put them that high on the sentience scale?" Gwendolyn asked, watching his expression carefully, and he chuckled wryly.

"I'm not any sort of xeno-anthropologist, so I wouldn't begin to know where to put them on the scale. I'm just saying they're a lot smarter than a lot of people—*most* people—give them credit for even now."

"It's interesting you should say that," Gwendolyn said. He looked a question at her, and she shrugged. "The Foundation hasn't taken an official position on the level of their intelligence, but Earl Adair Hollow's strongly inclined to agree with you, I think. And that poses a whole clutch of potential problems of its own. Among other things, there's the question Doctor Hidalgo's been raising for some time now. If they truly are the native sapient species of Sphinx, don't we have a responsibility to protect them from additional cultural contamination? The last thing we should want to do would be to make them into...clients of humanity. A species which depends upon humans can so easily become lost and adrift. Broken, actually. Obviously, that hasn't happened to Lionheart and the other 'adoptees.' Or, at least, if they've been damaged in any way, it's certainly not evident to *me*!"

She smiled, watching Nosey's expression as her carefully chosen words resonated with his own concerns over the possibility of the treecats' "exploitation."

"I may—we may—be worrying unduly," she continued smoothly, "and, frankly, I hope we are. But if the treecats are ever formally recognized as the native sapients of Sphinx, we could be looking at all sorts of legal, even constitutional, complications. I know it's early days to be concerned over that, but, as I've been saying, the Foundation takes the long view. The last thing any of us want is for the treecats to turn into the Star Kingdom's Amphors, Mr. Jones."

"Please, call me Nosey," Nosey said, his expression more than a little unhappy. "Do you really think that could *happen*? I mean, after they've already gotten as much publicity and notice as they have?"

"I'm positive it would never happen as a result of government policy, the way it did in Barstool!" Gwendolyn said quickly. "But that's where that 'private enterprise' angle comes in. I hate to say it, but there are always unscrupulous people who couldn't care less what happens to any animal—or sapient—that gets in their way. I'm positive people like the Forestry Service would watch for that sort of thing like shadow hawks but that doesn't mean some of it wouldn't happen anyway. And, again, there's Doctor Hidalgo's point." She shook her head, her expression pensive. "The more interaction there is between humans and treecats, the more likely we are to put our foot wrong and...damage them in some way."

"Steph would never let that happen," Nosey said flatly—so flatly Gwendolyn's eyes widened. "Neither would Karl or any of the others. For that matter, Doctor Harrington's the only reason Lionheart, Survivor, and Athos are even alive! And there's no way their relationship with their human partners is damaging them—trust me!"

"I do." Gwendolyn nodded, trying to hide an edge of dismay at Nosey's vehement defense of his friends. "And it may be that *individual* interactions between humans and 'cats—single humans and single 'cats—will prove highly beneficial to both partners. I'd say that seems to be the case with Lionheart and Stephanie, at least. I haven't had as much opportunity to see Survivor and Karl, but I'd be extraordinarily surprised if it wasn't the same in their case. But what's good for individuals may not be good for an entire species, Nosey. Only a tiny number of treecats will ever form bonds with humans, if what's happened so far is any indication. I know it seems that there's been a veritable *flood* of them, but given how many treecats there must be on Sphinx and the steadily grow- ing human population, it's obviously not going to happen on any sort of widespread basis. Which means the 'cats still living 'in the wild' won't have all of the advantages that come from bonding with a human, but could still suffer the damage that contact with a more advanced, more technological, and—let's face it—encroaching human population might inflict. That's what concerns me the most right now in terms of those long-term threats the Foundation keeps an eye out for."

"I can see that," Nosey said a little grudgingly, obvi- ously still a bit defensive of his friends. "And, for that matter, I'm sure it's one of the things Steph and Karl worry about."

"Of course they do!" Gwendolyn nodded vigorously. "But I think we all need to be thinking a bit proactively about this, Nosey. I'm sure that sometime in the not-too- distant future, the Crown will move to grant the treecats protected species status as a bare minimum, and that will definitely be a step in the right direction. But I think it's likely that, ultimately, we'll need a greater degree of separation, a wider firebreak, between humans *in general* and treecats *in general*."

"But how do we pull that off?" Nosey asked.

"Well, that's the problem, isn't it?" She shrugged slightly. "We don't know enough yet about their popu- lations or social organization to have any clear idea of just how much damage we may have already done...or might do in the future. Without that, it's hard to see how we could protect them from it, but that doesn't mean it isn't something we need to be thinking about as we learn more about them. And if they are, indeed, Sphinx's native sapient species, then finding ways to protect them from current and near-future human encroachment should certainly be high on our list of future priorities, don't you think?"

"I see what you mean." Nosey frowned thoughtfully. "There are still a lot of ifs and maybes in that, though. I mean, like you say, we still don't know enough about them to be making any kind of hard and fast decisions. For that matter, there are considerably less than a million humans on the entire planet at this point. We're not likely to be overrunning their habitat any time real soon!"

"I know that." Gwendolyn nodded. "And I'm not saying it's something we'll need to deal with tomorrow, or even the next day. But it *will* be something we need to consider, eventually, because the point of the exercise is to keep them *safe*, Nosey."

"I understand. And it's not like there's always a neat, clean solution to complicated problems." Nosey shook his head. "You've given me a lot to think about, Ms. Adair."

"Gwendolyn, please," Gwendolyn said with another smile. "Or just Gwen, if you're comfortable with it. And I'm sure quite a lot of what I've been saying would have occurred to you eventually."

"*I'm* not so sure of that," Nosey told her with a grin. "But I *will* think about it."

"Good! And stay in touch," Gwendolyn said. "As I said, we are always looking for leadership channels of public education, and I'm sure the"—she smiled broadly—"'Nose for News' could be very useful in that respect on Sphinx!"

3

IF THIS HAD BEEN A HOLOVID DRAMA, STEPHANIE'S testimony with its reminder that there was recorded evidence of Stormy's capacity for carefully planned malice would have been the turning point in the trial. However, since this was real life, the trial stretched for several more days. At one point, Stephen Ford managed to unnerve Jorge Prakel by insinuating that Jorge, not Stormy, was the guilty party, so that Jorge's testimony began to look unreliable. However, the counsel for the prosecution was not only skilled, she had the weight of facts on her side, including, but not exclusively, the images from Stephanie's uni-link.

The jury didn't rush, but the judge's instructions were clear, and when they came in and delivered their verdict that Erina Wether was guilty of premeditated murder, the judge did not hesitate to pass sentence.

Listening to the formula that stated that Erina Wether, having been found guilty of murder in the first degree and was sentenced to "hang by the neck until dead," Stephanie felt unexpectedly queasy. It wasn't that she regretted the part she and Karl had played, or that she hadn't understood what the end result would be if Stormy was found guilty. The formal words—as well as the expression of shock and panic that coursed over Stormy's face when she heard them and finally realized she wasn't going to get away with it—made it all real.

There was something different about looking for evidence, hoping it would be enough for a conviction, being part of laying out a plan of attack. There was something "hot" about that, like a chase or a fight. The law was not hot. The law was very, very cold.

And maybe, Stephanie thought, *that coldness is what we want, what we need to stay civilized. I've seen for myself what acting from heat, from temper, does. In the end, no matter how good it feels at the time, it's worse to act in the heat of the moment.*

So, even though she accepted the gentle pressure of Karl's shoulder against hers in a sort of invisible hug, Stephanie sat straight and tall, listening with stern attention as the words were spoken that would turn a living woman who she'd once actually liked into a soon to be corpse.

If I stay in the SFS, it's likely I'm going to sit in a lot more courtrooms, give a lot more testimony. The charge won't always be murder, thank goodness, but I'll always need to accept that in the end, I'm responsible to the legal code, not just to myself. There's no room for "better to ask forgiveness than permission" if I stay a law officer. I must always remember that I can only act within what the law permits.

When Stormy was led from the courtroom, Stephanie forced herself to watch. When she and Karl made their own exit, wordlessly heading off to collect Lionheart and

Survivor, Stephanie felt as if she was suddenly a lot older than sixteen going on seventeen.

But that didn't mean she didn't feel glad to have Lionheart there, patting her softly with his remaining true-hand, and buzzing a reassuring purr.

"What do you two think about taking a holiday before we go back to Sphinx?" Marjorie Harrington asked over breakfast the day after the verdict. She spoke with a sort of forced brightness, perfectly aware that Stephanie and Karl—even the treecats—were definitely subdued now that sentence had been passed. So much of their energy these last several months had been devoted to the case, and now it was over.

"By 'holiday,'" Marjorie went on, "I mean a real one. Our jaunt to Gryphon was supposed to be educational, as well as fun, sure, but it turned into rather more than any of us expected."

"We've been away from Sphinx quite a while," Karl began. "I don't know how Chief Shelton would feel about my taking more time off."

Richard cut in before Karl could get any further. "When I queried Chief Shelton, he said you're due back leave, because you ended up working much of your scheduled time off, even given our extending our stay on Gryphon."

"But my parents—" Karl began again, but this time Marjorie was the one to cut in.

"I've been in touch with your mother," she said. "All along, I mean, but especially over the last few days. Evelina was actually the one who first suggested that you needed to take some downtime. She was disturbed by how drawn you looked on the news vids. To quote, she said she knows 'perfectly well that as soon as Karl's been home for two days, he'll find himself drifting over to SFS headquarters, trying to catch up on what he missed. Probably the only way to make him rest is to keep him off planet.'"

Marjorie did a fair imitation of the slightly scolding tone Evelina Zivonik frequently adopted to hide her genuine affection for her large brood, which ranged from fully grown Karl to little Lev, who was nearly three.

"Well, I might stay away from headquarters as much as three days," Karl replied, laughing. "Or even four. Got to resynch the calendars, after all, then there's adjusting to the higher gravity on Sphinx. So, she and Dad really wouldn't mind if I took a holiday here?"

"I think they'd both be relieved," Marjorie said. "They miss you, absolutely, but after this long, they'd rather get you back rested and relaxed."

"I've been looking forward to seeing our friends back home," Stephanie put in, "even more since we had the chance to visit with Trudy and Nosey. Seeing them reminded me how much I missed everybody. But . . . I hate to say it, but you're right. Karl looks terrible. He really needs a break."

"Have you looked in the mirror recently, squirt?" Karl said, reaching over to knuckle her gently on top of her head. "You're too young to have circles like that under your eyes."

"Then you like the idea?" Marjorie asked. "Of a holiday? A real holiday?"

"Mom," Stephanie said, "you and Dad are the best. What do you have in mind? My only thought is that I'd really like to get out of the city."

"Then you should like this," Richard said. "A friend's offered us use of his holiday place right on Jason Bay. He showed me images of what he calls a 'cottage' and what I'd call a really nice split-level house. It's right on the beach, and has a boathouse with a few small craft we can use. Even better, it's not so far from civilization that you can't meet up with some of the friends you made when you were taking classes here, if you get tired of swimming and sunbathing and paddling about."

Stephanie, thinking of the long hours in the dry sterility of the courthouse, grinned ear to ear. "I don't think I could get tired of that. I love swimming in lighter gravity."

"Then let's consider it settled," Richard said. "We'll do some shopping for food—"

"And beachwear," Marjorie added.

"We have swimsuits," Stephanie reminded her. "We packed them for Gryphon."

"Practical suits," Marjorie sniffed. "I want one that will make me feel like I'm on holiday, not collecting specimens. And we'll need sunscreen, and shorts and sleeveless tops, and—"

Richard rolled his eyes. "Go shopping, but we head out for the cottage tomorrow morning. If we time things right, we should be in the water well before noon."

4

<I THINK,> MUSED KEEN EYES, <THAT I LIKE THE WATER *here better than I do in that other place. It does not tug as hard, and it is less salty. The fish are tasty, too.*>

Climbs Quickly looked to where his friend lay flopped along a made-log of some material that was very buoyant, and, unlike wood, did not soak up water. Death Fang's Bane and Shining Sunlight had given each of the People a log of his own, and had demonstrated how they could paddle about on them. This was a good alternative to swimming. Even though a Person's fur shed water very well, it did eventually become sodden.

The two-legs had made-logs of their own, as well as more elaborate constructions that let them sit in the water as if they were on land, not that Death Fang's Bane did much sitting. She swam, dove, and periodically surfaced under where Shining Sunlight "napped," spilling him into the water, whereupon he would chase after her, as if irritated.

The two were behaving like first-year kittens, and Climbs Quickly completely approved. Their mind-glows had darkened increasingly during the long days spent in the arguing place. Their moods on what had proven to be the final day of that vigil had been a strange mixture of triumph and something so complicated he was still trying to sort it out.

<It was as if,> Keen Eyes offered, sensing from the taste of Climbs Quickly's mind-glow that he was once again thinking over their two-legs' recent moods, <they had gone hunting and caught their prey, only to decide it was somehow distasteful, but they wanted it no less. Sometimes I wonder if we will ever truly understand two-legs and what drives some of their actions.>

<I do not think we will,> Climbs Quickly replied, <so I will be content that at this moment they both seem to be recovering from the cost of catching their prey.>

Today the two-legs were on shore, idly batting back and forth a small object over a long net strung between two poles. They didn't use their hands, but some sort of made thing that gave them the equivalent of longer arms and wider hands. The activity might have been training for some sort of hunting, but since there were no memory songs that showed two-legs hunting in that fashion, perhaps it was just a game. Certainly there was a great deal of laughter, since they kept hitting the small thing farther than they intended and then running after it.

A short time later, a flying thing came to a halt near the nesting place they were using. Seeing it, Death Fang's Bane's mind-glow lit with pleasure, and she made rapid mouth noises to Shining Sunlight.

<Visitors!> Climbs Quickly said to Keen Eyes. With visions of clusterstalk dancing in his head, he began paddling toward shore.

✧   ✧   ✧

Stephanie and Karl put aside their badminton rackets and hurried to meet the two men and one woman who were getting out of the air car: Allen Harper, Jeff Harrison, and Carmen Telford.

Allen and Carmen were Sphinxians who were studying on Manticore. When Karl and Stephanie had come to take part in the accelerated forest service course, Allen had been working as an assistant to one of the deans and had been assigned to help Stephanie and Karl find their way around campus. He'd been warm and friendly, and had even introduced them to Gwendolyn Adair, whose cousin's foundation was very interested in promoting the well-being of Star Kingdom wildlife, up to and definitely including treecats.

Since his graduate work was in geology, Allen hadn't been in any classes with them, but Carmen had been in their classes at the School of Forestry. Her family was very involved in logging, which was one of Sphinx's major industries. However, the Telfords were already looking to the future, and considered themselves custodians of all the lands where they did their work, not just of their Crown Oak barony. Carmen's studies were meant to keep the family business abreast of the "cutting edge," as she frequently joked, of the industry.

The remaining guest, Jeff Harrison, had been in their law enforcement classes. Although a native of Manticore, he'd been fascinated by treecats. As Lionheart had been the first treecat to leave Sphinx, Jeff had made a beeline for him. Stephanie, feeling no threat, only enthusiasm, had accepted his interest, knowing that the time would come when the treecats would need advocates.

Although all three of the visitors were four to five years older than Karl, they had taken the younger pair under their aegis without being in the least condescending, something which Stephanie, in particular, had appreciated.

Being fifteen and studying with college and even graduate students, as well as serving law officers updating their training, had been fairly intimidating.

"So, this is Survivor," Jeff said, hunkering down to offer the 'cat a piece of celery. Stephanie appreciated that Jeff had shown her and Karl the container first, in a mute request for permission. She granted this readily, having anticipated that their guests would likely bring treats, and so not given Lionheart any celery so far that day. Treecats could eat celery, and did so with great enthusiasm, but there were digestive consequences.

Clearly, Jeff's fascination with treecats hadn't ebbed one bit. Stephanie recognized the look of longing that she mentally dubbed "treecat envy." They were seeing more and more of that now that adoptions were occurring with increasing frequency, but Jeff was a good guy, not one of those who thought of the treecats as up for grabs was evident in how easily Lionheart and Survivor accepted him.

"Yep, that's Survivor," Karl agreed cordially. "Looking a whole lot better than when we first met, let me tell you."

"I've seen the images," Jeff said. "He's a whole lot less shredded, that's for sure."

"The treecats seem to be enjoying their time at the beach," put in Carmen. "Do they swim a lot back on Sphinx?"

"They definitely swim in rivers," Stephanie replied. "Scott McDallan calls his treecat 'Fisher,' because they met when Scott had an accident when out fishing, and the cat came to help. And because he does a *lot* of fishing—the pounce and leap sort—of his own."

"From what I've been reading in the Adair Foundation reports," Jeff added, "treecats are amazingly bright, at least as smart as a dog, I'd guess."

"At least," Stephanie agreed.

"The defense attorney for the Wether trial was a first-rate jerk," Jeff went on. "I'm taking an advanced criminology class with Dr. Flouret right now, great stuff. Flouret was solidly impressed with how you two used what you'd learned in his class, and absolutely livid when Ford tried to undermine the value of your testimony, just because you mentioned that the treecats were uneasy."

Jeff squared his shoulders and did a pretty good imitation of the professor. "'If Ms. Harrington had said her dog was uneasy, no one would question the validity of that statement but, because she's still a minor and treecats are a relatively unknown quantity, perceived by many to be 'cute,' Ford took a gamble. Happily, Ms. Harrington kept her head.'"

"I nearly didn't," Stephanie admitted. "But that's over. I want to hear all about all of all of your classes, but first do you want to go for a swim?"

"One vote here for swimming," Allen said. "This is a gorgeous beach."

"Another vote for swimming here," Carmen said, reaching back to grab a streamlined duffle from the air car. "Is there somewhere I can change?"

"Sure," Stephanie said. "You can use my room if you want. That way the boys can have the beach pavilion. C'mon." The young women trotted upstairs. When they reached her room, Stephanie darted in to grab her swimming gear from the dresser. "All yours. I'll change in my folks' room."

"Thanks." Carmen walked over the threshold, stumbled, then caught herself. "What the heck?"

Stephanie swung around to see Carmen had caught hold of the doorframe, a look of astonishment on her face.

"You've got the grav up in here," Carmen said, laughing. "I didn't expect that in a private house and got caught off-guard."

Stephanie moved as if to change the setting, but Carmen waved her back, still laughing.

"I keep the grav up for Lionheart, really," Stephanie hastened to explain. "We started doing this back when Karl and I came to take the courses here on Manticore, and Lionheart came with me. Dad pointed out that we didn't want Lionheart to get out of condition for higher gees, especially since he's already functioning minus one limb. So now the protocol is for the 'cats to spend enough time in a room where the gravity can be adjusted to Sphinx norm to keep them in shape. I benefit, too."

Carmen nodded. "No problem. I do the same in my dorm room, because I don't want to go home and need to use a counter grav unit like I'm a tourist. Like I said, it just caught me by surprise. I'll leave it set for Sphinx. Catch you downstairs."

Before they'd left Landing for Jason Bay, Marjorie had taken herself and Stephanie shopping for the sort of beachwear they didn't have much use for in Sphinix's much cooler climate. Remembering how hot Manticore could be, Stephanie had happily agreed, and even let her mom talk her into another swimsuit.

"That way you'll have one to use when the other is wet," Marjorie said. "That's practical, right?"

Both suits were dry today, and Stephanie dithered slightly before choosing the newer one. Although cut only a little lower in the neck and higher on the legs than the racing model one-piece she wore on outings to the Y in Twin Forks, the suit's ombre-pattern green managed to suggest that there was a lot less suit than there actually was. It felt just a little daring, and Stephanie had to resist tying her beach wrap firmly closed before heading downstairs.

She was glad she hadn't, because Carmen hadn't even bothered with a wrap, and she'd have had a lot more justification. Carmen's suit was a two piece that left little to the imagination. What fabric the suit possessed was in a golden yellow that went amazingly well with Carmen's dark skin and ash-blonde hair. Her build was the somewhat stocky, muscular type common to those born on Sphinx, but Carmen filled out the suit's triangular pieces front and back in a way that made having extra a definite asset.

I look like a complete kid next to her, Stephanie thought, *but at least I don't need to worry about falling out of my suit. Not that Carmen looks worried. She's enjoying the effect she's having on the guys.*

But Karl wasn't looking at Carmen. He was looking at Stephanie, a little grin quirking the corner of his mouth.

"I hoped you'd wear the green suit," he said. "I like that color on you."

Stephanie didn't know what to say. She hadn't even realized Karl had noticed that she had more than one suit. To cover a sudden fear she'd say something dumb, she tossed off her wrap and headed for the water, hoping it would cool what felt like a full-body blush.

It was a good day. Swimming segued into a game of volleyball, with Marjorie and Richard taking turns rounding out the sides. Then, when everyone was thoroughly sodden, and being dry seemed ideal, they moved onto the wide deck that faced the water and had less a meal than an extended cookout, the theme of which was experimenting with grilling just about anything that had caught Richard and Marjorie's attention when they'd been at the local farmer's market earlier that day. There was seafood, finny and in the shell, various burgers, sausages, and a variety of fruits and vegetables, as well as fresh bread.

Failed experiments were tossed to the wave cresters that soared overhead, their high-shrill voices seeming to call, "Me! Me!"

"I'm going to miss baking in standard gravity when we get home," Marjorie admitted. "I'm getting spoiled by how easily things rise, and how simple it is to make fluffy pastries."

"Oh, I dunno," Stephanie said, "I love your double dense cakes."

"Pick a flavor, and I'll make one for your birthday," Marjorie said.

"Is your birthday coming up soon, Stephanie?" Carmen asked. "How old will you be?"

"In January," Stephanie said. "I'll be seventeen."

"Ah," Allen said, putting on a portentous tone. "How quickly they grow up. Why it seems just yesterday that I was guiding around a wide-eyed fifteen-year-old."

Stephanie tossed an admittedly fluffy roll at him. He caught it and laughed.

"Seriously, though, it's hard to remember you're not even legal," he said, and Jeff laughed, as well.

"Tell me about it. Try being in class with her! Karl was pretty sharp, too. He only missed out on being labeled a Boy Wonder because Stephanie was even younger." He grew serious. "Karl, Steph, I was wondering, I've been thinking about applying for a post with the SFS. Would you put in a good word for me?"

"Absolutely," they said in unison, then started laughing.

"It started with the treecats, I'll admit," Jeff went on, "but I've gotten interested in a lot of other things that belong to Sphinx." His gaze slid toward Carmen, who did a very good job of hiding that she noticed.

"There are a lot of opportunities on Sphinx," Allen said, "and still a need for settlers, because not all of us who were born there plan to go back. Nothing against Sphinx, but my field is geology. I want to go exploring. Gryphon is actually pretty high on my list."

"Tell us about your classes," Stephanie said. "Seriously,

I want to know. College is coming up, and even if I opt for doing courses on the net, I still want to have a sense of what professors are best."

When the trio left well after dark, Stephanie noticed that Carmen took the back seat, rather than sitting up front with Jeff, who was driving.

"I think Jeff has a crush on Carmen," she said, "but I'm not sure if she does on him or not."

"It's hard to tell whether someone is just not interested or playing hard to get," Karl said. "I mean, you're pretty intuitive, but you aren't the greatest about noticing when people have crushes."

Karl turned and started walking along the beach away from the cottage. He trailed above where the waves left fingers of foam that gleamed with something slightly phosphorescent. Stephanie joined him, walking to his right, a little higher up the beach. The treecats romped along, splashing in the surf.

"You mean like I didn't notice Anders was falling for Jess?" she said. "Or that neither of us would have taken even a long-odds bet on Trudy and Nosey getting together?"

She wondered if Karl was thinking about Sumiko, his first girlfriend, who'd wanted them to get engaged even though they weren't out of high school. They'd been childhood friends and foster siblings, but Karl had never realized Sumiko was quite as ready to formalize the relationship as she was. When she'd died in an accident, his grief had been mixed with guilt that he'd disappointed her hopes.

Stephanie was so deeply lost in her thoughts that she almost missed what Karl was saying. When she realized, she couldn't believe it.

"I was thinking you've never noticed that I have a crush on you," Karl said, his voice low and steady. "A pretty serious one, if I'm honest with myself. And I want to be honest with myself, and with you. I think I've fallen in love with you, Stephanie Elizabeth Harrington."

Stephanie froze in her tracks, then scurried to catch up with him. She grabbed Karl's arm, conscious of the feel of him in a way she'd never been before.

"Me? Me? I thought, I thought if you had a crush on anyone it was Cordelia."

Cordelia Schardt-Cordova was the newest treecat adoptee, closer in age to Karl than Stephanie was, and, like him, from a large family of Sphinx natives. Cordelia and Karl had a lot in common, including having been children during the Plague, and having lost people close to them. And they both had treecats, too, which was a definite bonus.

Karl turned to face Stephanie, looking down at her. There was sufficient moonlight for Stephanie to see his face quite clearly. His oh-so-familiar features held a new expression that not so much transformed him as revealed a hidden part of his soul. He looked unwontedly serious, then his lips curved with a touch of a smile.

"You're not horrible, you know," he said. "You're actually really amazing. And you're much prettier than you give yourself credit for. And I've had a crush on you since...Oh, since before you decided to fall for Anders. I was actually working up the courage to talk to you when you made it clear your affections were centered elsewhere."

He put two fingers under Stephanie's chin and tilted her head slightly back so that despite the differences in their heights, he could look into her eyes.

"I spent a lot of time resenting that Anders was your first kiss. And then I decided that was stupid, because well...Y'know, Sumiko and I did at least get around to kissing."

"Oh," Stephanie said. Her heart was beating impossibly

fast, and she wondered if Karl's fingers had always been so warm, because she could swear they were burning her skin. She wondered if Karl was going to kiss her. Then she realized that, unlike the "heroes" of so many romances dramas, he wasn't going to kiss her without making certain he'd be welcome. That meant she had to say something, anything...

"I...Oh...I...Do you want to..." She started to say "kiss me," then chickened out. "Uh, date? Or something? I mean, like boyfriend girlfriend, not just best friends, because you've always been my best friend, human friend, I mean...You're not Lionheart, but you've always been more than Jess, and..."

You're screwing this up, Stephanie, she thought frantically. *But then Karl had an idea what he wanted to say, and this came out of nowhere for you, and now you're comparing him to a treecat, which I'm pretty sure is not what you're supposed to do.*

Karl started shaking and his hand dropped. To her horror Stephanie realized he was trying not to laugh.

"So, I'm bad at this!" she said, stomping one foot in irritation. Then, stretching up on her toes and putting her hands on his shoulders, she kissed Karl firmly on the mouth. She'd meant it to be just a little kiss, an introduction to kissing but, somehow, once they got started, she didn't want to pull her lips away. Happily, it didn't seem as if Karl did either. He put his arms around her. Half-lifting her off her feet, he repositioned her so that they could sink down onto the sand. That did a lot to get rid of the height problem. Stephanie let her arms slide around his shoulders, pulling Karl to her, and lips were parting and things were happening, and in a moment, it seemed as if stretching out on the sand would be a very good idea...

The cry of a sleepy wave crester coming in to roost on the beach pavilion roof broke the spell.

"Oh, you're not bad at that at all," Karl said, his eyes wide, his finger trailing down the side of Stephanie's face. He kissed her again, more deeply, then drew back. "I think you're very, very good, and are just going to get better, and we'd better stop or I'm going to be forgetting you're sixteen and not yet the age of consent, and all sorts of things."

But he kissed her again, less urgently, then laughed.

"To answer your question...Actually, I do want to date, like boyfriend and girlfriend and all that. Shall we give it a try? See if we can manage both as a couple, and as co-workers without ruining a beautiful friendship?"

Stephanie snuggled close to him, feeling as if she'd always sat in the shelter of his arms, his head lightly pillowed on top of hers. Her heart was slowing down, but she was aware of her pulse beating in all sorts of places where it had never beaten before.

"We're not going to ruin it," she said, confidently. "We're not going to ruin anything."

Tilting back her head, she kissed him again. Then she let him pull her to her feet, and with his arm around her, they walked slowly back toward the beach cottage, wordless and completely content.

<Is that bonding, two-leg fashion?> Keen Eyes asked, shaking himself hard, as if to remove the overwhelming sensations that were flooding him from Shining Sunlight along with the droplets of salty water.

<I think it is,> Climbs Quickly confirmed, comparing the sensations to those Swift Striker had shared when Darkness Foe had bonded with his mate.

<Will they mate now? Will we have two-leg kits soon?> Keen Eye's mind-glow held a fair element of trepidation. Courtesy of Shining Sunlight's large birth clan, he was

all too familiar with the noisy chaos that was the two-leg young.

Climbs Quickly considered what he was feeling from Death Fang's Bane.

<I do not think that our two-legs will immediately mate. I have never quite understood how and when two-legs are in season, but this feels like an awakening of awareness of a bond, especially on Death Fang's Bane's part. She has always been a bit slow in understanding things to do with others of her kind, perhaps because she has no littermates. Until not long ago, she did not even have friends close to her own age.>

<Even Shining Sunlight is her elder,> Keen Eyes agreed. <Or so I believe. It is difficult to tell, when one cannot count the rings on the tail or consult the memory songs for where in the cycle of seasons a kit was born.>

<I am relieved they have reached this awareness of each other,> Climbs Quickly said, basking in Death Fang's Bane's happiness. Her mind-glow felt as might the petals of a snowstar, unfolding toward the growing light of day, even if still encased in end-of-winter snow. <When Shining Sunlight began to spend less time with her, Death Fang's Bane's enjoyment of what she did was dimmed. I don't think she was aware of this, any more than one instantly notices when high clouds dim the sun. But that made the darkening no less real.>

<I always felt there was a bond between Shining Sunlight and Death Fang's Bane,> Keen Eyes mused, <even in the earliest days of my knowing them. I was more astonished to learn they seemed unaware of it than I would have been to discover they were a mated pair with several litters behind them. When I discovered that Death Fang's Bane's partner seemed to be Bleached Fur, I was astonished.>

<You met them later than I did,> Climbs Quickly said, <and the change came slowly. You helped. Before

you, there was a shadow over Shining Sunlight. When that was banished by his bond with you, I think he began to trust in his ability to shape a bond with another two-leg. But there was Bleached Fur. And then there was not. But even so, Death Fang's Bane and Shining Sunlight have taken so long to realize what has seemed obvious to all who know them.>

<About time!> Keen Eyes agreed. <About time!>

5

VIDOSLAV KARADZIC STOOD COURTEOUSLY AND SMILED, extending his hand across the table as Gwendolyn Adair walked into the small private dining room.

Like Gwendolyn herself, he was a direct descendent of a First Wave family. That was a significant social cachet even in relatively recently settled system like Manticore, although—again, like Gwendolyn—he held no aristocratic title or any hope of inheriting one. He was, however, related to two barons and a countess, and his family connections helped to explain his success as a management consultant, since they got him access to almost anyone when he needed it.

Gwendolyn understood how that worked, since she used exactly the same advantages in her own endeavors.

"Gwen! So lovely to see you, my dear!" Karadzic beamed. With his brown hair, brown eyes, and broad, cheerful face, he looked like anyone's favorite uncle, and he patted the back of the hand he held before he released it and waved her into the chair on her side of the table.

"It's been too long," he continued. "Tell me, what can I do for you or George?"

Gwendolyn smiled back, although she, for one, had never been taken in by his cheerful, artless expression. Then again, she knew him rather better than her cousin did. Although Karadzic had handled quite a few management issues for Earl Adair Hollow, all of them had been legal.

"Actually, I'm not here for George," she said, which didn't appear to surprise him. "My calendar says I am, so we probably do need to talk about a couple of issues the Foundation's having with one of its vendors, but the main reason I asked to meet you here is rather different."

"I'm shocked," he said mildly, and this time Gwendolyn snorted in amusement.

"I'm sure you are," she said. The dining room in Karadzic's private club had *excellent* security systems, which was one of several reasons he liked to do business here. Especially when the business at hand had any... questionable aspects.

"So, what seems to be the problem?" he asked in a more businesslike tone, and she grimaced.

"It's the damned treecats," she said.

"What? Is it possible you're telling me that you aren't really fully on board with George's efforts on their behalf? I'm shocked—*shocked!*" Karadzic's surprised expression might have fooled a particularly credulous six-year-old.

"Oh, come on, Vidoslav!" Gwendolyn rolled her eyes. "I'm sure you, of all people, know Angelique Frampton and I are considerably closer than dear George realizes. And I'll let you guess how she feels about the possibility of the treecats being declared Sphinx's native sapient species."

"Given how heavily invested she is in land futures on Sphinx, I don't have to guess," he said affably. "So should I take it that Angelique has approached you and your friend Morrow to do something about that?"

"I'm sure we're not the only ones she's approached, but yes. And the problem is that I have a ringside seat for how this is likely to play out in the end."

"Not well from her perspective, I'd wager."

"Got it in one." Gwendolyn nodded with a disgusted expression. "I'm fighting a delaying action, and George trusts me enough that I can keep the 'really-smart-animals-but-not-true-sapients' door open a crack even in his own mind. But that crack's getting steadily narrower, and the 'cats are getting steadily more visible. Especially since that business on Gryphon. Clifford Mulvaney's helping to downplay the *extent* of their sapience, but I doubt very much that we'll be able to keep that up a lot longer. It doesn't help that Stephanie Harrington is such an attractive and articulate spokesperson for them, either! She made Ford look like exactly what he was—a patronizing cretin trying to discredit her testimony by patting her on the head and telling her what a cute little girl she was. The only good thing about it is that for reasons of her own, and I suspect I know what they are, she and her friends have chosen to go slow on asserting the treecats' intelligence. In the end, though, that's not going to last. It can't."

"Then it would appear you face an insoluble dilemma, my dear," Karadzic observed.

"That's one of the things I've always liked about you, Vidoslav. How perceptive you are. Except that I don't believe there are any truly insoluble dilemmas if one can only find the proper angle of attack."

"Ah?" He raised his eyebrows in polite question.

"I'm not prepared to give up entirely on the notion that we can successfully argue that they aren't *fully* sapient," Gwendolyn said. "I admit the chance of that is fading, but it's not completely off the table yet. And my fallback plan is to back Hidalgo's position that they need to be protected from cultural contamination, which means we have to provide reservations for them, where they'll be safe from disastrous human contact."

"And said reservations will just happen to be someplace they won't inconvenience Angelique and her fellow investors?"

"Exactly. But it's always possible the fallback won't work, either. For that matter, it's always possible they'll be granted protected species status even if they aren't classified as fully sapient, which will automatically protect their habitat—their native habitat—as well. In fact, I'm willing to bet *that* one's coming at us sometime soon, now. So it's possible that I'll need a more...a more *permanent* solution to the problem."

"And you have such a solution in mind?"

"Well, it would be a pity if something happened to them, wouldn't it?"

"What sort of 'something'?" Karadzic asked. "Are you by any chance thinking in terms of a larger rendition of Muriel Ubel's unfortunate accident?"

"Oh, please, Vidoslav! That was a crude, utterly botched affair. Leaving aside how destructive of the rest of the local biosphere it was, the very scope of the disaster prompted an immediate response that mitigated most of the damage to the treecats themselves. And I'm sure the Sphinx Forestry Service is keeping an eagle eye out for anything else along those lines. Besides, it's not as if I want the little beasties to *suffer*."

"So what do you want?" Karadzic leaned forward, folding his arms on the table, his expression more intent.

"I'm looking for something...subtle. Something that might help encourage the treecats' champions to be in *favor* of isolating them from human contact. And something no one could ever trace back to me." Gwendolyn smiled. "That's why I've come to you. You're so *inventive* about these things. And you know so many people in all the most interesting places."

"I see." Karadzic leaned back again, rubbing his chin thoughtfully while he gazed sightlessly at nothing in particular. He sat that way for quite some time before his eyes refocused and he looked back at Gwendolyn.

"Did I ever mention to you that I know Joshua Muñoz?"

"At the Urquhart Group?"

"Yes. He and I are actually scheduled to have dinner next Tuesday on a different matter. It's possible he might be able to assist us with your little problem. For a reasonable fee, of course."

"Oh, of course! But I'd suggest you put it to him as an on-spec proposition. Angelique isn't the sort to lay money around on hypothetical projects. She'd probably trust me to greenlight any project, since that would keep her well away from it, but she's unlikely to put down even a down payment unless there's a reasonable probability of success. And she'll probably only pay in full if the plan—whatever it is—actually succeeds. Which means I'd need a well-organized, specific proposal. One I can be confident enough in that I'd feel justified in presenting it to Angelique, bearing in mind that if I sell her on it and then it falls through, the repercussions could be...unfortunate."

"That goes without saying, my dear." Karadzic smiled at her. "I'll get back to you after Joshua and I have our little tête-à-tête."

"That was...not bad," Trudy Franchitti said. "In fact, it was just as good as you said it would be."

"Told you so." She sat beside Nosey on the comfortable couch in his hotel room, her legs folded under her while she leaned her head on his shoulder, and he turned his head to kiss her dark hair lightly. "Pinocchio was always one of my favorite stories, when I was a kid. And this HD is actually an adaptation of a fairly late pre-Diaspora animation of it. I've seen a few minutes of the original that were digitally preserved, and given the limitations they had with things like CGI, it was actually pretty good. I do like this one better, though."

"I wonder why we lost track of it," Trudy mused. "I mean, I've seen...echoes, I guess you'd call them, of the same story idea often enough. So where did the original go?"

"I expect it just got lost in the underbrush." Nosey raised the arm that wasn't draped around her to turn off the HD with the remote. "I mean, we've got an awful lot of recorded history now. No way people could remember all of the children's stories that were ever written down."

"You're probably right." She nodded and snuggled a little closer. "I did like it, though. A lot."

There was something almost...wistful about her tone, and Nosey looked down at the crown of her head. He and Trudy were still discovering things about each other—a process he thoroughly enjoyed and planned to continue for the next, oh, fifty T-years or so—but he'd never heard quite that note in her voice before.

"I'm glad. I guess there's something in all of us that looks for that kind of change," he said in a deliberately thoughtful tone. "Something that makes us want to be more than we are, especially when it seems impossible."

"Maybe," she said.

He hugged her a bit more tightly and pressed another fleeting kiss to her hair.

"That wasn't what caught your attention in it?" he asked. "I mean, that's the classic element that all the critics would fasten on. If you're seeing something else,

I'd love to hear it." She raised her head enough to look at him, and he shrugged. "Hey! You know me. I'm always fascinated by the 'road not taken.' I think it's really cool when someone sees something the rest of the thundering herd misses, and you've actually got a pretty good eye for that kind of thing."

"Yeah—sure!" Trudy snorted. "Next thing you're going to be telling me I'm as smart as Stephanie!"

Nosey hid an inner frown. He knew about the original friction between Trudy and Stephanie, and knowing both young women, he wasn't surprised they hadn't hit it off in the beginning. But as he'd come to care more and more deeply for Trudy, he'd discovered something he suspected Stephanie hadn't twigged to. Not yet, at least. Which was probably because the one handicap from which Stephanie Harrington had never suffered was lack of self-confidence. She'd suffered the consequences of *too much* self-confidence often enough, but she'd never heard of the challenge she wouldn't accept.

And that could very well be the reason Stephanie had never realized that the person behind the flirtatious, challenging, often irritatingly superior and sometimes cuttingly sarcastic persona Trudy had presented to the world for so long—still presented, actually, except with those she'd come to trust—was driven by the exact opposite of Stephanie's confidence. She hid it well. It had taken months for her protective barriers to come down enough even for Nosey to realize it, but that lack of self-confidence, or maybe what it really was was a lack of self-*belief*, was there, deep at the heart of her. And he couldn't figure out why. She was gorgeous, she had a truly wicked sense of humor when it was fully engaged, and she was far, far more intelligent than she gave herself credit for . . . or allowed others to realize. And one way she'd managed to hide that intelligence from most people—at least until she'd become involved in the baka bakari mess and met Nosey—was to hide behind relationships with "bad boys" like Stan Chang and Frank Câmara. The only place she'd really let her mask slip was in her involvement with Wild and Free.

And now with him.

She'd let a handful of other people in, after the air car accident that killed Stan, but none of the others had seen as deeply beneath her inner barriers as he had, and now he sensed something stirring behind them.

"To be honest," he said lightly, "I suspect that very few people are as smart as Stephanie. Which, you may have noticed, didn't keep her from almost getting herself killed the day she and Lionheart met. Compared to mere mortals like myself, however, don't sell yourself short. You're not just smart, Trudy. Oh, you are—in fact, I think you're probably smarter than I am, and I'm not exactly a dummy myself—but what you are that's a lot more important than just smart is a good, caring person. You have what my mom always called 'the good heart.' That's why you spend so much time with Wild and Free. Although, now that I think about it, maybe the fact that you also spend so much time with *me* suggests that you aren't *quite* as smart as I thought you were."

She grinned at his last sentence, but the grin was short-lived and her eyes were dark.

He bent his head so that their foreheads touched and cupped the back of her head with his free hand.

"What's bugging you?" he asked softly. She stiffened, but he held her gently close. "I know something is. Tell me about it."

"There's nothing," she said quickly, and her voice was tauter than it had been.

"Yes, there is," he disagreed in that same soft tone. "And you don't have to tell me what it is if you don't want to, honey. But people do themselves an awful lot of damage when they keep things bottled up inside too long. Especially if they're hurtful things. Another thing my mom said to me, years ago, is that the knives that cut us most deeply are the ones we sharpen ourselves. She's a smart lady, my mom. I don't want you sharpening any more knives than you have to."

She sat very, very still for a long, silent moment. Then she sighed and let herself relax against his side once more.

"It's just that...that it wasn't Pinocchio's ability to become 'real' that I envied him for. It was Geppetto."

Nosey's eyebrows rose. That wasn't exactly the response he'd expected, and yet—

"Geppetto?" he repeated. "You mean for creating him in the first place?"

"No." Her voice was much lower and her shoulders drooped. "Or not just for that. I envied him because Geppetto loved him."

The last three words cut Nosey to the heart. He'd never heard that tone from her before, not even when they'd talked about Stan's death and her own terrible injuries. It was so...bleak. So empty.

He started to say something quickly, something comforting. But then he made himself stop. Made himself simply sit there, holding her, being there for her.

"I never had that, really," she said finally. "Not from *my* father, anyway. And I think that may be the thing I most envied—resented, even—about Stephanie and Jessica, back when we were constantly locking horns. Because they had what I didn't, and god, how I wished I had it, too."

Her tone was no longer empty. It was hard, bitter. Nosey wrapped both arms around her.

"Tell me," he said softly. "If you want to."

"I don't want to," she half-whispered, "but I think I *need* to."

"I'm listening," he promised, and saw tears in her eyes as she raised her head to kiss his cheek.

"I know you are. I know you always will be. That's the thing about you, Nosey Jones. You're such a good guy you just can't help caring about people, even when you try to hide it."

"That's me!" he told her. "Candidate for sainthood Nosey Jones!"

"I wouldn't go quite that far," she said dryly. "On the other hand, I think this is something I need to tell you because you mean so much to me. You need to know it, because I know—don't think I don't—that there are times I just seem to . . . go away in my own head. I'm working on it! But I don't want this—I don't want *me*—to side-swipe you somewhere down the road."

"Not gonna happen," he assured her. "I'm here for the long haul, lady. Where am I gonna find someone as gorgeous and smart as you are who's willing to put up with this schnoz?" He lifted one hand to tap his undeni-ably prominent nose.

"Yeah, sure." She rolled her eyes. "And I guess I'm glad you think I'm pretty," she continued in a softer voice, "but you know what? Sometimes I hate the way I look. I hate the way I act. I don't want to be me, because really, I never have been. Me, I mean."

Nosey's puzzlement must have shown, because she shook her head.

"Nobody ever let me just be 'me,' Nosey. I always had to be somebody else. Somebody my father could be 'proud' of. Somebody who always did the 'right thing,' even when she didn't think it was, because *he* did. Some-body who wore the right clothes, had the right opinions, knew where her place was. Somebody who made *him* look good. And someone who never, *ever* argued with him."

Nosey's jaw tightened. He'd crossed swords with

Jordan Franchitti himself, shamed him into doing the right thing more than once with the stories he'd posted to his blog. He knew Franchitti hated anyone who crossed him, just as he resented anyone who criticized him. Yet Jordan had always seemed to dote on Trudy. Anything she'd wanted, she'd gotten, and she'd been his darling, obedient little girl. Right up to the moment during the previous endless summer's terrible wildfires when she'd defied him to rescue her pets and then taken them to Richard Harrington for medical attention.

He'd obviously resented that, yet he'd seemed to accept it, even when Trudy signed up at Wild and Free, a "gooey-hearted" organization he despised. Yet—

"I don't like your father," Nosey told her now. "I never tried to hide that, and I'm pretty sure you've figured out how little he likes me. Which I figured was probably why he's so pissed that you and I are together now. But this sounds like it goes deeper than that."

"You didn't see me the day I turned up at Doctor Harrington's office with my animals during the fires," she said.

"No, I didn't even know you then," he agreed, frowning at the apparent change of subject.

"Might be a good thing you didn't—see me, I mean." Her bitter smile held no humor at all. "You're a lot more observant than most people. You might've noticed the bruises."

"Bruises." It was his turn to stiffen, and she nodded.

"I was really afraid Stephanie or her folks might notice them," she said in a low voice. "Or maybe a part of me hoped they *would* notice. I don't really know. But it's not their fault they didn't. I was in long sleeves, so the bruises on my arms didn't show, and I told them the one on my face was from running into a door on the way out of the house because of the smoke. It wasn't."

"Your father *hit* you," Nosey said and heard the iron-ribbed anger in his own voice.

"That was the face," she said. "The arms were finger marks, where he grabbed me and shook me when I told him I was going after them. He has big hands. The bruises were pretty dark."

"Oh, Trudy," he half-whispered as tears prickled the corners of his own eyes.

"Wasn't the first time," she continued in an oddly detached monotone. "The first time I remember him slapping me hard enough to knock me down I was about four, I think. I couldn't have been much older than that, anyway. It probably *wasn't* the first time, really, but I realized a few months ago that I don't have a single memory of him that's older than when I was four. Or I don't think I do. It's a little hard to be sure because they all sort of...blur together. And then there were the 'spankings.' I was thirteen before I realized most parents don't use belts when they 'spank' their daughters. But he was my father, and all fathers love their daughters, don't they? That's what everyone says, so it must be true...unless there's something wrong with the daughters. So, obviously, if mine didn't love me, it must be my fault. So I decided to be the very best daughter I could be, Nosey. I did what he told me to do, I wore what he told me to wear, I even thought what he told me to think, and everything was perfect... as far as anyone else knew."

"But what about—" he began, then chopped himself off, and she snorted harshly.

"Mom?" She shook her head. "Believe me, *I've* wondered where she was, a time or two. But be fair. They've been married twice as long as I've been alive, and do you think a man who'd smack a four-year-old around wouldn't do the same thing to his wife?"

"But she could have asked for help! Not just for her-self—for you, too!"

"She could have. She *should* have, and there are times I resent the hell out of the fact that she didn't. But I finally realized she'd sold herself the same ratio-nale I had. If he could treat her that way, then it had to be her fault. She's accepted that even more deeply than I ever did."

"What a pile of garbage," Nosey grated. "Nobody deserves that kind of treatment, Trudy. *Nobody!*"

"Easier to see from the outside than the inside," she told him. "Even now, there's a part of me that desperately wants him to decide I'm worthy of being loved after all."

"And what about your brothers?" Nosey demanded, his tone harsh. "They just stand around and think it's fine for him to be punching out his wife and his daughter?!"

"Why not? He did it to them, when they were younger, too. Not as much, as they got older, but a lot of that is because they grew up to be younger versions of him. Especially Ralph. Trevor's not as bad, but he's closer to my age."

"Then why haven't you moved out already?"

"It's not that easy, Nosey. It wasn't like a teenager could have set up on her own without people asking questions, now was it? And where would I have gone? Besides, he was *Jordan Franchitti*, and he'd made damned sure I knew how important, how influential, that made him. You may have noticed"—a tiny sliver of actual humor crept into her tone—"how he makes that point to just about everyone. Try growing up as his daughter and hearing it day after day after day at home. So there was never any question in my mind that he could make me come home again. Besides, who was going to believe me over him—take my word for it, or even care about it—when he dragged me home again if I ran away? And how do you think *he* would have reacted once he did drag me home?"

"But—"

"But somebody probably would have believed. Or at least looked into it." Trudy nodded. "Except that ten-year-old me and twelve-year-old me didn't know that."

"Well, you've damned well got somebody to run to *now*," he told her flatly.

"I know. And I know you've been hinting about that for quite a while now. But I need to be *sure*, Nosey."

"Sure that I love you?" He tried—hard—to keep the edge of hurt out of his voice and his expression. And given what she'd just told him, if anyone in the entire universe had reason to question whether or not someone who said he loved her really meant it, it was she. But—

"No, sweetheart," she said, raising her head to kiss him again. "I'm not worried about that. I just need to be sure in my own mind before I actually move in with you that I'm running *to* you and not just *away from* him. You deserve more than to be my hiding place. And I won't let you be just my hiding place. You're too important to me for that. Besides, I won't turn eighteen for another three months, so technically, I'm still a minor, and I'm not going to give him the ammunition to have you charged with contributing to my delinquency. Not"—she looked up at him again, and this time her smile was actually wicked—"that I'm not *thoroughly* delinquent already, especially when I'm with you!"

He gazed back down at her searchingly, looking deep into her eyes for a long, silent moment. Then, not entirely happily, he nodded.

"All right, I guess I can see that," he said. "But you won't be a minor much longer, so start thinking about it a lot harder. And in the meantime, if he ever—and I mean *ever*, Trudy—lays a finger on you again, you'd better tell me. I don't care if he's 'Jordan Franchitti.' I care about *you*, and I'm not letting anyone treat you that way again. You understand me?"

"It means the world to me that you feel that way," she said. "I've got to learn to stand up to him on my own, though."

"Of course you do. That's obviously the first step, but there's no rule that says someone—someone who loves you, like, oh, *me*—can't have your back while you do it."

"I know. It's taken me a long time to figure it out, but I know that now. Except that it's not the *first* step. Not really."

"It's not?" He frowned. "In that case, what *is*?"

"The first step, the really *hard* step, was to find someone who loved me. Who I *knew* loved me. And who I could trust enough for him to be the very first person I've ever told this to." She reached up, ran her fingers through his hair, and her smile was misty. "Thank you for being my first step, Nosey Jones."

6

THE REMAINDER OF THEIR HOLIDAY ON JASON BAY passed a little like a dream. Sunlight and swimming, the brilliant sparkle of stars in a dark sky echoed by phosphorescent-flecked night-dark waves, all were enhanced by Stephanie's new awareness of Karl as *her* Karl in a way he'd always been, although she was only realizing it now.

Stephanie didn't tell her parents anything had changed, but they figured it out. They weren't exactly clueless, after all. If Richard and Marjorie smiled softly at each other, held hands a lot more often than they did at home, well, Stephanie just felt quietly pleased by this evidence that even two people with a nearly adult daughter could still be in love. It felt nice, a wordless promise for her and Karl's own future.

But vacations, by definition, come to an end. All too soon, the four of them were packing up in preparation for heading back to Sphinx. They had more baggage than they had when they'd left something like nine months before, not only clothes for the needs of different worlds, but souvenirs and presents for the folks back home. In the end, the Harringtons rented a spare air car. Karl and Stephanie, along with Lionheart, Survivor, and the tree-cats' carriers, along with as much spare luggage as could be crammed in, drove it to the spaceport in Landing.

The autopilot did most of the driving, so Stephanie and Karl sat snuggled up against each other, watching as the now-familiar landscape of this part of Manticore whipped by, a blue-green blur very unlike the green and shadows of Sphinx.

"We probably should have scheduled more jaunts," Stephanie said, "but it was nice to be just us, quiet, not needing to worry about people gawking at the treecats."

"We'll have time for that some other visit," Karl said. "Lots of time. In days to come the treecats will be less of a novelty, and even when they are, we won't need to worry as much about having their every action misinterpreted or reinterpreted to their detriment."

"I love when you use big words," Stephanie said, adopting the languid tones of the heroine of a real howler of a holodrama they'd binge-watched with her folks in the evenings. Then she shifted back to her more usual voice. "I hope you're right. The interest in treecats certainly hasn't faded as the novelty has worn off. I think Jeff would have moved in with us if he could have. He's read every report, and had so many questions!"

"And his was just honest interest," Karl agreed. "It's not at all common to be right there when just how 'smart' or 'sentient' a species may be is in the process of being decided. And it makes you think—all of us, human-types, not just you, Steph—what it is that makes a person, rather than an animal. I find myself wondering if we humans even have the right to judge. I've known range bunnies who seem a lot more worthy of respect and preservation than, say, Frank Câmara, or the late, unlamented, Stan Chang."

"Not that I disagree," Stephanie said, "but let's just worry about the treecats, and save the question of what defines personhood for later."

After they'd off-loaded the luggage, and gotten Lionheart and Survivor in their carriers, Stephanie and Karl made their way to the terminal from which a shuttle to their ship to Sphinx would be leaving. They were nearly there when Stephanie stopped so fast that Lionheart's carrier bumped into her legs. Behind a shop window, she saw what appeared to be a male treecat, sitting upright. It held a freshly caught fish in one true-hand, and a carry net in the other. When it blinked leaf-green eyes, then turned its head to look at them, she expected to hear excited "bleeks" from Lionheart and Survivor. When they didn't react at all, she realized that the "treecat" was a life-sized robotic toy, and that the diorama was a come-on for Frontier Wilderness Tour's travel agency and gift shop.

"Visit Sphinx on your next vacation! True wilderness beckons!" the banner proclaimed in sparkling emerald-green letters. "Join our experienced docents on group tours, or arrange your own individualized excursion. Counter-grav equipment included!"

Stephanie drew closer to get a better look at the treecat toy. The sign next to it promised "All six limbs move! Makes realistic sounds! Extendable claws! Comes with carry net and a selection of xeno-anthropologically vetted accessories."

The animatronic treecat shared the window with a near-beaver and a rock raven, both wonderfully detailed. The near-beaver came with "chewable log" and robotic fish, while the rock raven "moves all four wings" and "can really fly!"

The diorama's background showed holo footage of a hexapuma prowling, as well as various herbivores browsing beneath the tree. Stephanie noted that hunting and fishing tour packages were available, as well as those devoted to ecotourism. There was even a potential settlement tour, more focused on residential areas, and land open for purchase.

"I know Sphinx's government favors promoting both settlement and tourism," Stephanie said, "but I had no idea stuff like this was being done—especially the way they're depicting the treecats."

"There's nothing in that diorama that hasn't been in various public domain reports," Karl reminded her.

"But that display," she motioned toward the window, suddenly glad that Lionheart and Survivor were concealed within their carriers, "is a lot easier to understand than one of Dr. Whittaker's or Dr. Radzinsky's papers. Worse, as the only tool users shown among the Sphinxian species, the treecats look way too much like what you and I know they are: Sphinx's intelligent, tool-using, indigenous inhabitants."

"I agree," Karl said. "I know you've been in favor of being cautious, but I think we're going to need to let a lot more people into the Great Treecat Conspiracy, and a lot sooner than we'd originally planned. Otherwise, if we don't get allies for the 'cats, the treecats of Sphinx may face the fate of the Amphors of Barstool."

The shuttle touched down on Sphinx in the twilight hour. Richard Harrington had slept much of the seven-hour voyage. Now, with the training of a much-in-demand veterinarian for whom all hours of the 25.62 were the same, he cheerfully set about directing the reclaiming of the family air car, triaging what luggage needed to come with them, and which could be delivered to the Harrington homestead by courier.

Tonight, Karl would be coming back to the Harringtons'. There he'd pick up his own air car and then fly to the Zivonik Barony on Thunder River in the morning.

Stephanie felt a pang of something very like fear at the idea of being separated from Karl. She didn't think the heaviness that shrouded her every motion had anything to do with being back in Sphinx's 1.35 gravity. In the back-seat of the air car, she snuggled up close to him, feeling the warmth of his arm around her shoulders as if she was in a private shelter.

That night, when they all went up to their rooms in the sprawling stone and timber house that was home, Stephanie thought about following Karl into his room. Not to *do* anything, she assured herself, just to keep him close for a few hours more.

She resisted, settling for a lingering good night kiss, and a "See you in the morning," before stumbling into her own room. Still dressed, she collapsed onto her own familiar bed and buried her face in her pillow. The linens smelled fresh, since Marjorie had paid her part-time assistant Naomi Pheriss to come by and get the place in order.

I'll brush my teeth and comb my hair in just a minute, Stephanie promised herself, before falling into a deep, dreamless sleep that lasted until pale early spring daylight crept through her window.

<*I think,*> Keen Eyes said to Climbs Quickly as the two People sat out on the limb on the golden-leaf where Climbs Quickly had his auxiliary nest, <*that we will be parting company soon. The mind-glows of our two two-legs echo with a sorrow and resignation that is as easy to interpret as the scent trail of a horn blade in rut. Shining Sunlight's mind-glow is conflicted. I do not think he wishes to part from Death Fang's Bane, but I think he wishes to see his birth clan with a different intensity.*>

<*I will miss you,*> Climbs Quickly replied. <*For hands upon hands of days, you and I have been the whole of each*

other's clan. Having you with me made this voyage from our own places much easier than when I went alone with only Death Fang's Bane's mind-glow to touch. We both tried, but there was not the faintest hint of another Person's mind-glow in either of those lands of different stars. I am glad, however, that I will soon be able to visit Bright Water again. I am sure that my sister, Sings Truly, will be eager for tales of our adventures to weave into her memory songs. I only wish I understood better the "whys" as well as the "whats" of what the two-legs do. As a scout, I feel as if I have walked a trail, seen the landmarks with only my eyes, without the deeper understanding my other senses bring.>

<I believe we will be together again soon enough,> Keen Eyes said. *<Shining Sunlight and Death Fang's Bane will not wish to be apart very long. I will luxuriate in being back among familiar scents and will try to figure out by the signs in plants and animals and the shape of the stars just how long we were gone. Not a full season turning, I think, but no matter how much time has gone by, surely no People have ever been on such a journey as we have been.>*

Karl forced himself to leave the Harrington homestead as early he could manage the next day. His excuse was that the flight to the Zivonik Barony would take several hours, and that his family had been pretty patient already, given that his return from Gryphon had been delayed at least three times already. Best he not arrive later than expected.

His real reason was more complex.

Although Stephanie was doing her best not to act any differently than she usually would when they parted, he could practically feel—even without Lionheart and Survivor's body language—how forlorn she was.

Best we get this parting over with sooner. I could take her with me, sure, but I don't want to com the folks with news that I have a new, serious relationship. Or show up with Stephanie, just in case they're not good with our being a couple. I can't see why they wouldn't be, but what if they're not? That could be super awkward. And I really want to talk with my mom without Stephanie wondering why I want to talk to Mom alone.

To her credit, no matter what she was feeling, Stephanie didn't even hint that she and Lionheart might come along.

"I'm going to take Lionheart to see his family," she announced. "The weather's perfect for hang gliding. And Jessica actually got time off from the hospital this evening, so we're going to hang out. You have a good time with your family. Want me to com Chief Shelton and see if I can set up a meeting with him for when you're back on duty?"

"Sure," Karl said, loading the last of his luggage in the back of his air car. With typical consideration, Richard and Marjorie had made sure his souvenirs and presents were among the boxes they'd brought from the spaceport. "But give me at least two, maybe even three, days or so for family stuff. And you should brief Jess and Cordelia about the upcoming expansion of the Great Treecat Conspiracy."

He squeezed Stephanie close one more time, extra tight. "I'll screen you. Probably more than you want, actually. I've gotten used to hearing you chatter, can't go cold turkey."

Another squeeze, another kiss—he still couldn't get enough of the feeling of her lips against his—then into his air car, Survivor taking the passenger seat. Lifting up and off and the little figure waving, waving, vanishing from sight. Karl nearly turned around to get Stephanie, to bring her with him, after all, but *I can do this without backup. Well, without backup other than Survivor. I'm glad to have him along.*

Karl's family was quite large, even though the Plague had done its part to reduce the older generation. There were six kids in his family alone: Karl himself, Nadia, Anastacia, Gregor, Larisa, and Lev. Given that Lev was only a couple years old, it was certainly possible Evelina and Aleksandr weren't done yet, either.

As things stood, little Lev knew Karl more as an interesting semi-stranger who was away from home as much as he was there, but Karl had shared his childhood with Nadia and Anastacia in particular. He still did what he could to help out, even if that helping was just pick-up and drop-off as he went about his rounds.

Nearly nine months was quite a while to be gone, though. The biggest shock was how much Lev had grown. Karl had known intellectually, as there'd been message packets back and forth throughout his absence, but while Karl had been away, the baby had become a toddler who peered at Karl in deep suspicion, before Evelina convinced him the towering giant was the same person as the person he'd visited with on the vid.

Nadia, who was only a little younger than Stephanie—something Karl hadn't really thought about, since Stephanie was such a different sort of person—was filling out, losing her coltish look and becoming distinctly pretty. To everyone's surprise, her relationship with Loon Villaroy was still going on. Loon was a couple years older than Karl, but seemed devoted to his younger girlfriend. Recently, they'd co-produced a water ballet to the mingled amusement and enthusiasm of live-entertainment-starved Twin Forks.

Another parallel with me and Steph, Karl thought. *Older guy, girl not yet legal. I wonder if Loon's being as careful about the whole "age of consent" thing as I've been? Well, that's one thing I'm absolutely not going to ask!*

Anastacia, more usually called Staysa, as Nadia was Dia, had shot up in the last couple of months. It looked as if she was going to be very tall and, like Karl, take more after their dad, Aleksandr than their mom, Evelina. She'd become active as an "older" member of the new SFS Explorers, and often escorted their younger sister, Larisa, to meetings.

The Zivoniks weren't into massive and varied culinary experiments like the Harringtons. There were simply too many mouths to feed to go for fancy, so they settled for massive and good. Karl's "welcome home" dinner featured prong buck ribs with Aleksandr's secret sauce, ice potatoes with sour cream and chives, and a roasted root vegetable platter. There was raw fish for Survivor, with celery for dessert. The humans had a varied selection of cut-out butter and spice cookies, slightly singed, courtesy of Gregor, Larisa, and Lev.

Karl was amused to see that in addition to the usual hearts, stars, and circles there were cookies made with a brand new "treecat" shaped cutter, which Gregor had found in Twin Forks.

Yet another sign of the increasing popularity of our little indigenous aliens.

Karl's first day back at the Zivonik Barony was a flurry of "Look at this!" "Did you know!" "Come see what we did with the feed barn." "What do you think of how we painted the porch?"

He did manage to announce that he and Stephanie were dating. He was more than a little surprised that the overall reaction was "What? You weren't already? Then it's about time you figured out you were. The rest of us had ages ago."

On the second day, he also managed to get his mom alone, taking advantage of Dia and Staysa going into Twin Forks with Gregor (swimming class) and Lev (playdate).

He was slightly startled—though he shouldn't have been—that Dia was handling the driving. Larisa had proudly donned her SFS Explorers "near-otter" hood and sash and gone off to a meeting of the Thunder River chapter, only mildly disappointed that she couldn't bring Survivor for show-and-tell.

"We're learning about near-beavers now," she confided, "not treecats. Near-beavers are very clever, and we're going to tour one of their dams later on, after the thaw."

Once the hullabaloo of departures was over, Karl joined Evelina in the kitchen and automatically started helping with prep for dinner: stew with meat from the prong buck that had provided last night's ribs, and more seasonal vegetables.

"Mom," he said hesitantly, "no one seemed surprised about me and Steph."

"Well, dear," his mother replied, shaking the cubed meat in flour and paprika, "you two have been spending a lot of time together, more and more since you took your job with the SFS. And maybe you didn't notice, but Alek and I certainly did, but when Stephanie started dating that nice Anders Whittaker, you did a lot of glowering."

"I most certainly did not!" Karl said, suspecting that he actually had.

"If you say so, dear," Evelina replied mildly. "It's so hard to figure out exactly what has teenage boys glowering. It seems to be a default expression. That's why Loon is actually something of a relief. He's gotten past that stage. He treats Dia like she really is that princess from the fairy tale they used for their ballet. We have the performance recorded, by the way. You really should watch it. Dia would be thrilled."

"I will," Karl promised. "Do you think Loon wants to marry Dia?"

"I do, but time will tell. Dia's young for her age in

many ways. I'd like them to wait until she's done with college, and I'd like that to be elsewhere, maybe even on Manticore. She needs to know about more than our corner of Sphinx. I felt the same way about you, which is why—even though we missed you—we were glad to have you go first to the ranger training course on Manticore, then off with the Harringtons to Gryphon. I do wish, though, that you weren't always getting tangled up in muggings and murders. It can't be good for your peace of mind."

Karl started laughing. "It really isn't, but if I'm going to stay a ranger, I don't think I'm signing up for a quiet life, just an interesting one." He paused, drew in a deep breath, and then said, "I was thinking...Stephanie turns seventeen in January. I was thinking about, well, maybe giving her a promise ring or maybe even, uh, well, um... proposing."

Evelina stopped browning the coated meat cubes to consider this.

"You've only been dating a short while," she said after a moment, "but you two have been through a lot together. January is a good four or so months away, and you've been living in each other's pockets these last nine months. That's more than many couples manage before announcing their engagement. Are you sleeping with her?"

"No!" Karl was offended. "She's a minor. I'm not. That could get awkward from a legal standpoint."

Evelina chuckled. "I see...Well, Stephanie is almost seventeen. That's the age of consent. I don't think it's a coincidence that you're thinking of proposals, then. You want her to know you're serious, right? Not just looking to get in her pants."

"Mom!"

"Karl, be realistic. I have six kids. Lev is almost three years old. Clearly, I have not quite lost my ability to feel passion." She relented. "I think it's a very nice idea that you want to propose, to make it clear to Stephanie you're not just after her body but you want all of her life, forever and on. But I don't want you to pressure her. If she wants to try sex without signing up for a life-long commitment, you should respect that. Remember how it felt when Sumiko pressured you for a ring? You don't want to do that to Stephanie, do you?"

Karl shook his head, then industriously began chopping root vegetables.

"No. I don't want to pressure Steph. Even though I think I did the right thing when I told Sumiko we needed to slow down, all of that, it hurts to be the one who has to draw the line. But I still want to ask Stephanie to marry me, and sooner, not later."

Evelina smiled and reached over to tousle Karl's hair in a fashion she hadn't done since he was Gregor's age.

"Then I have an idea. I have your maternal grandmother's engagement ring. Would you like to have it to give Stephanie? The setting may be a trifle old-fashioned, but the stones are flush with the band, which would be a good thing in the active lifestyle I envision you and Stephanie will be living."

"Seriously, Mom?" Karl's eyes widened. He'd actually been saving toward a ring, but he loved the idea of something that would create a link between not only him and Stephanie and some jewelry shop, but between his family and hers. Then he paused. "But is that fair to the other kids? I mean, there's only one ring, and six of us—now. There might even be more if you and dad keep remembering about that passion thing."

Evelina laughed, but that didn't hide the sadness in the depth of her deep grey eyes.

"Our families lost too many of our elders earlier than we thought we would because of the Plague," she said. "I have a velvet-lined box full of too many rings and bits of heirloom jewelry. If anyone seems worried you as the oldest child are getting an advantage over them, I'll make sure they know everyone will have an appropriate heirloom, even if that person never decides to marry. Sound good?"

"Sounds great!" Karl said. "Hold onto the ring for me? Like you said, I live a very active lifestyle. I'd be absolutely mortified if I lost such a treasure."

"I'll hold onto it," Evelina said. She twinkled, "I'll even have it cleaned, since we don't want Stephanie to get even a slight hint that you're considering proposing, and you two do seem to live in each other's pockets. Now, chop up those veggies. The stew won't wait, not even for romance."

SOON AFTER THEY HAD RETURNED TO THE NESTING place he shared with Death Fang's Bane and her parents, Climbs Quickly had been delighted to taste the distant but still discernable mind-glow of Shadow Hider, one of the scouts of Bright Water Clan. Climbs Quickly considered it a gift that he now had two clans—three, if one counted the two-leg family grouping of which he now was very much a member. His newer clan, which he himself had helped to make, was the scattered group of People who now lived most of their lives with the two-legs. Nonetheless, his birth clan, Bright Water, kept an equally important place in his heart.

Death Fang's Bane had always appreciated that and gone out of her way to make certain he was able to regularly visit with Bright Water Clan. They, in turn, had welcomed her, and had enjoyed watching her develop from the skinny little thing they had helped him to rescue from that death fang so long ago, to the young adult she was becoming, her always brilliant mind-glow now richer and deeper with the wealth of her many adventures.

When Climbs Quickly had a sense of Shadow Hider's location, he loped through the net-wood until they were close enough to mind-speak.

<*You are here again!*> came Shadow Hider's delighted cry. <*You warned us you were going far, but we had no word of you, nor did Keen Eye's clan of him. We did not worry because Dirt Grubber and Stone Shaper both said their two-legs were not in the least distressed, not even when Dirt Grubber and Windswept came to Death Fang's Bane's nesting place to do things in the plant places. We all agreed that if something horrible had happened to you, there was no way the two-legs would not know, and would not be sad. Still, you were gone a very long time.*>

<*Longer, I think,*> Climbs Quickly replied, <*than was planned, and neither Keen Eyes nor I are completely certain as to why, but I have wonderful experiences to share with you all. If the weather remains good for travel, I think we will be coming to you soon. I saw Death Fang's Bane checking the folding flying thing she uses when we make a visit.*>

<*If a visit does not happen,*> Shadow Hider said, <*then I feel certain that Sings Truly will once again push the patience of the other elders and insist on leaving our central nesting place to come to you. One way or another, the songs of your adventures will be shared.*>

But Climbs Quickly had indeed interpreted his Death Fang's Bane correctly. Shortly after Shining Sunlight and Keen Eyes had departed, she came to him, making mouth noises and waggling her linked hands back and forth in a fashion that did an amazing job of mimicking the folding flying thing in flight. Her mind-glow held many tastes: still a touch of the sorrow she'd felt when Shining Sunlight had departed, overlaid with notes of anticipation. From this, Climbs Quickly deduced that she was anticipating the proposed outing for itself, as well as for the pleasure she thought he would feel at seeing his birth clan again.

And maybe even as a distraction from her own welter of emotions.

He did his best to mimic her hand gesture with his hand-feet, making her laugh.

Not long after, they were aloft. Climbs Quickly was grateful for the warmth of the made-fur Death Fang's Bane had bundled him into as he enjoyed this peak wing's eye view of the world that had been his home for so long. The cold times had removed leaves from many of the trees, but there were some that kept long needles. Others, such as the golden-leaf, grew much thinner foliage in the cold times when so much of the world slept blanketed in snowdrifts far deeper than any Person.

Although the People made their nests in the trees, many of the creatures that they hunted tunneled beneath the snow, rarely coming to the surface. Climbs Quickly remembered lessons in how to tell when the crust of the snow would bear a Person's weight, how to listen for the burrow runners and grass runners beneath, and how to pounce without giving away the hunter's presence.

Even if he had not seen it from the air in previous cold times, Climbs Quickly would have recognized Bright Water's central nesting place because of the modifications that had been made to make it a better place to live during the times of deep snow. Like most People, Bright Water used the interconnecting net-wood to let them range safely throughout the region without touching the ground. However, larger trees made for better-concealed, more stable nests, a factor not to be overlooked when hunting birds like the death-wings and peak-wings soared out, seeking prey that was not deep beneath the snow.

The bright water that had given the clan its name was a rounded lake that supplied both water and opportunities to fish. Semi-aquatic hunters like the lake builders and sleek swimmers made holes in the ice, which the People then kept open for their own use. Climbs Quickly found himself thinking of the long sticks with string and hooks that the two-legs used for fishing, and wondered if the People might adapt this to their own needs, much as many now used the hard, bright not-rock scavenged from two-leg leavings instead of the traditional stone knives.

The People did not clear away or tramp down the snow beneath their nesting places, as the two-legs did around theirs, but there were several large outcrops of rock that the winds kept scoured mostly clear, and that was where Death Fang's Bane usually brought her folding flying thing in to land. Unable to even sense mind-glows, much less mind-speak, Death Fang's Bane always circled her folding flying thing over the area a few times before beginning her descent, apparently to give the People an ample opportunity to see that she was not a death-wing or a peak-wing or some other aerial threat.

Climbs Quickly had, of course, been aware of the wide variety of mind-glows from some distance out. As they had moved closer to the central nesting place, he had been exchanging mind-speech with Bright Water's inhabitants, sharing greetings, and answering questions.

<Welcome home!> came the cheerful greeting from Sings Truly, the clan's senior memory singer, and Climbs Quickly's own sister. In her own way, Sings Truly was as great an explorer as he was, although her challenges fell within extending the traditional limits of the customs the People had long followed.

<Climbs Quickly! Did you bring clusterstalk?> This was from Long Jumper, a youngling already notable for his considerable—some said "foolhardy"—daring. When they

had left for the faraway places, Long Jumper had been a mere kit, but the passage of time had noticeably strengthened his mind-voice. Judging from his outspokenness, he was no less of a risktaker. However, Long Jumper's query was echoed by numerous spikes of intense interest from the other younglings, no less eager, if somewhat less bold.

<Plenty for all,> Climbs Quickly reassured them, thinking of the bag of neatly trimmed stalks he'd seen Death Fang's Bane put in the folding flying thing's carry net.

Despite having done very little soaring since their departure, Death Fang's Bane touched down smoothly on the large rocky outcropping she had often used as landing place. Once down, she unstrapped herself and Climbs Quickly. He immediately loped off to touch noses with Sings Truly, who had scampered down the trunk of the golden-leaf in which she had her nest. After securing the folding flying thing, Death Fang's Bane seated herself on the wind-scoured rock to put on the big, flat foot covers that enabled her to walk over the snow almost as easily as did one of the People, whose already long fur grew thicker and longer in the cold seasons. The fur on their feet actually widened their feet, so their weight was more dispersed.

After Death Fang's Bane had finished donning her footwear, she took a few tentative steps to test her footing and balance. Then she went back to retrieve the carry bag that held the much-anticipated clusterstalk. She was striding lightly over the snow, heading to join Climbs Quickly when, from the overarching limb of the golden-leaf, Long Jumper decided to live up to his name.

<Catch me!> he cried out gleefully, his mind-voice full of images of a much smaller him and other kittens of his year clambering all over Death Fang's Bane, who in these memories was a near giant. The setting for Long Jumper's memories was leaf-turning time. In

them, a laughing Death Fang's Bane stood with her feet slightly spread, and firmly anchored on the forest floor. The situation now was much different, but a kitten who had not yet seen a full turning of seasons could not be expected to understand this.

Long Jumper plummeted down toward Death Fang's Bane. She raised her arms, either to catch him or to protect her face—perhaps both. The force of the treekitten's impact unbalanced the two-leg's unstable stance on her wide false feet. She toppled backwards into the several body-lengths depth of accumulated snow and vanished, the heavy white wetness covering both two-leg and treekitten with smothering cold.

Stephanie was pleased at how quickly her muscles remembered how to handle a hang glider in Sphinx's 1.35 gee, although she had needed to work harder at it than she would have before spending nine months off-planet. and even had to tweak her counter-grav to help her avoid a couple of patches of minor turbulence that would just have been fun when she was in full condition.

Working out isn't the same as living day to day in a heavier-grav environment, Meyerdahl mods or not. I hope Karl's being careful. He doesn't have the mods. Do I give him a hint or would that be nagging?

When they arrived in the area of the forest where Lionheart's family had their nests scattered throughout the surrounding trees, Stephanie grabbed a dense fortified fruit and nut bar from one of the side pockets of her snowsuit and downed it while folding up the hang glider and getting on her snowshoes. The calories helped some.

The Meyerdahl mods are great, but they do demand a price. Good thing Mom loves to experiment with new recipes, and there were still some of these in the freezer.

Stephanie's test walk on the snowshoes satisfied her that she hadn't lost her reflexes for using these either. Across the clearing, Lionheart was definitely enjoying his family reunion. Morgana, the female Stephanie was almost sure was his favorite sister—although Morgana could have been his mom, since female treecats didn't have the convenient rings which almost certainly indicated age on their tails, as the males did—had scampered down the trunk of the vast crown oak in which she had her nest, and was hanging head down, claws firmly anchored in the bark. Although there were no sounds but an occasional "bleek," Stephanie felt sure they were talking.

Stephanie was picking her way over the snow to join them when she heard high-pitched excited squeaks from above. Glancing up, she saw several treekittens, probably from some of last spring's litters, scampering back and forth in the over-stimulated fashion of juveniles of any species.

Like kids on their birthday, waiting for cake and ice cream, Stephanie thought fondly. *I bet Lionheart's told them I brought celery. I'd better hurry.*

She considered just switching on her counter-grav and drifting up to join the kittens, but that would have violated her personal code of ethics. As soon as she'd realized treecats were people, she'd resolved to treat them just like she would humans. So, just as she wouldn't have given candy to Jessica or Karl's younger sibs without asking for permission from their parents, that meant no celery for treekittens until their folks indicated it was okay.

"Cool your jets, kids," she called, and increased her pace.

"Bleek!" came a shrill cry from above.

Stephanie glanced up and was astonished to see a grey and white blur plummeting down, right at her. Automatically, she leaned back and put out her arms to catch him, forgetting that even a few kilos of treekitten coming down from that height would be like catching a hard-thrown ball. When he connected with her, she pitched backwards, further unbalanced by the large bag of celery she'd flung over her shoulder. Together they hit the snow which gave beneath them.

My fall alarm isn't going to register that, she thought. *We barely hit before the snow crumpled.*

The combined weight of Stephanie's gear and the force of the treekitten-turned-missile drove both of them down through the snowpack. Compacted snow tumbled into the hole they'd created, immediately burying them both beneath a considerable weight. The treekitten began to struggle frantically, and Stephanie wrapped her arms around him, holding him to her chest. Thankfully, the thickness of her snowsuit provided some armor, and the treekitten's claws were not yet the lethal scimitars of an adult.

He's pushing us deeper! Stephanie thought, her heart-beat hammering in her ears as the insulating snow cut off light and sound. Then she felt them drop about forty centimeters. They were momentarily surrounded by musty air, before the snow tumbled in after. *Did we hit a pocket? Maybe part of some burrowing animal's tunnel system, wood rats or chipmunks, one of those creatures that rarely surfaces once the snowpack is established.*

Stephanie had been trained in avalanche survival techniques. Oddly, this situation was little different. Holding the treekitten pinned to her chest with her left arm, she used her right arm and hand to open up a space over her face, then over his. People buried in snow usually suffocated before they froze, the moisture from their own breath turning into clinging ice that made further breathing impossible. At the same time, she wriggled her legs gently, working to create space around them so she wouldn't be cemented into place, as well as to provide an air space.

She tried to ease an arm down to reach the controls of her counter-grav unit, but the heavy snow was like being wrapped in wet bricks. Worse, the now-still treekitten provided an effective block between her and her belt. Unable to reach the counter-grav controls, Stephanie poked her arm in a straight line over her head, parallel with her torso.

If this is part of a tunnel, I might be able to poke through to it, get us a little more air.

Her questing fingers did find what seemed to be an open area, but she couldn't make a hole larger than a couple of digits before the snow started sifting down once more. She stopped probing and instead concentrated on breathing as shallowly as possible to make the air last.

Lionheart will get us out. I could make matters worse by struggling. Use up the air faster, for sure. The kitten is awfully still. I hope he's all right. He couldn't be dead, could he? Tears flowed unbidden from Stephanie's eyes, freezing on her skin and lashes. *I'd never be able to face his family if he is. Just a kid wanting "candy," just a dumb, eager kid.*

At least she had dressed not just for cold, but for the added cold of flight, so that although the snow burned against the exposed skin of her face, she wasn't in immediate danger of freezing. She clung to that reassurance. Lightheaded from lack of air she found herself fighting to keep from laughing.

I'll smother before I freeze. I guess that means I'll make a pretty corpse. Karl ... Two of your girls killed by this damn gravity, this endless snow.

But even as her imagination wove morbid fantasies as preferable to panic, Stephanie could sense the light, the warmth, she associated with Lionheart. He wasn't that far away. Heck, if some of what they'd speculated about treecats was true, he probably knew more about her situation than she did herself, including whether the furry weight she held against her chest was alive or dead.

Was she imagining those rhythmic vibrations from above? Surely the treecats would be working to excavate them. They'd have to know how to safely move snow, wouldn't they? This was their world, after all. Nonetheless, it was all Stephanie could do to trust, not to panic or flail about or do anything that could make the situation worse.

I'll believe it'll be all right. They'll get us out. Breathe slowly. Don't use up the air.

Only when an opening appeared over her head and cold air flooded in did Stephanie realize how thin her belief had been. Forcing open eyelids nearly sealed by frozen tears, she looked up to see Lionheart's bewhiskered face peering down at her, ears perked forward.

"Bleek!"

"Bleek yourself," she replied. She tried to sit up, but the motion only made more snow tumble down.

"Bleek! Bleek!"

"Got it. Wait. Be patient. Can you tell me if the baby is okay?" She dumped down more snow by gesturing with her head toward the bundle on her chest.

"Bleek." A reassuring sound, but without content. The treekitten didn't move. Was this because it was being told to hold still, or because it couldn't move, would never move again? Stephanie shut her eyes and practiced patience.

She wasn't very good at it.

When at last the treecats had dug them out—a task, she would figure out later, that had been complicated by the network of burrows that ran hither and yon under the snow—Stephanie checked her uni-link and estimated that the entire ordeal had lasted no more than ten minutes,

probably closer to five. The treekitten moved first, scrab-
bling out of her grip and leaping onto the snow's crust.
After that, Stephanie activated her counter-grav and used
it to lift herself clear of the snowy pit. Neither she nor
the treekitten were damaged, though Stephanie's face was
rosy from contact with the snow.

"Bleek!!" Lionheart said, bounding over to her.

Off to one side, the treekitten was being loomed over
by a brown and white female treecat who was probably
his mother. He hunkered down against the snow, his ears
flattened and his tail drooping. After what was apparently
the treecat version of a serious dressing down, the female
wrapped her upper two sets of limbs and her tail around
him and hugged him to her furry underside. The little
guy squeaked what had to be "Mom! You're squashing
me!" but Stephanie noticed that he was hugging her back.

I'll think I'll call him Tarzan, Stephanie thought.

Once Lionheart was certain Stephanie was recovered,
he very gently patted the sack of celery. Stephanie let her
counter-grav carry her up to one of the broadest limbs
of the crown oak, which gave her a place to sit easily as
wide as the trunk of many types of trees. As she distributed the treats, she watched to see if little Tarzan's
mother would let him have one. Apparently, his regret
was sufficiently sincere, but he did wait until the other
treecats got their celery sticks first.

He sat down next to Stephanie, leaning against her leg
so she could feel his purr. After he'd had a few nibbles,
he held out the shredded celery stick to her, tilting his
head beguilingly to one side.

"Bleek?"

Stephanie was enchanted all out of proportion. "Thank
you, Tarzan, but I have my own treats. You finish that off."

"Bleek!!" Tarzan responded ramping up his purr.

There seemed no reason not to finish their visit, so

Stephanie used her counter-grav to hover to a perch on a sunny tree limb, and watched the treecats go about their activities. A few were fishing out on the ice. Others were twisting fiber—mostly their own shed fur—into cords. She thought several of the females were rounding with kittens, although given the additional fluff of their winter coats, it wasn't easy to tell.

Stephanie and Lionheart flew home while there was still plenty of daylight. As they did so, Stephanie debated whether or not to tell Karl about what had happened, because he was sure to be upset—not at her, but at the situation. She decided to tell him, though, because protective lies were a lousy foundation for any friendship, and an even worse one for love.

As Karl listened his expression on the vid-screen was stiff with all the emotions he wasn't letting out. His first words startled her.

"I wonder," he said carefully calm, "if the treecats deliberately don't hunt the chipmunks and wood rats who tunnel in the areas where the treecats have their nests because that way the 'cats have a sort of larder for those times when snowstorms are so bad that going far to hunt would be dangerous."

Stephanie guessed that he was still processing all those horrible "what ifs," so she answered levelly, "Good thought. Maybe they even drop seeds or nuts down to draw the burrowers close, and encourage them to stay around. There's some support for that sort of behavior documented among creatures who are a lot less smart."

They discussed the possibility of setting up surveillance equipment next autumn, so they could do a detailed survey of the ways that treecats prepared for winter.

"At the very least," Karl said, "it would provide the SFS with guidelines for when we might provide supplemental feed, like we're already doing for some of the prong bucks and tuskalopes whose ability to range and forage has been impacted by human settlement."

Autumn, Stephanie thought, her lips shaping in a dreamy smile. *Nearly thirty T-months away that would be. T-years. Nice to be planning for the future.*

As they were signing off, Karl paused and quirked one of his sideways smiles. "In case I haven't told you, I love you, Stephanie."

He hadn't told her, at least not that way, not with that look in his eyes. Stephanie felt a tingle run through her and her breathing come unexpectedly short.

"I love you, Karl," she managed. "Lots. Sleep well. Sweet dreams."

"Of you," he promised. "Of you."

8

"STEPHANIE!" DR. SCOTT MACDALLAN SMILED INTO his com display. "I figured you'd be off in Twin Forks at the Red Letter, swigging down Mr. Flint's double chocolate milkshakes, not screening me the second day after you got back!"

"Oh, trust me, that's on my list, too," Stephanie assured him. "But there's something Karl and I have been thinking about, and I really need to get your input on it. We think it's a good idea, but it's not just our decision to make."

"Something to do with our furry better halves?" MacDallan asked, as Fisher hopped up onto the back of his chair and made bleeking sounds at Lionheart, who was curled neatly in Stephanie's arms.

"Absolutely," Stephanie said in an unwontedly sober tone.

"So tell me about it."

"Well, we're getting more worried about how visible the 'cats are, especially after that whole thing on

Gryphon." She grimaced. "It seems like Lionheart and I can't go anywhere without *something* happening, and we're thinking that's probably just going to get worse. So it seemed to us that it would be a good idea to approach Chief Shelton about how we might go about getting them assigned protected status."

"That sounds like a great idea!" MacDallan said.

"Yeah, but neither of us really feels comfortable lying to the Chief or even just misleading him. And we're definitely going to need his full-fledged support farther down the road. So it seems to us that we may have to... enlarge the Conspiracy."

MacDallan's expression tightened a bit, and he reached one hand up to touch Fisher's ears.

"So you're talking about taking off the mask—at least some—to him."

"Yes." She nodded. "On the other hand, Scott, he already knows a lot more than we've officially told him. Especially after what happened with Orgeson and the baka bakari. He's been really good about not pushing for more, which is one reason Karl and I are sure we can trust him. But if we want his full support—his most *effective* support—we have to tell him a lot more than we've ever told anyone else. For that matter, sooner or later, we'll probably have to confide in someone like Dr. Hobbard, too."

"And you'll have to convince them the 'cats truly do have a means of communication even if they don't use words. As in more than 'I can tell that he can feel what I'm feeling.'"

"Yes," she said again and met his gaze levelly.

MacDallan's tight expression turned into a frown, and Stephanie understood perfectly, because Scott MacDallan was the one human being who absolutely knew that treecats were capable of complex communication, and not just with their own species. But that knowledge wasn't anything that he could prove or demonstrate in a lab, and it hadn't been easy for the treecats to accomplish it in the first place. For that matter, the last thing he needed was to sound like some sort of lunatic freak. Or maybe, if he was lucky, just the freak part of that, without the "lunatic" for good measure.

"You want to tell them about the Stray," he said softly.

"I think we have to." She gave her head a little toss. "I know it won't actually prove how they 'talk' to each other, or the level of complexity they can handle. But it's really suggestive supporting evidence, and everyone knows you found out about Doctor Ubel somehow, so that's probably some corroboration of the fact that they told you about her."

"But it took hundreds of them to get through to me," MacDallan said. "And, like you say, there's no way to independently verify what happened. It was just me, Fisher, and the 'cats. And even with all of them cooperating, all they could really do was send me...pictures. Pictures with sound, some of them, but not anything really coherent. Enough to help me figure out at least some of what must've happened, but it's not like we were exchanging complex sentences, for God's sake!"

"Of course not. But, Scott, if they could get pictures through to a human, a totally different species, then you know they have to be exchanging information that's bunches more complex with other treecats."

"Probably. No," he shook his head, "certainly. But it's not something we'll ever be able to *prove*, not when nobody's ever been able to verify a single proven case of *human* telepathy. And I'll be honest, Steph. My family and I have had way more experience than we ever wanted with people who think we're nuts because we think we have 'the sight.'"

"I know, and we'll ask Chief Shelton—and anyone else we tell about it—to keep it confidential and explain why we want them to. But we need to lay our cards on the table with them, be as honest and open as we can, if we expect them to sign up to help us."

"I know," MacDallan sighed. Then he produced a crooked smile. "And, actually, Shelton won't be the first Ranger who knows what really happened."

"Frank Lethbridge?" Stephanie didn't sound particularly surprised, MacDallan noted.

"I've known him a long time. So when you first screened me, wanting to talk about the 'cats, I had a long talk with him. I needed a better feel for where you were coming from, where you might be headed, and I knew he and Ainsley had been involved in investigating your hexapuma incident. I figured he probably had the best perspective on what you might be after of anyone I knew, which made him the logical choice to ask. That, and the fact that he'd been involved with the Stray and Ubel." MacDallan shrugged. "I sort of told him the inside story on that whole business at the same time I asked him about you, and at least he didn't laugh at me. He hasn't been telling anybody about it over beers, either."

"Frank?" Stephanie blinked at him. "Scott, there's no way he'd ever—"

"Oh, I know that! I knew it before I told him, or I probably wouldn't have. I'm just saying that I've already come that far out into the open, and from everything I've heard Chief Shelton's a pretty understanding and trustworthy sort himself. If you need to trot out me and Fisher as 'supporting evidence,' I guess we'll just have to live with it. I take it you're going to have this conversation in person?"

"Oh, yeah! And not before we've talked it over with Jessica and Cordy, too. Jessica's coming out to the house this afternoon, and I promise I'll talk about it with her. She's had a lot of practice wrangling Harringtons and helping me restrain what Mom calls my 'intrepid impetuosity.'" She grinned. "Trust me, this isn't something Stephanie the Impulsive is going to run out and do on her own!"

"I'm relieved to hear it," he said dryly. "Do you need Fisher and me to tag along for the conversation?"

"Not if you're willing to trust us to get the story straight. I don't think we need to have anyone noticing a bunch of treecat partners trooping into SFS HQ unless they have an innocent reason to be there. But I wouldn't be surprised if he wanted to speak to you personally about it, maybe on the com."

"Oh, I think you can probably count on that." MacDallan's tone was even drier than before, and Stephanie chuckled.

"Okay," he said. "We're in. And I'll give Frank a heads up that his boss may want to talk to him. Maybe ask him a few pointed questions about his previous silence on this very issue."

"Oh. I hadn't even thought about that!" Stephanie's eyes widened, and she sat back for a moment, thinking hard. Then she shrugged.

"I don't think Chief Shelton'll get on his case about it. I mean, the Chief knows how long you've been friends, and he understands about things like that. It's one reason I like him so much."

"And the fact that you—and Lionheart—like him so much is one reason I'm willing to step out of the shadows with him. Not wildly enthusiastic over the notion, you understand, but definitely willing."

"Good." Her eyes thanked him. "I appreciate it, Scott."

"Hey, your credit's pretty good with me where the celery bandits are concerned."

"I appreciate that, too," she said, then cocked her head. "Can I ask you another question before I go?"

"That depends. Will it be equally seismic?"

"No, no! It's just that you said you talked to Frank after I screened you and before you and I actually met. Obviously, he didn't tell you to run the other way as fast as you could, but I have to admit I'm...curious about what he actually did tell you about the crazy little girl with the new pet that convinced you it would be 'safe' for the 'cats if you talked to me."

"Actually, the last thing he thought of you as was a 'little girl,' Steph, even then," MacDallan said seriously. "In fact, he told me that you'd probably be more determined, more willing to do anything it took, to protect the treecats than even I was."

Her eyes widened, and he nodded.

"Can...can I ask *why* he thought that?" she asked quietly. There were very few people in the universe Stephanie Harrington respected as much as Frank Lethbridge. If he'd told Scott that all that time ago, then—

"He thought that because of what you never told anyone about how Lionheart's family rescued you both," Scott said, equally quietly.

"What? What are you talking about?"

"The fact that they didn't kill the hexapuma."

"Of course they did!" Stephanie said almost fiercely, suddenly and irrationally angry as she remembered that horrible, terrifying afternoon. Remembered standing between Lionheart's broken, bleeding body and the hexapuma with her vibro-blade in her hand, knowing they were about to die before the rest of his clan arrived. How dared anyone suggest they hadn't saved her!

"Lionheart and I would both be dead if they hadn't killed it!" she added hotly.

"I didn't say they didn't *stop* it, Steph. I only said they didn't kill it."

"What are you *talking* about?" she demanded again,

and it was his eyes' turn to narrow. Was it possible she didn't know? That no one had ever told her?

"Steph, they didn't kill it; *you* did."

She stared at him in disbelief, and he smiled crookedly as her expression proved that no one *had* ever told her.

"I know they pulled it down, and I know that if they hadn't, it would've killed you and Lionheart," he said quietly, "but they didn't kill it. It was already dead; it just hadn't finished dying yet. You killed it when you stabbed it... from behind. You never told anyone else *that*, either, did you? Never told them you went after a hexapuma—a *hexapuma*, Steph—from behind with only a belt vibro-blade, broken arm, bad knee, and all."

Stephanie's face felt like a forest fire as she heard the soft, sincere admiration in his voice.

"You remember when Ainsley retrieved your vibro-blade?" he asked, and she nodded silently. "Well, she got there soon enough to walk the site before the scavengers pulled the carcass apart. She could see the damage you did, and if not one of Lionheart's relatives had ever showed up, it would have bled out, probably within minutes of killing you. And after Frank told me that, I knew *damned* well I could trust any twelve-year-old kid who was willing to do that to look after Fisher and all his friends, as well. So, if you and Karl think it's time to bring Chief Shelton on board, I'll trust you on that one, too."

"Barely home, almost killed, and with a new romance to report," Jessica said, wrapping her fingers around her mug of cocoa. "About par for the course with Stephanie Harrington."

"Hey!" Stephanie said in mock indignation. "That romance is a major landmark. I expected some excitement."

"Well, it's about time." Jessica laughed. "I mean, it's

been pretty obvious for a while that Karl has been head over heels for you. The rest of us—including Anders, if you must know—have had a betting pool as to how long it was going to take you to notice. I guess we all lose, since from what you say Karl had to tell you."

The two young women were sprawled in front of the fireplace at the Harrington homestead, where a fire that was for appearances and comfort, not heat—although having it available for heat if the power went down was a major reason there were fireplaces in every main room of the house—snapped and popped like a third member of the conversation. Stephanie's parents were both out, so Stephanie had revealed the Big News that she and Karl were dating—including some details as to just what a great kisser he was.

"Seriously? A betting pool?" Stephanie swung upright and stared at Jessica in horrified fascination.

"Seriously," Jessica laughed harder at the expression on Stephanie's face. "You two suit each other awfully well, better ever than you and Anders ever did. Face it, Anders was half in love with the Stephanie Harrington of his daydreams, even before he came to Sphinx, then—"

"Then I made the mistake of thinking my attraction to him—because, you've got to admit, Anders *is* gorgeous— was love at first sight," Stephanie admitted. "Honestly, romance stories have a lot to answer for."

After Karl—and Lionheart, of course—Jessica was definitely Stephanie's best friend, a friendship that had endured despite Anders dumping Stephanie for her.

I wonder if I didn't mind more because I was already realizing that Anders and I didn't quite fit. I mean, I missed him tons when Karl and I went off to Manticore for the accelerated training program, but it's nothing like how I'm missing Karl now.

Jessica was pretty, with a mane of wild auburn hair,

hazel-green eyes, and a pleasantly rounded figure. Like Stephanie and Karl, she'd been adopted by a treecat. Based on the number of rings on his tail, Valiant was somewhat older than Lionheart and Survivor, but not precisely elderly. Valiant had been a window into just how different from each other treecats could be. Although primarily carnivorous, like all treecats, Valiant was very interested in plants, and even had a garden and small greenhouse of his own at Jessica's family house.

Right now, Valiant and Lionheart were out examining Marjorie Harrington's extensive greenhouses. Although a lot of the quicker growing annuals had been left unplanted while the Harringtons had been off-planet, Marjorie had hired Jessica's mother, Naomi, to come and tend the perennials and biennials, as well as making sure Naomi knew she was welcome to harvest whatever she wanted for her large family. When Naomi had been alerted that the Harringtons were due back within a month, she'd planted seeds for the annuals, so they'd come home to find plenty of fresh herbs, greens for salads, and even some flowers, already established.

And celery, of course, but given that celery has a long growing period before it's ready to be harvested, I think Naomi must have kept plants going in rotation the whole time we were away. I'm sure Valiant appreciated that. The treecats always seem to like Mom's celery best.

"How was living on Gryphon?" Jessica asked. "Did the treecats do okay?"

Stephanie nodded. "We made sure they didn't lose their higher gee-conditioning, but the heat did make them shed a lot of their undercoats. Dad's suggested that Lionheart and Survivor wear their sweaters when they're outside; what with it still being pretty cold here, low temperatures could be a problem. Happily, the 'cats don't seem to mind wearing sweaters. They're not stupid."

"I'm glad to hear both of them did so well there," Jessica said, "because I'm thinking of applying to do my undergrad work off-planet. I'll have a better chance of getting into med school if I've done my pre-med in a cutting-edge program, rather than here where half the courses are virtual. And, of course, if I go, so does Valiant. I think he'd actually be interested in trying out an entirely new biome. Whenever we go to a different area, even here on Sphinx, he's always looking for new plants."

Stephanie thought, *And here's my opening to tell her about what Karl and I will be bringing up with Chief Ranger Shelton.*

She did so, keeping it short, because Jessica already knew the basics.

"I agree it's a good idea to get the treecats more protection," Jessica agreed when Stephanie had finished. "Having more guidelines in place when I'm thinking about moving off-planet for college will definitely be good for me and Valiant. Just tell me what you need by way of support for the new program and I'm there for you. I'm sure Cordelia will be, too. Cordy and I have hung out a lot while you were away, and she's a great person. If her family didn't need her so much, I think she might have joined the SFS, although right now she's pretty excited about her advanced courses in agriculture, agronomy, and forest management. They've just bought a starter herd of capri-cows, and Cordy's starting a dairy and cheesemaking operation."

"And is her sister, Dana, engaged yet?" Stephanie asked, awash in the glow of her own newly discovered love.

"Not yet," Jessica said, "and maybe not at all. Turns out that when they started talking long-term plans, like where to live and all, she and her boyfriend discovered some really big differences of opinion. And Mack Kemper broke up with Brad, though they're still friends. I wouldn't be surprised if they still hop in the sack time to time."

"Oh," Stephanie said, thinking *I hope this isn't how people are talking about me and Karl in less than a T-year from now. Dana was practically engaged to her guy when we left for Gryphon. What if Karl and I turn out to be like I was with Anders? What if it turns out we're better as friends?*

She saw Jessica looking at her with concern, and made herself stop brooding. "How're your little sibs? Several of them joined the Explorers, right? Are they still members? Any thoughts on how we should tweak the program?"

"They're all still members," Jessica re-assured her. "After you and Karl left for Gryphon, Chief Shelton assigned Moriah and Stephan Rosenquist to take over running things. They've done a great job and, as an added bonus, they breed Meyerdahl Rotties, and have a new litter of pups. It's a good thing all the pups were reserved even before they were born, because even if my family's income is doing a whole lot better than it was, we're not up to one of those. They eat as much as hexapumas!"

From there they went on to discuss how fostering wild animals via Wild and Free was filling the "wanna pet" gap in the Pherris household. Since this was the organization that Trudy volunteered for, it was pretty natural to segue to discussing that new romance.

"I get the impression Trudy's thinking about moving in with Nosey," Jessica said. "I think she's already spending a lot of time there. The Franchittis are still our landlords, and it's pretty clear that Jordan at least isn't thrilled to have the Nose for News dating his daughter. But she's past the age of consent, so there's not much he can do, other than throw her out, and since that would definitely end his ability to control her, he's in a bind."

"And Trudy's mom? What does she think?"

"Mrs. Franchitti's pretty much a cipher in that relationship," Jessica said. "I mean, we've been their tenants for years now, and I don't think I even know her first name. Wait...Maybe I do! Gertie, short for Gertrude. Trudy is named for her, but they call her Trudy to avoid confusion."

Stephanie once again felt grateful for not only how supportive her parents were, but that they were a team. When she'd been younger, she'd tried the "ask Dad" when her mom had said, "No," to something, and about the best she'd managed was a consultation, never one parent overriding the other just because they could. Karl's family worked a little differently, with Aleksandr running the farm, and Evelina running the house and supervising the kids, but they definitely collaborated on important things.

I wonder which model Karl and I would follow? Stephanie thought, then felt herself blushing that she was even thinking like that. She leapt to her feet.

"Almost time to start dinner. Let's go out to the greenhouse and make sure the treecats haven't eaten all the celery, then finish off the cooking."

Jessica pushed herself to her feet, and gave a lazy stretch. "Sounds good. And while we're at it, I want to talk college. I'm going to need scholarships, and I wondered if you'd help me research some options."

9

WHEN KARL CAME TO SPEND THE NIGHT WITH THE Harringtons the night before he and Stephanie were due to meet with Chief Ranger Shelton he was astonished at how exquisitely shy he felt.

It's not as if I've never slept over here before. I mean, I have my own parking space in the garage, and a bedroom that's had my clothes in the closet for years. And it's not as if Steph and I haven't been talking every night, as well as on and off during the day.

When Stephanie burst into the garage to greet him. Karl gathered her up in a hug, marveling all over again at how small she was.

I guess I never really noticed because her personality is so outsized, but she's positively dainty!

Stephanie held up her face to be kissed, and Karl bent down. Lips met lips, warm and intimate. He felt all too aware of the potential for even more intimacy. Neither of the senior Harringtons' vehicles were in the garage, and Stephanie was tugging him inside the house, saying something about how she'd made hot drinks, and built up the fire, and he was imagining holding her in his lap, sliding his hand up under her sweater when the incoming call beeped simultaneously on both their uni-links with the code that indicated the call was from Chief Shelton.

"Better get that," Karl said, trying to feel grateful that he'd been stopped before he started something that he wasn't certain he could stop. Or something like that.

Stephanie nodded and took the call.

"Hi, Chief Shelton. We're still on for tomorrow's meeting, I hope."

Chief Shelton grinned. "That's right. End of vacation for Karl, I fear. I screened you to find out if I was correct that tomorrow's meeting was related to treecats."

"That's right," Stephanie replied, puzzled. Chief Ranger Shelton rarely clarified things like that. He wasn't perfect, but his secretary, Francine Samarina, was an organizational genius.

"Sanura Hobbard's on planet, and since she's in charge of the official investigation into treecat intelligence, I thought you might like to have her sit in."

Stephanie moved her free hand out of sight of the pick-up in a thumbs-up gesture, then pointed at Karl and wobbled her hand in a "Thumbs-up? Thumbs-down?" gesture. Karl made a thumbs-up gesture, and Stephanie said, "That would be fine with us, sir. More than fine."

"Very good. Your appointment is for 9:30. I'll ask her to join us at 9:45. I have a couple of things to bring up with you first, shouldn't take long. Just a few departmental things."

Karl could have sworn the chief was trying not to smirk and fought down astonishment. Chief Shelton never smirked. It must be an artifact of the screening.

"Yes, sir!" he and Stephanie said together. And Karl

added, "And thank you, sir," although, for the life of him, he wasn't exactly sure what they were in for.

Stephanie's parents came home not long after, saving Karl from a renewed urge to investigate what Stephanie was wearing under her sweater, and what was under that. When Richard and Marjorie greeted him as they always did, warmly, like the son they hadn't yet had, Karl felt conflicted.

Are they saying, "We trust you not to overstep?" Or are they saying, "Help yourself?" Or nothing at all? Just because Stephanie and I have changed our relationship in our eyes, it seems as if we're just catching up to where everyone else figured we already were. Or something like that.

Whatever the case, although Karl permitted himself to give Stephanie a very warm goodnight kiss when they went upstairs, he didn't go into her room and she didn't come into his.

Which actually is weird, because before we were in and out of each other's rooms all the time, though not when we were changing or whatever. Now it's like we're drawing borders or something. I created this new tension, I'm pretty sure, with my speech about age of consent and all that. If this keeps going on, I may lose my ability to concentrate on anything else before Stephanie's birthday!

The next morning, Stephanie couldn't resist cuddling up to Karl in the air car during the flight to the SFS headquarters, though she was careful to make sure they didn't show up rumpled. Karl was wearing a fresh uniform, and she definitely didn't want him to look anything but his best.

When they got inside, Francine greeted them cheerfully. "So very glad to have you both back, and Lionheart and Survivor, too. It's been a little dull around here with only humans. I've buzzed the Chief, and he said to send you right in."

Stephanie nodded and put a small package on Francine's desk. "A souvenir, from Gryphon."

Then, leaving Francine to unwrap the little box, they headed back to Chief Shelton's office. Karl stepped back as always to let smaller Stephanie go in first. Chief Ranger Shelton hadn't changed much in the last year, except for maybe looking more tired than usual. He waved them to the chairs across from his desk, glanced at the time, and began speaking without further delay.

"We have just a few minutes, so let me start with a question. Via the rumor mill, I have heard that the two of you are dating, going steady, have become a couple, whatever term you prefer. Is this correct?"

"Yes, sir," from Karl, and "Gee, news sure does travel fast," from Stephanie. The grin that accompanied this faded when she saw Shelton lean back and sigh.

"Okay, so that means I need to brief you on the SFS policy for couples serving together, since you're both on staff. If we were on Manticore, you'd probably be congratulated, then put on different duty rosters so you wouldn't find yourself on the same patrol. Here on Sphinx, especially in the SFS, the situation is different. As you both know all too well, we're short-staffed. Many of our rangers quietly work extra hours without compensation, whether as volunteers or just making sure routine jobs in their patrol areas are taken care of, when routine gets pre-empted by an emergency. Often, they're forced to stay away from home.

"Karl's a good example. His legal address is still his parents' in Thunder River, but he often stays with you Harringtons. Stephanie often rides along with him on patrol. Well and good. However, now that you're a couple, and a young couple at that, there will be questions as to whether you're paying attention to your jobs or maybe 'canoodling' instead."

Thinking of how nice it had been to snuggle Karl on

the way to headquarters that morning, Stephanie felt herself blush. She hoped it didn't show. Karl shifted slightly, but his attention was on Shelton. Shelton paused, obviously to give them time to speak, but Stephanie decided to take her cue from Karl, and waited.

Shelton gave a slight smile, since he knew as well as anyone that restraint was not Stephanie's first response to any problem. "My policy is to place my trust in my rangers first, and not to assume dereliction of duty until that dereliction is proven. That applies to any couple, married or not. Which means it applies to you."

"Oh, thank you, sir!" Stephanie replied with a slight gasp.

"Don't thank me until you've tried it. This doesn't just mean refraining from inappropriate behavior while on duty, it means not bringing problems from home in with you to work. It means remembering the chain of command—and that the chain of command stops when you're off duty. We've had relationships break up over the inability to do all of these things. Don't make the mistake of believing I'm going easy on you. I'm making it harder, both for you to have a successful relationship and to do your job. Any questions?"

"Just one, sir," Karl said. "How do you deal with accusations of inappropriate behavior, especially if there's nothing to substantiate them other than someone's word?"

"We keep careful track of such complaints, but you don't need to worry about getting fired or penalized or yelled at just because someone says they saw you, say, making out in your cruiser. We check visual images for validity, and even if those are genuine, we'd ask you to explain. It might be you were off duty, for example."

"But for that reason," Stephanie said slowly, "we'd better be on our best behavior if we're in an SFS vehicle or Karl's in uniform."

"Precisely. I see you're putting your usual acute mental functions to work on this problem as you would with any other." He glanced at his desk com. "And Francine has signaled that Sanura Hobbard has arrived, slightly early, as I would expect of her. If you feel we've concluded the matter of what's considered seemly for serving SFS rangers who just happen to have the good sense to be in a relationship with someone who shares his or her interests and devotion to the goals of the service, then why don't we add a chair to our little circle, and you two tell us what this meeting is about."

Dr. Sanura Hobbard, the Chair of the Anthropology Department at Landing University, was a quietly attractive woman. Her brown hair was accented with auburn highlights, and her dark brown eyes were capable of looking intelligently interested while giving very little away. Way back when Lionheart had first entered her life, Stephanie had been inclined to think of Dr. Hobbard and the organization she represented as potential opponents, but as the years had unfurled and Stephanie had encountered real threats to the treecats, she had revised her opinion. Even so, today, facing the first time she was going to tell someone who wasn't already an adoptee or a member of the inner circle what she suspected about what the treecats were capable of, her heart started racing.

Stretched out along the back of her chair, Lionheart placed his true-hand lightly on her shoulder and gave a muted version of what Stephanie thought of as his "soothing purr." Having recently come to realize how she automatically reached up for Lionheart when she felt nervous, Stephanie gripped her teacup instead.

"So, did you like Gryphon?" Dr. Hobbard asked after

greetings had been exchanged. "Not what happened there, obviously, but the planet."

"I did like it, actually," Stephanie said, "although I think their weather would drive any residents crazy after a while. Once you get used to Sphinx's longer seasons, they're almost boringly predictable—at least in the Tannerman Gulf area—but on Gryphon, it's like they don't seem to have seasons as much as they have wildly unpredictable weather systems."

Dr. Hobbard laughed.

"I understand what you mean. I definitely prefer Sphinx or Manticore. How did the treecats do? Lionheart's been off-planet before, but other than gravity and temperature, Sphinx and Manticore aren't dissimilar. Gryphon would have been very different. Were they interested? Frightened? I can't imagine apathy. Apathy and treecat just don't seem to go together."

Karl leaned forward, every line of his body telegraphing his eagerness.

"Survivor was definitely interested in learning about his environment—often by sticking things in his mouth. I was pretty nervous at first, but then I noticed that, at least when it came to food, he had a remarkable tendency to limit himself to things we'd already sampled, maybe not sampled raw and wriggling, but definitely he was watching what he ate."

"Hmm..." Dr. Hobbard didn't look dubious. She knew Karl too well to accuse him of doting on his "new pet." Before they got too distracted by this new topic—or she chickened out—Stephanie thought they'd better dive into the topic they'd called this meeting to discuss.

"Listen," she said, then paused, worried she'd sounded bossier than a sixteen year-old probationary ranger should when addressing a couple of adults who happened to be a university department chair and the head of the SFS. But neither Hobbard nor Shelton seemed in the least annoyed, so she swallowed hard and continued. "Karl and I have been noticing just how much more treecats are on people's radar. Even as far back as our first visit to Manticore we had people asking us questions about them. I was even asked to give a talk for the Adair Foundation. The trial, though, especially since the treecats played a role in the whole thing, especially in saving us... Well, before long, it's not going to just be a few people here on Sphinx who think treecats would make great pets or at least want to go on a 'treecat watching' tour."

"So," Karl picked up as they had rehearsed, "we want to tell you some things we've learned about treecats that we think might influence your willingness to speed up getting some legislation passed to protect them from abuse."

Dr. Hobbard frowned slightly.

"Several xeno-anthropological study groups, including Dr. Whittaker's and the one sponsored by the Adair Foundation, have been studying the treecats' material culture," she said. "No one disputes any longer that treecats are tool makers, as well as tool users. Their stone tools are knapped, not just conveniently found, and their textiles are far more than heaps of twigs and leaves. Even more crucial is their use of fire. Very few 'animals' use fire, and those that do use it don't kindle their own fires, but adapt natural fires to their own uses."

"Like hawks that pick up burning branches," Stephanie said, "and use them to spread a fire, so that they can hunt the little animals as they flee from cover."

Hobbard nodded.

"So, I think we can feel certain treecats will definitely be placed somewhere on the 'sapient' scale. The question, as people like Clifford Mulvaney and Gary Hidalgo make unfortunately clear, is where on that scale. You're perfectly aware that the point that keeps coming up is the question of language. Other than a few noises, like that adorable, all-purpose 'bleek,' and a few shrieks and squeals, treecats are relatively silent. Many people—many *human* people—feel that the ability to communicate complex thoughts is a necessary part of being on the higher end of being sapient, intelligent, sentient... Whichever term you prefer."

Dr. Hobbard did that on purpose, Stephanie thought. *By showing how many words we have that provide slightly different variations of meaning for a single concept, she's showing what, to some people, treecats are apparently missing.*

"What if," Stephanie began slowly, really wishing she could reach up and hold onto Lionheart without looking like a complete kid, "treecats don't make a lot of sounds because they have other ways to communicate?"

"Are you thinking of scents or pheromones?" Dr. Hobbard asked. "Certainly, they use some of those. Even humans do, although we're largely unconscious of that element in our own communication. However, thus far we haven't had any evidence that treecats convey complex ideas via scent."

Karl raised one hand in a "stop traffic" gesture.

"Can you give us a moment to present our case? Not that we don't appreciate your input, but we want to explain how we came up with this theory. If we don't present our case right, we're just going to sound nuts."

"Sorry." Dr. Hobbard leaned back and laughed self-consciously. "I've been in so many discussions about where treecats should be placed on the sapiency scale that I forget myself. You two wouldn't have asked to speak with Chief Shelton—and agreed to include me—if you didn't think you had something new to offer."

"We do," Karl said. "And while we can't do anything to keep you from writing up what we're going to tell you as a paper for some journal or sharing it with one of your committees, we hope you'll understand why we've held back on sharing such a key point. To be honest, that decision—to hold back—was Stephanie's idea, originally, but all of us who have been adopted by treecats definitely agreed with her. We call it"—he grinned, despite his tension—"the Great Treecat Conspiracy. And we're"—he waved one hand in a gesture that encompassed not just Stephanie, Lionheart, and Survivor, but all the other adopted pairs—"about to invite you and Chief Shelton to join it."

Hobbard and Shelton looked at each other for a moment, then the Chief looked back at Karl, his expression speculative.

"Would it happen that Frank Lethbridge and Ainsley Jedrusinski are already members of this 'conspiracy,'" he asked.

"In a way," Karl admitted. "Neither of them's formally joined it or asked any embarrassing questions, but I know they both suspect something more than we're talking about publicly is cooking away in the background. Frank realizes that even more than Ainsley does, but I think you'll understand why he had a bunch of reasons for keeping his mouth shut. The biggest one, frankly, is that he's been protecting somebody. Not somebody who's done anything wrong," he added quickly. "Somebody whose family's had enough problems over the years for being 'different' and really, really doesn't want any more of them."

"Okay, I can accept that at least tentatively." Shelton nodded. "For that matter, I might as well admit I've had a few suspicions of my own." He glanced at Hobbard. "Doctor?"

"I don't know I'd go so far as saying I'd suspected there was an organized 'conspiracy,'" she said. "But it's been obvious to me from the beginning that you—all of you, but maybe *especially* Stephanie—have been . . . deflecting certain questions and speculation. Which, to be honest, was fine with me, in most ways, since I knew for a fact that anything Stephanie did was intended to protect the 'cats." She smiled warmly at the younger woman. "Which is why I haven't pushed harder and farther, young lady."

"I know," Stephanie said in a grateful tone.

"Well, in that case, why don't you get started on this recruiting pitch of yours?" Chief Shelton invited, and Stephanie drew a deep breath.

"Chief Shelton, when I told you I couldn't go to Manticore without Lionheart, I tried to make clear that I wasn't being a brat who *wouldn't*, but that I really *couldn't*. You took me at my word and didn't ask any questions, which I deeply appreciated. And my parents have pretty much done the same. So I figure you've already guessed at least parts of this. But the truth is that treecats are telempaths. When we say 'adopted,' we mean that literally, not like getting a pet from the shelter. Treecats can create bonds with other creatures, up to and including humans. We don't know how or why they pick their candidates, although a life-and-death situation often seems to provide the impetus. But there doesn't *need* to be a crisis. Survivor just picked Karl."

Karl nodded and reached up unselfconsciously to pat Survivor.

"And Survivor was definitely the one who did the choosing," he said, "and not because either of us were in any life-or-death situation. He'd had a bad time of it, sure, but by the time we bonded, he wasn't particularly threatened. It was just like he somehow saw or felt something in me that matched up with something in him. There was no bonding ritual or dance, or even any choice on my part. It just happened, kinda between one breath and the next."

Dr. Hobbard's fingers twitched, as if she were eager to take notes, but she restrained herself.

"Do you resent this one-sided decision? Do you feel violated in any way?"

Karl laughed.

"Not one bit. I feel like we were two parts of a jigsaw puzzle that just slid into place, filling in a picture that had been there all along."

"Amazing..." Dr. Hobbard sighed contentedly. "We'd certainly suspected the treecats' telempathy, but having you confirm that they can create an emotional symbiosis beyond their own species is very useful. Do all the other treecat adoptees agree that the treecats are telempathic?"

"They do," Karl confirmed. "In fact, one of the reasons just Stephanie and I asked to meet with Chief Shelton is so that he—now either of you—would have the opportunity to interview the other adoptees without our being present. We did tell all of them we were going to talk with you two, because they've all been part of keeping the secret we're sharing, but we all agreed that beyond that we wouldn't contaminate the sample any more than we have already."

"Amazing," Dr. Hobbard repeated. She clearly wanted to start speculating, but she had the good manners to press her lips together and gesture for them to continue their presentation.

"So our first point," Stephanie went on, "is that we believe part of the treecats' communication structure is based on telempathy. One reason they have mostly harmonious communities is probably because they can share emotions, really know what everyone else is feeling when it comes time to make decisions or settle disputes. Of course"—her expression darkened for a moment—"it's not enough to completely prevent things like the war that almost got Survivor killed."

"But," Karl added, "we're pretty sure their ability to communicate is more complicated than that. Based on observation, we think they also 'talk' to each other by speaking mind-to-mind. Basically, we think treecats are also telepathic. We can bore you to tears with examples, and we'll be happy to. For now, I'll just say that based on Occam's razor, the simplest explanation for a lot of what we've witnessed—including how they seem to 'spontaneously' share labor or cooperate in other ways—is that they talk to each other without making any sound."

"That all sounds reasonable and logical," Chief Shelton said after a moment. "Obviously it's all speculative at this point, though." He paused as Karl and Stephanie looked at each other, then raised an eyebrow. "It *is* speculative, isn't it?" he asked.

"Actually," Karl said slowly, "we have an incident we're pretty sure conclusively proves everything we've said so far. Unfortunately, it's not something that could be demonstrated or replicated in a lab or a field study. At least, not under any circumstances we can think of."

"Really?" Dr. Hobbard's eyes narrowed.

"You remember the Stray?" Stephanie asked, looking back and forth between the older adults, and both of them nodded. Shelton's expression was rather grimmer than Dr. Hobbard's, but then he'd been directly involved in the BioNeering investigation. Her involvement with the treecats had begun later than that.

"Well, there was a reason Scott went out to the BioNeering site, and it wasn't just because the Stray led him there. I know that's what he told everyone, but the real reason was that the treecats showed him what was happening there."

"*Showed* him?" Dr. Hobbard repeated sharply, and Chief Shelton sat forward in his chair, his eyes intent.

"It wasn't just the Stray," Stephanie said. "That evening, while he was still helping investigate the air car crash,

Fisher and the Stray between them led him out into the woods, and there were dozens of other treecats waiting for them—around a campfire, no less. Scott thinks there were probably at least a couple of hundred of them—probably more—all adults, all in one spot."

Shelton was frowning now, his eyes no longer just intent but afire with speculation. The Sphinx Forestry Service's database on treecats and the population size of a typical clan remained woefully incomplete and fragmentary, but what they did have suggested that a single clan would have been extraordinarily hard-pressed to produce that many adults in one spot. Not if they'd left *any* of their adults home to protect their nesting site and their treekittens.

"You're suggesting they came from more than one clan?" Dr. Hobbard put Shelton's thoughts into words, and Stephanie nodded.

"We think it's possible. Either that, or they thought what they were doing was important enough to bring virtually all the clan's adults together in the woods in the middle of the night. What we *know* they did was communicate with him."

"Communicate," Dr. Hobbard repeated very carefully.

"They . . . for want of a better word, they projected images into his mind," Stephanie said, hoping it didn't sound as outrageous to Dr. Hobbard as she thought it might. "Images of things he'd never seen, of the damage at the BioNeering site, and the sounds of human voices arguing. That's what took him out there in the first place. Him and Fisher and the Stray. He doesn't know for certain, but he thinks the images were from the Stray, not from the clan at the crash site—that the other 'cats were basically relaying them to him from the Stray—and that suggests that they can communicate a heck of a lot more than just emotions with one another."

Both Hobbard and Shelton were staring at her now, their eyes wide in astonishment, but their gazes switched back to Karl as he cleared his throat.

"The problem, of course, is that there's no way to prove any of that. Given that no one's ever been able to demonstrate telepathy in humans—and believe me, we've done our research on that since it happened—how are they going to detect it or measure it in treecats? And without the ability to do that, all we'd have would be Scott's unsubstantiated testimony. The fact that he did go straight to what Ubel had been up to after his encounter with the 'cats seems like pretty strong corroborating evidence to Steph and me that they told him about it, but he'd already given the 'I followed him there' explanation. That means the true version could be dismissed as an after-the-fact fabrication to bolster our argument for how smart they are. And as someone like that poisonous pain in the butt Ford would point out, we're prejudiced witnesses. It would be awfully easy for people who don't know us to suggest we're lying or paint us as lunatics. And especially if Scott claimed he 'heard voices.'"

"Which is exactly why Dr. MacDallan never told anyone else about it...except probably Frank Lethbridge," Shelton said.

"Pretty much, yes, sir," Karl confirmed.

"And if they are telepathic," Stephanie jumped back in, "it could explain not only the lack of verbalizations, but also why they seem even slower than the average animal to pick up human words. They have the concept of a noise indicating alarm, or a baby crying, or something like that. But they don't use words for things or ideas, so they're handicapped when it comes to picking up our words."

"Amaz—" Dr. Hobbard began, then cut herself off with a grin. "I think I've been overusing that word," she said, "but if you're right about that—about the telepathy, I mean—the consequences could be staggering. How do they actually communicate information? Telepathically, yes, but as discrete bits, the way we do in spoken or written language? Or do they simply . . . share a gestalt? How big are their data packets? Would they even understand what syntax is?" She shook her head. "The only thing I'm sure of is that their mode of data *sharing* would have to be as different from ours as their means of communicating that data to one another is."

"Survivor's learned to at least recognize a few words," Karl said, "but those are frequently repeated ones, like his own name. And I don't think he considers 'Survivor' his 'name.' I think it's more as if he thinks we humans have created a specialized cry of alarm, a sound that's meant to alert specifically him."

"And," Stephanie said, "if you think about it, really, it makes more sense than not. Even if we weren't dealing with the differences in 'data sharing' you just mentioned, Dr. Hobbard—and, to be honest, I hadn't gone as far with that in my own thinking as you seem to have—'Karl' sounds a whole lot like 'car.' 'Steph' like 'step.' If treecats don't use words, why would they sort out those noises that are so nearly the same? Actually, while we humans are judging their level of sapience and basing that on factors that include their inability to talk, well, I wonder if they're not doing the same thing when they look at us. Are they wondering why we're so incredibly noisy and if that means we're more like, say, tool-using prong bucks? Or maybe near-beavers, since we do build places to live."

Chief Shelton nodded slowly and rubbed his hands together in satisfaction.

"I like it. As an explanation of what we think is going on, I like it. Telepathy would explain why on a planet chock-full of megafauna predators that would just love to munch on treecats, treecats have been able to survive, to develop communities, and to evolve a relatively complex technology. They can talk up a storm without alerting the local hexapuma or peak bear to where they are!"

"I do too," Dr. Hobbard said. "And if we could prove that they're telepathic, it would be very useful in eliminating the complaint that their lack of a spoken or written language invalidates placing them higher on the scale. However," she grimaced, "as you just pointed out, Karl, there aren't any objective, replicable tests for telempathy, much less telepathy!"

"I think we might at least come up with tests for the empathy part of the equation," Stephanie said, "since we assume that the bond they made with us is telempathic. We already have a sense of the range of that bond and how sensitive it is, but I'm sure someone could argue that was all subjective. It would be better if you could come up with tests whose validity would satisfy you—and other xeno-anthropologists, of course—that we're not just imagining all of it."

"I'd love to design some tests," Dr. Hobbard said, "even if not for immediate publication. It would be good to lay some foundations before someone makes a public move against placing them higher on the sapience scale. That way we don't look as if we've created a theory on the spur of the moment to counter their arguments that the 'cats can't be very high on the scale because they don't communicate."

"Sounds like excellent tactics to me," Karl said. He gave Stephanie a sly grin. "If I hadn't been adopted, and Stephanie had started shooting off her mouth about how her wonder 'cat was as smart as a human—and telepathic, to boot—well, I might've just thought she was too eager to keep the limelight she'd earned as the discoverer of a very interesting new species."

Stephanie poked him with her elbow, but she also nodded to Dr. Hobbard.

"I agree," she said. "But, listen, there's a reason we didn't tell you about this until now. We've been worried about the risk to the treecats if it looks like they're about to be ruled the indigenous sapient species of Sphinx. There are a lot of people who hold land, or options on Crown Land, that actually belongs to the treecats, and we don't expect them to like hearing any of this." Her expression turned grim. "We don't want to see something like the Amphors right here on Sphinx."

"Do you really think that could happen?" Dr. Hobbard asked, but Stephanie noticed her tone was anxious, not skeptical.

"We don't know," Karl said. "But, as we see it, the most dangerous point isn't after the decision to give treecats some official standing, but during the critical period when proofs are being established. If the treecats aren't protected in advance, well, what happened on Barstool really might happen here, all over again."

"Not," Chief Ranger Sheldon growled, "on my watch! And that doesn't go just for treecats, but for any attempt to wipe out a species, whether it be a wood rat or hexapuma. The one is annoying, the other is dangerous, but they belong to this world, they're part of its ecosystem. We humans and *our* animals are the invasive species, and it's our job to learn to work within the Sphinx biome, not to wipe out what seems inconvenient and then later try and fix what we've done when we figure out how stupid we were."

Stephanie inhaled deeply in relief. She'd thought Chief Shelton would react this way, but it was one thing to hope, and another to have proof.

"First step," Shelton went on, "is to get some protections in place. I'm sure we can get them protected species status, as a minimum. Governor Donaldson's been worried about what might happen to them for a while now—I think some of those land speculators of yours have been leaning on a few of the Provisional Assembly's members, Steph—so I'm confident we can get her on board. And I need to have a talk with Jase Stamford and Liddy Johansen, too."

Stephanie stiffened slightly. Not because she had any doubt that Jason Stamford and Lydia Johansen, both members of the Provisional Assembly which constituted Sphinx's local government, wouldn't make good allies. Both of them had always been strong supporters of the SFS and its mission. But taking the question of the 'cats' sapiency to the Assembly—making it that big a part of the debate already swirling around them—

"Don't worry, Steph," Shelton said, reading her mind as clearly as though *he'd* been telepathic. "I won't have to share anything you and Karl have just told us to get them onboard. They're completely in the 'cats' corner already. And the 'cats aren't the only thing they're worried about. That's why Jase drafted the Wildlife Protection Act in the first place."

"We've heard about that . . . a bit." Stephanie's relief showed in her tone, but her eyes were still a bit worried. "I don't know as much about it as I should, though." She grimaced. "We were on Gryphon trying to not get murdered when he first proposed it, and we haven't seen much about it in the feeds since."

"That's because it hasn't gone a lot farther than that yet," Shelton said more than a bit tartly. "Mostly because Lautenberg and Peabody and their crowd have been keeping it tied up in committee. They're big proponents of maintaining the 'limited government which has always been so much a part of our Sphinxian heritage.'" This time he looked more like he wanted to spit. "They're really big on that 'roughhewn frontiersman' image, even if they were plenty willing to accept all the 'government intrusion' they could get during the Plague! Now that that's over, though, they don't want any more regulations than they can possibly avoid that might restrict anything they want to do on their own land. The truth is, I can't disagree with them about that in a lot of ways." He grimaced. "They *ought* to be free to make their own decisions on their land, and that's exactly what they see the WPA taking away from them. It won't, of course—aside from establishing things like protected species—but they regard even that as an intolerable 'intrusion,' which is why they're doing everything they can to keep it from coming to the Assembly floor for a vote. In the long run, they can't, and they know it, so in the meantime they're trying to water down its enforcement provisions."

Stephanie and Karl nodded. There were still a lot—way too many, in Stephanie's opinion—of unsettled details where the SFS was concerned. Its mission definition had blurred during the Plague Years, when the survival demands of a human colony hovering on the brink of extinction had trumped every other consideration. Worse, it had never been formally chartered by the Crown. The vital need for something like it was obvious to everyone, so no one had objected when Governor Donaldson's predecessor set it up, but it had always operated in something of a gray area, which was one reason its law enforcement powers were so limited.

The Wildlife Protection Act was supposed to rectify that. It would formally recognize the Sphinx Forestry Service as the paramount enforcement agency where all matters relating to the Sphinx biome were concerned, and it would spell out very specifically both the scope and limits of its mission and also the extent of its authority to shape natural resource management policies and to enforce existing policies and regulations. And, as she understood it, it would also just happen to significantly increase SFS's budget and funding.

That would be a good thing.

"I think the Governor's already more than a little irked over how long this has been delayed," Shelton continued, "so I'm pretty sure I can get her to push the Judiciary Committee to move on it. Jase is pretty sure it will pass once he finally gets it to the floor, and it includes specific authority to create a list of protected species. If we put the 'cats on the list, it would put us in a position to act on their behalf when and if the need arises without ever opening the can of worms where the degree of their sapiency is concerned. And if we do that, it'll give Sanura and her teams time to come up with the tests they'll need and design documentation for them."

They spent another quarter hour discussing possible approaches, then Dr. Hobbard announced that she had another appointment.

"I hate to cut this short," she said as she pushed back her chair, "but I really do have to go. Stephanie, I understand exactly why you and your friends have been going slow on putting forward exorbitant claims about the treecats' intelligence and how they communicate. Frankly, I think that was very wise of you, and I think it has to remain our policy going forward, until we are able to come up with some way to validate at least part of this in ways no one can ignore or sweep under the carpet. And I can't tell you how glad I am that you decided to finally trust us. I understand your reluctance, especially in the early days when it was just you and Lionheart, and then Scott and Fisher. But you're right that the 'cats need all the friends they can get. They're attracting attention, and not all of that will be eco-friendly tours or people wanting pets. Humans are very territorial beasts, and it's the job of the SFS and those of us who work with it to remind humanity that even if we've been on Sphinx for decades now, that isn't an excuse to abuse its original inhabitants instead of using the planet in the most responsible possible fashion."

She headed for the door. "Next meeting! Stay in touch!"

When Dr. Hobbard had left, Stephanie said, "Chief Shelton, what Sanura just said about reminding humanity made me think. We've heard good things about Moriah and Stephan Rosenquist." The Rosenquists were the couple who'd taken over running the SFS Explorers while she and Karl were off-planet. "Would it be okay with you if we set up a meeting with them, just to touch base, maybe volunteer to do a presentation or two when we're close to where there's a club meeting?"

"That would be an excellent idea." Shelton pulled up schedules on his desk display. "They're in the Twin Forks area currently. I've sent you their contact information. You can have an hour on the payroll to meet up with them."

"Thank you, sir," Stephanie and Karl chorused.

Karl added, "And we'll get out from underfoot. I'm sure Dr. Hobbard isn't the only person who has more meetings today."

Chief Shelton sighed. "You're right there. I've a glorious forty minutes before my next one, so the four of you should scoot and let me get prepared."

10

"DO YOU THINK STEPHANIE AND KARL WILL WANT TO take back running the Explorers?" Stephan "Rozie" Rosenquist asked his wife and fellow SFS Ranger, Moriah. "If so, I plan to protest to Chief Shelton. Sure, they got the club started, but we've put a year into making the idea real."

Rozie Rosenquist was a solidly built, fair-skinned man in his mid-thirties. He wore his dark brown hair and beard neatly trimmed, and carried himself like the soldier he'd been before their immigration to Sphinx. His eyes were a deep penetrating blue that could switch from amused to intimidating without warning.

"Don't forget why Chief Shelton gave us the job," Moriah replied with the same firm gentleness she used when working with her kennel of Meyerdahl Rottweilers and stable of riding horses. "You and I both appreciate that the Explorers gives us more time with Wade and J.C, and one reason he assigned us to run them was because we have kids the right age to be in the club. I don't think he's going to let anyone horn in."

Moriah was smaller than Stephan, with green eyes, light brown hair, and a fair complexion that summer sun dotted with freckles. She often wore a stocking cap, since she intensely disliked being cold. Today her cap featured rounded near-beaver ears.

"I don't know." Rozie got up to pace restlessly, emphasizing his points by making sweeping gestures with his coffee mug. "We've both seen Karl Zivonik at SFS meetings. He seems as nice a young man as you could want but, you've got to admit, that Stephanie Harrington seems sort of pushy. Rumor is that the post of probationary ranger was created because otherwise her family was going to sue the SFS after Stephanie was mauled by that hexapuma."

Moriah puffed out her breath. "Nonsense. I've spent a lot of time with Richard Harrington, what with the dogs and the horses, and he doesn't strike me as the sort to sue anyone over something like that. Besides, Cordelia Schardt-Cordova says Richard saved Barnaby's life after that encounter with the near-weasels."

Since Barnaby had started life in Moriah's kennels, that clearly settled the point of Richard Harrington's character for her.

"We're not talking about Richard Harrington, or Marjorie, for that matter," Rozie persisted. "We're talking about their probably over-indulged, in-the-eye-of-the-media-since-she-was-eleven, only child."

"Who has a treecat."

"Precisely. And, as Nosey Jones pointed out in his column last year, just about everyone who's 'been adopted' by a treecat also happens to be a friend of Stephanie's. I think she's a manipulator."

Moriah sighed. "If she is, she probably had to learn how to manipulate to survive. Not all of us get by on brawn and intimidation, my dear. Those of us who are petite need to learn how to handle the competition more subtly."

"You're not taking her side because you're both short, are you?" Rozie said with a laugh.

"I'm not taking her side because I don't think there's a side to take," Moriah countered. "Why don't you wait to meet her before you judge her?"

"I thought you and I might want to arrange our arguments in case Karl and Stephanie start hinting they want to start running the club again, that's all."

"So organize your arguments, but don't start the fight until you see if there's a fight to start. Now, hush. It's nearly three, and I bet that's them at the door. They both strike me as the type to be on time, or even a bit early."

Moriah was right. The door to the meeting room that doubled as headquarters for the SFS Explorers, mostly because it had a closet dedicated to club supplies, had swung cautiously open. Stephanie Harrington came in, followed by Karl Zivonik.

They were definitely a study in contrasts: Karl tall and dark, with the muscular build of the Sphinx native; Stephanie about Moriah's height, fine-boned, with an almost triangular face. Karl wore his SFS uniform, Stephanie a neat but practical outfit that evoked the uniform, especially in its more practical details, without attempting to imitate it. Their treecats weren't with them, and Rozie relaxed slightly at this sign that the pair weren't keeping the smart little creatures dancing attendance at their heels.

Introductions were pretty much a formality, but Stephanie and Karl offered their names as politely as if Rozie and Moriah weren't there specifically to meet with them. Then Karl shrugged off a daypack and took out a box bearing the logo of the Red Letter Café.

"We had to stop and do some shopping for Steph's folks," he explained, "and since Stephanie needs to be fed at least every couple of waking hours, we brought supplies."

Stephanie's boot tip lifted, as if she might be about to kick her partner, but she collected herself and settled for a cheerfully put-upon smile.

"Karl's not completely wrong, actually. We asked Eric Flint what you liked, and got a selection. Those bacon-wrapped cream-cheese-stuffed dates are incredible. Salty and sweet together. I'd somehow missed them before."

As anything with bacon got a high score from Rozie, they all settled around the table and dug in.

Karl began the conversation.

"When I was last home, my little sister, Larisa, couldn't stop babbling about how great the Explorers are. We wanted to thank you for taking the barest seed of an idea and turning it into something terrific."

"You gave us a good foundation," Moriah said. "Just the names you'd chosen for the different achievement levels gave us a strong sense of your vision for the group. I liked how you alternated flora and fauna, because the SFS is responsible for the care and protection of both. So many outsiders overlook that and think we're either for one or the other."

"I also liked how you didn't give predators precedence," Rozie added. "Emphasizing predators would give the wrong message, no matter how 'sexy' some people see anything with fur and fangs. It was also nice how you made the lowest level—the purple tulip—something we could work with in the classroom. Let me pull up images of the kids' starter pots."

Karl looked embarrassed.

"It's been a busy year, and we debated our choices so many times that I've forgotten what we settled on for the levels," he admitted.

"Purple tulips," Moriah began, ticking the list off

on her fingers, "then tuskelopes, after that range barley, near-otters, picketwood, hexapumas, tan apple."

She paused for breath, and Rozie took over, "Peak vultures, crown oak, treecats, spike thorn, mountain eagle, lace willow, and, finally, crag sheep. Probably my only complaint is that there isn't anything wholly aquatic in there. The health of the watershed is important, too."

"We did put in near-otters," Stephanie said anxiously.

"You did," Moriah said, "as I've pointed out to Rozie. He just wanted a fish. Also, lace willow grows best near water, so the watershed's covered there, too. Anyhow, it's not as if we're limited to the plants and animals on the list."

"I think Larisa mentioned that you have a trip planned for this spring to a near-beaver dam," Karl said.

"An abandoned dam," Rozie clarified. "Near-beavers may not be hexapumas, but they can be pretty fierce if they feel threatened. This dam was abandoned last autumn, and we figure it will survive the spring thaws. It's also way out in the boonies, several hours away from settled areas, so the kids should feel they're really getting out into the field."

"They're already excited," Karl reassured her. "We wanted to ask, can we help out with the club? Maybe give a talk or two?"

"It's going to be a while before it's warm enough you'll want to take the kids out into the bush," Stephanie put in. "A few new faces might help keep the excitement up."

With that, Rozie's apprehension that the Explorers might be poached vanished. The box of treats was emptied as ideas were tossed around. Moriah and Rozie both immediately understood why Stephanie and Karl were reluctant to put the treecats on center stage.

"We need *all* of Sphinx to be appreciated," Moriah said, "not just the one tool-using species. If Lionheart and Survivor come with you and want to look at the kids, that's great. Otherwise, you both have a lot more to offer."

"I'm really impressed by how well you understand kids," Stephanie said. "I'm an only and, basically, hopeless with them. Over the last few years, I've made friends who have tons of sibs, but to me kids still seem like weird little aliens."

Rozie nodded solemnly.

"Children are tiny sociopaths who will actively try to kill themselves or others, without knowing that's what they're doing," he said. "It's our job to keep that from happening and shepherd them into adulthood as productive members of society!"

"That works," Karl agreed. "My mom has been known to say—in her offspring's hearing—that if toddlers weren't so cute, they'd never make it past the 'grab and break' stage."

"You have two kids, right?" Stephanie asked. "Boys?"

"Yep," Moriah said, "four years apart from each other. Once Wade started moving on two feet, I realized that the amount of chaos kids can cause isn't additive, it's multiplicative. J.C. works out the plans, and Wade carries them out with an enthusiasm that has to be seen to be believed."

Karl laughed and nodded.

"That's about right. You two are definitely the best for this job. My sibs would try to argue with me, and Stephanie would swear off kids for life."

Stephanie didn't disagree. "Let's compare calendars and see where Karl and I can fit our schedules with yours," Stephanie said.

"Great," Moriah said, grabbing the last bacon-wrapped date from under Rozie's hand. "We've already got Cordelia Schardt-Cordova scheduled for our next meeting. She's going to talk about her experience with the near-weasels, then about her new dairy operation. We're going to finish off with a capri-cow cheese tasting."

"That sounds great," Stephanie said, making a note. "Maybe we can come in the next meeting after that?"

THE BRILLIANT SUN SPARKLE BOUNCING OFF THE DEEP, endless snow hurt Trudy's eyes a little even through the polarized sunglasses as she snowshoed her way toward the shed that held the power receptor, but that was fine. Given the lengthy Sphinx year, this was only her fourth winter, but even though she was glad it was winding towards its end, it was her favorite season in many ways. Blizzards on a planet with a gravity thirty percent greater than Old Terra's had to be seen to be believed, and they could be terrifying. Yet there was also a power and a majesty to those cataclysms that filled her with a sense of wonder and awe. And on windless, sun-burnished days like this, the purity of the snow, the quiet hush of winter stillness, turned the forest around the Franchitti barony into an enormous cathedral, with a lapis-blue roof upheld by the towering columns of near-pines and the nearly leafless, titanic crown oaks.

She'd always loved the forests of her cool, beautiful homeworld regardless of the season. And not just because of their beauty. She suspected that she loved them just as much as Stephanie Harrington did, but a part of her deeply envied the exploring joy that pushed Stephanie into them. For Stephanie, they were an enormous, exciting jewelry chest, just waiting to share its treasures with her, and Trudy understood that. That was part of her love for them, as well. But it was only *a* part, and the other, far bigger part was something she'd tried to deny even to herself for as long as she could remember.

They were her refuge. Her hiding place. The sanctum to which she could flee not just from her father's hectoring voice or his hard, hurting hands but from the entire life in which she'd been trapped for as long as she could remember.

It was hard admitting that to herself, even now. In fact, she'd managed to deny it in her own mind for as long as she could remember. Even when her envy had been part of the reason she'd deliberately picked quarrels with Stephanie, she'd hidden from the reason she loved the woods just as much as the woods had hidden her from her father. But her admission to Nosey had opened her own eyes, freed her to recognize too many things a younger, hurt, heartbroken Trudy had refused to admit or confront in the name of survival, and that was one of them.

Now she swung along the edge of the trees, avoiding the snow-coated, broad-based cones of the red spruces which intruded into the clearing at the heart of her family's barony. Like most of the First Wave holdings, the Franchitti claim was enormous, a bit smaller than the Zivonik claim but several times something like the Harringtons' freehold. And while her father was fond of explaining that titles of nobility were ridiculous and normally went by a simple "Mr. Franchitti," she knew he was secretly irritated that he was only a baron when other First Wavers with only marginally larger holdings were earls.

The majority of Sphinx's trees were evergreens of one sort or another—not surprising, given the planet's fifteen-T-month-long winters. The most notable exception was the crown oak, which (like the various species of its smaller cousin, the dwarf oak) was deciduous and essentially hibernated over much of the winter. The disappearance of the crown oaks' leaves, which formed the upper canopy of most of Sphinx's forests, accounted for the deep snow which buried those forests every winter, since it let the snowfall through. The near-pine, Sphinx's tallest evergreen—some of them were almost as tall as crown oaks—didn't drop its leaves in winter, but unlike most of its less-lofty relatives, the lower third of its trunk was branchless, which also let the snow sift through to heap about it.

The red spruce, which made up over a third of the forest understory at lower elevations, was far less lofty than the near pine—it seldom got much more than seventeen meters or so—but its densely needled branches began no more than a meter or so above ground level and rose in a steep-sided, snow-shedding cone. That meant that aside from a thick drift of fallen needles, the ground around the base of a red spruce's trunk was usually bare or only lightly dusted in snow, which formed a sort of natural snow tree well with a drop-off that could be as much as two meters or more lower than the snow around it. A much younger Trudy had amused herself by seeing how close to the edge of the snow precipice she could get before it crumbled and she slithered down through the red spruce's lower limbs into the sheltered area. Getting back out again through those dense branches, even with counter-grav, had been a challenge on more than one occasion, however, and she had no intention of hauling herself out of any trees' snowy embraces today.

There were even more of the spruces around the Franchitti barony than in other parts of the surrounding forest. Unlike some of his neighbors, Jordan Franchitti had been perfectly willing to log off the crown oaks and near-pines around the Franchitti farmhouse and its out-buildings, and not just so he could sell the lumber. That had opened the tree canopy, letting in more sunlight and giving faster, lower-growing species like the red spruce the chance to prosper. Trudy wished he hadn't allowed so much of the crown oak to be cut, given how many decades it took for replacement trees to reach maturity. The fact that it also allowed near-kudzu to invade the area didn't help any, either. Oh, there were enough prong buck and hexa-elk in the surrounding forest to keep it grazed back to manageable proportions...mostly. For that matter, cut and baled, it made excellent fodder for Old Terran herbivores, with a few judicious nutrients added to it. None of which made the parts of it the prong buck didn't eat any less of a barrier to mere human beings trying to get through or around it. Personally, Trudy preferred to dial up her counter-grav and just go over the intricately tangled thickets the fast-growing vines produced.

But there were at least a few upsides to her father's logging practices from her perspective. Among other things, trees like red spruce and its distant cousin the beech-fir produced seedpods and nuts, and that—coupled with the cover the near-kudzu offered to smaller creatures—had given Trudy a childhood filled with the teeming species which fed upon them. She'd spent literally days at a time watching foraging near-squirrels and Sphinx chipmunks scamper through the branches, not to mention the various avians who fed on the same seedpods or nuts...or the raptors, who fed upon the near-squirrels and chipmunks.

But even that came with a downside on the Franchitti barony, she thought more glumly, slogging steadily across the snow toward the power receptor, and grimaced down at the LED flashing on her uni-link.

Like the warning light on the main panel in the house, it was only a blinking yellow, not the steady amber of imminent failure, so the problem—if there truly was one—was probably minor. She'd been tempted to ignore it and let one of her brothers deal with it when they got back from their hunting trip with her father, and she probably would have if she hadn't been able to guess how *that* would have worked out when Jordan got home. Even if the link to the power satellites went completely out, they had ample generator backup to keep things up and running for days. Not that her father would see things that way. And he'd probably add something cutting about how little time she spent at home anyway, these days, and how she obviously couldn't be bothered to contribute a few minutes to keeping the barony up and running. And then—

Stop that, she told herself. *It won't be all that long before you* do *move out, and then you'll never have to put up with him again.*

She held that thought to herself, like the memory of a beloved, long-nosed face, and smiled into the icy sunlight.

Leaf Racer scampered along the net-wood's bare branches in a cautious, fast-moving blur. Every season had its own dangers for the People, and it was well to remember that the winged hunters could see their prey far more easily with no leaves to hide it. The cold itself was seldom an issue for the People, given their warm, thick coats, but even that could change if one was injured with none to aid. Most clans lost a hunter or two during the long, endless days of ice and snow, and Leaf Racer did not intend to be one of them.

Still Water would be most *unhappy with me if I allowed something like* that *to happen,* he thought cheerfully. *She would not be the only one, either. Prey Finder would have an unkind thought or two if he lost one of the clan's better hunters!*

He bleeked a soft laugh as he pictured Golden-Leaf Clan's senior hunter glowering at his vanished hunter. The fact that Prey Finder was Leaf Racer's grandsire would only make the older hunter even grumpier! Especially if it happened on an unauthorized trip like today's.

Still, even Grandsire would probably forgive me for "creeping off on my own" today. He loves Still Water as if she were his own kitten. Not that he is alone in that!

Leaf Racer paused, close to the main trunk of the current net-wood, and sat upright, grooming his whiskers as he thought about his mate. He had thought, when he was younger, that he understood what a lifemate bond was. He had tasted enough of them from the outside, after all. But he knew now that until his own mind and soul had entwined with Still Water, he had tasted only an echo of the reality. The depth of her love warmed him on the coldest day, welcomed him home again after the longest hunt, and the glow of her was always there in the back of his mind, shimmering deep at the heart of him, like sunlight on water, wherever he was.

Which, after all, was the reason he was here today, he reminded himself and allowed himself another soft mental chuckle. He could always trust Still Water to do things her own way!

Most kittens were born late during the new leaf days of each season turning. Some were born a little earlier than that, during the last of the mud days. But leave it to Still Water to bear her first litter of kittens before the cold days fully surrendered their icy grip upon the world! It wasn't unheard of, and the memory singers and the clan's healers knew how to deal with kittens born out of season. In fact, clans embraced the opportunity to spend all their effort spoiling just a single litter, and mothers with no young of their own could be counted upon to curl themselves around another's kittens if sire and dam were called away. Indeed, Leaf Racer had teased Still Water about deliberately becoming pregnant simply because she knew how the entire clan would turn out to coddle the only mother they had.

She had swatted him across the head for that one, he remembered cheerfully.

But the truth was that he intended to do all the spoiling she could possibly require, and one of the things she had always loved—and had recently developed a far stronger craving for—were the seeds of the gray-bark tree. They were only just now coming to full ripeness, but he intended to fill his carry net completely before he headed home to her.

The distant cry of a cloud slayer came to him, and he cocked his head and ears, tracking the sound. The winged hunters were large enough to take one of the People, but most were wise enough to seek easier prey, and this one seemed to be headed away from the clearing which was his destination. Still, he sat motionless a short while longer, giving it time to take itself elsewhere before he resumed his journey along the net-wood.

The trees about him thinned as he approached the two-leg nest place. Once, and not all that long ago, he would never have approached it in daylight. But the People had learned a great deal about the two-legs since Climbs Quickly of Bright Water Clan had bonded with one of them. One thing they had learned was that there were evildoers among the two-legs, which meant caution was still in order, but they had also learned that those like Death Fang's Bane and her friends would punish evildoers who harmed the People. Besides, the secret of the People's existence was a secret no longer, which meant that it was no longer necessary to skulk about, hiding in the dark. Not that Leaf Racer intended to take any chances. And because the two-legs of this nesting place had cut back the golden-leaf and green-needle trees, the lower-growing gray-bark trees had sprung up in abundance. It would not take him long to fill his carry net, he thought.

I told Ralph that circuit breaker needs replacing, Trudy thought bitingly as she studied the diagnostic readout on her uni-link. *But did he listen to me? No, of course he didn't!*

Her older brother, Jordan Ralph Franchitti, Junior—Ralph, for short and to distinguish him from his father—was, in fact, very *like* his father. Which meant he was stubborn, resented any potential criticism, and was firmly convinced of his own infallibility. And he was also firmly convinced that he knew how to handle any task better than anyone else on the entire planet—except, of course, for his father. So when Trudy had suggested that perhaps he needed to tighten his maintenance schedule just a bit he'd promptly filed it as "Sister's Advice: Ignore All."

To be fair, the circuit breaker wasn't in any danger of immediate failure, but the winter weather hadn't done its reliability any favors. Trudy was tempted to simply go ahead and replace it herself, except that Ralph would immediately take that as a silent criticism of his own capabilities and be impossible to live with for at least a week.

That was another thing she wasn't going to miss when she moved in with Nosey.

She considered the circuit breaker a moment longer, then tapped the command that turned off the warning light...this time. Hopefully the next time it tripped, Ralph would be here to deal with it himself. In the meantime, she'd just quietly log it and go on her way.

She closed the panel, stepped out of the sturdily built shack which housed the receptor and protected it from the worst of Sphinx's sometimes ungentle weather, and shut the door carefully behind her before she kicked her feet back into the snowshoes to start back to the main house.

Leaf Racer leapt from the net-wood into the thicket of tangle-vine around the closest gray-bark tree. A Person was small enough to squirm through the densely woven tangle-vine, and it offered the shortest path to the gray-bark without requiring him to burrow his way through the snow. Of course—

Trudy's head snapped up as she heard the sudden, high-pitched squeal. For a long moment, she had no idea what it had been, but then it sounded again, and her eyebrows rose in surprised recognition.

She turned toward it, slogging swiftly across the snow, and her eyes narrowed as she saw snow cascading from the tangle of near-kudzu as something thrashed deep inside it.

Damn *you, Ralph!* she thought bitterly. *You and your stupid traps! If you had a single ounce of—*

She cut the thought off. It wasn't as if it was the first time she'd had it, nor was there any way she was going to change it. Not since her father completely agreed with Ralph. After all, he'd done exactly the same thing when he was younger.

One of the reasons he'd been so willing to log off the crown oaks around the homestead was to increase the habitat for things like prong buck and hexa-elk. Not because he cared about their well-being, but to bring them closer to home, where he could find them without long hunting trips by air car. And it also provided habitat for Sphinx's smaller creatures, like range bunnies, near-weasels, Sphinxian raccoons, and—especially—near-sables. Like their Old Terran namesakes, near-sables' pelts were highly valued, especially by those enamored of "fashion-able" winter wear. The red spruce dominating the area around the main house was a smorgasbord for all those species, and Ralph's traps brought in a welcome trickle of dollars.

But those traps weren't as selective as they might have been. Not that it bothered Ralph—or their father—when something less valuable got itself trapped. After all, they liked range bunny stew, and there were plenty more where that one had come from. And there were plenty of scavengers to deal with the less tasty unfortunates who fell into one of the traps. In this case, though—

Leaf Racer made himself stop thrashing as he tasted the two-leg mind-glow moving rapidly closer. Its con-cern was evident, although the powerful edge of anger he tasted under the concern puzzled him. From what he sensed, it seemed unlikely the made-thing which had snapped shut on his mid-limb belonged to this two-leg. It had obviously been left here by *a* two-leg, however, and Leaf Racer castigated himself for not detecting it before it bit him. He had been too focused on the seedpods he'd come to harvest, let his caution lapse, and this was the result! Prey Finder and Finds Things, Golden-Leaf's senior scout, would take his ears when he got back and confessed to *this* blunder!

He had already tried his own claws and his flaked-flint

knife, but the made-thing's tether was too tough and the gray bark limb to which it was anchored was too thick for him to simply gnaw off. Worse, none of Golden-Leaf's other People were close enough to hear his mind-voice when he called for aid, which meant there were none to help him. Not until he had sensed the two-leg's presence and squealed to attract its attention.

And did you stop to consider that it might have been this two-leg who left this trap here? he asked himself now. *Of course not! You are going from strength to strength today, are you not?*

Trudy reached the tangle of near-kudzu and leaned close, parting the vines cautiously. Something like a near-weasel or a near-sable was capable of a nasty bite, and the sables, especially, boasted claws that were longer than and almost as sharp as a treecat's. Her thick, warm gloves would protect her from most bites, but her snowsuit, for all its warmth, was less tough than they were. If this was what she was almost certain it was, that probably wouldn't be a problem, but she'd learned a lot—some of it the hard way—about approaching frightened or trapped animals, and if it *wasn't* what she thought it was . . .

"Bleek!"

Her frown disappeared when she heard the welcoming cry, and she pulled the vines confidently apart. From the sound of it, the victim of Ralph's trap hadn't been badly injured, thank goodness! Not that Ralph would have worried about it one way or the other. The banked glow of her anger burned hotter as she thought about how her brother would have shrugged and dismissed any concern over what might have happened.

"Bleek!"

The final curtain of near-kudzu parted, and she saw

the treecat. The snare had closed around the wrist/ankle of its right mid-limb, not its neck, only because it clearly hadn't been interested in the bacon with which Ralph had baited it. On the other hand, the 'cats were smart enough that if it *had* been interested in the bait, it would undoubtedly have approached it far more cautiously than a near-weasel or a sable. In fact, it looked a lot like it had simply stepped on the snare, and she felt a surge of relief as she realized it truly wasn't seriously injured.

Leaf Racer looked up at the towering two-leg and sampled the cascade of its emotions. The anger was stronger than ever, in some ways, but it was overlaid by a burst of relief. Relief that he himself wasn't hurt, he realized. And then that relief was followed by something that tasted very much like amusement.

"And here I thought all treecats were so observant and careful in the bush!" Trudy told the captive as it—he, from its coloration and markings—gazed up at her. "How in the world did you just *step* on it? It almost serves you right for not watching where you were going!"

The mouth noises meant nothing to Leaf Racer, but the amusement flickering behind them did, and he twitched his ears in resignation. No doubt the two-leg was wondering exactly what Prey Finder would ask him about when he returned to Golden-Leaf's nesting place. But it was also bending closer to examine the made-thing, and Leaf Racer raised his hand-foot as high as the tether would allow.

Trudy examined the snare and reached for her vibroblade. Then she paused.

"Crap," she said, and shook her head in disgust. If she cut it, then Ralph would realize she had. It wasn't as if anyone else in the Franchitti clan would have turned a trapped animal loose! And if he did, he'd be pissed, and then her father would be pissed, and God knew she'd had enough of that kind of grief in her life already. So—

Leaf Racer wished that could follow the two-foot's thoughts the way he could follow its emotions. They were... tangled, those emotions, but they were certainly strong and clear, and he sensed far too much pain lurking in their depths as it examined the made-thing. It reached for what he recognized from other clans' descriptions as a knife, even though it had no blade, but then it made another mouth noise and paused. It grasped his mid-limb gently, just below the elbow, and turned it as it bent closer to the made-thing.

There you are, Trudy thought as she found the recessed release button.

"Too bad you didn't know what to look for, Fuzzy," she told the treecat. "You'd have been out of here in a heartbeat if you had. So"—she tapped the catch beside the button—"pay attention so you can do this for yourself if there's a next time!"

Leaf Racer's eyes followed the two leg's finger. It was obviously showing him something, although he had no idea what, but then his ears flattened as it pressed a small round shape and the made-thing biting his wrist suddenly let go.

"Bleek!"

It sounded very different this time, and Trudy laughed in delight as the treecat raised his mid-limb and carefully examined the area the snare had closed upon. He flexed the fingers and thumb of his hand-foot as if testing them, then into a neatly seated position, wrapped his tail around his feet, and looked up at her in obvious gratitude.

"You're welcome," she said, extending one hand to him. "And I'm sorry Ralph's stupid trap caught you. Although"— she smiled as he gripped her index finger firmly—"if you'd been paying attention, it wouldn't have caught you anyway, now would it?"

"Bleek."

Trudy reminded herself that she was scarcely the treecat expert Stephanie Harrington was, but *that* bleek sounded almost rueful to her. If Nosey was right about the 'cats' ability to sense human emotions, then it probably *was* rueful, given the tenor of her own feelings at the moment.

Now that he was free of the made-thing, Leaf Racer took the time to truly sample the two-leg's mind-glow, and as he did, his ears perked in respect. It was very, very strong, that mind-glow. Stronger than almost any Person's mind-glow he'd ever tasted, despite the darkness stranded through its brilliance. Or possibly *because* of the darkness? He considered that for a moment and realized it was true. The brightness was even brighter not just because of the contrast but because it must triumph *over* the shadows. Such darkness almost never afflicted one of the People, not with so many other People and mind-healers about them. This mind-glow must burn even brighter to drive back the shadows which tried to choke it.

His heart went out to the two-leg as he recognized the courage that lonely, isolated battle must require and tasted the blazing power it created. He felt none of the drive to reach out to it, embrace it, as those like Climbs Quickly who had bonded with the two-legs had done, but still its brightness beckoned to him. And so did its welcome, its amusement and happiness at seeing him. It was...nice, that welcome.

"Now what brought you out here today?" Trudy mused aloud, then grimaced. "Of course! You're out foraging, aren't you?"

Leaf Racer knew the two-leg was asking a question, and frustration surged as he realized there was no way he could know what the poor mind-blind creature was trying to say. But then it turned and raised one of the gray bark's branches. It shook it hard enough to shake away the snow and made more mouth noises as it pointed at a cluster of seedpods.

"This is what you're looking for, isn't it?" Trudy said, and her grimace turned into a broad grin as the treecat started unwrapping the cargo net from its torso. "Okay, since Ralph's dumb trap bit you, I guess the least I can do is help you harvest!"

Leaf Racer bleeked happily as the two-leg began plucking seedpods from the gray bark. Its hands were much bigger than his, and he spread the carry net as the two-leg dropped the pods into it.

It took longer than Trudy would really have expected to fill the net as full as the treecat—she'd decided to think of him as her Fuzzy Friend from the denseness of his winter coat—obviously wanted. In fact, she was a little surprised that he could handle the weight of the packed net as easily as he clearly could. But it was full, eventually, and he moved it to his back, slipping his mid-limbs through a pair of loops that would keep it there.

He sat back up on his haunches, gazing at her. Then he reached out, patted her gently on the knee, and pointed—unmistakably pointed—back into the surrounding forest.

"Home's that way, is it?" she asked, then pointed at the farmhouse. "That's home for me. Right now, anyway."

The treecat's ears twitched, and she wondered if that meant that he'd understood that she'd understood where he was pointing. She hoped so.

Then the 'cat turned and leapt back into the picket-wood, landing lightly and gracefully despite the weight of his cargo net. He paused again, looking down at her, and she raised one hand in an abbreviated wave.

"Come back and visit again," she told him. "But next time, be more careful! I may not be here to get you un-trapped!"

Leaf Racer tasted the fresh amusement—and welcome— in the two-leg's mind-glow. It was truly amazing how... *comfortable* the two-leg tasted. The flow between them might be nothing like the consuming brilliance in the memory songs already circulating about Climbs Quickly and Death Fang's Bane, but it was... warm, like sunlight on green leaves. It felt good. And, he realized, this was something he needed to explore. The possibility of making *friends* with a two-leg had never been part of those memory songs. Or not, at least, unless the two-leg in question was already a friend of one to whom a Person had bonded. He thought about that for a moment, and then raised a true-hand as the two-leg had raised its.

"Bleek!" the treecat said, and Trudy blinked as it returned her wave.

Then it turned and flowed away into the picketwood. She watched it go with a sense of regret, but also with an odd serenity. And, somehow, she knew she'd be seeing him again.

12

"IT'S GOOD TO SEE YOU AGAIN, NOSEY!" GWENDOLYN
Adair said cheerfully as Nosey Jones crossed the shuttle
pad with his overnight bag in hand. The transit time
between Sphinx and Manticore was only a bit more than
seven hours at the moment, but Gwendolyn's invitation had
included attendance at a couple of Adair Foundation PR
events on the Star Kingdom's capital planet. That meant
spending at least one night here on Manticore before
returning to Sphinx. In fact, that was the only real fly in
his ointment, since he and Trudy had planned to meet
Karl and Stephanie for dinner at Eric Flint's restaurant.

"It's good to be here again," he said, mostly truthfully, as he shook the hand she offered him. "In fact, it's
a little flattering."

"Like I told you last time, we regard you as a valuable
ally," she replied. "And the eye I've been keeping on your
demographics only underscores that. Your audience on

Sphinx has grown steadily since the baka bakari incident, and now the way you covered the Wether trial from a Sphinxian's perspective has expanded your visibility here on Manticore, as well. In fact, that's one reason George—I mean, Earl Adair Hollow—agreed with me that getting you into the press pool for the Foundation's events this week was a good idea."

"Now I really am flattered," Nosey said with a smile.

"Everything I've just said is deserved," she told him, then released his hand and waved toward the exit. "I've got an air car waiting to deliver you to the hotel and let you get settled before this evening's first event. I'm afraid we'll be talking about the new Jason Bay fishing regulations instead of anything really exciting." She made a small face as they stepped out of the terminal and her air car's autopilot delivered it to an open slot in the valet zone. "It's important, don't get me wrong, but people generally seem to have more trouble getting excited about fish than they do over something 'cute and cuddly' like a treecat! Trust me, that makes fishing regulations a lot harder to sell."

"I can see where that might be true," Nosey chuckled.

The air car doors opened and they climbed aboard. Gwendolyn checked the navigation display and glanced at Nosey.

"There's a nice little restaurant—Dempsey's, it's called—in the same tower as your hotel. If I've got the time conversions right, we're probably actually coming up on suppertime for you back home. I've tentatively booked us a table, if you'd like to grab something to eat before we check you into your room."

"That sounds great," he agreed gratefully, and she nodded.

"That's the plan, then," she said.

✧　　✧　　✧

Dempsey's wasn't quite what Nosey had expected. It had obviously begun life as a bar, not a restaurant, and the floor was covered in what looked like woodchips. He raised an eyebrow at Gwendolyn as the young man at the entry stand tapped a slate to summon one of his servers.

"Part of the original owner's notion of rustic charm," she told him. "Back on Old Terra, bars and saloons used to cover the floor in sawdust to soak up any unfortunate little accidents like spilled drinks or dropped food. The custom's been revived on quite a few of the planets we've settled since then, including right here."

"The health department doesn't have a problem with that?" Nosey asked a bit quizzically.

"Completely cleaned and recycled every day after closing, sir," the youthful host put in with a grin. "It's not all that hard, once you get the janitor bots programmed for it. And the truth is, that we do still occasionally have those 'unfortunate little accidents' Ms. Adair mentioned, even today. One of our servers dropped an entire tray of filled beer steins just yesterday, as a matter of fact. Close to four liters of lager." He rolled his eyes. "Talk about messes!"

"I wasn't criticizing," Nosey said. "Just curious!"

"Which, between you and me, is the reason Granddad decided to put it down in the first place," the host said. "And he was right. *Everybody's* 'curious' when they first hear about it, and it's a hook that intrigues people into dropping by. The trick is to hook them with good food and better service once you've got them in the door."

Nosey nodded, and the young man handed them off to a slightly older young woman whose close physical resemblance made it obvious she was his sister, or at least a cousin. She ushered them to a table in one of the smaller side rooms.

"Thank you, Sylvie," Gwendolyn said as she settled into a waiting chair.

"We're kind of between rush hours right now," Sylvie replied. "You should have this section pretty much to yourselves." She grinned. "I figured you probably had Foundation business to discuss, so I might as well find you some privacy in order to deserve the generous tip I know you're going to leave."

"Oh, of course!" Gwendolyn laughed. "And, seriously, thank you for thinking of that."

"We try to take care of the regulars, ma'am," Sylvie told her. "Your usual drink order? Tanapple juice and an ice water?"

"Sounds good."

"And you, sir?" Sylvie looked at Nosey, and he chuckled.

"I don't usually think about tanapples off Sphinx, but that sounds pretty good to me, too."

"Good! I'll be back for appetizer and entrée orders in a minute or two."

She headed off, and Nosey leaned back in his own chair.

"They really do know you here, don't they?" he said.

"I spend too much time meeting with people in restaurants," Gwendolyn replied. "Which is not, by the way, a subtle way of telling you how onerous I find 'wining and dining' *you*, Nosey! But when you eat out as much as I do, you learn the difference between good and bad service pretty quickly. You also try to cultivate the former whenever you can, and Dempsey's staff is really, really good."

"I can tell."

"Well, I might as well feed you someplace I like. Go ahead and call up the menu. Just about anything on it is good!"

Nosey nodded and brought up the tabletop menu. It offered a greater variety than he was accustomed to finding in eateries back home on Sphinx, but his were simple tastes, and by the time Sylvie returned, he'd made up his mind.

"The Everything-on-It Burger sounds good to me," he said with a grin. "I have a friend back on Sphinx I want to be able to describe it to in loving detail. She's got the Meyerdahl mods, and it's exactly what she'd be ordering if she were here."

"Sides?"

"Salad with peppercorn and fried onion rings."

"Salad first, or with the entrée?"

"Salad first, I think."

"Sounds good. And tell your friend if she ever decides to drop in that we offer endless refills on onion rings and French fries."

"If I tell her that, she'll bankrupt you," he said with an even broader grin, and Sylvie laughed. Then she looked at Gwendolyn.

"It's a little early for me," Gwendolyn said. "My friend here's on Sphinx time, so I needed to get him fed. Just bring me an appetizer portion of the guacamole and chips, please."

"You've got it," Sylvie said, and headed for the kitchen.

Nosey sipped the sweet, tart tanapple juice appreciatively, then set down the glass.

"You said when you invited me that the 'cats are back on the radar here on Manticore again?"

"That's probably putting it a bit strongly, but the truth is they've never really dropped back off since the trial. And the fact that the automatic review of Ms. Wether's sentencing will wrap up next week is only throwing things back into the public view again. Not as much as before, obviously, but people will be talking about them. I imagine the fact that you're from Sphinx and so closely associated with the 'cats in people's minds here on Manticore is likely to get a few questions about them thrown your direction, too."

"I hadn't really thought about that," Nosey said. "I

guess I'm too used to being the one writing the stories to think about ending up in one myself!"

"Visibility, Nosey. Visibility." Gwendolyn shrugged. "You're a journalist. You know that's what makes a spokesperson successful. She has to have enough visibility for anyone to actually hear what she's saying. The fact that you've got more of that than most where the 'cats are concerned helps make you a more effective advocate for them."

He nodded.

"Anything new about deciding how sapient they are?" he asked. "Here on Manticore, I mean. I've been trying to stay tapped in, but I've got plenty going on back on Sphinx, and day-to-day life tends to get in the way of keeping track of things over here."

"Nothing planet-shattering," Gwendolyn said. "The groundswell towards the notion that if they *aren't* truly sapient, they're very smart animals at the very least is still gathering strength, I think. But it hasn't been that long since your last visit, so there haven't been any significant changes." She shrugged. "What I *am* seeing worries me on a couple of fronts, though."

"Why?" Nosey's eyes narrowed, and she shrugged again.

"The first is that I think there's likely to be more pressure by the people who find the notion of treecat sapiency 'inconvenient' to push harder and faster on research about them. That would be more intrusive, which would obviously increase the degree of cross-cultural contamination, but even more to the point, rushed studies are usually easier to manipulate. Or they make it easier to confirm the researchers' initial positions and biases rather than rigorously testing those positions' validity, at any rate. And the second is that I'm hearing very quiet whispers about an effort to . . . remove inconveniently located treecat clans. For their own good, of course."

"What do you mean 'remove'?" Nosey asked in a sharper tone.

"That *is* the interesting part, isn't it?" Gwendolyn grimaced. "Most of the proponents aren't really big on the details of how it would all work, which, frankly, is the aspect of it that bothers me. I very much doubt that finding a way to move entire treecat clans without traumatizing them as a community would be remotely as simple as some of the people talking about it seem to think. Assuming they really think that at all, of course. But the truth is that there's a lot to be said for . . . creating firebreaks. Providing separation between the 'cats' ranges and the areas we humans are developing for our own use."

"I can see that," Nosey acknowledged. "But how do we do that?"

"Well, one way would be to establish . . . game preserves, for want of a better term. Or maybe even 'reservations,' although that term's got some unfortunate historical connotations. But whatever we *called* them, they'd be areas that were off-limits to any human incursion—reserved and preserved for the treecats' sole use. We don't know enough yet about their populations or social organization to have any idea how best to go about that—like I say, that's what worries me about the people currently starting to talk about it—but it's still something we need think about as a possible future option. And if they are, indeed, Sphinx's native sapient species, then reserving sufficient areas on Sphinx—even helping them migrate to areas far enough away from current or future human encroachment to be safe—might be the best way to protect them over the long haul."

"I see." Nosey frowned thoughtfully. "I can't say I like the thought of making them move just to get out of our way, though."

"I know it might seem like that's what we'd be doing,"

Gwendolyn said sympathetically. "For that matter, there's a degree of validity to looking at it that way. But that's not the point of the exercise, Nosey. Frankly, humanity's record with 'inconvenient' indigent species suggests that they *will* be encroached upon as soon as someone gets around to it. Much as we'd like to prevent that from happening, history suggests it won't be easy. And the point of the exercise is to keep them *safe*."

"I can see that, I guess." Nosey shook his head, his expression glum. "That still doesn't mean I like it."

"It doesn't have to be traumatic for them. In fact, I think you and Stephanie and the 'cats' other friends on Sphinx could play a major role in keeping it from being traumatic. If it comes to that, I mean." She shrugged. "Hopefully, it won't, but if it does, figuring out where to locate their safe zones, their 'reservations,' I suppose, will be one of the tougher aspects of the operation. Obviously, it would be a Crown decision, in the end, but I know the government would want input from all the stakeholders, which would automatically include the SFS and, almost as automatically, the Foundation. If we were on the same page about how to manage the transition with the least repercussions for the treecats we'd be in a much better position to guide the process."

Nosey's eyes narrowed as he thought about that. He sat that way for at least a full minute, then shook himself as Sylvie arrived with his salad and Gwendolyn's guacamole. She set them on the table, refreshed their drinks from a juice carafe, and disappeared again, and he looked back at Gwendolyn.

"I definitely agree that we need to come up with ways to protect them from human intrusion," he said more enthusiastically. "The notion of setting up areas reserved solely for their use is certainly one way to go about that, too. I'd been thinking more in terms of telling people

they couldn't just move in on the treecats' existing territories, but I can see where that could be hard to work
out. We don't know anywhere near enough about them
yet, but it does sound as if they tend to stay in one place
for fairly lengthy periods. At the same time, though, their
territories *do* shift, and as far as I know, we still don't
have anything like a definitive handle on the population
densities any given territory can support."

"Those are the kind of details we need people like
Stephanie to be digging out back home on Sphinx,"
Gwendolyn said. "And they're the kind of information
we'd absolutely have to have before we could even begin
setting up reservations for them, whether the reservations
in question are where they've already settled or in virgin
areas of the planet far away from human incursion."

"That much I can certainly see," Nosey said, then
snorted. "You seem to give me a lot to think about each
time we meet, Gwen! I hope you're not going to sprain
my brain before I escape back to Sphinx!"

"Oh, I think your brain will be just fine," she reassured him, and scooped up guacamole on a corn chip.

"So, what do you think?" Karl asked.

He sprawled in the old-fashioned, tipped-back recliner
in his room in the Harrington farmhouse. It was a family
relic which had traveled to Sphinx from Meyerdahl, but
it was in his room because it was also one of the few
old-fashioned, unpowered chairs in the house that actually
fitted someone his size. In fact, it was a bit large even for
him, a fact of which Stephanie totally approved, since that
made it possible for her to curl up in it on his lap with
a pair of highly satisfactory arms wrapped around her.

Lionheart and Survivor were a bit crowded, lying
across the top of the chairback, but the faint, almost

subliminal hum of their buzzing purrs made their own approval of the furniture abundantly clear.

At the moment, however, Stephanie was in a less than purring mood of her own. She and Karl had just finished viewing Nosey's com message from Manticore, and both of them were definitely in two minds about it.

"I think I hope Gwen's being overly pessimistic," she said after a moment. "I really don't want the notion of 'treecat reservations' floating around any sooner than we can help! Have you heard anything about it that I haven't?"

"You've heard everything I have," Karl replied. "That may be at least part of what Patricia Hamilton was getting at with the Chief last week, though."

Stephanie nodded with a thoughtful frown. Governor Donaldson had responded strongly and favorably to Chief Shelton's desire to push harder on the Wildlife Protection Act, but Patricia Hamilton, Donaldson's chief of staff, struck Stephanie as less enthusiastic about the idea.

"I thought she was just suggesting that we wait until the Assembly transitions into the planetary parliament," she said, and Karl nodded.

At the moment, the Provisional Assembly elected by the citizens of Sphinx had strictly limited authority. The Star Kingdom's Constitution provided that all three of its planets would eventually have their own planetary parliaments. Until that happened, there was only one official Parliament, the one seated in Landing. The local parliaments (which might well end up called something else, to avoid confusion with the *Star Kingdom*'s Parliament) would have authority to enact planetary laws, so long as they posed no constitutional conflicts, once they officially came into existence. Until that point, any laws the Provisional Assembly might enact were subject to review and override by the national Parliament.

The Constitution had established threshold population

levels at which the transition would occur, but the Plague's ravages had pushed the deadline back, and Sphinx's population was only now beginning to approach it. It would probably reach it in the next planetary year or so, in fact, if the demographic curves held steady. Of course, that meant it could take up to another five *T-years*.

"That's what I thought, too," Karl said. "In fact, I still think it's what she was talking about. What I'm less certain about is whether that's because she doesn't want to get into a potential squabble with Landing until *our* parliament has its feet under it, or if she just doesn't see the point in rushing into anything when we'll be able to handle it completely locally in another couple of T-years."

"She really doesn't seem to feel as much...urgency as Chief Shelton does," Stephanie acknowledged unhappily.

"Steph, nobody else in the entire Star Kingdom feels as much urgency as we do!" Karl told her with a quick hug. "On the other hand, I'd have to say she might be more in favor of something like this reservation deal Gwen's apparently talking about than we'd like. I know at least some of the Governor's councilors would be, anyway! Especially Tatum."

Stephanie nodded even more unhappily. Anthony Tatum was Coordinator of Commerce on Governor Donaldson's Advisory Council. That made him the closest thing to a Minister of Commerce Sphinx had, and the fact that he really, really wanted to attract additional industry to Sphinx was abundantly clear. At the moment, all Sphinx had to offer to Manticore or anyone else—exclusive of tourism, at least—were forestry products and fish, neither of which generated a lot of tax revenue. Unfortunately, Tatum was rather less concerned about protecting the planetary environment from the potential consequences of new industry. He was notably cool about environmental impact statements, for example, which made him a natural ally for people like Assemblyman Lautenberg and Assemblywoman Peabody. And in Stephanie's private opinion, the fact that he'd grown up with Jordan Franchitti was another strike against him. If there was anyone on the entire planet who'd cheerfully banish all of Lionheart's relatives to "reservations" as far as possible from any "desirable real estate," it was undoubtedly Tatum.

"Well, whether or not she's right to be worried about it this early on, you and I both know the suggestion's going to be made sooner or later," she told Karl, resting her cheek on his chest. "And to be honest, I wish Nosey didn't sound quite so . . . enthusiastic about the notion himself."

"Fair's fair, honey," Karl said. "I wouldn't say he's *enthusiastic* about it, but he's obviously thinking about it as a way to provide refuge for the 'cats if everything else goes south on us."

"But that's *wrong*," Stephanie said.

"Of course it is, but neither he nor Gwen know as much as we do about the 'cats." Karl shook his head. "It's a lot easier to talk about 'reservations' and 'game preserves' when you don't think you're talking about real, fully sapient *people*. And for all of Gwen's and the Adair Foundation's dedication to protecting the environment, even a lot of the Foundation's directors still think of them as smart, clever *animals*, not people. For that matter, sometimes I think Gwen thinks of them that way herself."

"Really?" Stephanie's tone was troubled, and he shrugged.

"Again, fair's fair. She's seen more of Lionheart and now of Survivor than most anybody else on Manticore, but she really hasn't seen that much of them. For that matter, Nosey doesn't know as much about them as you and I have learned. Or Cordelia, or Jessica—or, especially, Scott!"

"That's true," Stephanie acknowledged. "I guess we've just been seeing so much of Nosey since the baka bakari episode that I'd forgotten he's still pretty much an outsider in a lot of ways."

"So maybe it's time we changed that," Karl suggested. "I think it's obvious Gwen sees him as a valuable ally for the Foundation and for at least what she thinks is best for the 'cats, and I have to say, she's probably right. We tend to think of him as 'just' Nosey because he's our friend, but he actually does have a lot of subscribers, you know, and the list is growing steadily. I think he really is going to be one of the major newsies here on Sphinx. In fact, he may be already! But if she's thinking about recruiting him, then we should probably be thinking the same way. Especially since we still can't tell her everything we think we know about the 'cats."

"Add him to the Conspiracy, you mean?"

"That's exactly what I mean," Karl agreed.

"That's actually a pretty good idea, even if I'm not the one who had it," Stephanie told him with a grin. Then the grin faded a bit. "The truth is, I'd almost forgotten he wasn't already a Conspirator. Officially, I mean. But he's no dummy, and I think he'd probably be a good add even if he wasn't an aspiring newsy."

"In that case, let's run it by the others before he gets back from Landing," Karl said, then chuckled suddenly.

"What?" Stephanie asked him, raising her head enough to look him in the eye. "I know that evil chuckle. What did you just think of?"

"Well, we are talking about 'Nose for News' Nosey Jones," Karl replied. "I can hardly wait to see the way his nose quivers when he finds out what nobody else has ever reported about the treecats...and that we've sworn him to secrecy before we tell him. I can't decide whether he'll hate it or love it."

"Oh, that *is* evil," Stephanie said with a giggle of her own. "I like the way your mind works, Mr. Zivonik!"

"What? You only love me for my *mind*?" Karl managed a quite serviceable stricken expression, and Stephanie laughed again, harder.

"I love you for your mind among *other* things," she told him, and kissed him firmly.

13

"WOW."

Nosey Jones looked back and forth between Karl and Stephanie, then at Lionheart and Survivor, curled across the back of the armchair his hosts shared, and his eyes were wide.

"Just . . . wow," he repeated and shook his head. "I always knew there was stuff you guys were holding back. Stuff you shared with Cordelia after Athos adopted her but never told anyone else. And I've always suspected Doctor MacDallan had more input in the background than most people realized, even after the Stray. But *this*—!" He shook his head again. "Wow."

"You understand why we never told anybody all of this, though, right?" Stephanie asked a bit anxiously, holding onto Karl's hand as she perched on the chair's well-padded arm. Nosey doubted she even realized she was holding it, and her eyes were dark. "Why we're so worried about how the rest of the Star Kingdom may react if what we think is true ever comes out?"

"Especially since we can't think of any way to prove any of it," Karl put in. "If there were something we could take into a laboratory, or a court of law, and conclusively *prove* the 'cats are as intelligent as we think they are, or even that they can communicate complex concepts without a spoken language, that would be one thing. I think after what happened to the Amphors, nobody in the Star Kingdom would be willing to sign on for anything remotely like a repeat performance if we *could* prove it. But we can't. And that means—"

"And that means everybody with a vested interest in doing the treecats dirty would line up their own 'expert witnesses'—however much they had to pay them to say the right things—to dispute your 'wild, ridiculous, unvalidated, impossible to verify speculation,'" Nosey interrupted grimly, and Stephanie's shoulders sagged in relief.

"That's exactly what we're afraid would happen," she said.

"And," Nosey smiled crookedly, "it wasn't something you could tell me until you'd seduced me into the proper mindset, given that 'The Nose for News' would probably blab it to the heavens. Or to every reader of his blog, at least!"

"Actually, it was less—a lot less, after we got to know you a bit better—a question of which side you'd come down on, or whether or not we could trust you, than it was that we already knew you were a treecat supporter," Stephanie told him a bit somberly. "We didn't have to convince you to be that. The articles you were already posting showed you were concerned about them, wanted to protect them and prevent them from being exploited. To be honest, there was a while there when I wanted to strangle you because of the way you were speaking out against people making 'pets' out of treecats."

Nosey raised an eyebrow and cocked his head, and she snorted.

"Trust me, I was *totally* on board with your discouraging people from hunting them down as pets! The thing was, though, that I already knew nobody's going to catch a 'cat—or even see one in the bush—unless it's the 'cat's idea. And in other ways, we wanted as many adoptions as we could get."

"Strength in numbers." Nosey nodded.

"Exactly." Karl nodded back vigorously. "We want as many advocates for the 'cats as we can get. But at the same time, there's a sweet spot, a balance point where the numbers of adoptions give us those advocates but don't become so 'common' that people who don't actually know the 'cats assume they *are* pets. If they weren't, then why would so many people have them?"

"I can see that." Nosey pursed his lips. "On the other hand, I think you'd need a lot more adoptions than you're likely to get before the downside of 'too many pets' started outweighing the advantages of advocates."

"That's probably true," Stephanie said, then surprised Nosey with a chuckle.

"What?" he asked.

"Just something Doctor Hobbard told me day before yesterday," she said with a wicked smile, and Karl snorted beside her in matching amusement. Nosey made a "tell me more" gesture, and she shrugged.

"You remember Doctor Bolgeo?"

"Tennessee Bolgeo? The guy who was trying to kidnap the treecats before you stopped him?"

"Well, it wasn't really me so much as Lionheart's family and the hexapuma they chased straight into him." Stephanie's amusement faded a bit, and she shook her head. "Honestly, that's the one thing I really regret about it. It wasn't the poor hexapuma's choice to go after him, and I hated having to kill it to save him."

"I'm sure *Bolgeo* appreciated it," Nosey said dryly.

"Oh, I'm sure he did, too." Stephanie grinned as her sense of humor reasserted itself. "And when Lionheart's family shredded his hostile environment suit, I think he got a clue about what they could have done with him or to him instead of the hexapuma. Even with his trank gun, he couldn't have kept them from swarming him under, and—trust me—he figured that out sitting there while I kept Lionheart's relatives from eating him until Karl and Scott could get there!"

"I'd really like to do an interview with you about that," Nosey said thoughtfully. "I've thought about that a couple of times, over the years. I think it would be really interesting."

"*I'd* like you to do an interview with me, but not one for publication," she replied, and his eyebrows rose again. "The fact that the treecats went and rounded up the hexapuma to attack the human who was trapping and kidnapping them is pretty strong evidence of their ability to work together and plan things on the fly. That would have to help the argument that they're fully sapient. At the same time, I don't want to be handing their enemies ammunition, and I guarantee you someone would get all hot and bothered over the fact that they'd sicced a 'man-eating monster' on him!"

"Damn straight they did!" Nosey said. "I'd've done the same thing!"

"Yeah, but what Steph was giggling about is a request Doctor Hobbard got a couple of days ago," Karl said. "I think she might not have mentioned it if we hadn't taken her and Chief Shelton fully into the GTC, but I also think it tickled her as much as it does Stephanie. Not to mention the fact that it could actually turn out to be really, really useful."

"And 'it' happened to be exactly what?" Nosey asked a bit tartly.

"Sorry!" Stephanie waved an apologetic hand. "We're not trying to be mysterious, honest. It's just that it turns out Doctor Bolgeo really is a credentialed xeno-biologist, and while he did figure out that the 'cats were perfectly willing to have the hexapuma kill him if that was what it took to get their relatives back, he also figured out that when they...peeled him, they were very careful about inflicting any significant damage. That they were going easy on him. You know that when they brought him up on charges, he pled guilty?"

"Of course." Nosey shrugged. "I would've looked for a plea bargain, too."

"That's the thing," Stephanie told him. "He didn't. Take a plea bargain, I mean."

Nosey looked at her, and she shrugged.

"It's not like the sentence for trafficking in 'exotic animals' was all that heavy, really," she said. "I mean, it's more than just a slap on the wrist, but it's not like they'd be sending him to prison for years and years and years, and they couldn't charge him with anything else without opening that whole can of worms about just how intelligent the 'cats really are. I'm pretty sure what *he's* concluded about their intelligence, though. They gave him three T-years jail time and then two T-years of community service, which was about the max he could have gotten, but he's getting out of jail four T-months early for good behavior, and he's formally requested that the parole board allow him to do his community service with the Forestry Service. Specifically, helping us study the treecats."

"What?" Nosey stared at her.

"Yeah, that was my first thought, too," Karl said sardonically. "But Steph here actually thinks it could be a good idea."

"Why?"

"Because he's already spent a lot of time studying them," Stephanie said very, very seriously. "And because I think he genuinely accepts that they are sapients, in every sense of the word. He's not a *bad* man, really. I mean, he's nothing like someone like Ubel or even Orgeson and her thugs. From what Doctor Hobbard says, the thought that he might have been kidnapping an actual intelligent being to sell into what amounted to slavery really bothers him. And"—she met Nosey's eyes levelly—"I think he's probably done some figuring out of his own about how they communicate, too. Which means he knows any tree-cat who gets stolen and sold off-world, taken away from Sphinx, will never be able to communicate with anyone he knows and loves ever again. I think that bothers him, Nosey. I think it bothers him a lot. And if it does, somebody with his background—especially somebody used to thinking in twisty ways who could help us counter *other people* who think in twisty ways—could be really, really useful to us."

"If you're right about him, then, yeah. He probably could," Nosey said slowly. "And if you're not, you'd certainly be in a good position to keep an eye on him!"

"A point not lost upon Chief Shelton," Karl said dryly. Nosey glanced at him, and he shrugged. "Stephanie the Impetuous has already taken the notion to the Chief. He was...pretty incredulous there at the beginning. He's had some experience with Steph's tendency to come at things headlong, you might say."

"Hey!" Stephanie reached high enough to smack the top of his head, a not insignificant reach for someone her height. "I'm a lot better than I used to be! I'll have you know I think a long time before I just plunge ahead nowadays!"

"Yeah—a whole thirty seconds!" Karl shot back.

"That's not true, and you know it. I spent an entire

minute thinking about it before I talked to Chief Shelton. In fact, it was closer to *ninety seconds!*" She raised her nose with a sniff as Karl and Nosey both laughed...and both treecats joined in as well.

"Oh, much more cautious than you used to be!" Nosey nodded soberly. "I see that now."

"Good!" Stephanie told him, then leaned back against Karl again.

"One of the reasons we wanted to get you on board with the Conspiracy," she said more soberly, "is that we think Gwen's right about your growing profile, both here and on Manticore. Don't take this wrongly, but you don't really have all that much competition here on Sphinx yet, so your footprint here is probably inevitable. But your coverage of the trial and the way Gwen and the Foundation have introduced you to the people worried about our biosystems really has increased your visibility. And when people actually view your stuff, they find out you're a pretty sharp cookie. You're not a half-bad writer, you don't go off half-cocked, you check your facts, and you're honest. We'll need that on our side when the time comes to go public, and getting you into the mix as early as possible will only make that even more effective."

Nosey nodded, trying—unsuccessfully—to hide how pleased he was by her evaluation. Especially because he knew she meant it.

"At the same time, we didn't want you climbing on board this 'reservation' idea she brought up with you," Stephanie continued. "On the face of it, it makes a lot of sense, and the idea usually starts out with all the good intentions in the world. As a way of saving and preserving an indigenous people. Or that's the way it gets sold to governments, anyway. But when you look closer, the whole notion of reservations has what you might call a checkered past. The people who originally owned the land don't tend to get to keep the good bits...which is exactly what a lot of their proponents *really* had in mind from the beginning." Her expression hardened. "I've done some research on this, and some of it—no, a *lot* of it—hasn't been very pretty. I like to think we'd do a better job of it here than people did elsewhere, but people are people, Nosey."

Her somber expression belonged on an older face, he thought.

"Dad says the problem is that history is full of people who insist on repeating really bad ideas because they sound like they ought to be so good. The fact that they've never worked out that way when people actually tried them only convinces the people who want to repeat them that the folks before them didn't 'do it right.' He says that happens with economics and political systems more than almost anything else, but it's also happened way too often with reservations, with indigenous species, with animals that ought to have been protected. Gwen may be right that we could end up in a situation where that would be the best of the bad solutions left to us, but I don't think we want to be suggesting it this early."

"I can see that...sorta," Nosey said after a moment. "I know she means well, really wants to look out for the 'cats, and she really knows her stuff about biosystems and habitats. Remind me to tell you what she told me about the hexapumas sometime. But you may be right about its being too early to be bringing up the notion of reservations. Especially if it means relocating the 'cats off of the ranges they've already established, rather than creating reservations around their *existing* ranges."

"Which is pretty much exactly what Chief Shelton thinks would happen—moving them, I mean," Karl said.

"To be honest, I think Gwen figured it would probably come to that, too," Nosey replied. Then he looked at Stephanie. "So the Treecat Conspiracy wants me not to get behind and push that idea?"

"Pretty much." She nodded. "I think it would probably be fairer to say we'd prefer someone everyone knows is friendly to the 'cats not be the first to bring the idea up. It's going to *come* up, we all know that. But we'd prefer for it to be something we could present...measured arguments against, let's say, without having had somebody on 'our side' propose the idea—as far as public opinion would be concerned, anyway—in the first place."

"That much I can *definitely* see." Nosey nodded. "Okay, I can get on board with that. But since you're bringing me in, should I take it that you're also considering... broadening the ranks of Conspirators?"

"Some." Karl nodded. "Folks like Chief Shelton, Doctor Hobbard, Frank Lethbridge, Ainsley Jedrusinski—people like that—we have to have on board if this is going to work. But we don't want to get too carried away about it. We're trying to keep it very low-key and under the radar until we've been able to amass the best evidence and arguments in the 'cats' favor we can come up with."

"Makes sense. I would like to suggest you consider telling Trudy about it, though." He saw Stephanie's expression go blank and shook his head. "That's not just because I'm in love with her, which, by the way, I am. It's because she's smart—a lot smarter than I think too many people give her credit for—and she's also deeply committed to protecting the planetary environment and especially the animals that live in it. You know that. I think she's probably more than halfway to figuring out at least two thirds of what you two just told me, too. And—"

He started to say something more, then stopped and waved one hand. Stephanie looked at him very thoughtfully, then glanced at Karl.

"I have to say I've seen a lot more depth—and pain, I

think—in Trudy since Stan was killed than I ever would have expected when we first met," Karl said quietly. "I think too many people here in the Star Kingdom have had too much experience with losing people they loved, or just cared about. I don't think Trudy ever really *loved* Stan—not the way you love her or I love Steph"—his arm tightened around Stephanie—"but she cared about him. Losing him, especially that way, hit her hard, and it shows. And I think there's something else going on down inside her, too."

He held Nosey's gaze levelly, but Nosey refused to confirm what he might be thinking. What Trudy had told him she'd told *him*, not anyone else, and nothing in the universe could have brought him to betray that confidence. But he'd always known Karl had a tonne of what his mother called "people sense." He wouldn't be a bit surprised if Karl saw deeper—and more clearly—beneath Trudy's surface than most did.

"I have to agree with Karl—that I've realized there's a lot more to Trudy, a lot more *good* stuff, than I ever realized when all I wanted to do was punch her in the snoot," Stephanie said with a slight smile that somehow lightened Nosey's heart. "And everything you just said about her protective side is certainly true. But there's another thing, too, that I'm not sure even you've thought about."

"Like what?" Nosey asked.

"She's a Franchitti." Stephanie gave her head a little toss. "Honestly, I don't much like the Franchittis, especially her father. And he doesn't much like us. For someone who makes such a big thing out of downplaying the fact that he's a baron like Karl's dad, he's awfully fond of pointing out that First Wave status of his family and beating us newcomers over the head with it, too."

"You're afraid she'd side with her family?" Nosey's tone

was sharper than he'd intended it to be, and Stephanie shook her head quickly.

"I think exactly the opposite, Nosey. I've thought that ever since she went back into the fire to rescue her 'pets,' and everything I've seen out of her since, especially what she's done with Wild and Free, only reinforces that. I don't like the thought of how adding her to the GTC might... complicate things with her family, but if we *did* bring her into it, she'd bring that whole First Wave thing in on *our* side of the debate, as well." She smiled nastily. "I would pay good money to see her father's expression when she stands up and says treecats are people, not animals!"

"So would I," Nosey said feelingly. *And for a lot of reasons you don't know about, Stephanie,* he added silently.

"I think this could be a good idea," Karl said with a nod of his own. "But we're being pretty careful about who we invite into the Conspiracy, Nosey. A lot of the initial nominations are coming from Ms. Impetuous here"—Stephanie swatted him again, this time with a giggle—"but we're getting input from all of the others, or as many as we can, at least, before we extend any actual invitations. Give us a day or two to kick this around with the others and we'll get back to you. Deal?"

14

"*THERE* YOU ARE!" TRUDY SAID AS A CREAM AND gray shape appeared out of the winter-bared picketwood. "I wondered if you'd turn up today."

Leaf Racer sat fully upright on the net-wood branch and groomed his whiskers at his two-leg friend. He had paid much greater attention to the memory songs from Bright Water Clan since the two-leg freed him from the made-thing, yet he had found nothing within them that was quite like his connection to this two-leg. The flow between them was strong and almost intoxicating, yet nothing at all like the deep lifemate bond Climbs Quickly had formed with his two-leg. It was obvious Bright Water Clan had recognized that when he requested their songs, as well, and Sings Truly, Bright Water's senior memory singer, had requested that Golden-Leaf Clan send back memory songs sharing Leaf Racer's experiences in return.

He was more than happy to honor her request. Especially, he thought with an inner chuckle, when it meant his own clan elders were willing to send him to spend time with "his" two-leg instead of castigating him for avoiding his other duties.

The memory songs had also allowed him to taste Climbs Quickly's frustration at his inability to mind-speak with Death Fang's Bane, and he understood it completely. The Bright Water scout was obviously correct, in Leaf Racer's opinion, that the two-leg mouth noises were the best the poor creatures could do to communicate with one another. How anyone could share complex thoughts and meanings through such a wretched interface was more than he could imagine, but clearly that was what they did. And judging from all of the marvelous made-things they used in such profusion, it worked far better for them than a Person could have believed.

He would have loved to ask Shadow Eyes about that, just as he longed to ask her about the constant descant of sorrow that darkened her two-leg-blue eyes so often. She was so young—he had realized on only his second visit that she was just out of two-leg kittenhood—which made the darkness even worse in so many ways. One so young should not be burdened with such deep, long-held grief and unhappiness, and he longed to understand it. As it was, he could not even truly speculate as to its cause, which was especially maddening when he would have done anything he could to alleviate it. But the shadow in her soul could not damp the joy she felt each time he came to visit, and now he dropped back to all six hands and feet and scampered across the net-wood toward her.

Trudy watched Fuzzy Friend flow closer, and her skin itched with the urge to hold out her arms to him as she'd seen Stephanie do so many times with Lionheart. But Fuzzy Friend hadn't indicated he wanted that degree of closeness—not yet, at least—and she'd spent too much time with wild animals to force an embrace upon him. Now he came to rest on one of the picketwood's lowest branches, right at her left shoulder, and made soft, welcoming sounds at her.

"That's not how you talk to each other, is it?" she said, holding out one hand, fingers extended. "It's just how you get us poor, dumb humans' attention!"

The treecat cocked his head and leaned forward to brush her fingertips with his nose, and she felt a tiny, impossible to define...tickle at the edge of her mind. Or she thought she did, anyway. Maybe she was just fooling herself. The envy she'd realized she'd always felt for Stephanie Harrington was stronger than it had ever been before. Yet there was no bitterness in it. Not this time. She and Fuzzy Friend might not share the depth of Stephanie's bond with Lionheart, but they had something else that Stephanie didn't have. They had this friendship. This sense of welcome. And she was barely eighteen T-years old, which meant she and Fuzzy Friend would have years and years for that friendship to deepen the way she already sensed that it would.

The only downside, as far as she was concerned, was that Nosey's house was well over an hour away by air car, which undoubtedly put it far, far beyond Fuzzy Friend's range. Which meant that to spend time with him, she'd have to come "home," and it was only when she'd realized she would pay even that price to continue this friendship that she'd also realized just how steep a price it would be. Because every time she came back to visit with him, she would also revisit her childhood, and all she really wanted to do was to slam that door behind her and nail it shut.

But Nosey was probably right about that, too, she thought. However badly it hurt—and it was going to hurt a *lot*, she already knew that—she had to face that childhood. She had to deal with it. Not as a helpless child victim, but as an adult. And so maybe Fuzzy Friend was a blessing in still another way, because of the additional motive their friendship would give her for confronting the demons of her past.

What are you thinking, Shadow Eyes? Leaf Racer wondered as he tasted the deeper, darker hurt in his friend's mind-glow. *Are there* no *mind-healers among the two-foots to see your pain? To taste it and heal it? How does your kind endure being locked up inside your own hurt this way? And how do you find the courage to reach out as you have reached out to me from the depth of such pain?*

He crooned softly and leapt gently from the net-wood to her shoulder.

Trudy froze as Fuzzy Friend's weight hit her shoulder. He was heavy enough, even with her counter-grav, that she wondered how anyone as petite as Stephanie—even someone with Stephanie's genetic mods—could carry Lionheart everywhere she went with such apparent ease. But that question was tiny compared to her sense of awe. Despite everything, she couldn't help thinking of the treecats as wild animals, and her love for everything wild and free welled up within her when Fuzzy Friend leaned to press his muzzle against her parka's hood. And as he did, she felt a sudden insight open before her. One of the reasons her heart had always cried out to the rich, intricately varied wildlife of her homeworld, she realized, was because its denizens *were* wild and free. Especially *free.* Even on her darkest days, they'd told her—shown her—there was an entire world beyond the dreary bars which imprisoned her. And they'd offered to share that freedom with her.

As Fuzzy Friend was sharing it with her now.

"Thank you," she whispered, daring to raise one hand to caress the treecat's sharply pricked ears. "I wish we'd met—"

"So, this is where you've been sneaking off to!"

Leaf Racer's head snapped up as the unexpected mouth noise, far deeper and . . . uglier, somehow, than his friend's mouth noises, cut through the windless cold. He felt Shadow Eyes stiffen, tasted the bolt of old, cold darkness and even fear, that went through her, and a very soft snarl rumbled gently, almost inaudibly, in his chest.

Trudy's nostrils flared. Ralph. Why did it have to be *Ralph*? Couldn't he just leave her in peace even *once*?

She stood very still for a moment, her fingers gentle on the treecat's ears, trying to will him into stillness as that soft, rumbling sound vibrated against her own ear. She knew only too well how Ralph felt about her "stupid softheartedness" for all of the "dumb animals" running around Sphinx. After all, he'd taken a vicious delight in showing her exactly that since she was a little girl. A chip off the old Franchitti block, Ralph was, she thought bitterly.

And there's not a single thing I can do to make this turn out well, she thought.

She turned slowly to face him and forced her expression to remain calm as she raised one eyebrow.

"I haven't been 'sneaking' anywhere," she told him, not entirely truthfully. "I've taken care of all the chores

Mom asked me to do today. So it's not like I'm avoiding anything."

Except you and your stupidity, she added silently.

"You and your stupid little critters," Ralph said disdainfully. Then he cocked his head and frowned thoughtfully. "Actually, though, maybe it's just as well I ran into you out here. You've given me an idea."

A fresh spasm of dread went through Shadow Eyes. Leaf Racer tasted it, although he had no idea what might have caused it. Except that it was coming from the much larger male two-leg who had imposed himself so disagreeably upon her. Leaf Racer might not be able to understand mouth noises, but he understood the sharp-edged glitter of cruelty in the other two-leg's mind-glow only too well, and his ears flattened. He had no business inserting himself into two-legs' quarrels, and he knew it. But if *this* two-leg wanted trouble—

I am watching you, tasting you, Mind Canker. If you harm Shadow Eyes, it will not go well for you.

Trudy saw the amusement in her brother's eyes. She knew that particular shade of delight only too well. Not that complaining about it had ever done any good. A much younger Trudy had made the mistake of telling her mother about Ralph's petty cruelties and viciousness, and her mother had told her father. Who'd been amused by it. Who'd told her mother "the girl has to grow up, learn to stand up for herself." And who'd promptly kicked her flat any time she'd tried to do just that.

Until she'd learned to stop trying.

She knew Ralph was goading her, pushing her to ask what his brilliant "idea" was so he could hurt her with it, whatever it was. And she knew she shouldn't. That giving him what he wanted would only make it worse. Yet she'd been his victim too long and too often. It was as if he'd somehow programmed her to walk into his petty cruelties over and over again.

Besides, even if she didn't ask, he'd tell her anyway.

"And just what kind of 'idea' has finally managed to break through to you?" she asked, and the cutting edge of her own tone surprised her.

A trace of surprise flickered in Ralph's eyes. He wasn't accustomed to timid little Trudy showing a bit of backbone, and he didn't like it. He especially didn't like it because what he heard in her voice was entirely too much like contempt.

"Well," he said spitefully, "the furriers in Yawata Crossing pay top dollar for winter sable pelts. I bet I could get a lot more for *treecat* pelts."

A bolt of sheer, white-hot fury ripped through Shadow Eyes' mind-glow, and Leaf Racer stiffened on her shoulder. His claws flexed in their sheaths, his ears flattened, and the soft, rumbling snarl of his rage grew louder. But Shadow Eyes' hand tightened, pressing down, and he tasted a sliver of fear that seemed aimed at *him*—to be *for* him—and so he made himself remain motionless.

"First," Trudy heard herself say, "treecats are way too smart to get caught in your stupid traps, Ralph. For that matter, they're too smart for someone as dumb as you to catch in the first place. And, second, that would be the worst idea even *you* ever had. You know how hard the Forestry Service's been studying the 'cats. How do you think someone like Chief Shelton would react if you started trying to trap them for their pelts?"

Ralph's face darkened.

"Who gives a shit what Shelton wants?" he shot back. "Thinks he's so high and mighty, trying to tell us what we can and can't do on our own property. In our own woods! We're *First Wave*, damn it—what gives a Johnny-Come-Lately like him the right to tell *us* what to do? He can take that crap—and, yes, that little bitch Harrington—and shove them up his ass sideways! If I want to kill every single one of those frigging animals, there's not a damned thing he can do about it. He sure as hell can't *stop* me!"

"Oh, no?" Rage flared through Trudy, stiffening her spine, lifting her up with a defiant strength unlike anything she'd ever tasted before. "I'd like to see you tell him that. But you won't, will you? Oh, no, not you! Not *Jordan Ralph Franchitti, Junior*! Just like you'd never open your mouth about Stephanie to someone like Karl Zivonik, because you know exactly what he'd do to you, don't you?"

Incandescent fury roared up within Ralph.

Jones, he thought. *This is all that son-of-a-bitch Nosey Jones's fault. Filling her head with nonsense. Constantly putting down him and his father—her entire family—in that lying blog of his, and the disloyal little bitch just eats it up with a spoon! And now—*

"Listen, you," he snarled. "You tell your friend Zivonik if he wants a piece of me all he has to do is ask! I'll kick his ass sideways!"

"I'd pay money to see you try," she told him coldly. "I know exactly how that would end...and so do you!"

Leaf Racer quivered under the hammer blows of anger flashing back and forth between Shadow Eyes and Mind Canker. The sheer power of their emotions was almost impossible to bear, and a corner of his mind wondered how *they* endured it?

And then he realized. Because they were mind-blind, they *couldn't* taste it the way he did. There was no . . . reflection. No echo they could perceive from one another. And so the fury, the anger, boiled only higher and higher when, among the People, others would have intervened to separate them long before this point. But where would it lead? From the Bright Water memory songs, Leaf Racer knew that at least once Death Fang's Bane and Shining Sunlight had been physically attacked by other two-legs on that other world to which they had traveled. From Mind Canker's mind-glow, he was not far from that point!

"You little bitch!" Ralph snarled, his face dark with fury. "Somebody should kick *your* ass!"

"That's about your speed, isn't it," Trudy said coldly. "Beating up girls half your size. Lot easier than facing up to someone who might actually be bigger than *you* are, isn't it?"

A part of her couldn't believe what she was saying. But the rest of her flamed with a sort of joyous, fury-shot elation as she said it at last.

He stared at her, his mouth partly open, as if stunned into involuntary silence, and she bared her teeth.

"I'm through being your punching bag, Ralph. Nosey's right about you, and I should've seen it long ago. You're so brave hunting prong buck with a high-powered pulse rifle, or trapping sables and range bunnies in your snares, and God knows you're brave enough to knock me or even Trevor around! But underneath it all, you're a *coward*, Ralph. And I'm not only through with letting you threaten or frighten me—I'm through with *you*."

Ralph's darkened face went suddenly white, and his right arm drew back as he cocked his fist. Trudy knew from experience what that fist felt like, but this time she only glared at him, refusing to cower. Let him hit her. This time she was ready to take her bruises to Twin Forks and—

Mind Canker raised his hand, mind-glow boiling with an appalling brew of anger, shame, and something very much like fear. The power of it hammered Leaf Racer with almost overwhelming force, but he tasted the moment Mind Canker decided to attack Shadow Eyes. Perhaps it was unfair to call it a "decision," for the whirlpool of the two-leg's mind-glow was too intense, too chaotic, for anything as conscious as a decision. But that didn't matter.

"Orr-OWWWWWWWWWW!"

The sound ripped out of Fuzzy Friend. Trudy had never heard anything like it, and the sheer volume of it, so close to her ear, was stunning. But there was no mistaking the warning—and the fury—in that rippling, tearing-cloth snarl. The 'cat's ears were flat, lips drawn back to show its bone-white canines, and the claws on its raised true-hands radiated ivory menace.

Ralph Franchitti leapt backwards, eyes wide with sudden terror, the hand he'd balled into a fist raised in front of him like a frail, protective shield against the green-eyed, bristling fury on his sister's shoulder. His snowshoes tangled, and he went down in a jarring heap, half-stunned despite the deep snow's softness, as he stared at Fuzzy Friend in full-bore panic.

Trudy's hands flashed up to restrain the treecat, but even as she touched him, she realized Fuzzy Friend hadn't even tried to lunge at Ralph. His warning was clear, and she had no doubt what would've happened had Ralph carried through and actually punched her, but Fuzzy Friend had himself too well under control to actually attack *before* Ralph struck her.

Tears spangled her eyes as she sensed the treecat's determination to protect her. To stand up with her against the threat. Friends, she'd heard once, were the people you *knew* you could rely on and who knew they could rely on you. Who would always be there for you. And in that moment, she realized how very few true friends she'd ever had.

And how desperately she wanted more of them.

But she held onto Fuzzy Friend and shook her head.

"No," she told him. "Don't get involved in this! The last thing you or any of the 'cats need is to give someone like him the opportunity to lie about how you 'attacked him for no reason at all.' And trust me, that's exactly what *he'd* do!"

Leaf Racer tasted the concern in her mind-glow—concern for *him*, far more than for herself. He didn't understand all the reasons for it—he couldn't understand, given the impenetrability of the two-foots' mind-glows—but he recognized its strength and sincerity. His ears came up, his claws retracted, and he turned his head to look at her.

"Go," she said softly, lifting him from her shoulder, putting him back into the picketwood while Ralph floundered, two-thirds buried in two meters of Sphinxian late-winter snow and sinking deeper with his own struggles. "Go now. I'll be okay. You go back to your clan."

The treecat hesitated, looking between her and Ralph.

Then he raised one true-hand, touched her cheek gently, and turned and flowed back along the picketwood.

She watched him go until he disappeared, then drew a deep breath and turned back to her brother as Ralph finally started to claw his way up out of the snow.

His head came up, and his eyes darted around frantically, searching for the diminutive foe who'd struck such terror into him. She could almost see the residual panic rising from him like smoke, but then he realized Fuzzy Friend had disappeared and panic turned into something else.

Humiliation. She could taste it, see it in his eyes. Humiliation and seething hatred at the creature who'd inflicted it upon him.

"Where is it?" he snarled, still more than half-buried in the snow. "Where is the little bastard?! I'll kill the son-of-a-bitch!"

"He never did a thing to you!" Trudy exclaimed. "He was only—"

"Those little monsters are *dangerous,* damn it!" Ralph shouted at her, his face dark with rage. "I swear to God, I will *kill* that little son-of-a-bitch the next time I see it!"

"Oh, no you won't!" she spat back. "You listen to me this time, Ralph Franchitti! If you harm a single treecat, especially that one, I promise you it will be the worst mistake you ever made in your life."

"Oh, and what are *you* going to do about it?!"

"I don't know what *I'll* do about it, but I know what the SFS will do. He knew you were going to hit me, and he was protecting me. So you'd better believe I'll protect *him*. And I know people who'll help me do it!"

"Then you'd better get them on the com now," he told her in a raw, hating voice. "Because I don't give a damn about any of them. Anybody's got a right to shoot dangerous animals who come onto his land, and that little bitch Harrington's always talking about how they killed a damned *hexapuma* to save her, isn't she? That proves how dangerous they are, doesn't it? Well, fine!" His eyes glittered. "I'll just shoot me a 'dangerous animal.' Like to see your precious SFS hammer me for *that*. That little bastard is *dead* the next time I see it!"

Trudy glared down at him, then turned and snow-shoed for the house—and her air car—leaving him to dig himself out of the snow unassisted. She heard him still shouting after her, but she ignored it. She was done being terrified of him.

And yet, even from within the fiery cocoon of her own rage, she felt an icicle of fear. Not for herself, but for her friend. Ralph was the coward she'd called him. If she'd ever doubted that, if his bluster had ever hidden it from her, she knew better now. But Fuzzy Friend was only one, small treecat, and she never doubted for a moment that Ralph would kill him if the chance came.

15

NOSEY'S UNI-LINK PINGED.

The icon of an incoming com blinked on his air car's HUD, and he smiled as he recognized the ID tag.

"Accept!" he said, simultaneously enabling the autopilot so he could accept the visual, not just audio. The com window opened in the center of the HUD, and his smile grew broader.

"Hi, honey!" he said. "I was just on my way—"

He paused, smile fading, as Trudy's expression hit him.

"Honey?" he said in a very different voice. "What's wrong? What happened?"

For a moment, she didn't answer. She only looked at him from behind that shuttered face of Sphinx granite. But then the granite crumbled. Her lips trembled and she scrubbed at sudden tears with the heel of her hand.

"Trudy?"

"Nosey, I...I'm sorry." She shook her head and drew a deep breath. "I didn't mean to com you and...and then just . . . just *cry* at you. I'm sorry. I shouldn't have bothered y—"

"Stop."

He made the word come out quietly, despite the way his heart twisted within him. *Not again, honey,* he thought. *You are* not *going to apologize again for needing me.*

She looked at him, and it was his turn to shake his head.

"First," he said, "I happen to love you. That means you can com me anytime, anywhere, for any reason. Second, you wouldn't be 'crying at me' unless something was badly wrong. The truth is, Trudy, you don't cry *enough.*"

"Enough?" she repeated in a surprised tone.

"Enough," he repeated. "I'm still finding out things about you, and most of them are wonderful, but one thing I've discovered is that you lock things down inside. Until you told me, I didn't know what a crappy childhood you'd had, but now that you have, I can see the scars, honey. And one of the scars is that you hide things from the world. I can't stop you from doing that, but you need to understand that I don't want you *ever* hiding things that hurt you from *me.* I won't have you dealing with that kind of pain all by yourself—not anymore! You're the most important human being in my entire world, sweetheart. As far as I'm concerned, we're in this together, whatever comes our way, for the long haul. If I need to lean on your shoulder, I will. And if you need to lean on mine—or *cry* on mine—that's what it's here for. So tell me what it is?"

She stared at him for a long, still moment, and his heart almost broke as he saw the wonder in her eyes when she realized he meant every word of it. That she was truly that important to him. God knew he'd told her so before, but for her, it was a fresh revelation every time. It was like her entire world kept resetting to the one in which no one loved her because she wasn't *worth* loving. He *hated* that part of her, the one that leapt on any hope that might even suggest she could be of value to someone and beat it to death with a shovel because *hope* was the most painful, dangerous thing in her life. But he was making progress against that demon. He knew he was, and he saw the confirmation when she drew another, far less ragged breath, and nodded, those eyes thanking him for being there, accepting that he truly loved her.

"It's Fuzzy Friend," she said. "I'm worried about him. No, that's not right. I'm *scared* for him."

"Scared?" Nosey cocked his head. "Why?"

"It's Ralph," she replied. "Fuzzy Friend came for a visit, and this time he actually sat on my shoulder, like Lionheart does with Stephanie." Despite her distress, she smiled a bit mistily. "It was so cool, Nosey! But then"—her smile disappeared—"Ralph came along. You know how he is."

Actually, Nosey suspected, he didn't know how Ralph Franchitti truly was. He'd thought he did, but that was before he'd found out about Judy's childhood. Unless he was sadly mistaken, the sewer in Ralph's soul ran even deeper than he'd thought it did.

Which, admittedly, would take some doing.

"What happened?" he asked.

"He was just . . . being him." Trudy's lips tightened. "Making his sick, nasty jokes."

"What kind of jokes?" Nosey's eyes narrowed.

"Well . . ." Trudy paused, then shrugged. "He saw Fuzzy Friend on my shoulder, and he made a stupid joke about selling treecat pelts to the furriers in Yawata Crossing. He said he thought he'd get a lot more for them than he got for sables."

"He what?!" Fire flashed in Nosey's eyes, not least because he doubted it had been a "joke" at all. That was exactly what someone like Ralph Franchitti would actu-ally *do* if he thought he could get away with it. "If he tried that—!"

"I know Chief Shelton and the SFS would be really, really down on that, and I told him so. And that really pissed him off." She shook her head again, eyes dark. "He said there's not anything they can do about it if he shoots or traps treecats on our own property. I told him he'd better not count on that, and he got even madder. He started really...hassling me."

Nosey opened his mouth. Then he closed it again, while the fury burned still hotter within him. She wasn't leveling with him, even now. He could tell. There was something a lot worse than just "hassling" behind those darkened eyes. But even now she wasn't going to open up about it, even with him.

Oh, sweetheart. The so-called "men" in your life have really torn apart your ability to trust anyone—even me—haven't they? How did I get lucky enough for you to let me in?

He wanted to push her, get her to tell him everything, but he couldn't do that. Not over the com. He needed to be close enough to hold her when he did.

"And then?" he asked instead.

"And then I think Fuzzy Friend thought I was in trouble, because he snarled at Ralph. I mean *really* snarled, Nosey! I'd never heard anything like that out of a 'cat, and—well, it scared the hell out of Ralph. He jumped back, landed on his ass in the snow, two-thirds buried. I'm pretty sure he actually peed himself." She shook her head, and despite her distress Nosey recognized the satisfaction in her tone.

"So far, that sounds like a *good* thing to me," he said. "Obviously, there was more to it, though."

"Yeah." Trudy grimaced. "Ralph didn't like having shown how scared he was. What a *coward* he is. By the time he started digging his way out, I'd gotten Fuzzy Friend to go home, so all of a sudden he was all *brave* again." The sarcasm in her tone was devastating, but her expression was drawn. "He started cussing and shouting about what 'dangerous animals' treecats are, and about how vicious, and about how he's going to *shoot* Fuzzy Friend the next time he sees him! I told him the SFS would really come down on him if he did that, and he said he doesn't care. Anybody has a right to shoot dangerous animals that come onto his land! I know he was mad, but I'm scared, Nosey." She stared at him appealingly, her mouth trembling again. "I think he means it. I'm scared he *will* shoot Fuzzy Friend—or any other treecat he sees—as soon as he gets the chance!"

Nosey's stomach knotted. He knew damned well she still hadn't told him everything that had happened, but he totally believed she was right about Ralph.

"I think you're right to be scared," he said. "Your dad and brother are the kind of people who kill things just for the fun of it. Maybe killing something like a hexapuma makes them feel tough, but they'll kill *anything* just to prove they can. And unlike the true *hunters* I know, they've got *zero* respect for the animals they hunt. They don't go after them on foot, don't think about culling the herd, don't hunt for food, don't give a single, solitary damn about conserving the species. Hell, they shoot hexapumas from *air cars!* But the fact that they can kill even 'pumas doesn't make them 'tough,' Trudy. And the fact that *they* think it does makes them stupid, instead. Killing is easy. Saving lives, keeping something alive when it's hurt or sick or scared—that's a whole lot harder, honey. As I see it, you and the Wild and Free people are a hell of a lot tougher than Ralph or your father could ever be!"

"You mean it?" She stared at him from the com, her eyes wide. "Really?"

"Of course I do!" Nosey raised one hand, making a "gun" from his forefinger and thumb. "Bang! Dead. Creature shot from a distance with a high-power rifle." His lip curled. "What's tough about that? How much guts does it take to squeeze the trigger from a tree stand or the *air*, for crying out loud? But dealing with a wild animal that's hurt and afraid up close, getting it out of the snare, trying to get it to someone like Doctor Harrington when it doesn't know what you're doing, when it's terrified enough to bite or claw hell out of you for trying to help it? That takes courage, Trudy. Something your father and your brother wouldn't recognize if it bit them on the ass!"

"You mean that?" she repeated.

"I'm a reporter," he told her with a crooked smile. "As a rule, I think I usually express what I'm thinking fairly clearly. Was there something about that you didn't understand?"

"No." She surprised him—both of them, probably—with something very like a giggle. "No, I think I got it. And the truth is, you're a pretty special kind of guy, Nosey Jones. In fact, I think you're pretty fantastic!"

Oh, honey, he thought. *I'm glad you think that, but the fact that you do says way too much about the "guys" you grew up with.*

"I'm not any more special than you are," he told her sincerely. "And, getting back to Ralph and Fuzzy Friend, I don't doubt you're right to be worried."

He frowned, thinking hard. Stephanie and Karl hadn't authorized him to bring Trudy into the Great Treecat Conspiracy—not yet; he was sure they'd get to that, but they hadn't yet. So he couldn't tell her everything without violating the confidence they'd placed in him. But—

"Look," he said, "you know I've been working on another deep-dive story about the 'cats' for a while now? That that's what I was on Manticore with Gwendolyn Adair about?"

He raised an eyebrow at her, and she nodded.

"Well, after I got back, I had a talk with Karl and Stephanie, too. Kind of bringing them up to speed on what Gwendolyn had to say. And, being the nosy"—he flashed her a smile—"reporter type that I am, I've been noodling over what they had to say since I left the Harrington place, thinking about how much of it to put into my next blog. And I'm going to follow up on it with Chief Shelton, as well. From what I can already tell you, though, I think Ralph's in for an unpleasant surprise where the treecats are concerned."

"He is?" Trudy looked like she wanted desperately to believe him, but he could see the doubt in her eyes again. That damnable doubt of someone who'd found out the hard way how agonizing hope could be when it was snatched away yet again.

"Oh, I'm pretty sure he is." Nosey allowed himself a nasty smile. "Trust me, he does *not* want to find himself at odds with Chief Shelton, whatever he thinks at the moment. And that doesn't even count Stephanie and Karl! Personally, if I were him, I'd rather take my chances with a hexapuma with a sore tooth than have all three of them after my worthless butt!"

"He said there wasn't anything Chief Shelton could do about it."

"He might even have a point about that . . . now," Nosey replied. "But things can change, Trudy. And I think there are some *serious* changes coming where the 'cats are concerned. In the meantime, I'll for sure bring up Ralph and Fuzzy Friend the next time I talk to any of them about the story I'm working on."

"That would make me feel at least some better," she admitted.

"Where are you right now?" he asked.

"Actually," she said with a small smile, "I'm in the air headed for your place. About fifteen minutes out, now."

"Well, you just keep on flying then, young lady," he told her with a considerably broader smile. "I'm still about thirty-five minutes out, myself, but if you wanted to light the fire and dust off that rug in front of the hearth, maybe toss a couple of pillows out there, I'll bet I can make you feel a *lot* better after I get there."

"Promises, promises!" Her laugh melted Nosey's heart. "Don't think I won't hold you to that, mister!"

"I'm counting on it," he assured her.

"Then I'll see you then," she said in a softer tone. "And if I haven't mentioned it lately, I love you a lot."

"Both ways, Trudy. That works both ways." He smiled. "In the meantime, I've got a couple of com calls I need to make. So, I'll see you in a few."

"You betcha," she said. "Bye."

The com window went blank. Nosey smiled crookedly at it for a moment, then cleared his throat.

"Com Stephanie Harrington," he told the air car's computer.

Stephanie looked up from the handheld as her uni-link pinged.

At the moment, she stood in a storeroom in Copperwall Animal Hospital, her dad's veterinary clinic, with boxes and bundles piled all around her. She'd been coming to Twin Forks just about every day to help at the clinic, since Richard's partner, Saleem Smythe, was taking a well-earned break after handling the practice solo while the Harringtons were away. Given his shorthandedness in Richard's absence, both Doctor Smythe and the hospital's technicians had been focused on patients, not paperwork, so a lot of routine stuff had piled up, and at the moment Stephanie was buried in an inventory check. Which, since Salvo Ciambrone and Keagan Henson, the two vet techs on duty today, were both assisting her father right now, had become a solo chore... again.

It wasn't the most boring thing she'd ever done, but it came close, and she was grateful for the interruption. She was also a little puzzled, though, when she saw the caller ID. Nosey had left his conversation with her and Karl barely an hour ago—she'd barely had time to get back to the clinic and bury herself in the inventory again. So why was he screening her so soon?

She shrugged and tapped accept.

"Hi, Nosey! What can I do for you?"

"Am I interrupting anything?"

"Darned right you are—and thanks."

"Excuse me?"

"Still catching up on the clinic's records and stuff," she told him, "and that traitor Karl decided it was more important to tidy up routine paperwork over at SFS than to help me take inventory." She glowered with mock ferocity. "He just says that because I make him get the stuff off the tall shelves down where I can scan it."

"Is it really that bad?" Nosey asked with a chuckle.

"Let's just say that computer inventory is great if everyone remembers to swipe things when they remove them. But when there's an emergency, routine's the first thing to slip." Stephanie grinned and pushed a brown curl out of her eyes. "And I've gotta say, even if it's a pain doing this catch-up, I like my dad's staff even more for where their priorities are. So, what's up?"

"I'm afraid it goes back to what you and Karl just finished discussing with me," he said, and any trace of humor had vanished from his tone and his expression. "I just finished a com conversation with Trudy, and she's worried. And now that she's told me why, so am I."

Stephanie stuck one foot under the stool she used to reach the higher shelves in Karl's absence to hook it close. Then she settled onto it and her eyes narrowed.

"Tell me," she said simply.

He did. In fact he told her everything Trudy had told him. What he didn't tell her were how many reasons Trudy had to fear violence from her father and brother. He couldn't—not without violating not just Trudy's confidence but her trust. He told her everything else about Ralph's threats, though, and Stephanie's eyes got colder and harder with every word.

"So, the reason I screened you," he finished, "is to find out—for me, not just for Trudy—whether or not we really can do anything to protect the treecats, keep Ralph from shooting them, even if they're on private land?"

"Darned right we can," Stephanie said flatly. "Protecting wildlife is a problem as old as the first governments that declared there'd be hunting seasons for certain types of game rather than permanent open hunting on all of them. Here in the Star Kingdom, it basically boils down to this: the landowner owns the *land*, but the wildlife is considered the property of the Crown when it comes to management and protection, because things like that—policies like that—have to extend beyond any one person's property line. Ralph's right that landowners have the right to protect themselves and their livestock from predators, and there aren't as many restrictions on that—yet, at least—here in the Star Kingdom as there are someplace like Meyerdahl, where humans have been on the planet for over a thousand years. That's what the Wildlife Protection Act will let us clarify and fix."

"Soon enough to protect Fuzzy Friend?"

"That's probably trickier, but I think if the Chief goes back to the Governor and gets her to push a little harder, yes."

"You'll talk to him, then? And can I tell Trudy you're going to? She's really worried, Stephanie."

"Sure." Stephanie nodded. "I'll even shoot you a copy of the draft bill to show her, but I'd appreciate both of you keeping it confidential. Most of the terms have already leaked over into the public record, but we're trying to get all the i's dotted and t's crossed before we go public with the full text. Partly because of people like the Franchittis, to be honest. I'll guarantee you some of them will think it's a terrible idea, and they won't be shy about screaming about how it 'tramples on their rights' as landowners. Especially the First-Wavers, to be honest. That's the last thing we need when people like Oscar Lautenberg are already dragging their feet just as hard as they can."

"Oh, trust me, I understand *that*. In fact, it's probably paranoid of me, but the reason I didn't want to go directly to Chief Shelton with it myself was that I didn't want to create any connection between Trudy and the complaint."

For a lot of reasons, he added silently.

"I understand." Stephanie nodded. "One of the biggest problems law enforcement faces is that no one wants to make a problem worse by complaining about it. And because they're afraid of who they might piss off if they do. I think that's why newsfeeds like your 'Nose for News' get so many comments. You've already 'complained,' and that makes it safe for other people to speak out, too."

"I think you're right," Nosey said. "That's certainly one of the things I always hope will happen. But, speaking of news, what's up with the SFS Explorers? I meant to ask you and Karl about that, and it completely slipped my mind when you sprang the Conspiracy on me. Will you be running the Explorers now that you're back?"

"No way." Stephanie shook her head. "Moriah and Stephan are doing a great job—better than I would, I think, since they actually have kids, so they know what kids like. Karl and I will be doing presentations about Gryphon and Manticore, with images from our trips, though. That should be fun."

"Good! Can I print that?"

"I don't see why not."

"I will, then. And now, I'll let you get back to your incredibly exciting inventory-taking."

"Oh, thank you *ever* so much! How can I ever repay you?"

"Just try not to hurt me too much," he said with a grin. "I've heard about your temper!"

16

"I DON'T LIKE THE SOUND OF THAT AT ALL," CHIEF Shelton said grimly, tipping back in his office chair and looking back and forth between Stephanie and Karl. "Not at all."

"I didn't think you would, sir," Stephanie said, not trying to hide her relief that he didn't. "I don't know Ralph anywhere near as well as I know Trudy, but I have to say, the little bit I do know about him, I don't like very much."

"That, Ranger Harrington, is because you have a brain that functions," Shelton said dryly. "The younger Franchitti boy, Trevor, isn't all that bad. In fact, until Trudy got involved with Wild and Free, I'd have said he was the best of the bunch. But Ralph and their old man?" He shook his head. "Just between the three of us, the only reason I wouldn't feed them to a hexapuma is that they'd poison the poor critter!"

Stephanie's eyes widened slightly, because that last sentence hadn't been just a joke.

"At the moment, unfortunately," Shelton continued, "most of what Ralph was telling her is accurate. That'll change, once the act gets passed. To be honest," he grimaced, "I really expected that to've been introduced in the Assembly, at least, by now."

He sat for a moment, fingers of his right hand drumming on the desk, then nodded to himself with a curiously decisive air.

"All right," he said, raising his left index finger at them, "it's time for you two to be flies on the wall. Under normal circumstances, I'd shoo you out before I placed this call, but you've been pretty central to getting us this far. And, to be honest, I trust your instincts. I'd like to have you listen in and see where you think we all are."

Stephanie glanced at Karl, one eyebrow raised, and he shrugged back. Then he looked at Shelton.

"Sir, if this is something that's above our pay grade, or something we shouldn't know anything about, then we'd be perfectly happy—"

"No, I want you both here. But I also want you being here as dutiful junior rangers, not as members of the Great Treecat Conspiracy. I think you'll understand what I'm talking about in a few minutes."

"Whatever you say, sir," Stephanie said, and Karl nodded.

Shelton nodded back, then punched a com combination on his desk unit from memory. He sat for a moment, watching the display, then smiled as a somehow familiar looking blonde, blue-eyed woman appeared upon it.

"Good afternoon, Chief!" she said with a smile. "What can I do for you?"

"Good afternoon, Pat," he replied, and Stephanie realized why the woman had looked familiar. She was Patricia Hamilton, Governor Donaldson's chief of staff. "I'm sitting here with Ranger Zivonik and Ranger Harrington, and

I'm screening you because of something they've just been discussing with me. In fact, I wondered if I could speak with the Governor—or with you, for that matter—about the status of the WPA."

"You mean you want to find out why it still hasn't been reported out to the Assembly after all this time, don't you?" Hamilton responded with an expression which was less than amused.

"I wouldn't have phrased my own concerns quite that bluntly," Shelton replied with just a trace of a smile. "Now that the point's been raised, though, yes. That's really what I was wondering about."

"I know Ms. Harrington and Mr. Zivonik are determined to look after the treecats' best interests," Hamilton said. "Should I assume their presence means you're currently screening because of something that involves the treecats?"

"I think you can safely assume, that, yes."

"I suspected it did. And I have a great deal of respect for their feelings and their views. I have to ask, though, if there's a specific reason why the status of the Act is assuming greater urgency at this moment?"

"Actually, there is," Shelton replied. "And they're not the only ones who feel that way. I'm feeling more than a little concerned myself, based on reports I've been hearing and some conversation that's come to my attention."

"What sort of conversation?" Hamilton's blue eyes had narrowed.

"Let's just say that it included someone who thinks treecat pelts are the next big thing in the fur trade."

"What?" The one-word question came out sharply, and Hamilton straightened in her chair. "Did you say treecat *pelts*?"

"I did, indeed." Shelton's smile was wintry now, his eyes as cold as a Sphinxian winter sky. "And this is precisely why we need the Act reported out, Pat. Right now, there wouldn't be a single thing I could do if somebody turned up in Twin Forks or Yawata Crossing with an entire rack of treecat pelts. Not...one...damned...thing."

"May I ask who you heard this from?"

"I would prefer not sharing that information," Shelton said in a careful tone. "It was made available to me confidentially, and there could be some...significant personal repercussions for the person who shared it. I will say, however, that the comment came from one of the First Wave families and that I absolutely believe the individual who suggested the possibility is fully capable of acting on it."

Hamilton's eyes narrowed further. Stephanie could almost see the thoughts chasing themselves around behind those eyes. And then they widened slightly, as if the chief of staff had added two plus two and gotten a four named Franchitti.

"I see," she said. "You do realize that without a name associated with the suggestion it won't carry as much weight in certain quarters as it should?"

"If we're at the point of worrying about whose toes we might be stepping on with this sufficiently to stall the act indefinitely, then I think we have a problem," Shelton said levelly.

"I didn't say that," she replied. "What I said is that as a threat to the treecats, the fact that we can't or won't *name* the threat will make some people wonder how serious it actually is. Or *claim* they wonder, at any rate. I don't happen to be one of them. I'm just observing a fact of political life. And whether we like it or not, getting something as fundamental as the WPA enacted is a political effort."

"Understood." Shelton nodded. "And I don't want to sound like I'm jumping down your throat, Pat. But I have some worried people here at my end, and given how long and hard they've worked on this whole situation, I'd like to be able to give them some idea—and have some idea myself—how much longer we think the process will take. And, frankly, just how urgently it's being pressed."

"Totally fair," Hamilton said, then sat back and pinched the bridge of her nose in silence for several seconds.

"Look," she said then, "I'm fully aware that you—and, I presume, Rangers Zivonik and Harrington—think I'm one of the people who hasn't been pressing this as urgently as you all believe it ought to be pressed. And, to be honest, that's not unfair of you. Nor are you wrong to think I'm not looking forward to the opposition of assemblymen like Oscar Lautenberg. I do expect quite a food fight when the Act comes to the floor—one that could delay its actual adoption more than any of us would like—but I also expect it to pass, and it's definitely not the reason I haven't been pushing this just as hard as you'd like. Why the Governor hasn't been pushing it is hard as you'd like.

"The *reason* is that we're probably less than two T-years away from transitioning to an actual planetary parliament, and until we do, anything the Assembly passes is subject to review, modification, or outright nullification by the Kingdom Parliament. And if we move forward with the kind of comprehensive protections the WPA would let you put in place for the treecats—and which I happen to strongly agree they need—and the Kingdom Parliament decides to nullify the WPA, then we'll have a hell of a time getting them put back in place. I wouldn't go so far as to say I've been trying to deliberately slow-walk this, but if you think I haven't been getting behind and pushing as hard as I could, you're right. Which doesn't address the concern you've just brought me, because if somebody's really thinking that way—and, yes, Chief

Shelton, I think I can pretty much figure out who that might be—we don't have two T-years to waste."

She looked out of the display at all three of the people in Chief Shelton's office and her nostrils flared.

"Given that, we need to rethink our strategy," she said after a moment. "Your proposals are currently incorporated into the WPA, an Assembly bill that would give them the force of planetary and Kingdom law. I think that's exactly where we need to be in the end, too. But getting that through the Assembly in any kind of expeditious timeframe's already going to be difficult, and there are more than enough special interests involved to go crying to the Kingdom Parliament to get it overturned if it steps on those toes you were referring to a minute ago, Chief. So I think the solution may be to step back a bit."

"Meaning what, exactly?" Shelton asked.

"What you and Jason Stamford have put together at this moment—and, yes, Chief, I know *exactly* who he's been using as a 'sounding board,' so don't pretend your fingerprints aren't all over the draft bill—is an excellent, well-thought out, comprehensive set of wilderness protection regulations. That's part of the problem—they're *comprehensive*. The WPA covers too much to just be sort of rubberstamped by the Assembly, and, frankly, it increases the SFS's regulatory authority in ways that quite a few of our fellow subjects—including an unfortunate number of First Wavers—will resent the hell out of because of its 'intrusiveness.' And it's that resentment which is likely to send somebody crying to Landing and get the entire WPA nullified by the Kingdom Parliament. Are you with me so far?"

She looked past Shelton, her eyes focused on Stephanie and Karl, and Stephanie felt herself nodding slowly.

"So are we asking for too much?" Shelton said.

"No, you're asking for it too *soon*," Hamilton corrected

him. "Which, admittedly, is another way of saying too much, I suppose."

"So your suggestion is—?"

"Let me sit down with the Governor and talk this over with her, but I think the solution might be an Order in Council. A very *focused* Order in Council—one that deals solely with the treecats at this point. If we—"

She paused, then cocked her head.

"Yes, Ranger Harrington? You have a question?"

Stephanie felt her face heat. She really, truly hadn't intended to intrude into this conversation at all. Really she hadn't! But—

"I'm just confused, a little," she said. "Why would an Order in Council be better than an actual Assembly act? I mean, how would it be any different?"

"In enforcement terms, it wouldn't be different at all," Hamilton said. "But if Governor Donaldson and her Council issue an order under her executive authority as planetary governor, it could go into effect tomorrow. It wouldn't have to be debated in the Assembly, which would prevent a lot of the...obfuscation I'm afraid we might face there. And although it would still be subject to review and even revocation by the Kingdom Parliament, it's only a single facet of the entire Wilderness Protection Act. In other words, invalidating it wouldn't invalidate the rest of the package I think we're all in agreement needs to be enacted eventually."

"And if it was revoked—a process which would burn up at least a few T-months of that two T-years you were talking about—it would be only that 'single facet,'" Chief Shelton said thoughtfully. "Which means there'd be a lot less of a fight, or at least a lot less in the way of someplace to stand, for people in the new planetary parliament who might oppose its reintroduction as an *amendment* to the WPA."

"Exactly," Hamilton said. "I realize what we're talking about will still leave a lot of gray area, especially where safeguarding the treecats' ranges is concerned, but if the Governor proclaims protected species status for them, it would at the very least put an end to any casual trapping or hunting where they're concerned, and I think that's got to be the most important point right now."

It was Shelton's turn to raise his eyebrows at his two youngest rangers. Stephanie looked at Karl for a moment, then back at Hamilton.

"Yes, ma'am," she said. "That's definitely the most important thing right now."

"I'm glad we're in agreement." Hamilton allowed herself a smile, but then it faded. "The way things are set up right now, however, the Governor really needs a majority vote of her Council if she's going to issue a formal Order, and at the moment, the vote would be three-to-two against."

"Tatum, Stokowski, and . . . Eulenburg?" Shelton said, gazing thoughtfully up at the ceiling.

"I always knew you had good political instincts, Chief," Hamilton agreed wryly. "It's probably not too surprising Tatum's worried about the entire WPA and its probable 'chilling effect' on some of the industry he's trying to attract.

"Stokowski, on the other hand, is more worried about the treecats, specifically, than anything else in the package, I'm afraid. As Coordinator of Education, she could care less about industrial development, but she's another First Waver. I don't think she's as worried about any options someone may hold on Crown Land as she is concerned about what the recognition of a native sapient species might do to the already existing boundaries of Sphinx landowners. Like her own family, for example.

"And then there's Eulenburg. As Coordinator of

Justice, he's basically Governor Donaldson's lawyer, which means he's looking very, very carefully at any legal precedents we might be setting, especially in the run-up to the formal recognition of the planetary parliament. And, to be honest, I think he's what you might call a legal minimalist. From where I sit, it looks like he's trying to limit any executive overreach before the new parliament gets to vote on the actual planetary law code. Limiting the Order in Council to just protected status for the treecats would probably put his mind at ease. By the same token, though, he's made his opposition to the WPA as a whole clear enough that it would probably take at least a couple of weeks for him to back out far enough to support the Order.

"Fitzroy, MacGilloway, and Burlaka have always supported the SFS and all three of them are strongly in favor of the WPA. But Fitzroy's off-planet dealing with a family emergency and won't be back for at least a couple of T-weeks, which is why I said that at the moment the vote would be three-to-two against, and it'll stay that way until Fitzroy gets home. Unless I can work on Eulenburg and get him turned around sooner than that."

"And what do you think the odds of turning Eulenburg really are, seriously?" Shelton asked.

"It's a crap shoot, frankly," Hamilton replied. "I'll see what I can do. Worst, we wait until Fitzroy gets home, the council vote ties, and the Governor would cast the tie-breaking vote, but I'd really move on this sooner if we can convince him. Would you be available to bend his ear about the treecats if I called you in, Chief?"

"Of course I would!"

"Good! And what about you, Ms. Harrington?"

Hamilton's blue eyes turned to Stephanie, and for just a moment, even her brashness faltered.

"*Me*? Talk to a member of the Council?"

It came out much closer to a squeak than she might have preferred, and Hamilton's lips twitched.

"I know how...eloquent you can be, Ms. Harrington. And I suspect most of the Star Kingdom's aware of how passionate you are about the treecats. I think there's a very good chance Councilor Eulenburg might be impressed by your arguments, especially if you brought Lionheart along with you. And if you could refrain from being *overly* passionate in your presentation."

Stephanie heard something very much like a smothered chuckle from Karl's direction and managed not to turn her head and glare at him. Instead, she looked back at Hamilton and nodded.

"Yes, ma'am. I can do that," she said.

"Good," Hamilton said...and this time Stephanie heard a smothered chuckle from Chief Shelton, as well.

17

"HAVEN'T SEEN YOU IN A WHILE, JORDAN."

Jordan Franchitti lowered his beer stein and looked up as the well-dressed, blond-haired man stopped beside his table in the First Steak's main dining room. The restaurant's name was a play on words, and it was really more of a private club than a restaurant, since its clientele consisted almost entirely of First Wave families. Franchitti was a charter member, as it were, as was the man standing beside him.

"Most likely because I haven't been in in a while," he said with a smile. He raised his right foot and used it to push the facing chair back from the table. "Why don't you sit a spell, Tony?"

"Don't mind if I do."

Anthony Tatum settled into the offered chair, tipped back, and looked around the dining room. The First Steak embraced a deliberately rustic decor, with plank-topped tables, unvarnished wooden floors, and paneled walls decorated with mounted prong buck heads, stuffed silver hawks, and hexa-elk antlers. A snarling peak bear's head held pride of place above the bar, and an old-fashioned log fire blazed on the central hearth below a freestanding, cone-shaped copper hood.

And a series of wall plaques ran around the entire large room, right at eye level, with the names of First Wave Sphinxians the Plague had claimed.

"You're drinking more of Nate's crappy beer, aren't you?" Tatum asked with a smile, looking at Franchitti's stein.

"Hey, sooner or later he's gonna get it right," Franchitti replied with a somewhat broader smile. "Somebody's got to buy enough of it to at least keep him trying. Seems like the least I can do for him."

"Guess so." Tatum looked around, caught the waiter's eye, pointed at Franchitti's beer stein, and made a drinking motion with an imaginary stein of his own. The waiter nodded and began drawing a fresh stein.

"God knows somebody's got to look after Nate," Tatum continued, turning back to Franchitti. "Boy still doesn't have the sense to come in out of the snow."

"Oh, I expect he's got *that* much sense. Not much more, mind you!" Franchitti replied, and Tatum laughed.

The Plague's death toll had hit everyone on Sphinx hard, and the bonds formed between the childhood friends who'd survived it ran deep. The Tatum claim bordered the Franchitti claim, and Nate Tillman had been fostered with Tatum's family after his own parents and younger sister died. Tatum wasn't sure where Nate had caught the bug that had led him to the brewmaster's trade, but he was determined to make a go of it. And, to be fair, his current effort wasn't half bad. Not that he wasn't hell-bent on making it still better.

"Where've you been?" he asked Franchitti now.

"You're pulling my leg, right?" Franchitti looked at him across the table. "Winter, remember? I mean I know it's *technically* spring, but I'm guessing even *you*'ve noticed all the snow out there. Lotta stuff needed taking care of around the place and for the last couple of T-months I've been marking timber for Carter and bush-hogging the way in for the logging crews, when the snow allows."

Tatum nodded. Carter McKinsey was another First Waver, and his logging business had begun finding a reasonably lucrative market on Manticore itself. Mostly for specialty woods, like red spruce with its darkly veined red wood or rock tree, both of which were prized for decorative woodwork. Crown oak commanded a decent price, as well, though, and a single mature tree could provide enough timber to build an entire respectable-sized house out of.

And, of course, he thought disgustedly, the whiners were complaining about "slash and burn" logging practices even on a man's own land.

"What?" Franchitti said.

"What do you mean, 'what'?"

"You got that bellyache look in your eyes, there," Franchitti told him, then took another sip of beer. "The kind that says something's pissing you off. More crap on the Council?"

"That obvious, was I?" Tatum shook his head, then accepted his own beer with a nod of thanks. He waited for the waiter to take away Franchitti's empty plate before he sampled it, then smiled. "Be damned if Nate's not getting better at this!"

"Told you." Franchitti chuckled. "So, what's the Council been up to now?"

"More of the same," Tatum sighed and shook his head again. "I swear, there's times Flo Donaldson sounds an awful lot more like some damned newcomer than a

First Waver. If I didn't know she was born right here on Sphinx, I'd think she was one of those bleeding hearts like that pain in the ass Adair Hollow back on Manticore! And there's times I think Pat Hamilton's even worse." He took a morose swallow of beer. "Which doesn't even mention His High and Mightiness Shelton!"

Franchitti's eyes narrowed. He'd had his own run-ins with Gary Shelton and didn't much care for the man, but Tatum sounded especially disgusted.

"There a reason all those people're keeping company in your gripe session, Tony?" he asked with a crooked smile.

"I just—" Tatum began sharply, then stopped and inhaled deeply. "I just get so tired of trying to do something to bring a little prosperity home to Sphinx, maybe even put some money in people's pockets," he said in a more measured tone. "We got a whole planet here—a mighty nice one, in my opinion. And there aren't a whole lot of people on it. It's not like there's not plenty of more crown oak where the ones Carter logs off came from! And people like us, Jordan—the First Wave families—we paid cash for what we've got. There's too many of us buried in Sphinx dirt. And here comes the newcomers, the Johnny-come-latelies, and they figure they can tell us what to do with our own homeworld. And they're so damned smug and sanctimonious about it when they do!"

"Got that right," Franchitti agreed. "So what are they up to this time?"

"You remember I told you about that Wildlife Protection Act Jason Stamford wants to introduce? I sent you a copy of the first draft, didn't I?"

"Yeah. Can't say I paid a whole lot of attention to it, though." Franchitti shrugged. "Knew I wasn't going to like much of anything in it and didn't see much point in pushing my blood pressure till it was actually introduced. Why? He planning on bringing it to the floor?"

"I don't think he's stupid enough to put it in front of the Assembly just yet," Tatum growled. "Too many First Wavers like you and me in the Assembly. Will be, for a while, too. Thank God."

Franchitti grunted in agreement, although, if the truth be known, he was less confident of that than Tatum chose to be. Oh, the First Wave families still commanded a majority in the Assembly, and they would for a while...probably. According to the Constitution, someone had to pay taxes for at least three Manticoran years—just over five T-years—before they were eligible to vote. But that restriction had been set aside at the height of the Plague in light of the need to attract warm bodies, and especially those with the most desperately necessary skills. That meant that too many of the newcomers whose immigration the Crown had subsidized had been able to pay enough of their own passage costs to gain the franchise on arrival, without any waiting period at all. That special exception to the franchise qualifications had come to an end, thank God, when the Crown formally declared the end to assisted immigration, but coupled with how brutally the Plague's death toll had hammered many of the First Wave families, the descendants of the Star Kingdom's original settlers constituted less than sixty percent of the total population, and the percentage was even lower on Sphinx than on Manticore.

"That bad, is it?" he asked a bit more mildly than he actually felt. "Maybe I should have read through that draft you emailed me."

"It's not all that bad in terms of the restrictions it sets up directly. For that matter, some of it's probably a damned good idea in the long run," Tatum conceded grudgingly. "The problem's how much room for growth it includes. It 'regularizes' the Forestry Service's authority, for example."

"Wonderful!" Franchitti rolled his eyes. "Bunch of busybodies are already a big enough pain in *my* butt!"

"Well, it's going to get worse if Stamford's bill passes. Among other things, there's provision for SFS enforcement powers to cross over into private land, not just Crown Land."

"The hell you say!" Franchitti set his beer stein down hard. "Nobody's coming onto *my* land and telling me what I can and can't do just because he's got some shiny badge to wave around! I'll shoot the first one who tries!"

Tatum nodded in sober agreement, although he'd known Franchitti long enough to recognize the degree of angry bluster in that last sentence.

"It specifically sets up some other stuff, too," he told his friend. "Like I say, some of it actually makes at least a little sense, I guess, and I probably wouldn't be so upset if the SFS was still going to be restricted to Crown Land. Hell!" He shook his head. "That's damned near ninety percent of the entire planet right now." He grimaced. "You'd think that should be enough to keep even Shelton happy, wouldn't you?"

"There'll *never* be enough to keep someone like Shelton happy," Franchitti half-snarled. "Just look at how he dotes on that little bitch Harrington!"

Tatum's eyebrows rose at Franchitti's choice of noun and the genuine, searing anger in that last sentence. It surprised him, actually. He'd always known how bitterly Franchitti despised the entire Harrington clan, but that was more than a little harsh even for him! But then, as he thought about it...

"How's the family?" he asked as casually as he could. "Haven't seen Trevor—or Trudy, now that I think about it—for a while. Not to talk to since that air car accident when the Chang boy killed himself, really. I know she got banged up pretty bad, herself. I hope she's doing better?"

"Why do you think *I'd* know?" This time there was nothing halfway about Franchitti's snarl. "Spending more and more of her time with that pain *Nosey* Jones. And Harrington and her crowd, which is probably worse." He shook his head, his expression a mix of anger and disgust. "Girl's thinking with something besides her brain right now, and then there's that whole Wild and Free crap. Trying to score points with all the newcomers and all the bigmouth meddlers who think they know so much more than people like you and me do!"

Tatum nodded understandingly, although the sheer power of Franchitti's anger took him a bit aback. He'd known about the growing friction between Jordan and Trudy, but he hadn't realized just how angry Franchitti was over it. And he hadn't known the girl was spending time with Jones. That *really* had to frost Franchitti, he thought, given what the "Nose for News" had said about him upon occasion.

"Sorry to hear that," he said sympathetically. "Probably going to be even more of that going around, though, now that the Plague's behind us and people don't see as much need to pull together if we're all going to make it through."

"You can say that again," Franchitti muttered moodily, then shook himself. "But getting back to Stamford and this 'wildlife' act of his. How soon do you think he'll go ahead and bring it to the floor?"

"I don't know." Tatum grimaced. "I'm thinking he'd like to move as quick as he can, but Flo's been dragging her heels. Up until yesterday, I'd have said she either didn't want it passed at all, or at least didn't want it passed until we've got a formal planetary parliament to sign off on it."

"Until yesterday?" Franchitti cocked his head, and Tatum snorted.

"Oh, she's not going to start pushing for a vote on the WPA anytime soon, but from what she was saying yesterday, she *is* going to push out at least some of what it wants as an Order in Council."

"What?" Franchitti looked at him. "She can *do* that?"

"Actually, she can do pretty much anything she wants, as long as a majority of the Council's willing to sign off on it." Tatum shrugged. "She's technically still a Crown appointee, even if she did have to be approved by majority vote here on Sphinx, as well. That means she answers to the Crown until the planetary parliament's up and running. And that means she's a mighty big hexa-frog in a mighty small pond right now. Truth to tell, she's been pretty careful about how she used that authority. But I think she's going to pull out the stops this time. Probably not until Fitzroy gets home from Manticore, but once he does—"

He shrugged again.

"What part of this 'WPA' is she looking at?" Franchitti asked intently.

"Mostly it's the damned treecats," Tatum said in a tone of profound disgust.

"Oh, *damn*. Not the frigging *treecats*!"

"Well, fair's fair, there's a lot of pressure to go slow and cautious where they're concerned," Tatum pointed out. "And don't forget she's a Crown appointee. The way the Adair Foundation and the other pointy-headed intellectuals are whining about Barstool and the Amphors, the Crown's likely to give her a lot of slack where they're concerned."

"Oh, give me a break! They're *animals*, Tony. No way something that size is 'intelligent.'" Franchitti rolled his eyes again. "The way everybody's sucking up to the miserable little pests makes me want to puke."

"Never said I disagreed with you," Tatum said mildly. "Doesn't change the way people are talking about them, though. And I'm pretty sure Shelton and his bunch have been pounding Flo's ear over them. So what I think she has in mind is to give them protected species status."

"What does that even mean?" Franchitti demanded. "Protected species. I mean, I've heard people throw it around, but nobody's ever told me exactly what a 'protected species' is!"

"That's probably because there aren't any yet, at least on Sphinx. But it's coming, and probably not just for the treecats eventually. And to be honest, even if I don't want to admit it, there's probably going to be cases where it's actually justified. Not here and not yet, of course, but... eventually."

"So how would it work?"

"Depends on exactly how it ends up structured. Most often, though, it means it's illegal to hunt or harm whatever the hell's been declared 'protected.' Oh"—Tatum waved one hand—"there's exceptions if something's actually attacking somebody, or—usually—exceptions for hunting licenses, if it comes to population management or things like that. But for the most part, it means you can't even kill the critters if they're killing your chickens. Or, in this case maybe, stealing your celery."

"Not even on my own *property*?"

"Anywhere," Tatum snorted.

"And just who's going to stop me?" Franchitti demanded scornfully. "Assuming, of course, that anyone even knows I'm doing it!"

"The way it looks to me from the little Flo's told us so far, she'd probably give that authority to Shelton and the SFS. Eulenburg seems to be a little antsy about that, since the Forestry Service is officially restricted to Crown land right now. But he's agreed that if a blanket protected species designation gets handed down, somebody's gotta enforce it, and at the moment, SFS is all there is. So until and unless somebody back on Manticore gets around to overruling her, Flo can probably make it stand up."

Franchitti eyed him incredulously for a long moment, then grunted.

"Well doesn't that just take the cake? Any idea what kind of penalties a man would face assuming he was so far gone he'd go ahead and tell Shelton to pound sand?"

"Depends." Tatum waved his hand again. "Usually it's a misdemeanor with a fine big enough to make sure *anybody*'ll think twice before he does it. Sometimes, if they're really serious, there's even jail time involved. Come to that, technically, Flo has the authority to make it a felony, not just a misdemeanor. And if she does that, you could be looking at some serious jail time. Maybe as much as five, ten T-years."

"For shooting an *animal*? Especially one that, according to Harrington and her suck-ups, can pull down adult hexapumas?"

"I'm just telling you what I know and what I've heard so far," Tatum said. "I don't know she's really going to push it, but if she does, I don't think anybody here on Sphinx would be able to stop her."

◆　　　◆　　　◆

"You think the Governor might really do that? Bring in this...'protected species' bullshit?"

"I don't know, Ralph," Jordan Franchitti told his son as the air car headed away from Twin Forks and back to the Franchitti barony. "Tony Tatum seems to think it's likely, though."

"Well, damn." Ralph shook his head disgustedly, and Franchitti looked away from the HUD for a moment.

"Something going on here that you might like to share?" he invited.

"Well, it's just that there's been a bunch of treecats

hanging around the place," Ralph said. "Didn't see any point bothering you about it, but we're missing three or four chickens and I've seen their tracks around the rabbit hutches, too."

"You think they've been getting to the chickens?" Franchitti frowned. "Don't much like the sound of that."

"Like I said, I hadn't seen any point bothering you with it," Ralph shrugged. "Figured I'd just take out a shotgun and deal with it. For that matter," he smiled at his father, "I'd been thinking I could probably pick up some extra pocket change selling treecat pelts."

"Not if you're taking them with a shotgun, most likely," Franchitti said dryly. "Kind of messes up the coat when you hit something that size with a half dozen flechettes."

"That's why I was thinking about traps. Problem is, they really are pretty smart critters. Lot harder to catch than sables, for example."

"For God's sake don't say that where any of Shelton's assholes might hear about it!" Franchitti implored.

"Yeah, that's probably not a bad thing to keep in mind." Ralph nodded. "Did Uncle Tony have any idea when this 'protected species' order might actually get itself on the books?"

"Nah." Franchitti shook his head. "From the sound of things, it's still going to be at least a couple of weeks before Donaldson's likely to have a majority on her Council. Once she does, though, he seems to think she'll move pretty smartly with it."

"I see."

Ralph Franchitti turned away, looking out the side window at the glittering white vista of a Sphinx winter, and his eyes were as cold as the ice and snow below them.

"Well, in that case," he said after a moment, "if we want to discourage them from raiding our henhouse, I might just need to be getting on with it."

18

"I'M GOING TO BE A LITTLE LATE, SWEETHEART," NOSEY
said from the tiny display on Trudy's uni-link. "That
delivery to the Alfonso place is running over."

He grimaced, and Trudy nodded. Although the reporter's side of her lover's life ate up more and more of his
time, he continued to make deliveries, especially of pre-
scriptions and medical supplies, to the local community's
scattered holdings. And not, she suspected, just to "keep
my ear close to the ground" as a reporter, whatever he
might say. He did it because it needed to be done and
because, at the bottom of it all, he had a deep and abid-
ing need to help people. That was one of the things she'd
discovered she most loved about him.

"How much later, do you think?" she asked.

"Not more than fifteen, twenty minutes."

"Okay. I've still got some light stuff to pack. But,
trust me, I'll save the heavy stuff till you're here to lend
your brute male strength!"

245

"That's me!"

Nosey's tiny image bent his arm and flexed his biceps, and Trudy giggled. Nosey was long and lanky, yet still somehow brought the adjective "wiry" to mind. He would never carry the muscle mass of someone like Karl Zivonik, but no one lived on Sphinx without becoming far more muscular than those who lived in lighter gravity fields.

"Ooooh! Do you really think you're manly enough to carry these incredibly heavy loads?" she laughed, rolling her eyes at him.

"Not a doubt in my mind," he assured her firmly. "Besides, I'm bringing reinforcements."

"What kind of 'reinforcements'?"

"I ran into Karl and Stephanie this morning. They wanted to come out and talk to you a bit about Fuzzy Friend. I think they're hoping Lionheart and Survivor can convince Fuzzy Friend to lead them back to his clan."

"That sounds like a good idea to me. As long as no one tells *Ralph* where they are, anyway," Trudy finished a bit darkly.

"Trust me, that's definitely not on their agenda," Nosey reassured her. "But they did want to drop by while you were there, since that seems to be what brings Fuzzy Friend to visit. And I figured it wouldn't hurt to have a semi-official presence when I turned up. Just in case your father or Ralph gets antsy about my helping you pack."

"I made sure neither of them would be here," Trudy said. "But I'm sure that between Karl's size and Stephanie's mods, they'll be able to carry anything my knight in shining armor is too wimpy to hoist."

"You do such wonders for my male ego," he told her with a chuckle.

"Trust me, your male ego is just fine. Muscles alone do not make a man."

She batted her eyes at him, and he laughed.

"Anyway, they'll be a few minutes behind me, probably. So I should have the opportunity to sweep you into my manly arms and devour your face with kisses before they get here to ruin the party."

"Maybe you should write bad romances instead of news copy," Trudy suggested with a gurgle, and he laughed again.

"I'm multitalented. I can do both. And I fully intend to make a down payment on that particular bit of purple prose when I get there."

"Then I'll see you when you get here," she said. "Love you!"

"Ditto!"

The display blanked, and Trudy looked around her room. It was far neater than it had been for most of her lifetime, and a warm but somehow bittersweet glow enveloped her as she thought about why that was. The treasured keepsakes and clutter of stuffed animals which had all too often soothed a sobbing girl into sleep had disappeared into the packing cases stacked beside the door. The bed was neatly made...even though she would never sleep in it again. The closet door stood open, its contents folded into other carry cases, and her precious store of hard copy books—there weren't all that many of those, but she'd loved them since she was a little girl, losing her unhappiness in their printed pages—and all the other memorabilia she'd assembled in her eighteen T-years were packed into the heavier cases she'd teased Nosey about.

She'd turned eighteen and become legally adult four days ago. It still felt more than a little scary, but her life was officially her own now, and a sort of joyous trepidation filled her as she contemplated that.

Today would be the last load, and she really could have packed all of it into her own air car. It would've been tight, but she could have done it. Except that she wanted

Nosey here for the final trip. She wasn't sure why, really, just as she'd found it difficult for quite a while to decide why her emotions seemed so bittersweet. It wasn't because any part of her wanted to stay. She knew that much. Just as she knew—and knew Nosey knew—that at least part of her decision to move in with him was actually a decision to move *out* of this room on her family's barony. To get away from all the dark, strangling memories.

And just as she knew that wherever she went, those memories would go with her. One way or the other, they would go with her.

Nosey was right about that, too, she thought, leaning back against the wall and folding her arms as she made one last painstaking visual check to be certain everything was packed. She *did* need counseling, from someone who didn't love her as much as he did. Someone who could be an impersonal professional when they started unraveling the poisonous, knotted tangle of her childhood. She couldn't afford to simply run *away*; she needed something to run *to*, and that had to include more than "just" Nosey. He might be her rock, her fortress, but he deserved someone who wasn't so crippled and damaged she *needed* him first and foremost as a stronghold. Oh, he'd be that—and he'd offer her his support without stint or limit. She knew that, too. But she refused to be the wounded bird unable to fly on her own, because he deserved better than that.

And so did she. That had actually been the hardest part. To accept that she deserved better. She wondered if she ever would have accepted it without him, and that, too, was one of the reasons she loved him so much.

Well, standing around here's not getting the car loaded, she told herself, and grabbed two of the lighter boxes and headed for the garage apron.

❖   ❖   ❖

<I did not realize it was quite this far,> Still Water said. <Somehow the journey never seemed to take so long in your memories!>

<Well, I would not like to suggest that a hearty scout, such as myself, journeys more swiftly than one who stays home and weaves carry nets,> Leaf Racer replied with an edge of loving laughter.

<That is wise of you,> his mate replied dryly, although he tasted her own laughter over their lifebond.

<Perhaps the clan should rename me,> he said thoughtfully. <Which would you think was better—Abundant Prudence or perhaps simply Brilliant Mind?>

<Neither does you true justice. I think perhaps Addled Wit would be more suiting.>

<You wound me,> he said sorrowfully.

<Not yet ... but give me time,> she replied, and he paused, bleeking laughter, until she caught up with him and he could wrap his tail and one of his arms around her.

<You will be such a wonderful stern, loving mother,> he told her softly, and she nestled against him. <Even if your timing is not of the best,> he added, and it was her turn to laugh as she nipped his ear.

<We are near Shadow Eyes' nesting place now,> he said more seriously. <I do not know if she will be there, but I am hopeful. Until I am certain that she is—and that Mind Canker is not—you must remain behind, my love.>

He tasted her acknowledgment, although it was farther short of full agreement than he might have preferred. Still Water had always been a law unto herself. Had her mind-voice been only a tiny bit stronger, she would undoubtedly have been a memory singer, like her own mother's mother. As it was, despite her relative youth, she was the clan's chief weaver, and one day, he was certain, she would be one of Golden-Leaf Clan's elders. That independence was one of the things which had drawn him to her in the first place, but there were times when it could be more than a bit...not *frustrating*, although that came close. Perhaps "worrisome" would have been better.

And perhaps you spend too much time worrying because of how much you love her, he told himself. *She is not a kitten, and you are not her ancient elder! It is just that the thought of a world without her in it terrifies you so.*

He was careful not to think that out loud, but she sensed it anyway, and nuzzled her nose against his cheek.

<*I will be good,*> she promised him, and he returned her quick caress with an inner laugh before he went bounding away through the net-wood.

He was careful as he made his way along the still-bare limbs. It had been obvious to him for some hands of days that Shadow Eyes was leaving her nest place. He could taste that in her mind-glow, although it was overshadowed by confusing tides of happiness and sorrow and dark memory. How he wished they could mind-speak one another! There was so much darkness down inside her, so much hurt, and he longed to help her heal it. But the joy he'd tasted within her on the single occasion when the two-leg he had named Heart's Glow, the male two-leg who was clearly her mate, had come to help load some of her possessions into her flying thing made him hope she would heal herself without him. Certainly she would do better once she was away from Mind Canker and Anger Cloud!

His own mind-glow darkened as he thought about *those* two. It had taken him some time to realize Mind Canker was Shadow Eyes' elder sibling and Anger Cloud was actually her sire, and the realization had shaken him. It was proof of how different the two-legs were, because no clan of the People could have tolerated the way in which Anger Cloud clearly thought about—and treated—Shadow Eyes. Not out of *any* adult, far less a kitten's sire! Kittens were to be treasured, to be loved, to be nurtured. They were not to be used as something to vent one's own anger upon. And, above all, they were not *owned*. They were not possessions which had no right to choose their own way, make their own decisions. They were not—

He made himself stop. There was nothing he could do about the way in which Anger Cloud and Mind Canker had done their best to blight Shadow Eyes' mind-glow, and he knew from his single taste of Heart's Glow that he would never permit another to treat her so. He *approved* of Heart's Glow, and he was happy Shadow Eyes had found him, even if it did mean she would be moving to Heart's Glow's nesting place and away from his own range. From things he had tasted from her, he hoped she would be returning for occasional visits, but he was well aware that his opportunities to visit with her were winding to an end.

So was Still Water, and she had pressed him for an opportunity to taste Shadow Eyes for herself. To meet her mate's beloved two-leg friend before Shadow Eyes moved away and before her own kittens precluded this sort of journey. And, in truth, Leaf Racer was happy she felt that way. He wanted her to meet his friend, to taste the fascinating ripple and flow of the two-legs' mind-glows in person.

But he would not expose her to Mind Canker. Neither to his mind-glow nor to the vicious anger he had tasted in *that* two-leg. In many ways, Leaf Racer considered Mind Canker's obvious hatred for him, personally, a thing of honor. It was largely because he had offered to defend Shadow Eyes, he knew, but there was something else inside the two-leg. Something that reminded him of a lairing death fang, or even a needle-fang's blood-crazed hunger in mating time. He had watched for Mind Canker on his scouting rounds since their first encounter, and he had observed him on more than one occasion. Enough to know Mind Canker enjoyed killing. Not just when he had to, but whenever the opportunity presented itself.

The sooner Shadow Eyes was away from Mind Canker, the better, he thought grimly as he reached the edge of the clear space around the two-legs' nesting place.

"So, you can hardly wait to go climb into his bed, can you?"

Trudy froze. She hated that reaction, but it was instinctive as she heard Ralph's nasty-toned voice. She'd done her best to time this last trip when neither he nor their father would be home, but he'd obviously returned sooner than she'd expected.

She drew a deep breath, trying to pretend her heart rate hadn't just quickened, then straightened from where she'd been loading the air car's cargo compartment and turned to face him.

"Whose bed I sleep in—or do anything else in—was never any of your business, Ralph," she said. "It certainly isn't now."

"Even if the nosy, opinionated, self-appointed 'crusader' hates our family and everything we stand for? Even if he's only sleeping with *you* to put his thumb into Dad's eye? You *really* think there's any *other* reason he would?"

The scornful contempt in his tone would once have turned her into a mouse, shrinking away from his contemptuous anger. She felt some of that stir deep inside, even now, but it was overlaid by a burning anger of her own. She welcomed that angry strength, but she also reminded herself to keep it tamped down.

"I know you'd like to believe that," she told him. "In fact, you'd like *me* to believe it. But I know better, and so would you if you weren't so bigoted and full of your own importance. Nosey may not be First Wave, but he cares more about the future of Sphinx than you *ever* will."

"Oh, *sure* he does!" Ralph sneered. "All those damned newcomers do, don't they? Riding to the rescue? Coming to 'help' us so we all owe them for it? Well, I've got news for you, Sis—*I* don't owe them a single damned thing! Hell, three quarters of them didn't even pay their own way here! What gives them the right to tell me what I can or can't do on my own planet?"

"So, we're back to that again," she said, shaking her head.

"Damn straight we are!" Ralph turned to face her fully, and her stomach clenched as she saw the shotgun held under his right arm. "They can cram all their holier-than-now worries and rules sideways, for all I care. Me? I'm going to go shoot me some snow-hens. Unless I see any treecats, that is!"

Her face tightened as she felt the sincerity in that last sentence. His anger over the way Fuzzy Friend had terrified him had never gone away. It had only festered, and his hatred for the treecat had grown steadily more overt since he'd found out about Governor Donaldson's proposed decree granting the 'cats protected species status. That was one of the reasons—indeed, the *main* reason—she'd tried so hard to avoid him and her father whenever she was home rather than crashing with a friend or Nosey. Fuzzy Friend seemed to know when she'd returned, more often than not, and the last thing she wanted was Ralph in bloody-minded mode when that happened.

"I'm telling you again, that would be a really bad idea," she said as calmly as she could. "I know at least part of it is you're doing it to spite me, Ralph. You made that clear enough. But if you start killing treecats, I *guarantee* you you won't like the consequences."

"Oh, screw the consequences!" He bared his teeth at her. "I'll take my chances. Especially before Donaldson gets around to screwing everything up!"

"Ralph, whatever you think—" she began.

<*Do not come closer,*> Leaf Racer warned Still Water. <*Mind Canker is here, and he is angry with Shadow Eyes for some reason.* Very *angry.*>

He let his mate taste a reflection of the vicious anger boiling inside Mind Canker and felt her shock and revulsion.

<*How can his fellow two-legs tolerate that?*> she asked. <*It is like a cloud of poison!*>

<*They are mind-blind,*> he replied. <*They cannot taste one another. If they could, then surely the two-legs' elders would have intervened long ago. But that is one reason I fear for Shadow Eyes. I do not think she realizes just how blood-mad Mind Canker truly is.*>

<*Then it is well she is moving away, even if it may mean you can no longer visit her,*> Still Water said. <*It is enough to make me doubt the wisdom of any closer contact with all two-legs! If something like this can dwell among them without their even realizing it, then perhaps it is no wonder the evildoer who slew True Stalker was able to wreak her evil despite all the good two-legs could do to prevent it.*>

<*You are not the first of the People to think that, my love,*> he replied. <*And I fear there is much truth in that concern. But the two-legs are here now, and there are so many more of the good two-legs. Bright Water is on the true scent in this, I think. We must make friends and allies of the good ones, because they are not leaving our world, and we will need friends to resist the evildoers among them.*>

<I know that. It does not make me enthusiastic for it, however. To meet your friend, yes. That I look forward to eagerly. But I do not think I will seek to find and know many others among them. I will leave that for the more adventurous. Like you.>

She sent him a warm glow of love, only slightly tempered by lingering distaste for the glimpse into Mind Canker's mind-glow he had shared with her, and he returned it. Yet even as he did, he crept closer to Shadow Eyes, flowing unobtrusively along the net-wood. He did not truly believe Mind Canker would physically attack Shadow Eyes, but as he tasted the red fury of the two-leg's anger he was less certain of that than he would have liked.

"Well, speak of the devil!" Ralph interrupted Trudy in mid-sentence. "Guess what I see, Sis?"

Trudy's heart seemed to stop as her brother snapped the shotgun up and wheeled away from her.

"Always seems to come slinking around whenever you're here, doesn't it?" Ralph continued sadistically. "Thought I didn't know that, didn't you? But I figured it out, and I programmed the cameras to look for him. And there he is."

He brought the shotgun to his shoulder, and Trudy leapt towards him. But she was too far away.

"Say goodbye, Sis!"

The savagery in Mind Canker's mind-glow peaked. It blasted over Leaf Racer like a scorching wind funnel of hatred, and he knew the two-leg was prepared to kill. But he did not know *who* he was prepared to kill, and concern for Shadow Eyes sent him racing along the net-wood until he saw the thunder-barker in its hands, saw it swinging in his direction.

<*Leaf Racer!*> he heard Still Water mind-cry. <*Do not!*>

He sensed her racing through the net-wood toward him.

<*Stay where you are!*> he told her, even as he halted his run toward Shadow Eyes and leapt for another net-wood trunk. <*Come no cl—!*>

"*No!*" Trudy screamed. "No, *please!*"

BLAAMMMMM!

The thunderous concussion slammed her ears and a hammer slammed her heart as Ralph fired. Whatever his other failings, Ralph Franchitti was an excellent shot, and the treecat's last-second swerve didn't save it. A tornado of flechettes in a tightly grouped pattern hit Leaf Racer almost squarely center of mass.

Very little of his body was left intact.

<*Leaf Racer!*> Still Water mind-screamed as her mate's mind-glow was ripped suddenly and brutally away. <*Leaf Racer!*>

She streaked through the net-wood despite the heaviness of her pregnancy, racing towards him. There was nothing she could do. She knew that. It didn't matter. All she felt in that instant was the desperate need to reach him, to be there, to hold him. And so she put her head down and flew along the net-wood like a mad thing.

Nosey Jones felt a happy glow as he saw the Franchitti parking apron through his windshield and prepared to set down. The sooner he got Trudy away from her family's "loving arms," the better. And he intended to see to it that she *stayed* away from them unless the future contact was on her terms. She'd had to put up with enough—

A guillotine chopped his thought short as he got close enough to see what was happening. For just an instant, he couldn't believe his eyes, but then he was slamming his air car down on the apron in an emergency landing. He didn't waste time opening the canopy, either. He hit the jettison button with his right thumb and blew it off even as his left hand unlocked his shoulder harness.

"Damn you, Ralph! Damn you to *hell!*" Trudy shouted, lunging for the shotgun while tears streamed down her face. "He never hurt you!"

"And now he never will!" Ralph laughed, twisting at the hips to avoid her efforts to grab the shotgun. "Serves the little prick right!"

"I'll—!"

"You'll *what?*" he sneered. "You won't do a damned thing, Sis. Not one damned *thing*, and we both know it! Oh, look! There's another one!"

Still Water reached the edge of the clearing, keening in horror and grief as she saw her mate's mangled body. She flung herself from the net-wood, too caught in her own agony to taste the two-leg mind-glows. Yet even so, she felt the fury and the grief flooding out of Shadow Eyes.

She raced to Leaf Racer, gathering his broken, bloody body into her arms, put back her head, and wailed.

Trudy had never heard such grief, such anguish. The cry of the smaller, dappled female treecat—the one she somehow realized instantly had been Fuzzy Friend's mate—went through her like a jagged-edged dagger. And even as the 'cat wailed, even as she held Fuzzy Friend's ripped and torn body and rocked on her haunches, Ralph's shotgun was swinging toward her.

"*No!*" Trudy screamed, and lunged between them. "Don't you dare, *damn* you!"

"Move!" Ralph snarled. He tried to step around her, but she moved, keeping her body between him and the wailing 'cat. "Get out of the way, or so help me—!"

"No!" Tears streaked Trudy's face. "Not this time!"

"You little—!"

Ralph stepped toward her, took one hand from the shotgun, and shoved her violently aside. She stumbled, going to one knee with brutal power in Sphinx's heavy gravity. She cried out sharply in pain, and he grinned triumphantly as he put both hands back on the shotgun. But she lunged back to her feet somehow, despite the stabbing hurt in her knee, and this time she was close enough to get her own hands on the weapon. She grabbed it, trying to wrench it out of her brother's hands.

"No, damn you! *No!*"

She almost succeeded. Surprise flashed through Ralph as Trudy, who'd never dared to raise a hand in self-defense, however uppity she'd grown of late, actually attacked him. That wasn't supposed to happen. That wasn't what she was supposed to do, and for a moment, he couldn't truly believe she had. But his grip tightened on the shotgun, and he turned, trying to wrench it out of her grasp so he could finish off the second treecat.

"Let go!" he snarled. "*Let go, Trudy!*"

"No!" she screamed again, clinging with all her strength. But Ralph outweighed her by at least fourteen kilos, and he got his back into it.

He twisted, throwing her away. She hit the parking

apron's ceramacrete again and this time her left wrist broke. Pain flared through her, but somehow she hurled herself to her feet yet again, reaching for the shotgun with her good hand.

Ralph saw her coming and swung the weapon in a short, vicious arc before she could touch it.

"*Ralph!*" Nosey bellowed.

A distant, shocked corner of his brain realized he'd stopped running toward Trudy and her brother. Like the majority of Sphinxians, Nosey had always been at least familiar with firearms, and he'd always carried one on his rare forays into the bush. But he'd never carried one for defense against his fellow humans. Not until Lyric Orgeson's thugs had attacked him, anyway. Since then, he'd decided that wasn't going to happen again.

Now the ten-millimeter automatic from his belt holster was in his hands as he found himself with arms extended in a stable triangle while he captured Ralph Franchitti in his sights. An icicle went through him, a horrified realization that he was truly aiming a lethal weapon at another human . . . and an even colder icicle as that same distant corner of his brain realized he truly was prepared to squeeze the trigger.

That was when Franchitti butt-stroked Trudy with the shotgun. It hit her squarely on the right side of her face, and her head snapped violently to the side and she went down, dark hair swirling, without a sound, just as Nosey shouted her brother's name.

Franchitti whirled towards him, eyes wild in a fury-darkened face, and the shotgun was still in his hands. Nosey didn't know what the other man meant to do. It was entirely possible *Franchitti* didn't know what he meant to do. But what he'd already done was bad enough, and the shotgun's muzzle levelled as it moved in Nosey's direction.

KerrrrrAACCCK!

The pistol bucked in Nosey's grip before he consciously realized he'd squeezed the trigger. He rode the recoil, brought the sights back on target, and Franchitti was still turning toward him, shotgun coming level.

KerrrrrAACCCK!

A second shot cracked out and a second shocking crimson blotch appeared on Franchitti's parka. But he was *still* on his feet, still held the shotgun, and the back of Nosey's brain clicked like a computer, repeating what his instructor had drilled into him.

"Guns aren't toys, and they're not status symbols. They're tools—serious tools, for life-or-death situations—and no one is ever justified in shooting at all unless the situation is so bad that it justifies killing. Never forget that. But if you do shoot, if you find yourself in that situation, you go on shooting until the threat is neutralized."

He squeezed the trigger again.

19

"TRUDY! *TRUDY!*"

Nosey's voice floated to her from far away, from someplace beyond the stabbing pain in her wrist and the throbbing agony of her face. She blinked, but her right eye wouldn't open and her left eye's vision was blurred, spangled with light flickers that made it impossible to focus.

"Trudy!"

She was in his arms as he knelt on the parking apron, she realized. But how? Why did her face hurt so much? What—?

Her left eye flared wide. Fuzzy Friend! The other treecat!

"Fuzzy Friend!" she shouted, and it came out in a whisper. "Fuzzy Friend!"

The agony in her face was nothing beside the agony in her heart, and she thrust with her right hand, fighting to push herself to her feet.

Nosey tried to restrain her, but she pushed harder,

with even more determination. Her right knee was obviously injured and he heard her whimpering in pain, but he realized he couldn't stop her and found himself helping her stand, instead. He kept himself between her and the sight of her brother. It was easier, given her focus on her treecat friend.

She started forward, leaning heavily on him and dragging her right leg as they staggered through the snow. Nosey knew he really should be more worried about Ralph, about whether or not he was still alive, needed medical attention. But he wasn't. He was far more concerned about Trudy, and if that said bad things about him as a human being, he was prepared to live with it. He put an arm around her, helping her as she went to her friend, and grief and a white-hot, passionate fury flared in his heart as he saw the second treecat—the smaller, *female* treecat—holding that mangled body in her arms and wailing.

"*Oh, Fuzzy Friend,*" Trudy whispered in a broken voice. "Oh. How *could* he? How could even *Ralph*—?"

She went to her good knee in the snow, right leg stretched awkwardly to the side, and reached out a trembling hand, but Nosey grabbed her forearm. She turned to look at him with her good eye, and his heart twisted with another, different grief as he saw the side of her face. Her eye was swollen shut, the shape of the shotgun's butt plate was a dark, livid mark across a cheekbone that was already puffing and bruising. Unless he was badly mistaken, that cheek was badly broken, and he felt a fresh stir of rage. But—

"Wait," he said. "You don't know how she's likely to react after all this." His own fury at what Ralph had done darkened his tone. "I wouldn't blame her if she decided she hated *all* humans!"

"He's my *friend*," she said in that same broken whisper. "And she's . . . she's—"

"And you're already hurt," he told her as gently as he could. "Let me."

She looked at him, and then, slowly, nodded and lowered her hand.

"Hey, there, lady," he said softly, reaching his own hand towards the 'cats. "I know. I *know*, believe me. But he's gone. I'm sorry, but he's gone. Let us help you, please."

Still Water heard the mouth noises even through the terrible shroud of her grief, even through the darkness beckoning to her, promising her an end to pain if she only followed Leaf Racer. He was gone. The light of her world was *gone*, and in its wake there would be only emptiness. Only grief and loss, made infinitely worse by the memory of what had been torn from her. Darkness, an end, would be so much better than *that*! Yet even in her anguish, she felt the unborn mind-glows of the kittens in her womb. If she ended—if she *allowed* herself to end—they would never be born, and that last loving echo of Leaf Racer would disappear with them.

She hovered, torn this way and that by the conflicting riptides of grief and love, unable to find her way out of the pain, and the siren song of the darkness grew stronger. It, at least, offered her peace, an escape. A way to be free. She yearned toward it, and then she heard the mouth noises.

They were two-leg mouth noises, and she wanted, more than she had ever wanted anything in her life before, to hate *all* two-legs. Leaf Racer had told her Mind Canker was not like other two-legs, but she did not care. They—the two-legs—had taken him from her, and she would never forgive them. She would rip out their lives with her fangs and claws! She would—

She looked up at the two-leg beside Shadow Eyes,

lips drawing back to bare her fangs, claws slipping free of their sheaths, prepared to rend and tear.

And then the two-leg's mind-glow washed over her, and she froze. Shadow Eyes' grief was a wind funnel fit to rip even a golden-leaf from the ground, torn with sorrow for the loss of her friend, but this two-leg's mind-glow was different. It had never met Leaf Racer, never known him the way Shadow Eyes had, and yet in its own way, its grief, its sorrow was even deeper and sharper. Even in that moment, Still Water sensed that there was more than what had happened to Leaf Racer in the two-leg's tempestuous mind-glow, but whatever drove it, it was focused on *her*. It was filled with pain, with regret, with anguish and guilt, with blazing fury for what Mind Canker had done to Leaf Racer, and with a concern for *her* that was deeper than the sky itself, broader than the tallest golden-leaf. That mind-glow reached out to her, and her claws retracted and her eyes squeezed shut as she laid Leaf Racer gently, gently upon the ground and stretched her arms to the two-leg crouched over her.

Karl Zivonik's com chimed, and he frowned as Trudy Franchitti's ID came up in the corner of the display.

"Trudy?" Stephanie said from beside him in the cruiser's front passenger seat. "We're only five minutes out. Why's she screening you now?"

"I don't know," he replied as she voiced his own thoughts. Then he shrugged and tapped the display. "Yes, Trudy? What can we—?"

"Hurry, Karl!" Trudy's voice sounded horrible. "Oh, please hurry! Ralph shot a treecat, and then...and then he hit me with the shotgun, and then Nosey got here, and...and—"

"Hold on! We're coming!" he snapped, and hit the

button that activated the cruiser's siren and strobed its transponder to clear the air in its path, then shoved the throttle fully forward to send it screaming through the icy air at well over the speed of sound.

"We'll be there in two minutes, Trudy," he heard Stephanie saying from beside him. "Are you all right?!"

"Yes. No! I don't know!" Trudy's voice was ragged, shaking. "But...but Nosey shot Ralph. He...he had to. And I don't think Ralph's *breathing!*"

Stephanie's face tightened and she looked at Karl. Then she drew a deep breath.

"Hold it together for another minute, Trudy. We'll be there, I promise!"

Trudy looked up with a vast surge of relief as the SFS cruiser came screaming in from the west. It flared at the last instant, riding its counter-grav down in an emergency landing, and the canopy popped almost before it hit the ground. Its camera drone deployed automatically as the canopy opened, and Stephanie Harrington flung herself out of the passenger side, followed an instant later by Karl Zivonik from the other side, with Lionheart and Survivor right behind them.

The two rangers looked around, and then without a word spoken, Karl was racing toward Ralph's body while Stephanie sped across the snow toward Trudy and Nosey, followed by both treecats.

"Oh, Stephanie!" Trudy sobbed as the other young woman went to her knees beside her. *"Oh, Stephanie!"*

"It's okay, Trudy. We're here now." Stephanie embraced the young woman who'd once been the farthest thing from a friend she could imagine. "What happened?"

She looked at Nosey, but he didn't answer. She started to repeat the question, but a keening wail cut her off.

There were two of those wails, actually, coming from Lionheart and Survivor, and Stephanie's heart twisted as realized Nosey was staring down at the dappled body in his arms. A treecat. And not just *a* treecat, but a female. One whose bloodstained winter coat and slenderness couldn't hide the evidence of her pregnancy.

"It was Ralph," Trudy said bitterly through the treecats' lament, and Stephanie glanced over her shoulder. Karl was on one knee beside Ralph, ripping his parka open, his medical kit by his side. "He *killed* Fuzzy Friend, Steph! Did it just to hurt *me*! And then...then *she* came, his mate. She has to be! And she cried—oh, Steph! She cried her heart out!" Tears welled from Trudy's good eye. "And Ralph—he was going to kill her, too! I tried to stop him, but he hit me, and then Nosey—"

"Okay. Okay," Stephanie said soothingly. "I understand. But—"

She reached across, touched Nosey gently on his forearm, and his head snapped up. His eyes suddenly regained focus and he looked around for a moment before he found Stephanie. Then his arms tightened around the treecat he held, cradling her against his chest as he stared at her. Lionheart and Survivor crowded up beside him, no longer keening but crooning as they stood high on their true-feet to stroke and caress the treecat he held.

"Stephanie?" He sounded dazed. "When'd you get here?"

"Just a minute ago," she said. "Are you all right?"

"I...I think so. I'm not sure. I—Oh, my God, Stephanie! I *shot* Ralph!"

"Trudy told me. Just focus for me, Nosey. Focus. Are *you* all right?"

"Yes. Yes!" Nosey shook himself. "Don't worry about me, take care of Trudy!"

"We will. But first we have to see about Ralph. You stay here with Trudy. Right here! Got me?"

"Yeah, sure. Of course!"

"Good. Before I do anything else, though, where's your gun?"

"I don't—" Nosey began, then stopped. "It's right here, in my holster. Funny. I don't remember re-holstering it."

"Reflex," she told him. "That and good training. Give it to me, please."

Nosey took one hand from the treecat—Lionheart had to move aside to let him—long enough to draw the pistol and hand it to her butt-first. His hand went back to the huddled treecat the instant she took it from him. She handled it carefully and noticed that he'd remembered to reset the manual safety before he returned it to his holster.

And I bet he doesn't remember that, *either,* she thought with a stab of sympathy. *Poor Nosey! I never liked Ralph. If I ever knew anybody personally who* deserved *to get shot, it was him, but this is going to get ugly.*

She ejected the magazine, released the safety long enough to clear the chamber, and slid the pistol into her parka pocket. Then she drew another deep breath and looked down at Lionheart and Survivor. Lionheart looked back up at her, as if he'd felt her eyes upon him. For a moment, they only looked at one another, but then Lionheart raised his remaining true-hand and pointed to Karl.

So maybe that means he and Survivor have this, she thought. *God, I hope so! But when all of this hits the fan—*

She nodded to the treecat, then hurried across to Karl.

"Doesn't look good," he told her, his voice grim, as she went to her knees beside him. "One shot through the shoulder, the other two chest wounds. And at least one of them hit a lung."

"But he's still alive?" she asked urgently.

"For now." Karl's expression was grim. "Twin Forks' First Response is en route, I've got coagulant in all three wounds. That's stopped the bleeding, and I've injected the blood expander. I've got the remote med sensors on him, too, but I think we're more likely to lose him than not, Steph."

"I hate that," she said softly. "Ralph's always been an ass and a bully, and I hate the way he goes around killing anything that gets in his way, but this—" She shook her head. "I don't want to see anybody killed."

"Me neither. But if I'm reading what happened here right, then— Well, let's just say I'd have shot his sorry ass, too."

Stephanie looked at him quickly as she heard the searing anger in his voice, but he wasn't looking at her. He was looking at where Nosey sat on the ground beside Trudy. She had both legs stretched out flat in front of her now while he wrapped one arm around her and she pressed the unbroken side of her face into his shoulder and sobbed, but his other arm still cradled the surviving treecat. Even from here, they could hear their companions' comforting croon, and his eyes were harder than flint.

"Maybe so, but it's going to be a mess," she said. "And we're right in the middle of it, Karl." She smiled crookedly. "First officers on the scene."

"And both of us with emotional ties—one way or another—to everyone involved in it." He nodded. "Plus treecats. Couldn't we just once do something the easy way? Just *once*, Steph!"

"I'm working on that," Stephanie told him. "So far it doesn't look real good."

Karl chuckled harshly, then shook himself and drew a deep breath.

"Okay. You stay here with Ralph. Nothing much we

can do until the EMTs get here but keep him warm. I"—he looked across the snow to Trudy and Nosey—"have to go do something I'm really going to hate."

<How did this happen?> Keen Eyes demanded as he and Climbs Quickly crowded as closely as they could to the female in Needs to Know's arms.

<I do not know, yet,> Climbs Quickly replied, <except that this is Still Water, Leaf Racer's mate. And that Leaf Racer>—he looked at the mangled body beside Needs to Know—<has been slain with a two-leg weapon.>

He tasted Keen Eyes' surprise that he knew Still Water and her mate, but he did not, truly. Sings Truly had shared the Golden-Leaf memory songs with him, however, and Leaf Racer had possessed a powerful mind-glow for a male. His lifebond to Still Water had been no small part of its strength, and Climbs Quickly had tasted its power in his memory songs. Now the memory of those songs flashed between him and Keen Eyes—along with the sick darkness of Mind Canker's mind-glow—and he tasted his friend's horror . . . and anger.

<Even People sometimes kill one another,> he reminded Keen Eyes, turning his head to look at the other Person. <You know that far better even than I!>

<True,> Keen Eyes conceded, and Climbs Quickly tasted the strand of apology weaving into his friend's raging grief and anger. <Even so—>

<Death Fang's Bane and Shining Sunlight will dig the truth from its burrow,> Climbs Quickly said firmly. <That is a two-leg task, and they will see to it that justice is done. For now, though, there are things we must do. Still Water must stay, Keen Eyes. If only for her kittens, she must stay.>

<But she cannot even hear us!>

<Not yet. But we must keep trying, and I think she will *hear* us. If only she stays long enough to.>

"Nosey?"

Nosey looked up and found Karl standing beside him.

"Ralph?" he asked, his voice harsh through Lionheart and Survivor's soft croons.

"Still alive," Karl said. "I don't know if he'll stay that way, though."

Nosey looked down at the crown of Trudy's head as she pressed even more tightly into his shoulder. Then he looked back up and nodded. A part of him felt vastly relieved that Ralph was still alive, but the immediate shock and adrenaline rush were fading, and the realization of what he'd done flowed through him like a deep, dark tide.

"I didn't want to," he said. "I *tried* not to."

"I believe you," Karl said with quiet simplicity, and turned to Trudy. "I can see the face, Trudy. How badly are you hurt besides that?"

"Not as bad as the last time you rescued me." She actually managed a tiny smile with the left side of her mouth as they both recalled the air car crash which had so nearly killed her. "I don't think it's good, though," she admitted in a pain-shadowed voice. "My knee won't bend and my wrist hurts...a lot."

"But you're not bleeding anywhere?"

"No."

"Then I think we wait till First Response gets here where you're involved." Karl reached out and moved a strand of black hair from Trudy's forehead. "Like you say, it's not like last time, and the EMTs are already inbound. I think"—he flashed a smile of his own—"it's even Stan Eisenberg's crew again. And I think he'd agree we should stop making a habit of this."

"I could get on board with that," she said with another fragile, fleeting smile. Karl patted her shoulder, eyes warm with approval of her courage. But then they darkened again, and he turned back to Nosey.

"I believe you didn't want to shoot him," he reiterated, "but you know what I have to do now."

"Yeah." Nosey managed something that was almost a smile. "Yeah, I've covered a few other shootings for the *Oracle*, haven't I?"

"I believe you have. So, let's go have a seat in the cruiser."

"Wait!" Trudy's head snapped up. "What? What are you talking about?!"

"It's procedure," Karl told her. "We have to arrest him."

"*Arrest* him?" She jerked straight, still seated, her arms tightening around Nosey. "He was protecting me! Protecting *her*!" Her chin jerked a nod at the treecat huddled against Nosey, streaked with the dead 'cat's blood, eyes still closed, still keening softly, almost inaudibly. "If he hadn't—"

"I believe you," Karl said. "All I have to do is look at the side of your face, and I believe you. But that doesn't matter right now. Until this is sorted out, I have to take Nosey into custody while we investigate. For that matter, I'm not sure exactly who's going to have jurisdiction. I expect it'll be Sheriff Torrente—we're in his county—but SFS was first on the scene. What matters right now, though, is that it's the same procedure no matter who has jurisdiction. Nosey has the presumption of innocence, but until we've investigated and determined he was legally justified in shooting, I have to take him into custody."

"But that's not *right!*"

"Nobody said it was, sweetheart," Nosey said gently. "But Karl's right. And it's especially important that we dot every 'i' and cross every 't' because he and Steph are friends of mine."

"But—"

"It'll be fine," he told her, rather more positively than he actually felt. "Here. You take her. She needs someone to hold her."

He held out the treecat to her, and her eyes widened. Then she extended her own arms, but the treecat squirmed away from her. It clung to Nosey, sinking the tips of its claws through his parka, pressing its muzzle into his chest. Lionheart and Survivor's comforting croon strengthened, and Karl's eyes narrowed.

"I... don't think you'll have much luck handing her to Trudy," he said, and Nosey looked back up quickly. He started to open his mouth, then stopped.

"Oh, Lord," he said, and it was a soft, genuine prayer. "I didn't—I never thought—"

"Thinking about it isn't usually part of the process," Karl said wryly. "And this is going to be... interesting. The first female 'cat to ever bond—and I'm pretty sure that's what she's just done—and she's obviously pregnant, to boot."

"And it happens in the middle of all this," Nosey sighed. "Wonderful."

"Yep, even more spectacular than Steph and Lionheart, some ways. Messier, anyway." Karl shook his head, then held out one hand. "Come on. We'll get you into the cruiser and into 'custody.' But I think we can justify taking her with you on the basis that she's probably in shock and may need veterinary attention."

"Thanks." Nosey took the proffered hand, and Karl helped pull him to his feet. Then Karl looked down at Trudy.

"We'll need a statement from you," he told her. "Are you in shape to give one?"

"Damn straight I am!" she said fiercely. "Like I said, Nosey was protecting me and the 'cat."

Karl winced ever so slightly, and Nosey's eyes narrowed. Then it was his turn to look at Trudy.

"I don't think defense of a treecat is going to help us very much, honey."

"Nosey, you can't go coaching the witness," Karl said sternly, although an observer might have wondered if his heart was fully in it.

"Of course not."

Nosey nodded, but he was still looking at Trudy. She looked back for a moment then nodded in return, and Nosey turned back to Karl.

"I think you said I'm under arrest," he said, raising one eyebrow, as another incoming siren announced the arrival of the Twin Forks EMTs.

20

THE EMT VAN SLAMMED TO A STOP ON THE PARKING apron and a three-person team piled out of it. They raced across to where Stephanie knelt beside Ralph's motionless body, lugging their equipment and a counter-grav stretcher as they came.

"Am I glad to see you guys!" Stephanie said as Stan Eisenberg, the team leader, went to his own knees beside her. "Is this as bad as Karl and I think it is?"

"That depends. If you think it's really bad, yes," Eisenberg replied. He carried a handheld, tied to the med sensors Karl had attached to Ralph. He'd clearly been monitoring it on the flight out from Twin Forks, and at least two of the icons on it pulsed an angry red. "We've got to move quick, Steph!"

"I've already got all the visual records I think we're going to need." Stephanie waved at the camera drone deployed from the SFS cruiser. "Go ahead and do whatever you have to."

"Good! We need to get him prepped for transport ASAP. Chris, I'm showing the nanite blood expander, but he'd lost a *tonne* of blood before Karl got them into him. Get the IVs started while Janet and I rig the stretcher tent."

"What about Trudy?" Stephanie asked.

"Trudy?" Eisenberg looked at her. "All we caught was the gunshot victim."

"Over there." Stephanie pointed to Trudy, who stood leaning awkwardly against her and Karl's cruiser. Her counter-grav was cranked up almost to max to reduce the weight her legs had to support and her right hand cradled her left arm across her chest. "We didn't know she'd been hurt when Karl first called it in."

Eisenberg looked at the other young woman for a moment, then nodded.

"I'll handle the tent, Janet," he said. "You go take a look at Trudy."

"Right." Janet Allen nodded back sharply and headed for the cruiser.

"What the hell happened here?" Eisenberg demanded as he activated the stretcher's control panel and the heated environmental tent opened above it.

"We're still working on that," Stephanie said, which was true as far as it went.

"What happened to Trudy?"

"We're working on that," Stephanie repeated in a slightly harder-edged voice.

Eisenberg turned his head and gave her a sharp look. She looked back levelly, and after a moment his eyes narrowed. Then he looked at Nosey sitting in the backseat of the cruiser and his expression hardened.

"Oh, crap. *This* is going to be a mess," he muttered, and despite herself, Stephanie's lips twitched at the universality that prediction appeared to be well on its way to attaining.

She started to reply then turned to look up as another SFS cruiser dropped out of the air and onto the apron. Frank Lethbridge and Ainsley Jedrusinski climbed out of it, and she felt an undeniable surge of relief as the senior rangers arrived.

"Caught your call and figured we might drop by, since we were in the area and all," Lethbridge told her with a crooked smile.

"Thank goodness you're here! This isn't the kind of thing I expected to be handling a lot of as a ranger," Stephanie admitted.

"Rangers handle whatever they have to handle," Jedrusinski told her. "And this is your and Karl's call. We're just here for support, and so far it looks like you and he are doing fine."

"I hope so," Stephanie said, watching Chris Charles, the third member of Eisenberg's team, cut away Ralph's parka sleeves and start a pair of IVs. Then he and Eisenberg lifted the wounded man quickly but gently onto the stretcher, secured the straps and sealed the environmental tent. "I hope so."

"All you can do is all you can do, Steph." Jedrusinski laid a hand on Stephanie's shoulder, and her tone was almost gentle. "And a lot of times, it won't be enough, no matter how hard you try."

"I know." Stephanie's nostrils flared as she inhaled deeply. "I think the one thing we forgot to do was call this into Sheriff Torrente."

"Don't worry," Lethbridge said. "You did your part when you called it in to us, and Dispatch followed SOP and cross-routed your EMT call to him. It's in his jurisdiction, but—guess what?—he doesn't have any officers in the area. It would take his nearest deputy at least thirty minutes to get here."

Stephanie grimaced in understanding. Counties on

Sphinx tended to be big. Duvalier County was no exception to that rule, and Torrente's deputies were spread at least as thin as every other law officer on the planet, with predictable consequences for response times.

"Given that, and since you and Karl were already on site, Duvalier Sheriff's Department's asked us to go ahead and take lead on this," Lethbridge continued. "It's formally our case."

There was something just a little odd about his tone. Stephanie looked a question at him, and he shrugged.

"I think the original suggestion that he leave it with us might have come from Chief Shelton."

"Chief Shelton?" Stephanie repeated.

"Treecats," Lethbridge said, and her eyes widened in sudden understanding.

"Yeah, that's got the potential to get ugly," she said. "Karl and I—"

"No!"

A raised voice interrupted her, and all three of them turned towards Trudy as she shook her head sharply.

"That wrist's broken," Janet Allen said. "I can already tell that. So is your kneecap, unless I'm completely mistaken, and I'm pretty sure your cheek—"

"I'm not going anywhere!" Trudy told her. "I'm staying here!"

"But—"

"No!"

Lethbridge and Jedrusinski looked at Stephanie, eyebrows raised, and she shrugged, never looking away from Trudy and the EMT.

"I really think you should come with us," Allen said. "There could be other damage I'm not seeing, Trudy. We need to do a complete exam, and we can't do that out here."

"I'm not leaving Nosey!"

Nosey said something from inside the cruiser, and Trudy glared at him.

"No!" she repeated for the third time.

"Janet!" Eisenberg called from the van hatch. "We've gotta lift *now!*"

Allen looked at him, then back at Trudy with an expression of baffled frustration and concern. Then she shook her head.

"If you decline treatment, it's on you," she warned.

"I understand that."

"Well..." For a moment, it looked like Allen was going to argue with her. Then she shook her head again. "Okay, girl." She touched Trudy lightly on the shoulder. "Guess I might be stubborn, too. But you get your butt to the docs as quick as you can. And"—she glanced over her shoulder at Stephanie—"make sure the rangers get imagery of your face. You understand me?"

"Yeah, I do," Trudy replied.

"Good luck, then!"

Allen patted her shoulder again, then turned and ran for the van. She jumped through the hatch, and the van started lifting even before she had the hatch sealed behind her.

"I hope they get him there in time," Stephanie said quietly.

"You two did all you could to make that happen," Jedrusinski began, "and—"

She cut herself off and all three of them turned as a civilian air car came scorching in and landed on the crowded parking apron. The hatch popped open, and Stephanie's jaw tightened as Jordan Franchitti leapt out of it. She glanced at the senior rangers, and Jedrusinski twitched her head towards Trudy. Stephanie nodded, and walked across to stand beside her own cruiser, leaving Lethbridge and Jedrusinski to deal with Franchitti. It might be her and Karl's investigation, so far at least, but the last thing they needed was to inject Franchitti's intense dislike for her into what would already be an... unpleasant conversation.

"What's going on here?" he demanded, red-faced with anger. "What's all this nonsense about Ralph?"

"There's been an altercation, Mr. Franchitti," Lethbridge said. "Your son's been shot. I'm afraid he's pretty seriously wounded, but Twin Forks First Response is transporting him to the hospital now. And your daughter's been injured, as well, although she declined transport to stay on the scene."

"Shot? *Shot?!*" Franchitti repeated, his face going even darker. "Shot by *who*? Why?!"

"We're working on that now," Lethbridge said. "Rangers Zivonik and Harrington were first on-scene. They have the shooter in custody, and we'll be taking him and any witnesses into Twin Forks for questioning. Until we've done that, it's way too early to draw any conclusions about what's happened out here."

Franchitti stared at him, his eyes wide. Then those eyes moved to Karl and Stephanie's cruiser. They narrowed as they saw Nosey in its back seat, and something very like triumph flickered in their suddenly ugly depths.

"That bastard Jones did it, didn't he?" he snarled. "He tried to murder my son!"

"It's too soon to draw any conclusions," Lethbridge repeated in a flat, hard tone, and Franchitti's gaze snapped back to him.

"The hell it is! We're standing on *my* property, Ranger! That means that bastard's a trespasser, with no right to be here! And certainly no right to try to murder a member of my family *while* he's trespassing!"

"It's too soon to draw any conclusions." This time Lethbridge's voice was a bar of hammered steel. "We'll get to the bottom of it. We'll determine what happened. But until we do, you might want to be careful what kind of allegations you go throwing around."

"Bullshit!" Franchitti snapped. "I'll see that little prick *hanged* for this!"

Stephanie's eyes blazed, but she knew enough to keep her mouth shut as Lethbridge looked at Franchitti with thinly veiled contempt.

"You're a father whose son has just been shot," the senior ranger said. "I can understand why you're angry. But this is a matter for law enforcement and the courts, not for you and me to decide standing here today. And I have to say, if I were you, I wouldn't be standing here anyway. I'd be headed for Twin Forks and the hospital... and my son."

Franchitti glared at him, but then he nodded curtly and turned away.

"Trudy!" he snapped. "Come on. We're going to Twin Forks!"

Stephanie saw Trudy's good eye widen with fear. For Nosey? For herself? Stephanie couldn't tell, but she felt the tension quivering through the other young woman when she put a hand on her shoulder. Anger swirled inside her, but she reminded herself she was an officer of the court. She had no business interjecting her own dislike for the man into the already tense situation.

"I'm sorry, sir," Karl said, "but she needs to come with us."

"What are you talking about? I'm her *father*!"

"I realize that, sir. But she's also the only witness we have. She needs to come with us so we can take her statement and figure out what happened here."

"What *happened* here?!" Franchitti's face contorted. "What happened is that that bastard"—he jabbed an index finger at Nosey—"just tried to *murder* my son!"

"We don't *know* that's what happened," Karl replied. "That's why we need her statement."

"Then tell him, Trudy!" Franchitti transferred his glare to his daughter. "Tell him your precious boyfriend just tried to murder your brother!"

Trudy shrank from her father's furious eyes in something far worse than even her physical hurt. Memories flooded through her, dark and strangling and terrifying. Memories of a far smaller, terrified Trudy, sobbing in fear and pain as Jordan Franchitti towered over her with those same angry eyes and a raised hand. Of shouted curses and sudden blows. They clogged her throat, threatened to drag her under, those memories. But then she felt Stephanie's hand tighten on her shoulder and something flickered inside her. She glanced at Nosey with her working eye, saw the anger and the anguish on his face, all blended with his shock as he grappled with the fact that he'd very probably just killed another human being, and the flicker became a flame.

"No, Daddy."

Franchitti jerked back as Trudy looked him square in the eye.

"What did you just say?!" he demanded.

"No." Trudy's voice was a thing of icy steel. "Nosey didn't try to murder anybody. He was defending *me*—and probably himself, but mostly me."

"What are you *talking* about?"

"I'm talking about *this*, Daddy!" Trudy jabbed her right index finger at the bruised and broken side of her face. "I'm talking about how Ralph butt-stroked me with a shotgun! I'm talking about how Nosey got here just in time to see him do it, and about how Ralph tried to shoot *him* when he did!"

Franchitti stared at her, his furious expression suddenly blank with shock. Silence hovered for a long, still moment, broken only by the still-audible sound of the crooning treecats. Then he shook himself.

"Don't talk crazy!" he snapped.

"I'm not," she said flatly. "And I'll tell the rangers and the sheriff and the courts *exactly* what I'm telling you now. Ralph attacked me, and Nosey shot him to stop him!"

"You lying little tramp!" Franchitti snarled. "You'll say anything to save the man you're sleeping with, won't you? Even lie about how he tried to murder your brother! What's wrong with you? Don't you even *care* about your own family?!"

"Care about my *family*!" Trudy barked a laugh, and her open eye flashed blue fire. "You can actually *ask* me that? Well the answer's really simple, *Daddy*. First, I'm going to tell the truth instead of whatever lies you want me to tell. And second, you've never given me a single reason *to* care about you. It took me years to figure out it wasn't my fault when you beat me or told me how worthless I am, how *stupid* I am. But I did. Damn straight I did! So don't expect me to lie about Nosey when he's the one—the *only* one—who's ever tried to protect me from you and Ralph!"

"That's ridiculous." Franchitti's expression tightened with fresh anger, but there was just an edge of fear to keep it company, and his eyes darted from Trudy to Karl and Stephanie before he could drag them back to his daughter. "Why are you making up lies like this?"

"I'm not lying, and you know it," she said flatly.

"Of course you are! Just trying to save the skin of the worthless piece of crap you're sleeping with! I'll bet Ralph caught your precious 'Nosey' trespassing! That's what *really* happened, isn't it? And when he did, I'll bet your *boyfriend* pulled a gun on him. Just the kind of thing he *would* do! And if Ralph hit you with a shotgun, it was probably because you were trying to keep him from *defending* himself!"

Trudy stared at him, then shook her head.

"I don't know what world you live in, Daddy, but I am *so* glad I'll never live in it again! You know perfectly well that's not what happened!"

"I know it's more likely than this . . . this *fairytale* you're spinning!"

Trudy laughed scornfully, and her father flushed even darker and raised one hand.

"Mr. Franchitti."

Karl never raised his voice, but Franchitti froze at the cold, hard granite at its core. He looked at Karl, then lowered his hand, tried to look as if he'd never raised it.

"All right," he said in an over-controlled tone. "I see how it's going to be. You're going to lie about what happened, and your *friends*"—he shot a furious, hate-filled glance at Karl and Stephanie—"will pretend to believe you and lie their own asses off to cover for *their* friend, the worthless piece of shit who just tried to murder your own brother! Of course they will. But it won't work, Trudy." He shook his head, curling his lip. "It's going to be obvious to everyone what's happening. If Ralph dies, I'll make it my life's work to see the bastard who killed him hang. And if he *doesn't* die, then it'll be his word against yours, and I think he'll have just a little more credibility than someone lying to protect her *lover*."

"You think that?" Trudy's voice was soft, and she looked at Karl and Stephanie. "Don't let him go into the house," she said.

"What?" Franchitti blinked. "What are you going on about *now*?"

"Ralph configured the cameras to watch around the

house so he'd know if Fuzzy Friend came to visit me and he could kill him." Trudy never looked away from Karl and Stephanie. "I'll bet you they caught every single thing that happened—*all* of it, from the moment he killed my friend. And if it did, then it for *damned* sure"—she turned back to look at her father at last—"recorded everything I just described to you. Don't give him a chance to wipe the files, because I *guarantee* you he will."

"I— That's a lie!" Franchitti said. "I'd never—"

"I'm afraid we'll have to examine that imagery, Mr. Franchitti," Karl said.

"Don't be ridiculous!" Franchitti snapped. "Those video files are private property. You've got no right."

"If they're evidence in a potential crime, then, yes, we do have the right to examine them," Karl said inflexibly.

"I'll see you in hell first!" Franchitti shouted.

"No, you won't. And we *will* examine that imagery."

Franchitti's fists clenched at his sides. Then he drew a deep breath.

"*Fine.* Suit yourself!"

He turned to stalk towards the house, his stride hard and purposeful.

"Stop, Mr. Franchitti," Karl said.

"Why?" Franchitti snapped back. "I'm on my own property, I can go wherever I want!"

"This is also a potential crime scene, and I have reason to believe you intend to tamper with evidence relevant to what happened here. I can't let you do that."

"No? Well, you can't *stop* me, either! This is private property, not Crown Range, and you and all the rest of you damned rangers have zero authority on private property! So screw you, Zivonik!"

He started towards the house again.

Karl took two quick strides after him and put a hand on the older man's shoulder.

Franchitti spun around. His right fist shot towards Karl's face, but Karl's left forearm blocked the blow. Franchitti snarled, and his knee came up sharply, only to be blocked by Karl's thigh. The older man lost his balance and stumbled backward, arms flailing for balance.

"Calm down," Karl advised him flatly as he caught his balance, but Franchitti only spat on the ground and charged.

"You son-of-a—!" he began, arms spread wide to grapple with the younger man.

Karl sidestepped, caught one arm in midair, and twisted. An instant later, Jordan Franchitti was flat on the parking apron, Karl's kneecap was in the small of his back, and both arms were twisted behind him.

"Let *go* of me!" he bellowed.

"I'm afraid he can't do that, Mr. Franchitti." Frank Lethbridge's voice was colder than the Sphinx winter. "You're under arrest."

"Under *arrest*?" Franchitti twisted his head around to glare up at the older ranger. "Are you out of your minds! You can't arrest *anyone* here—it's *private property!*"

"Yes, it is. It's also a potential crime scene, and the Duvalier Sheriff's Department has formally passed authority to investigate it to the Forestry Service because they were unable to get a deputy here in a timely fashion. That means we do have jurisdiction under the unified planetary law code. And you, Mr. Franchitti, are not complying with the lawful directions of the law enforcement personnel investigating what happened here. Not only that, you just attempted to assault an officer."

Franchitti stared at him, and Lethbridge looked back levelly. Then looked at Karl.

"Cuff the prisoner, Ranger Zivonik," he said. "Then escort him to my cruiser."

Karl nodded, and Lethbridge moved his gaze to Trudy.

"I believe you're still a legal resident here?" he said. She nodded, and he smiled thinly. "In that case, Ms. Franchitti, would you save us the delay of getting a search warrant by authorizing us to enter the premises and showing us where the cameras' imagery is stored?"

21

"WELL, THIS IS GOING TO BE A DUMPSTER FIRE," AIN-sley Jedrusinski said while she watched Lethbridge balancing Trudy as they hopped towards the Franchitti house and Karl "escorted" a furious—and handcuffed—Jordan Franchitti to the older rangers' cruiser. Stephanie looked up at her, and Jedrusinski shook her head with an off-center smile.

"Something like this has been coming for a long time with Franchitti," she said. "I didn't expect anything this... spectacular or quite this soon. I expected it *after* the protected species order was officially issued, but I knew darned well there'd be fireworks. He's the kind of idiot who gives all First Wavers a bad name." She shook her head. "I'm a First Waver myself, and *I* resent the hell out of the way he treats anyone whose grandparents didn't arrive on the *Jason*."

"I know." Stephanie nodded, but her eyes were troubled. "I don't like what Trudy just had to say to him, though. Not if it means what I think it does."

"I think it means *exactly* what you think it does," Jedrusinski said grimly. "Could explain a few things I've wondered about over the years, too."

She gave Stephanie a sharp look, and Stephanie nodded again, her expression sober. Then she looked at Nosey, still bent over the treecat in his lap but watching Trudy limp away with worried eyes.

He knew, she thought, and her heart twisted while her mind replayed every interaction with Trudy, every time Trudy had hidden behind cutting sarcasm or disdain or scornful pride in her family's history. *Trudy trusted him enough to tell him. Oh, I* wish *she'd trusted someone sooner!*

"Can you and Frank take over the on-scene investigation when they get back with the imagery?" she asked.

"Won't be a whole lot to do, probably," Jedrusinski replied. "The Duvalier SD's forensics van is en route, and they'll do a more comprehensive survey of the scene, but I doubt they're likely to turn up anything your drone didn't already pick up. And, frankly, if Trudy's right about the cameras, this is one case where the 'forensics' are about as cut and dried as they come!" She arched an eyebrow. "You're thinking about getting that little lady"—she pointed her chin at the female treecat—"to your dad, aren't you?"

"Yeah, but it's going to be complicated." Stephanie grimaced with more than an edge of anxiety. "From the way Lionheart and Survivor are acting, and the way she won't let go of Nosey, I think we've got another bonded pair here. And if we do—"

"And if we do, we can't separate them."

Jedrusinski nodded, and Stephanie felt an enormous flash of gratitude that she and Lethbridge had become members in good standing of the Great Treecat Conspiracy. The older ranger raised a hand, tapping her lips with her index finger as she thought, then shrugged.

"There's likely to be some procedural issues if the two of you just haul the suspect in a potential murder—regardless of what Trudy has to say—off to your father's clinic. Especially given that all three of you are friends and everyone knows it."

"I know." Stephanie's nostrils flared. "But I don't like how...broken she seems. I mean, it doesn't look like she's responding at all to Lionheart and Survivor, and I've never seen another 'cat act that way. If she and Fuzzy Friend were mated, and I think they have to've been, what does that *mean* for a telempath? I know the bond between me and Lionheart means we can't be separated, and I've always assumed the bond between mated treecats has to be a lot deeper and stronger. But it looks like it may be even deeper than I'd imagined. She looks like..." Stephanie looked up at Jedrusinski and bit her lip. "It looks like she's just going to...go out, like a light with no power. Like the only thing still holding her is whatever's going on between her and Nosey."

"Which means we can't separate them," Jedrusinski repeated. "Oh, Lord, Stephanie! Can't *anything* be simple around you?"

"Hey!" Stephanie summoned a smile. "This is one you can't blame on me, Ainsley! Karl and I just happened to be in the area."

"And if you hadn't, Frank and I would've caught the call, and things would be a whole lot simpler," Jedrusinski shot back. Then she sighed and raised her uni-link. "Call Chief Shelton," she told it.

"Calling Chief Shelton," the uni-link responded. A moment passed. Then—

"Yes, Ainsley?" Chief Shelton said from the small display. "I've been monitoring the video feed from Karl and Steph's drone. What was that business with Karl and Jordan Franchitti?"

"Apparently there may be visual imagery of the entire confrontation, Chief. We're pretty sure Franchitti intended to erase it. Karl explained why he couldn't."

"And Franchitti, being the piece of work he's always been, took a swing at Karl. Wonderful!" Shelton rolled his eyes. "This just keeps getting better and better, doesn't it?"

"At least the imagery should make what went down pretty open-and-shut," Jedrusinski pointed out. "In the meantime, though, we've got a problem."

She looked at Stephanie, then pointed at the still-hovering drone, and then at Nosey in the cruiser. Stephanie nodded and drew a finger across the touchpad on the remote strapped to her wrist, and the drone swiveled in Nosey's direction.

"Is that—?" Shelton asked.

"Yes, sir. Looks like the whole thing started when Ralph decided to murder a treecat. Trudy tried to stop him and he clubbed her with his shotgun . . . just as Nosey arrived on the scene. And that 'cat in his lap is probably the dead 'cat's mate. And she's pregnant."

"Oh, hell," Shelton grated.

"Exactly. Stephanie wants to take the 'cat to her dad for examination. And this is the first time we've ever actually seen half of a mated pair of treecats survive the other's death. Like Steph says, we don't know if she *will* survive, long term, if the bond between 'cats goes as much deeper than the one between them and humans as we think it does. Either way, though, Steph is right. We *need* to get her to Doctor Harrington ASAP, Chief."

"Then take her!"

"It looks like she may have bonded with Nosey."

"Oh, *hell*." Shelton's voice was even darker and harsher than before.

He frowned, obviously thinking hard, then raised his voice.

"Stephanie?"

"Yes, sir." Stephanie moved closer to Jedrusinski, into her uni-link's field of view.

"You're our most experienced 'cat expert. How bad is it?"

Stephanie bit her lip for a moment, abruptly feeling very young, but then her shoulders squared.

"Bad, sir. She's obviously under a lot of stress, and she's not responding to Lionheart and Survivor at all, so far as we can tell. I think she'd already be gone if not for Nosey."

"And we don't want her aborting under the stress, even if she makes it herself." Shelton nodded. He might be a law enforcement officer, but he was also a ranger and knew his animals.

"All right. Trudy's still there, you said, Ainsley? She didn't head into Twin Forks with the EMTs?"

"No way she was leaving Nosey," Jedrusinski said dryly. "She's banged up pretty bad herself, too, though. Janet Allen said she's got a broken wrist and maybe a broken kneecap to go with it, and her face doesn't look good." The ranger's lips tightened. "Looks like Ralph hit her pretty good, Chief. I'll be *real* surprised if her cheekbone's not broken, too."

"Some apples fall even closer to the tree than others," Shelton said grimly. "I'm guessing no one's taken her official statement yet?"

"No, sir. She's given a partial account of what she says happened, and according to that, it sounds like a pretty clear-cut case of self-defense. But no formal statement yet. Not from her or Nosey."

"And we can't have Karl and Stephanie taking statements from either of them, given their known friendship." Shelton rubbed his forehead, then sighed.

"Okay. Ainsley, I want Frank and Karl to stay on-site

until the forensics team is done. I want you to swap off with Karl in his and Steph's cruiser. Then I want the two of you to fly directly to Doc Harrington's clinic—my authority—with the female 'cat...and Nosey. I'm guessing you won't be able to pry him and Trudy apart, so you'll probably have to add her to the party. Once the courts and lawyers get involved, this could get sticky, so you're taking Nosey formally into your custody, and you're bringing him directly to Twin Forks to our offices for processing, but you're taking advantage of the same trip to get the 'cat to the vet and Trudy to the hospital as quickly as possible, understand?"

"Yes, Chief."

"And the main reason you're along instead of my just sending Steph and Karl, frankly, is for you to be able to testify under oath that there was no collusion between them and Nosey or between Nosey and Trudy before we take formal statements from both of them. And there won't be any collusion, either, will there, Ranger Harrington?"

"No, sir!"

"I was confident there wouldn't." He smiled approvingly at her. "In that case, I'll see you when you get here."

<*I fear for her kittens,*> Keen Eyes said quietly to Climbs Quickly.

<*As do I,*> Climbs Quickly replied.

Neither of them had the sensitivity of a memory singer, but they could taste the frightened mind-glows of Still Water's unborn kittens well enough to recognize how they were responding to their mother's distress. He pressed closer beside her, giving her the closeness and warmth of his body as much as of his mind-glow, and he felt Keen Eyes leaning close from her other side. He tasted just an echo of awareness from Still Water's shuttered mind-glow, just enough for him to feel confident she knew they were there, even if she refused to hear them. But she remained dark and closed. Except—

<She needs *Needs to Know*,> he said, tasting the way her wounded mind-glow strengthened and waned in time with the two-leg's gently stroking hands. <*We must be here for her when—if—she returns to us, but we are not the ones who will* bring *her back.*>

Stephanie didn't much like the thought of leaving Karl behind, but she understood Chief Shelton's thinking. Now she stood beside Jedrusinski as Lethbridge and Trudy came back toward them. From the slump of Trudy's shoulders and how heavily she leaned on Lethbridge, despite her counter-grav, it looked as if the adrenaline which had supported her must be fading, and a deep wave of sympathy washed through Stephanie as she watched the young woman hobble closer.

The two senior rangers had conferred over their uni-links, and Lethbridge helped Trudy head straight to Karl and Stephanie's cruiser.

"You ready?" Jedrusinski asked her.

"I'm more than ready. And I never want to see this place again," Trudy said bitterly.

Stephanie surprised both of them by putting an arm around her and squeezing tight. Trudy's good eye gleamed suspiciously bright for a moment, and she ducked her head in a nod of gratitude.

"Then let's get into the air," Jedrusinski said. "Two things first, though. One, did you find the imagery and copy it? And, two, you understand that you and Nosey are *not* to discuss what happened here with each other at all until we've had time to take your formal statements? That's important, Trudy."

"Yes," Trudy replied. Jedrusinski quirked an eyebrow, and Trudy snorted. "Yes, it looks like the cameras caught it all. And, yes, Frank already read me the rules about 'colluding with my boyfriend.' Which, to be honest, won't be the easiest thing I ever did. Or *didn't* do, anyway."

"I know." Jedrusinski nodded sympathetically. "In that case, climb aboard."

"—so we're inbound now," Stephanie said. She'd commed her father the instant they were in the air, and he nodded on her cruiser's com display. "Karl had to stay behind," she continued, "but Survivor's with us, and he and Lionheart are both crooning to her like mad."

"Land on the rear apron when you get here," Richard Harrington said. "Meet me in Room Three. We have all the necessary equipment there. You say the boys are crooning to her—is she relatively calm?"

"She's *too* calm," Stephanie said. "She's like a limp rag, Dad. I think it's been too much for her. I'm worried..."

And worried about Nosey, too. He shot someone and bonded with a treecat in the same afternoon. At the same time! *Now the treecat may die, or lose her babies, and he's holding her so* gently. *But he's normally so chatty. Seeing him crumpled up like this...it's like he's sick with her pain.*

"I understand," Richard said gently. "Just get here as soon as you can."

Richard Harrington's experience with injured or traumatized treecats and the humans who worried about them stood him in good stead when the SFS cruiser grounded behind Copperwall Animal Hospital. He and Danielle West, Copperwall's senior tech, were waiting, and he didn't complain about the crowd that four two-legs and three treecats made of his examining room, although he looked very carefully at Trudy and shook his head with an edge of disapproval before he directed her into one of the room's two chairs.

"Sit," he said firmly, as Danielle brought the diagnostic systems online. "And you're not getting out of that chair until Steph or Ainsley is ready to take you to the hospital. Is that clear, young lady?"

"Yes, sir," she said, sinking into the chair. It was one she'd sat in many times since joining Wild and Free, and she managed a quick, pain-shadowed smile as she sat this time. She stretched her right leg straight out in front of her and arranged her left wrist carefully in her lap while he took a cold pack from a cabinet and crushed it to activate it. He handed it to her, and she pressed the cold compress gingerly to the right side of her face with a grateful nod.

"I mean it, Trudy!" he told her more gently.

"I know. And I'll be good. Promise."

"Good," he said, then turned to Nosey.

"All right. Can you put the lady down on that table? Put your hand near her head, so she can feel you're there, catch your scent." He glanced at Lionheart and Survivor. "And you fellows need to give me some room. Dani and I can't help her if we can't move her!"

His shooing gesture toward Stephanie communicated more than his words, but Stephanie bet that the treecats had picked up on his calm, matter-of-fact acceptance of the situation.

That and Lionheart and Survivor know firsthand that Dad would never hurt a treecat, or any animal. Maybe they can tell this poor lady to trust him.

Whatever the reasoning, both Lionheart and Survivor backed away from Richard's patient. Lionheart climbed to his accustomed place on Stephanie's shoulder, and in

Karl's absence, Survivor accepted Jedrusinski's offered arms. Neither of them looked away from the huddled, limp 'cat on the examination table for an instant, though.

The examination didn't take long. Everyone present, except Nosey, had at least some experience reading the images that came up on the wall screen as Danielle adjusted the female treecat's position with gentle hands while Richard worked the ultrasound around her middle.

"She's definitely pregnant," he said. "I'd estimate three kits, although the angle's less than ideal. There may be a fourth tucked away back there. We'll probably be able to confirm that one way or the other when she's less stressed." He looked at Nosey. "Seems you're in a unique position Mr. Jones. Not only do you have a bonded treecat, you're going to be a foster father."

"How soon?" Stephanie asked. "And how much care will they need?"

"It's not as if we had a lot of data about treecats and how independent their kittens are at birth," Richard replied. "But based on what we do know about Sphinx wildlife, and your observations when you've gone visiting with Lionheart, I'd estimate that we have a little over a couple of T-months. Which makes me wonder about the timing. Everything we've seen so far—bearing in mind that we still haven't seen all that much—indicates that treekittens are normally born late in the spring, probably because there's more food to support the nursing mothers then. But this little lady seems to have decided to ignore that!"

"Well," Nosey said, speaking for the first time, in a weak shadow of his usual ebullience, "hopefully I won't be in jail when the babies come."

"That's what we all hope," Richard told him with a smile, straightening and glancing one more time over the diagnostic unit's readouts. Then he shrugged. "As nearly as I can tell, there's nothing physically wrong with her.

She's definitely stressed, and that has a lot of potentially not-good consequences, but there's no physical *injury*. With a different patient, I'd probably recommend quiet, seclusion, and rest, but with a treecat—especially one that seems to have bonded—I think it's a lot more important for her to remain with you, Nosey. And probably to have these two"—he twitched his head at Lionheart and Survivor—"available to help soothe her. But there's so much we don't know about how their bonding process works that I really can't offer much in the way of a prognosis at this point." He looked Nosey in the eye. "We'll all do our best, Nosey, but in the end, most of it's going to depend on her."

"I know." Nosey gathered the still limp treecat into his arms once more, holding her close. "I know."

Silence fell for a moment, but then Jedrusinski cleared her throat.

"I hate to say this, Nosey, but I really do have to get you and Trudy over to HQ for your statements. And, Trudy, I know you're stubborn, but will you *please* let us get you a human-type doctor?"

"Your office is right next door to First Response," Trudy said with a smile that was only a little wavery. "They can take a look at me, but I want to get my statement made before anybody takes me to a hospital and drugs me or something. And"—she looked Jedrusinski in the eye—"I want to have everyone see me like this—*just* like this—when I record my statement."

"You *are* a stubborn one, aren't you?" Jedrusinski shook her head with a smile. "Okay, if that's the way you want it. Are you ready to let me take your patient over to SFS, Doctor?"

"I'd rather get her out of a situation that's likely to stress her even more," Richard said, as Danielle helped Stephanie and Nosey wrap his patient in a soft, heated blanket, "but under the circumstances, yes. Just please make sure there are as few loud noises and bright lights as possible."

"—and that concludes the witness's statement, recorded by Chief Ranger Gary Shelton, Eleventh Month, Ninth Day, Year Sixty-Four After Landing."

Chief Shelton tapped the stop key and sat back behind his desk. Under the circumstances, he'd decided he'd better take Nosey's statement in person, just to make sure there were no loose ends flapping around. Now he folded the camera back into its receptacle with a deliberate air.

Nosey had tried to sit straight as he gave his account and then answered Shelton's follow-up questions, but he'd kept slumping. The adrenaline had worn off a while ago, and the coffee Stephanie had brought him couldn't seem to touch his bone-deep weariness. He thought he might be in shock . . . and wondered if the shock was just his or if he was feeling that of the treecat nestled in his lap. At least she was no longer utterly limp, he thought around the ache in his heart, but she was still huddled tightly against him, just her head protruding from the warm cocoon of her blanket, and kept her nose and eyes buried beneath his left hand, as if trusting him to block out the world. Still, he thought—hoped—she might be getting a bit better. She was purring now, at least. It was a faint, reedy ghost of the robust buzz Lionheart or Survivor normally produced. And it *wasn't* a purr of happiness, either. He was sure of that. It was closer to the soothing purr domestic Old Terran cats used, purring to themselves when they were injured or even when dying, but at least it was there, and as his right hand stroked along her back, he felt himself floating somehow on that buzz.

Don't give up on me, Lady. You've got a lot to live for.

"How's she doing?"

Shelton's voice made Nosey twitch, but the treecat never moved, except to shift slightly so that his hand stayed over her head.

"Not really well, I'm afraid," Nosey said, remembering that Chief Shelton, like him, was one of the newer recruits to the Great Treecat Conspiracy. "She's grieving. I think losing her husband must've been like an instant amputation. I'm not flattering myself, but I think I'm the only reason she didn't go with him. I think she grabbed for me as something like a tourniquet. A way of clamping something tight to stop the bleeding."

Chief Shelton nodded thoughtfully, but he also frowned.

"Don't sell yourself short. She picked you, not Trudy. If they really are empaths—and I'm pretty sure they are—I suspect that may have been because she felt your anger at Ralph. Maybe your protectiveness. I'm not slighting Trudy, but after skimming her statement and taking yours, I'm pretty sure she was in shock herself. Who could blame her? Assaulted by her own brother, the treecat she'd befriended shot in front of her—shot because that sad, pathetic, *sadistic* excuse for a brother wanted to hurt *her* when he did it? I think if the lady in your lap had grabbed onto Trudy, in the shape she was in then, it would've been like a drowning swimmer pulling a rescuer under. They both would've drowned. And, Nosey, you're the reason *neither* of them did. That treecat didn't pick you because you were 'convenient'; she picked you because you were strong. She and her babies need a friend and protector, and I think she sensed you could be both those things."

Nosey shook his head, not so much in denial as in bemusement.

"I was furious. I got there just in time to see Trudy and Ralph fighting over the shotgun. And then he *hit* her. She went down so *hard*, and the rage just *filled* me.

But even then I didn't want to *shoot* him, only he still had the shotgun, and—"

He stopped himself, drew a deep breath.

"I wish I'd at least been able to stop him before he killed Fuzzy Friend. Or hurt Trudy. But I was too late for that. And now—" He shook his head again. "Her family's never approved of our relationship. Now I've made that even worse, and—"

"Stop that!" Shelton said so sharply Nosey's head snapped up in surprise. "I'm not a judge, and I'm not a jury, but I *am* a cop. And I'll tell you now exactly what I'll tell a judge or a jury if it comes to it. You're the only reason that lady in your lap and her babies are still alive. That may not matter to people who don't realize or want to accept just how smart treecats are, but you're also very possibly—in fact, *probably*—the only reason *Trudy* is still alive. Ainsley managed to convince her to make her statement from the hospital while they worked on her, and she forwarded the preliminary report while I was taking yours. Her wrist's broken into more than fifty pieces, Nosey, her right kneecap's fractured, and the term Doctor Flambeau used to describe the right side of her face is 'shattered.' It's going to take reconstructive surgery to put her cheekbone back together, at the very least, and there may even be some permanent damage to her right eye, for God's sake! And I've watched the video footage from the Franchitti cameras, too. I think if you hadn't shot Ralph, he *would* have shot you, and after that God knows what he'd have done to Trudy! I'm pretty sure he was already less than rational, and that's the kind of thing that leads to multiple homicides, even—or even *especially*—of family members. You didn't make things 'worse.' More *complicated*, maybe, especially with the 'cats in the middle of it, but not worse."

"But—"

"Look, the natural thing for any decent human being to do after shooting another human being is to wonder what you could've done differently. I understand that, and it's likely nobody will ever be able to convince you to stop second-guessing yourself about it. Not completely, anyway. But personally, speaking as somebody more than twice your age who's been a cop of one sort or another for over thirty T-years, I don't think you had any other option. And as far as Trudy's relationship with her family is concerned, if a quarter of what she told Ainsley in *her* statement is accurate, ending it as sharply and completely as humanly possible is the best thing you could possibly do for her."

"Really?"

"That's the way I see it," Shelton said firmly. "And because it is, I'm going to . . . strongly suggest to Judge Pender that she set minimum bail and let you go home instead of putting you in lock-up. In fact, if it were up to me, I'd probably just release you on your own recognizance, but it's not my call. On the other hand, she'll probably take my recommendation—she usually does—although I expect she'll insist on an ankle monitor to make sure you stay home until we decide whether or not to file formal charges. If Ralph doesn't make it, we might have to rethink that, but Doctor Flambeau also told me they think he's going to pull through after all."

"Really?" Nosey repeated, sitting straighter, eyes brightening.

"Really." Shelton nodded. "There's an old saying that comes to my mind at the moment where he's concerned. I probably shouldn't share it with you, but sometimes 'the Devil looks after his own.'" He grimaced, his eyes hard as agates. "I always knew he and his father were both miserable excuses for human beings, but I never suspected for a moment the way they've apparently treated Trudy since she was a little girl. If anyone *had* known—" He shook his head. "The truth is, Sphinx would be a better place without either of them on it."

"I can't say I disagree, but I don't want to be the one who took either of them off it," Nosey said. "You really think Judge Pender will let me take this little lady home? That'd be good. I've been really worried about her. I think Steph and the others are right that we can't be separated, and I don't think a jail cell would be good for her."

"That's precisely what my experts have said." Shelton allowed himself a wry smile. "Several times. Formally and informally. And that's another reason—a strong reason—I'm going to suggest to the judge that since you're no danger to anyone except possibly Ralph Franchitti, she should grant you bail."

"Thank you, sir!"

"It'll still take some time to process the paperwork," Shelton said. "It always does. By the way, do you have a name for the treecat? It would make filling out reports easier. Stephanie's been referring to her as 'the widow,' but I think it's unfair to define anyone merely by their relationship to another person. Especially to someone who's deceased."

"You have a point." Nosey considered, and a name bubbled up. "How about Dulcinea? That's the name of Don Quixote's lady. But it also means 'sweet,' and I'm sure she is."

"Don Quixote?" Shelton frowned and rubbed one eyebrow. "Wasn't he that Pre-Diaspora guy who fought against wind power?"

"I think you may be confusing him with someone else." Nosey surprised himself with a smile. "I'm thinking about the original. He did fight with windmills, but that was because he thought they were giants, not because he opposed wind power."

"Still doesn't sound all that tightly wrapped to me, Nosey."

"Maybe not, but he believed in ideals. And he took on the windmills because he thought it was his job to protect people." Nosey shrugged. "Well, I've been called quixotic a time or two, and after taking on Ralph Franchitti—and now this lady—I'm certainly living up to the name!"

"Dulcinea it is, then." Shelton made a note. "Very positive. Now, I'm going to need my office, so why don't you take yourself and Dulcinea over to the canteen while I fill out the forms to make my recommendation to Judge Pender. I'll even spare Stephanie and Lionheart to keep you company."

"Thank you, Chief. I very much appreciate that." Nosey rose, cradling Dulcinea in his arms. "Come along, sweet lady. Come along."

22

<I THINK PERHAPS SHE MAY BE PREPARED TO HEAR *us now,*> Climbs Quickly told Keen Eyes as Death Fang's Bane settled down near Needs to Know in the two-leg eating place.

<*I hope so, but I do not wish to intrude,*> Keen Eyes replied. <*You have at least tasted her mind-glow through Leaf Racer's, though. Do you truly think she is ready?*>

Climbs Quickly considered carefully. Keen Eyes was right; although he had never tasted Leaf Racer directly, his bond with Sings Truly meant he had tasted the Golden-Leaf memory songs more deeply than most. And he *had* tasted the strength of her bond with Leaf Racer, if only in its echoes, and so he knew how wounded she had been by her lifemate's death. And as he cautiously tasted her mind-glow now—

<*I do think so,*> he said. <*It is clear she has bonded with Needs to Know—that is the only reason she did not follow Leaf Racer—and the bond has grown stronger. More*

*than that, I taste her spirit awakening once more as she
leans upon it. But that bond is still new to her. I think she
will need to hear the mind-voices of other People, as well.>*

<Then let us see,> Keen Eyes said.

Death Fang's Bane rose and poured the hot, rich-
scented brown liquid most two-legs treasured into two
of the not-clay holder things. She handed one of them to
Needs to Know and kept the other for herself as she sat
beside him once more and began making gentle mouth
noises at him. Climbs Quickly moved from the round-
topped platform between the two-legs and eased his way
into Needs to Know's lap.

The two-leg looked down at him and stopped stroking
Still Water long enough to run one hand down Climbs
Quickly's spine. Climbs Quickly buzzed a purr at him,
then reached out and very gently touched Still Water's
mind-glow.

<We are here, Still Water,> he told her softly.

<I know.> She lifted her head from under Needs to
Know's other hand and looked at Climbs Quickly. *<I
know you from the Bright Water memory songs, Climbs
Quickly, and I tasted you and another even in the darkness. I knew you were there, helping to hold me. But the
emptiness—>*

*<It is not the first time I have seen a Person lose his
or her mate,>* Climbs Quickly said gently. *<The hole it
tears in your mind-glow is always deep, even when your
mate leaves you from sickness or old age and you knew
you must lose one another. When he is snatched away as
Leaf Racer was, the wound is terrible.>*

<I wanted to follow him so badly.> Climbs Quickly
could barely hear her soft mind-voice.

*<Of course you did. But you did not, and it may be
selfish of me, but I am glad you did not. And that you
have bonded with the two-leg who is a friend of Death*

Fang's Bane. We who have bonded with two-legs have become our own new clan, and you are the first sister to join us here. Welcome, heart-sister.>

Her ears came up, and he felt her heavy heart lighten just a bit more as she tasted the sincerity of his welcome... and that of Keen Eyes, as well. Which reminded him—

<This is Keen Eyes,> he said. *<He is bonded to Shining Sunlight, who is—or will be; we are still trying to understand exactly how this works among two-legs—mated to Death Fang's Bane.>*

<I greet you, heart-sister,> Keen Eyes said, and Still Water sent a ripple of matching welcome to meet him.

<I have heard of Shadowed Sunlight and how he came to shine, instead,> she said.

<He is strong, my two-leg,> Keen Eyes replied.

<He is,> Climbs Quickly seconded, *<and he is good for Death Fang's Bane. The power of her mind-glow grows only greater whenever he is near. And your two-leg is just as strong, in his own way, Still Water.>*

<He is!> she agreed fiercely. *<That is how he caught my mind-glow when I tried to follow Leaf Racer.>*

<When we first met him, he had been badly injured by two-leg evildoers,> Climbs Quickly said. *<There was much pain—and fear—in his mind-glow that day. Yet even then there was also courage and that fierce need to know new things and to right things which have gone wrong that is so much a part of him. And today he has shown all of us—and himself, I think—a new strength I do not think he believed he possessed.>*

<Yes, he has much courage, more than he thought he did,> Still Water said. *<I tasted the fear in him as he confronted Mind Canker, yet he never hesitated, and I do not think that even now he truly understands how much courage it took to act despite his fear. But it is more than just courage. He is... a protector. He reminds*

me of a little flyer who will challenge even a cloud slayer to protect its nest, yet there is more still. The little bird is protecting her own young; this two-leg had never met Leaf Racer, never met me, but when he saw Leaf Racer slain, I felt the rage that filled him. It was not simply for Shadow Eyes, although his love for her made it still greater. It was rage because . . . because what Mind Canker had done was wrong. *Was* evil.>

Climbs Quickly found himself nodding his head in the two-leg way, even though Still Water had no need of that to taste the profound agreement in his mind-glow.

<*And then, after he had felled Mind Canker, he was filled only with concern for Shadow Eyes . . . and for me. Especially for me.*> Climbs Quickly tasted her sense of wonder. <*His love for her was like a bright, clear flame, yet his concern for me was like a forest fire, for he feared I would follow Leaf Racer. He did not know that I would not use fangs and claws upon him after another two-leg had slain my mate—indeed, he feared greatly that I would!—yet he reached out to me, anyway. Held me. Kept me from going.*>

Climbs Quickly shivered as he tasted the memories, so hot and fresh in her mind-voice.

<*Shadow Eyes is a good name for Walks in Shadow,*> he said. <*That was what Leaf Racer named her?*>

<*Yes. But I think she is beginning to step out of the shadows. Not as the memory songs say Shining Sunlight did, because her shadows are different. Darker.*> Climbs Quickly tasted Still Water's inner shiver as she recalled Walks in Shadow's wounded mind-glow.

<*We think the same,*> Keen Eyes told her. <*And that, too, is also due in no small part to Needs to Know.*>

<*I understand why you named him Needs to Know,*> Still Water said. <*Leaf Racer had named him Heart's Glow, for the way Shadow Eyes' heart filled with light whenever*

he was near. Yet I think perhaps neither of those is truly the best name for him.>

<He is your two-leg now, to name as seems best to you,> Climbs Quickly told her with a ripple of laughter.

<He is indeed my *two-leg!>* Still Water returned with a pert spurt of answering laughter Climbs Quickly was glad to taste. *<It would be well for all of you to remember that!>*

<Be sure we will!> Climbs Quickly assured her in mock terror, and she laughed again, despite her sorrow. But then she grew serious once more.

<I think a better name for him is Protector,> she said, *<because that is what he wants most in all the world to do. To protect those he cares about, yes, but not just them. To protect ideas, and to protect* anyone *who has no protector of her own.>*

Climbs Quickly considered that carefully, and as he did, he realized how clearly and deeply Still Water had seen into her new bondmate. Needs to Know—no, Protector—was not like Shining Sunlight or Death Fang's Bane. He did not like confrontation, was not armed with Death Fang's Bane's joyous anticipation of battle, was not the quiet, unflinching warrior Shining Sunlight was. Yet he would always stand to protect those things—those people, both People and two-leg—for which he truly cared. His heart would never let him do anything less.

<You are right,> he told Still Water.

"Nosey!"

Nosey looked up quickly from his conversation with Stephanie as Trudy burst into the Forestry Service canteen. She limped heavily on a cane, despite her counter-grav's support, but she made a beeline towards him. He started to rise, but—

"Stay where you are!" she commanded. "The last thing your new friend needs is to be jostled around!"

She crossed the room to him and leaned close, braced on her cane as she threw her left arm around him to hug him so tightly it was hard to breathe for just a moment.

He got an arm around her, hugging her back, and she laid the uninjured side of her face against his cheek.

"God, it's good to see you!" he said. "I didn't know if—"

"Ainsley dragged me to Doctor Flambeau. Flatly refused to take my statement until I went." She snorted, then shrugged. "He turned me loose five minutes ago, and Ainsley told me where to find you. She says they're going to recommend a low bail and letting you go home?"

"That's what Chief Shelton said. He sent me out here to wait while they do the paperwork. And"—he nodded his head sideways—"Stephanie and the boys came along to keep me and Dulcinea company."

"Dulcinea?" Trudy released him and reached down to touch the dappled treecat in his lap very gently. "That's a wonderful name!"

"Well, I think it describes her pretty well, anyway," Nosey said with what felt like his first genuine smile in days.

Dulcinea raised her head, looking up at Trudy with bottomless green eyes, then nudged her nose lightly against the offered hand and bleeked softly.

"I'm so sorry," Trudy half-whispered to her. "Fuzzy Friend was my friend. I tried to stop him, but—"

"She understands," Nosey said. Trudy looked at him, and he shrugged. "I can't tell you how I *know* she understands, but I do. Truly! I'm not just saying that to make you feel better, sweetheart."

"No, he's not," Stephanie said. Trudy moved her gaze to her, and it was Stephanie's turn to shrug. "I don't know if it's some kind of leakage from the bond or if it's just reading body language, but I'm always pretty sure what Lionheart's feeling. I doubt it's going to be any different for Nosey and Dulcinea."

Trudy nodded, then settled into an empty chair at the same small table, and Stephanie examined her carefully. The other young woman's left wrist was encased in a plastic cast, another cast or knee brace swelled her pants leg, and Stephanie didn't like the way she seemed to favor her left shoulder, but the truly spectacular damage was to her face. The contusion had darkened and swollen, although the hospital had managed to get her right eye to open again. Barely.

Nosey was looking at her, too, trying unsuccessfully to hide his own pain at seeing her injuries, and she reached across the table to lay her hand on his forearm.

"Hey, it's okay," she said. His eyebrows arched doubtfully, and she actually laughed. "It's okay!" she repeated. "You don't have to worry about telling me I look like crap!"

"You *don't*—!" he began, then stopped and shook his head. "Okay. Got me."

"I love it that you're worried about me, but I'm going to be fine," she told him. "Doc Flambeau wants me back in tomorrow, but we're old friends now, and he wouldn't have let me go if he didn't think that. I'm gonna be limping for three or four T-weeks, 'cause of how much slower quick heal is on bone repairs, but at least *it* won't need surgery. This"—she touched the side of her face very gently, then returned her hand to his arm—"isn't in quite as many pieces as the wrist, either, but it's a bunch worse than the knee. They'll need to go in and put it back together, too. And they had to drain the edema on my eyelid before I could get it back open, but all of *that*'s going to be fine, too, eventually. Well, I've got a bruised cornea, too, and he's a little worried about my septum, but we'll keep an eye on both of those. If they need fixing, we'll fix them, and the pain meds mean nothing's hurting—well, not hurting *bad*—anymore. The important thing is that you kept it from being any worse, Nosey. And you kept Dulcinea alive." She shook her head. "Nothing else matters."

"It does to me," he told her, reaching out to brush his own finger gently against her swollen face.

"That's because you love me, doof," she told him softly.

"You two do realize you're embarrassing me, don't you?" Stephanie put in, and both of them looked at her, then laughed.

"That's better," she said. Then she leaned back in her own chair and her expression sobered. "So, what do you do now, Trudy?"

"That's a good question," Trudy said, yet she seemed oddly serene.

"And?" Stephanie invited.

"And I'm going ahead and finish moving in with Nosey."

"Are you sure, sweetheart?" Nosey asked. She cocked her head, and he sighed. "You know how much *I* want that, but neither of us ever expected anything like this. After everything that happened today, if you do—"

"Hush," she said.

He looked at her, and she shook her head.

"I know where you're going, but the one thing I'm not doing—ever—is going home again." That serenity never left Trudy's tone, but now it was wrapped around a core of iron. "I admit I wasn't planning on a complete break— I was too . . . programmed for that—but I was already leaving, Nosey. And I plan on spending the rest of my life with *you*. That's what matters. All this"—she waved her right hand in a circle that encompassed the canteen around them—"only underlines all of that. Believe me, I'm not looking back. Ever."

"What about your mom? Trevor?"

"Trevor's a year older than I am, Nosey. If he wants to see me, he'll know where to find me, and he's got my com combination. Same for my mom." Trudy's eyes darkened, but her tone never wavered. "I hope my father doesn't take it out on her, but the truth is that she knows what she ought to be doing about it, just like I did. Neither one of us did it, until today, but we both knew deep inside what we *should've* done. Maybe—I hope—she'll realize she can do the same, after today."

Stephanie reached across to pat Trudy's thigh comfortingly, and the left side of Trudy's mouth smiled wryly at her.

"Guess we sort of let the Franchitti dirty laundry out of the bag, didn't we, Steph?"

"Guess so," Stephanie agreed, patting her leg again. "I never knew, Trudy. I wish I had."

"I wish you had, too. And I wish I'd told you—or anyone else—about it. But you know, one of the reasons I was such a pain—and, yeah, I know I was—was because of how much I envied you. You've got two wonderful parents, Stephanie Harrington. Hang onto them."

"I will—promise!" Stephanie smiled at her.

"I think we've got a few logistics problems, though." Nosey's matter-of-fact tone tried unsuccessfully to hide his own deep feelings. "Like your air car and mine, Trudy. Somehow, we've got to get them both to my place. Well, *our* place, now!"

"Not a problem," Stephanie said before Trudy could reply. Both of them looked at her, and she shrugged. "Karl and Frank flew your car into town on auto pilot, Nosey. It's in Sheriff Torrente's impound lot. It'll need a canopy replacement, but it's hangared and out of the weather right now, so it should be fine till then."

"Really? That's great! But that still leaves Trudy's car.

I don't like the thought of her going out there to get it after what's happened."

"She doesn't have to. Trudy, give me your keys. I'm pretty sure Chief Shelton will authorize us to go pick your car up for you, if you like."

"I'd like that a lot," Trudy replied. "There's still a few boxes of stuff in my room that I'd really like to have, too, but they mean a whole lot less to me than Nosey does. And they're not worth ever setting foot on that land again."

"You're sure?" Stephanie asked. "If you want to give me a note authorizing me to pick them up, we can get them the same time Karl and I get your air car."

"I'd rather you didn't have to put up with—and *argue* with—my father," Trudy said. "He'll raise all kinds of hell and refuse to let you onto the property, note or no note!"

"Well, if we hop out this afternoon still, that won't be a problem," Stephanie said, and smiled wickedly at Trudy's questioning expression. "He's being formally charged with refusal to obey the lawful instructions of a law enforcement officer, assaulting an officer, and resisting arrest. I'm pretty sure he'll be able to make bail when the paperwork's filed, but for some reason, Chief Shelton's working on Nosey's first. With all that going on, and late as it is already, I'll be surprised—*really* surprised—if he's able to get your father's filed until late tonight. Or even tomorrow morning."

"Really?" If Trudy was upset by the news, it certainly didn't show in her tone, Stephanie thought wryly.

"For sure. And the assault charge is pretty serious. He never actually managed to hit Karl, but attempted assault and actual assault are the same thing in the eyes of the law. So if you want to write that note, we'll be glad to grab your stuff."

"I'd really appreciate that." Trudy said gratefully. "If you're sure."

"How many times do I have to say it?" Stephanie demanded, and Trudy smiled at her. Then she looked back at Nosey.

"I asked Doc Flambeau about Ralph before I headed over here," she said. "He says they've got him stabilized and they're pretty confident now that he's going to pull through."

"Thank God!" Nosey seemed to sag in his chair, and Dulcinea sat up in his lap, shrugging out of the blanket at last to lean back against him and croon softly. He looked down at her, his eyes soft, and then looked back up at Trudy. "I never liked Ralph, and I never will, but I never wanted to kill anybody, either. The thought that I might have was—I don't know how to describe what it was."

"You did what you had to do," Stephanie told him. "Which I imagine won't prevent the occasional bad dream about it. Heck, I still have nightmares every so often about the hexapuma! But it's not like he didn't have everything that happened to him coming."

"You're so right about that, Steph!" Trudy said. "In fact, I'm wondering if I can charge him with assault."

"Of course you can! Trudy, he clubbed you across the face with the butt of a shotgun. That was *after* he broke your wrist knocking you down the first time! That's aggravated assault and battery with bodily injury, at the very least, and that's a felony. And I'm not a lawyer, but I did take the basic law enforcement courses on Manticore, so I think you'd have a pretty good case charging him with assault with a deadly weapon, given that it was a *shotgun* he hit you with!"

"Which probably couldn't hurt Nosey's case, either, could it?"

"I think you can safely assume it wouldn't," Stephanie said in a dry tone.

"Hey, you don't have to do that just to help me!" Nosey protested.

"Shut up. You don't get a vote!" Trudy told him fiercely. "This is part of my bridge-burning exercise, Nosey. If it helps you, too, so much the better, but this is for *me*."

"You go, Trudy!" Stephanie said around a gurgle of laughter. "I think you could lodge the complaint with me, but it would probably look better if you swore it out with somebody who's not one of your buddies."

"Are we buddies, Steph?" Trudy asked softly. "Really?"

"Really," Stephanie assured her, and patted her leg again. "And if you ever need to borrow some parents, I've got a couple who'd be happy to help out."

Still Water tasted the joy flowing through Shadow Eyes. There was much sorrow and pain threaded through it, yet those dark strands were lost in the brilliance of the two-leg's happiness and a glowing wave of triumph.

<*She is no longer Walks in Shadow or Shadow Eyes,*> she told Climbs Quickly and Keen Eyes. <*Not now. Now she is Walks From Shadow.*>

<*She is, indeed,*> Climbs Quickly agreed. <*And I think Walks From Shadow and Protector will be interesting mates for each other. And good clan mates for your unborn kittens.*>

<*It seems a day for changes,*> Still Water said after a moment. <*I never thought I would bond with a two-leg. Now I feel a stranger to myself. Leaf Racer is gone, and I feel . . . Not that I have betrayed him, because Leaf Racer would be the first to tell me to live and to make certain our kittens thrive. But as if the Still Water who ran through the forest this morning to meet her mate's strange friend is someone other than me.*>

Climbs Quickly stroked his whiskers, considering what she had said.

<*She is still you,*> he replied, after a moment. <*She

is the foundation upon which the you of this moment stands. You are not a stranger to yourself; you have simply transformed in order to live. Many creatures do that, even among the People. Do you know Stone Shaper's song?>

<I have heard of him in the memory songs. He is the member of your clan who lost both his mate and his mind-voice to the gray death and exiled himself. He bonded with a two-leg not long ago.>

<We will never know all of Stone Shaper's story, because he cannot tell it to us,> Climbs Quickly said. <But I have seen the place where he battled the needle-fangs. I do not think he fought to live that day. Indeed, I think he might have welcomed death, but he rose above it to fight to keep Awakening Joy from dying. Yet in that battle for another's life, he found his own reason to live, not just survive. So have you. You reached to live because of the small mind-voices whispering within you, but I think you will find a new life for yourself, as well.>

23

"THIS IS RIDICULOUS," JORDAN FRANCHITTI GROWLED as he strode into the office. "I can't believe Tucker is serious about this!"

"I'm afraid he's entirely serious," the tall, well-dressed man behind the desk said as he stood to greet his client and indicated the comfortable chair in front of his desk. "I told you he would be."

"And I told *you* to fix it."

Franchitti glared at the attorney who'd represented his family for the last thirty-five T-years as he dropped into the chair, and Jackson Ostapenko managed to not glare back. It wasn't easy. Over the years, the Franchitti family had been one of his more litigious—and lucrative—clients, but Jordan's father, Alan, the first Baron Franchitti, had been a far less . . . choleric individual. He'd actually been known to be reasonable upon occasion. Jordan, not so much.

"This isn't a wildlife violation or a traffic fine, Jordan," the attorney said. "It's not a misdemeanor. You and Ralph are both facing *felony* charges. In your case, failure to obey an officer of the law is a misdemeanor; assaulting one of them is a felony, though, and one that carries up to three T-years."

Franchitti started to open his mouth, but Ostapenko continued levelly.

"That's bad enough, but Tucker"—Alvin Tucker was the Crown Prosecutor for Duvalier County—"has indicated he's prepared to accept a plea deal, where you plead to the misdemeanor and get probation and the Crown drops the felony charge. Frankly, I think that's far and away your best option here.

"But *Ralph* is facing potential attempted murder charges. Even if we manage to avoid that, he's definitely looking at threatening someone with a deadly weapon, aggravated assault and battery, and assault with a deadly weapon with serious personal injury. Those are all felonies, Jordan, not misdemeanors, although brandishing— that's the technical term for threatening someone with a weapon—is only a class III offense. The maximum sentence for that's only three T-years. But he could be looking at up to thirty T-years on the others."

"He had every right to defend our property against trespassers," Franchitti protested.

"Jones wasn't trespassing." Ostapenko managed not to roll his eyes. "I've already told you that. Your daughter, a legal resident on the property, had invited him onto it."

"But Ralph didn't know that!"

"Nor did he inquire," Ostapenko said flatly. "I'm afraid the video makes that crystal clear, Jordan. As such, Jones had a legal right to defend himself with deadly force. It took about three minutes for Tucker to reach that determination after viewing the imagery. Whether or not the charge will be upgraded to attempted murder is still undetermined, pending the grand jury hearing. But he'll definitely be arraigned on the lesser charge."

"What if Trudy testifies she *didn't* invite the bastard?"

"She's already testified in a sworn deposition that she did. I don't think a retraction at this point would change a thing."

"So he's going to get away with almost murdering my son?" Franchitti demanded.

"In the eyes of the law, even if he'd killed Ralph it wouldn't have been murder. But, yes, it's already been determined that no charges will be filed against him."

"Great. Perfect!" Franchitti glowered balefully. "This entire planet is going straight to hell!"

Ostapenko only looked at him, and Franchitti made himself sit back in his chair and draw a deep breath.

"All right. So the way the *law* is written we can't charge him. But where the hell does that 'personal injury' crap come from? Ralph never even touched him!"

Ostapenko abruptly sat back in his own chair, and his eyes narrowed. He started to reply, stopped, then pinched the bridge of his nose and closed his eyes.

"Have you spoken to your daughter?" he asked after a moment.

"What?" Franchitti's face darkened. "She's... angry right now. Not rational. She's not returning my calls. Why?"

"Because"—Ostapenko opened his eyes—"*she's* the one who filed the assault charges."

Shock blanked Franchitti's expression, and the attorney felt something that was almost—almost—pity as he sat there, waiting for his client to process the information.

"That's... that's *crazy*," Franchitti said finally. "He's her own *brother*!"

"Which doesn't change the fact that he assaulted her with a shotgun." An edge of compassion softened Ostapenko's tone. "Nor does it change the fact that she suffered serious bodily injury. Or the fact that the Crown has video imagery of the entire event."

"He was trying to shoot a dangerous animal, and she got into his line of fire. Obviously, he had to move her, and—"

"Jordan, I know how you feel about the treecats, but that's not going to fly." Franchitti clamped his jaw furiously. "It *might* have flown for the first treecat, but even that one was moving *away* from him when he fired. Convincing a jury it was attacking him would be... difficult. But the one that your daughter was protecting was just standing there, motionless, beside the first one. There's no way we could possibly convince anyone it was any sort of threat that justified his knocking her to the ground even the first time, far less when he hit her with his weapon."

"But she was trying to yank the gun away from him," Franchitti argued. "She was wrestling for it with him. For all he knew, it was likely to go off in the struggle. He *had* to get control of it back from her!"

"She wasn't even touching it when he hit her with it, so that's not going to fly, either," Ostapenko said in a tone of hard-tried patience.

Franchitti stared at him, as if unable to comprehend what he'd just heard. There was silence for a long moment, and then Franchitti shook himself.

"I'm sure it's all a misunderstanding. I'll talk to her. She'll withdraw the charges."

"If she does, then the charges—the potential charges—against him will be substantially lighter," Ostapenko said, although he strongly suspected that Franchitti would find himself disappointed in that respect.

"So what's our next step? Until I talk to her, that is."

"Formal arraignment," Ostapenko replied. "Given the situation, Tucker has agreed to hold the arraignment hearing—both hearings; yours and Ralph's—until he's out of the hospital and able to attend. My best information at the moment is that we're looking at a T-month or so for that?"

"Probably a little less." Franchitti grimaced. "We nearly lost him, but the doctors say he's responding well to the quick heal. Better than they expected, actually." His mouth twisted. "This is the first time he's been injured badly enough to need it."

He did not, Ostapenko noticed, offer a progress report on his daughter.

"In that case, I think the thing for us to do is a little preliminary exploration of that plea deal Tucker's offering in your case. We can probably get that nailed down between now and the arraignment. Ralph's case is more complicated, though. I'll need to get with him and hear his side of things before we make any decisions about that."

For all the good it's going to do, he carefully did not add aloud.

"In the meantime, and I know it's going to be hard, given your obvious feelings, it's important you keep a low profile about this."

Protest flickered in Franchitti's eyes, and Ostapenko raised one hand to wave an index finger.

"Listen to me on this one, Jordan. The only thing venting about this on your part is likely to do is to prejudice your case and Ralph's. You're a prominent member of the community—a First Waver and a baron—and you've got a lot of friends and, frankly, people who owe you favors. If you go around talking to them about this, it could be a serious problem if this comes down to a jury trial. Anything you said might be considered an attempt to prejudice the jury pool, and that will definitely weigh against you. And to be honest, that's not the worst that could happen. If Tucker decides he needs to apply for a change of venue *because* the jury pool's been prejudiced, the case will probably be moved to Landing, where any jury's likely to be a lot less sympathetic to Ralph's actions throughout this thing. The people who live there aren't farmers or hunters anymore. They don't spend as much time around guns as we do, and they're likely to be prejudiced in favor of the animals Trudy was trying to keep Ralph from shooting."

Especially, he thought, *the video of that female treecat holding the dead one and wailing.*

Franchitti glowered at him, but then, finally, he nodded.

"And stay far away from Jones," Ostapenko added. "Don't forget, that's one of the conditions Judge Pender imposed when she granted bail. If you violate it, she *will* put you back in cells until your arraignment. And might very well refuse to sign off on any plea deal with Tucker. She's not the sort to stand for any nonsense."

"I've got it. I've got it, okay!" Franchitti said. "The little bastard's going to get away with it and I can't even punch him in the mouth. Or not yet, anyway."

"I didn't hear that," Ostapenko said. "And, frankly, I'd better *not* hear it."

Franchitti snorted harshly, but he also nodded again.

"Good. In that case, there's some paperwork before I formally approach Tucker about the plea bargain."

Ostapenko punched up the forms on his desktop, and Franchitti leaned back in his chair and glowered at the universe in general.

24

JORDAN FRANCHITTI STRODE ANGRILY ALONG BESIDE the bailiff as he was escorted into the courtroom. He looked over his shoulder at a double row of seats occupied by friends and family, and his eyes narrowed as he saw the empty chair beside his wife. Then he stepped through the rail between the gallery and the well and took a seat at one of the counsel tables. The dock, spaced equidistantly between the counsel tables and located directly before the high, elevated judge's bench, was unoccupied, but the dark-haired man already seated at the table stood as he approached.

"Where's Ralph?" Franchitti asked before the lawyer could say a word.

"He'll be here shortly," Ostapenko told him. Someone less irate than Franchitti might have noticed the brief pause before the reply and might even have recognized the irritation behind it. Franchitti, however, had other things on his mind.

"This is all bullshit! I still say I never assaulted that little prick!" he snarled, and Ostapenko sighed.

"We've been over that," he said. "But if you want to withdraw your plea deal, that's fine. We can go to trial. And you'll lose."

This time even Franchitti recognized the sorely tried patience in the attorney's voice. His face darkened and his lips tightened, but then he forced himself to inhale deeply.

"I know. I know!" He waved one hand. "And I know you're right...'under the law.'" His sarcasm was withering. "It is bullshit, but I understand we're minimizing the damage."

Ostapenko nodded. That was one way to describe a misdemeanor conviction as opposed to a felony conviction. And probation as opposed to incarceration. In fact, Ostapenko had been more than a little surprised the Crown had been willing to accept the plea. True, young Zivonik had handled the older Franchitti's attack with humiliating ease, but the fact that Franchitti clearly had intended to erase critical evidence in what could very well have turned into a trial for murder—and made a royal pain out of himself the entire time he'd been in custody—wasn't the sort of thing that usually inclined Tucker—and, more importantly, the no-nonsense judge in charge of the case—toward unmerited clemency.

Of course, there was more than one Franchitti in the mix today, he reminded himself, and looked up as the side door opened and Ralph Franchitti was escorted to the same table by a uniformed sheriff's deputy. Unlike his father, Ralph wore an orange jumpsuit. He was still pale and moved carefully, although after three weeks of quick heal he was well on the way to full recovery from his wounds.

Franchitti glared at the deputy—he seemed to be doing a lot of glaring today—then enveloped his son in a bear hug.

"Ralph," he said. "This is all bullshit."

"I know," Ralph said, but his eyes were shadowed and his face was gaunt. His fingers trembled ever so slightly, and his voice had lost most of the boisterous arrogance it normally shared with his father's.

"Don't worry. I talked to Trudy," Franchitti said. "It'll be okay."

Ralph nodded, but doubt clouded his eyes. Unlike Jordan, he'd been denied bail. Of course, he'd spent all but two days of the three weeks since he'd been shot in the hospital, but after Doctor Flambeau released him from treatment, he'd been moved to the Duvalier County jail and held there. Which was another part of the mountain of bullshit in his father's eyes.

"So when do we get this show on the road?" Franchitti growled, looking back at Ostapenko as he and Ralph seated themselves.

"Won't be long now." Ostapenko glanced at his chrono. "Judge Pender runs a pretty tight courtroom, and—"

"All rise," the bailiff intoned. "The Duvalier District Court is now in session; the Honorable Judge Katie Pender, presiding!"

Ostapenko was already standing. Both Franchittis rose, Jordan with a hand under Ralph's elbow, as if to steady him, as Judge Pender stepped through the doorway to her chambers. She was not much taller than Stephanie Harrington, with a head of flaming red hair, but there was no doubt who was in command here as she seated herself behind the bench. She looked out over the courtroom, then rapped the old-fashioned gavel once, sharply.

"Be seated, please," she said, and shoes and clothing rustled as the spectators in the gallery obeyed the polite command. She let them settle, then glanced at the clerk of court, who'd quietly entered the courtroom at the same time she had and taken a seat at his computer console at the same time the others sat. The clerk looked up and nodded to indicate his readiness, and Pender turned back to the bailiff.

"Call the first case."

"Case Number One-Seven-Three-Two-Four, Your Honor. The Crown versus Jordan Ralph Franchitti, Baron Franchitti. Refusal to obey the lawful instructions of an officer of the Crown."

"Is the accused present?" Pender asked.

"Here, Your Honor," Ostapenko replied, standing once more and laying one hand on the elder Franchitti's shoulder.

"Is the Crown prepared to proceed?"

"We are, Your Honor." Alvin Tucker, the Duvalier County Prosecutor, was a square-shouldered, weathered looking man at least twenty-five centimeters taller than the diminutive judge, with a deep, rumbling voice.

"Very well," Pender said. "Proceed."

"Your Honor, the defendant has chosen to waive trial and plead guilty to the charges specified. Accordingly, the Crown is prepared to recommend probation rather than press for any jail time."

"I see." Pender looked at Ostapenko and Franchitti. "Does the defense concur in the Crown's statement?"

"We do, Your Honor," Ostapenko said.

"Baron Franchitti?"

"I do, Your Honor." Franchitti couldn't keep his angry disgust entirely out of his tone, and Pender's eyes narrowed ever so slightly, but she nodded.

"Very well," she said. "In that case, the Court sentences the defendant to one Sphinxian year of probation and two hundred hours of community service with the Forestry Service."

Franchitti's face darkened. He started to say something, but Ostapenko's hand on his elbow stopped him.

"Is there a problem, Mr. Ostapenko?" Pender asked.

"It was the defense's impression that the Crown intended to ask only for the probation, Your Honor," Ostapenko said after a moment.

"That is correct," Pender replied. "However, having reviewed the case and the evidence, it is the Court's opinion that something more than simple probation is in order."

"If Your Honor is referring to the charges which were dropped—"

"I am not," Pender interrupted him, her gray eyes cold and hard. "As the Crown Prosecutor has dropped those charges in view of the defendant's plea, those actions are not relevant to the Court's decision. What is relevant to the Court's decision is the Court's belief that the defendant did, indeed, intend to erase critical evidence in a possible capital murder trial. This was not a case of someone at a traffic accident arguing with the investigating officer or someone under the influence refusing to comply with his instructions. It was a case of someone who fully intended to deliberately destroy that evidence. As such, the Court feels it is appropriate to require the defendant to spend some time working with law enforcement in order to gain a better understanding—from the inside, as it were—of why his actions were so grossly improper. If he feels the sentence is inappropriate and prefers to go to trial on the assault charge instead, that is, of course, his option."

Ostapenko looked down at his client. Franchitti's jaw clenched and his eyes blazed, but he managed to keep his mouth shut, and the lawyer turned back to the judge.

"Understood, Your Honor. My client has no desire to withdraw his plea."

"Very well. In that case, it is so ordered." Pender's gavel cracked sharply. "Next case, Mr. Bailiff."

"Case Number One-Seven-Three-Two-Five, Your Honor. The Crown versus Jordan Ralph Franchitti, Junior. Brandishing a Weapon, Assault and Battery, Aggravated Assault with Serious Bodily Injury, and Assault with a Deadly Weapon."

Jordan Franchitti stiffened in his chair as the charges were read out.

"Is the accused present?" Pender asked.

"Here, Your Honor," Ostapenko replied.

"Is the Crown prepared to proceed?"

"We are, Your Honor," Tucker rumbled.

"Very well," Pender said. "Proceed."

"Wait a minute!" Franchitti blurted, surging to his feet. "What kind of nonsense is this?!"

"Sit down, Baron Franchitti!" Pender snapped, banging her gavel.

"No! This is bull—nonsense! My son never assaulted that bastard! Never even *touched* him!"

"Baron Franchitti!" Pender cracked in a sharper, angrier voice. *"Sit down!"*

Ostapenko gripped Franchitti's shoulder, urging him back into his chair. For a long, teetering moment, it appeared Franchitti would ignore him. But then he settled slowly back, glaring at the judge.

"Better," Pender said in icy tones. "Be aware that you are perilously close to contempt of court and additional time in jail, Baron!"

Those icy gray eyes held him with frozen contempt for a long, still moment, then turned to Ostapenko.

"Mr. Ostapenko, have you failed to acquaint the accused and his father with the specifics of the charges against him?"

"No, Your Honor. I've acquainted both of them." Ostapenko looked at his senior client with something less than approval. "I have copies of all our correspondence if the Court would care to examine them."

"But that was before—" Franchitti began, then stopped.

He turned his head, glaring at the empty seat beside his wife.

"Yes, Baron Franchitti?" Pender invited.

Franchitti opened his mouth, then closed it again. He sat there for at least thirty seconds, his eyes fiery enough to burn holes in asbestos, then shook his head.

"In that case, may we proceed?" Pender said. "Mr. Prosecutor?"

"Your Honor, the Crown contends that on Eleventh Month, Ninth Day, Year Sixty-Four After Landing, the accused, Jordan Ralph Franchitti, Junior, did knowingly and intentionally—"

Trudy Franchitti's uni-link chimed.

She looked down at it, and her mouth tightened in distaste, not surprise, as she saw the caller ID.

"Well, he's out of the courtroom," she said, and Nosey's arm tightened around her as they sat on the couch together with Dulcinea curled across both their laps, buzzing a gentle purr.

"You don't have to take the call, sweetheart," he told her. "For that matter, you can let it go to record and view it later."

"No, I knew this was coming." She shook her head. "He couldn't believe I meant what I said. I told him. I told Ostapenko. But despite all that, he *really* thought that at the last minute—"

She cut herself off, pressing her lips firmly together. Then she inhaled deeply and tapped accept.

"Trudy!" her father snapped from the display the instant it came alive. "Where were you? What the hell do you think you're doing?!"

"Exactly what I told you I was going to do," she said flatly.

"Don't you take that tone with me!"

"What tone would that be, Daddy?" she asked. "The 'I don't understand why you can't understand a simple "no" tone?' Or the 'would it be better if I'd just said, "Hell no!" tone'?"

Rage suffused her father's expression.

"You listen to me, Trudy! You march your butt down to that courthouse and withdraw those charges right now, you hear me?!"

"I can tell you no just as many times as you can tell me to do it, Daddy."

Trudy's eyes flashed, and Franchitti's jaw clenched. Up until that very morning, he'd believed—*known*—his daughter would capitulate in the end, just as she always had. That she was only waiting until the charges were read, enjoying the revenge of making Ralph sweat, before she told the judge she'd decided to drop them.

"This is insane!" he barked "He's your own *brother*!"

"He's the sadist who murdered my friend right in front of me and got away with it because the protected species order wasn't promulgated until two days later," Trudy said in a deadly cold voice. "And he's the *brother* who shattered my wrist into fifty-five pieces, fractured my right knee, crushed my right cheekbone with the butt of a shotgun, damaged the retina of my right eye, and probably would've killed *me* if Nosey hadn't stopped him. I hope you're satisfied with the man he's grown into, *Daddy*."

"I—" Franchitti began, then stopped, glaring at her in incredulous fury.

She met his rage with equally powerful, soul-deep anger, and silence hovered for several breaths.

"If you turn against your family—" Franchitti began then.

"Oh, no. You might say I'm *protecting* my family," Trudy interrupted.

"What?!"

"I haven't filed charges against *you*, Daddy," she said, her voice suddenly soft. "Not yet."

"What are you talking about?"

"I never told anyone who gave me all those bruises over the years," she said. "I always said they were from sports injuries. When I dropped sports, if people saw them, I let them think Stan had gotten a little rough. That was unfair to him, really. He only hurt me by accident. *You* did it on purpose."

Franchitti's silence was louder than any shout.

"I have images," she told him almost dreamily. "I'm a girl. Remember how you always reminded me of that? A stupid, empty headed, sniveling girl too dumb to come in out of the snow, you said. Among other things. Well, 'girls' keep diaries, Daddy. So I did. And I took selfies. Years and years of selfies."

"Faked—altered," Franchitti croaked, looking like someone who'd thought he was hunting range bunnies only to see a hexapuma explode from the burrow.

"No, they aren't, and forensics will prove it."

Her father stared at her, then squared his shoulders.

"You listen to me," he said. "If you don't drop the charges against your brother, or if you try to pass off all this . . . ridiculous nonsense to anyone, I'll—your brother—will file charges against your precious boyfriend for attempted murder!"

"The Prosecutor and the courts have already determined it was a legitimate use of deadly force, Daddy. Or did you miss that bit?"

"Then I'll sue his ass!" Franchitti barked. "I'll drag him in front of a civil jury and sue him for everything he's got or ever will have!"

"And you'll lose," Trudy said. "I've already discussed it with Nosey's attorney. No charges were brought against him, but Ralph's been charged with threatening *him* with a deadly weapon, and you and I both know the evidence will sustain that charge. His conviction—and he *will* be convicted, Daddy—will grant Nosey immunity from any civil charges you might want to bring."

"You don't know that—*any* of that!"

"You won't be able to change reality to suit you, Daddy. Not this time. But you go right ahead and try. And when you do, I *will* file charges against you for battery and child abuse. And for *spousal* abuse, as well."

Her blue eyes met his lethally with the last sentence.

"What are you talking about now?" Franchitti demanded, but something flickered in the depths of his own eyes.

"You know exactly what I'm talking about. You're not going to use her for a punching bag anymore, either. And I'll know if you try to."

"You'll never see your mother again, if I have any say in the matter!" he snapped.

"Oh, yes I will," Trudy told him coldly. "I'll be screening her regularly. And if she doesn't take my calls, or if I see any sign you've been beating on her again, I'll ask my law officer friends to execute a wellness check."

"On what possible pretext?"

"I did mention my diary, didn't I, Daddy?" He paled. "Well, there are entries about Mom in it, too. And the photos I took after some of her 'accidental falls.' I know she never had the courage to tell anyone how you treated her out there, all alone, where no one—no one *else*—could hear you screaming at her. But I knew. I *always* knew.

"And if I ever have any reason to so much as *suspect* you've laid another finger on her, I'll drag the great Baron Franchitti back into court and see you convicted as the kind of cowardly monster who beats little girls until they're black and blue and punches his wife if she does anything he doesn't like. And, by the way, I already checked with Doctor Flambeau. He went back through all my medical records from before the air car accident with Stan. He's prepared to testify that, now that he knows to look for it, he's found—and documented—clinical evidence that would substantiate my allegations that those 'sports injuries' your little girl suffered for so many years were nothing of the sort. You might want to think about that, too, *Daddy*."

"So you truly are turning on your own family!"

"No, I'm walking away from what *should* have been my family. Because you always kept it from being that, really, didn't you? But I finally know what a family is supposed to be...despite you."

Franchitti glared at her for a long, ferocious moment. Then the display blanked abruptly, and Trudy sighed. Her taut shoulders relaxed, and she leaned back, pressing the side of her head against Nosey's shoulder. Dulcinea rose in their laps, sitting upright to bump her head under Trudy's chin, and Trudy ran a hand gently down the 'cat's spine.

"It's not really the end, you know," Nosey said. "With family, there is no end. For better or worse, they're still family. Even if they only live in the back of your head."

"It probably isn't," Trudy acknowledged. "But there's a lot of other stuff living in the back of my head where he's concerned that I'm going to have to deal with, too. And chromosomes and genes aren't what really make a family." She turned her head on his shoulder to kiss his cheek gently. "You've helped me figure that out. Thank you for being you, Nosey Jones."

"Hey," he brushed his lips across her hair, "it's what I'm here for. And whatever else it is, it's also a beginning. Now it's you and me and Dulcinea...."

"And soon," Trudy kissed him again while Dulcinea's purr buzzed louder and happier, "kittens will make seven!"

25

"ANY THOUGHTS ABOUT WHAT YOU WANT TO DO for your birthday this year, Stephanie?" Marjorie Harrington asked. She and Stephanie were in one of the Harringtons' extensive greenhouses, picking a mixture of native and Terran imported greens to go in that night's salad. As usual, at least part of dinner would be an experiment, since Marjorie used her family to taste-test new finds and hybrids. "This year the weather's still pretty cold, so we can't do a big outdoor bash like last year."

Stephanie placed some leaves of a new variety of lace lettuce in a basket.

"I'd love to have a party, especially after being away for so long. And especially 'cause everyone's gonna feel the need for a break after Ralph Franchitti's trial wraps up, I sure *hope* it'll have wrapped up by then, anyway!"

"I'm pretty sure it will have." There was immense satisfaction in Marjorie's voice. "Judge Pender's only scheduled two days for testimony, since there are only three witnesses, and that video imagery is totally conclusive evidence, you know. I don't think any 'jury of his peers' will be able to look at that and not decide pretty darn quick, so I'll be astonished if it's not over by the end of the week."

"I think you're probably right," Stephanie agreed, "and I have been thinking about who to invite. And I've at least touched base with a lot of my Twin Forks area friends, but what with getting caught up with classes, then stuff for the SFS, I haven't had time to see people like Xadrian."

Marjorie smiled.

"Just remember, we do have indoor room for a fairly large party, and we can fold down the snow porch panels on the patio for overflow. Still, I think it would be wise to limit the guest list a bit."

"Well...Let's see, not only does Xadrian love a party, she's really a lot of fun. If we moved some of the furniture in the living room, we could even have dancing."

"We could do that, or we could use the dining room for dancing." Marjorie tapped her chin with a dirty fingertip, leaving a smudge. "We could set up refreshments in the kitchen. People always end up in the kitchen anyhow."

"Or what about the patio for dancing and the living room for just visiting?" Stephanie said. "The furniture there's our most lounge-worthy, anyhow. And maybe we could open up that room we've talked about making into a home office, and put some games or puzzles in there."

"Sounds good," Marjorie agreed. "What do you think about some team activities? Design teams that include people who don't know each other well, so we don't end up with anyone feeling left out?"

"I like it...Maybe start with that, and save dancing for later, when the ice is broken."

Later, when Stephanie started making her list, she began with the members of the Great Treecat Conspiracy. Of course, Irina would come with Scott. And since the GTC included both Nosey and Trudy after the disaster on the Franchitti claim, both of them obviously had to be on the list.

Still sorta amazing how much I actually want to invite Trudy. I would even if she wasn't dating Nosey, after the way she's stood up to Ralph and her father! I never would have thought she and I could ever be friends, but now I think we may end up almost as close as me and Jess!

Hmmmm... Since I'm inviting Cordelia, maybe I should add her "brothers," Mack and Zack? They're right about Karl's age, just a little older than me. What about Karl's sister, Dia? That would mean inviting Loon Villaroy, too. I don't know him that well, but if I'm going to be "seeing" Karl, I'd better remember he comes with a lot of other people. If I invite Dia, I should probably invite Cordy's sister, Natalie. They're good buddies. But maybe I should make their age the cutoff for the younger kids.

Then there was Toby from the hang-gliding club. She hadn't really had a chance to catch up with him since she'd been back. He always seemed to be working. Oh! And she couldn't forget Chet and Christine.

How many people should she include from the SFS? Ainsley and Frank, definitely, and Chief Shelton. And Dr. Hobbard, if she was on-planet. Of course, they were also members in good standing of the GTC now, too. It would be nice to invite Moriah and Stephan, too, but maybe inviting them could wait until later in the spring, when the party could be moved outside. That might be more fun for the kids.

Stephanie looked over to where Lionheart was drowsing draped over one of the cushions on her bed.

"I just realized that I'm thinking about having a

party for no reason other than it would be fun. That's a change, isn't it?"

Lionheart opened one leaf green eye, rolled onto his back, and fell asleep again.

Stephanie laughed, and went back to making lists.

26

"WELL, THIS IS ONE PATIENT WHO'S DOING *EXTREMELY* well, I think," Richard Harrington said, and smiled at Nosey and Trudy across the examining table while he rubbed Dulcinea's ears and she pressed back against his palm. "So far as I can tell, mother and babies are doing just fine, although I think we have a T-week or more than I'd originally estimated till arrival time. She's handling the supplements all right?"

"I don't think she much cares for the vitamins, actually," Nosey confessed. The vitamins in question were Sphinxian analogues, not the Terrestrial version Sphinx's human interlopers required. "She understands we want her to take them because they're good for her, but it's not real high on her list."

Dulcinea looked up at him from the table and bleeked, and Trudy chuckled.

"Fortunately, she's just as greedy where celery is

343

concerned as any of the other 'cats," she said. "So we just sprinkle it on a stalk and she swallows it right down."

"We're not really supposed to bribe our patients to take their meds," Richard said, trying to keep a straight face in the process.

"Oh, don't go there, Doctor Harrington!" Trudy shook her head. "I know *exactly* how many pill pockets you've issued me for patients at Wild and Free!"

"Yes, but those aren't for our *sapient* patients," Richard replied in a more serious tone, and Trudy nodded soberly.

Her inclusion in the Great Treecat Conspiracy was barely a single T-month old, but she'd embraced it enthusiastically. In fact, Richard thought, she'd seen it as part of that new family she was building. His own mood darkened, and his fingers stroked Dulcinea's silken pelt gently, as he thought about all Trudy had endured. About all he hadn't realized she was enduring. Intellectually, he knew it wasn't his fault he hadn't guessed the truth about all those "sports injuries" and "accidental falls." All her excuses had been reasonable enough, and God knew falls in Sphinx gravity produced pretty spectacular bruising! But whatever his intellect told him, his heart would never forgive him for not having put two and two together, especially given Jordan Franchitti's personality.

"Actually, we're not 'tricking' her at all, honey," Nosey put in. "I guess pill pockets are kind of sneaky, since the idea is that the poor critter won't even realize it's being medicated. But *this* little lady"—he reached down and lifted a purring Dulcinea into his arms, and she rubbed her muzzle against his cheek—"understands what we're doing perfectly well. So it's just like that old nursery song my mom used to sing me."

"Nursery song?" Trudy looked at him intently, and he touched her cheek with one hand.

"Nursery song," he repeated. "Don't worry. She's already promised to send you a whole raft of them, sweetheart."

"Good!" Trudy said, reaching up to cover his hand with her own, and her eyes had softened. There'd been very few "nursery songs" in Trudy's childhood, just as there'd been very few fairytales. That was an omission she fully intended to repair in *her* children's lives.

"Which one were you thinking about, Nosey?" Richard asked in a tone that deliberately failed to notice the look in her eyes.

"'A Spoonful of Sugar,'" Nosey said. "As in, 'a spoonful of sugar helps the medicine go down.'"

"Wiser words were never spoken," Richard agreed. "In fact—"

"Excuse me, Doctor," Keagan Henson interrupted over the examining room intercom, "but you have a com call. From off-planet."

"Off-planet?" Richard frowned. "Who is it?"

"I'm afraid I don't know," Henson replied. "It's from *Vulcan*, but I don't recognize the com combination and nothing's coming up on caller ID. I can take the call and find out, if you'd like?"

"No, that's okay. I'm just about done here, anyway. My patient is disgustingly healthy, and her pets are about to take her home."

"I am *not* Dulcinea's pet, Doc!" Nosey protested.

"Then tell me that with a straight face," Richard shot back, and grinned as Nosey chuckled. "See? You can't. Because just like Steph, you know the truth, whether you'll admit it or not!"

"Guilty—guilty!" Nosey conceded, and tucked an arm around Trudy as they headed for the door.

Richard smiled as he watched them go, then walked down the short hallway to his own office. The attention light on his com display blinked at him as he seated himself behind his desk, and his smile segued into a frown, because he didn't recognize the com combination, either. Of course, there were a lot of people in the universe who'd never called him before, he told himself with a snort, although why any of them would be calling him from what was turning into Sphinx's primary orbital platform eluded him. There was only one way to find out, though, and he touched the acceptance key.

A face appeared on his display, and Richard Harrington abruptly sat back in his chair in disbelief.

"Well," the man on his com said with a chuckle, "it looks like I've finally managed to startle you into silence, Richard!"

"So what's this all about, do you think?" Karl asked as the SFS cruiser settled toward the Harrington parking apron.

"And what makes you think I might have any better idea about 'this,' whatever 'this' is, than you do?" Stephanie shot back. "If I were younger and still staying home more, I'd've figured somebody had brought in a really interesting critter that needed some home care and Daddy was bringing him home for me to administer it." She sighed. "Actually, I kind of miss that. I think I envy Trudy a little bit because she gets to do so much of it with Wild and Free."

"Hey, we have to give up some things to do the ones that are more important," Karl told her, and leaned over to kiss her cheek lightly as he powered down the cruiser. "It's kind of like pushing the fledgling out of the nest, although your folks and mine have been a lot gentler about it than, say, a silver hawk. But if it's not that, what is it?"

"There you go again, assuming I'm psychic or something! If I were, we wouldn't need the GTC, now would we?"

Stephanie shook her head and opened her side of the canopy, and Karl grinned at her.

"Depends on what kind of psychic you were. I mean, if you were what's-her-name—Cassandra, that's who I'm thinking of—you'd know exactly what to do and nobody would pay you any attention!"

"I'm sure there's a reason I love you," she told him, "but just this minute, it seems to have slipped my mind."

"I'm sure it will come back to you again later."

"You go right on thinking that," she said, and linked arms with him so she could lay the side of her head against his shoulder. Well, against his biceps, actually, given the difference in their heights.

"I believe I will," he replied, bending his head to kiss her curls.

"Behave yourself, Mr. Zivonik!" Her severity was somewhat undermined by the gurgle of laughter which accompanied it.

They continued across the apron to the side door, accompanied by Lionheart and Survivor, and Marjorie Harrington opened it as they stepped up onto the snow porch.

"Took you guys long enough," she said. "I expected you at least fifteen or twenty minutes ago."

"Took a little longer than usual to sign off the end of shift paperwork," Karl replied, and Marjorie's eyebrows rose at his curiously satisfied tone.

"And why would that be?" she asked.

"Because day after tomorrow is Ralph Franchitti's sentencing," Stephanie replied. "You were right about how long the jury would need, Mom. Took them about three hours to find him guilty on all counts. That won't be announced until Judge Pender sentences him, though. She asked Karl and me to submit our own 'impact' statements on Fuzzy Friend's murder—from the perspective of the Forestry Service, now that the 'cats are officially a protected species, not just because we've both been adopted by treecats."

"Does Trudy know yet?"

"I don't think so," Karl replied, glancing at Stephanie who shook her own head. "I think they're probably telling her and Nosey first thing tomorrow. I know she's already written her victim impact statement. With a little help from Sphinx's leading journalist, I suspect."

"Well, good for them! Come on in, both of you."

"What's this big surprise of Daddy's?" Stephanie asked as she and Karl followed Marjorie into the house. "For that matter, where *is* Daddy? I didn't see his air car out there."

"He didn't tell me what the 'surprise' is, either," Marjorie said. "My first thought was that he's come up with some kind of special birthday present for you, but it's still four days till your birthday, and I don't see him pulling up the curtain for the big reveal this soon, do you?"

"Daddy?" Stephanie laughed. "I don't think there's anybody in the entire galaxy better at keeping his surprises hidden until exactly the right minute. Or what *he* thinks is exactly the right minute, anyway!"

"He does have a sometimes...questionable sense of timing—and humor—doesn't he?" Marjorie agreed affably. "Which, I might point out, is apparently hereditary."

Stephanie rounded her eyes innocently, and her mother laughed.

"Come on into the kitchen. I've got dinner in the oven and, by the strangest coincidence, I happen to have an entire platter of fudge brownies that are still warm and just a little gooey."

"Great!"

Stephanie grinned and made a beeline for the kitchen.

"Hey! I get at least *one*!" Karl called as he followed her.

"If you snooze, you lose!" she replied, and Marjorie shook her head.

"Good luck, Karl! You'll need it."

In point of fact, Karl got no less than three of the brownies, which given Marjorie Harrington's Meyerdahlian idea of portion sizes, were more than enough. His diminutive girlfriend, on the other hand, devoured six of them and looked wistfully around for more.

"You gotta have somewhere to put supper," Karl told her severely.

"But that won't be for *at least*...I dunno, thirty minutes *after* Daddy gets home," Stephanie replied plaintively. "I'm likely to faint from starvation before then!"

Lionheart and Survivor bleeked with laughter from their perches, and Stephanie shook an index finger at them.

"Don't you mock my famished, weakened condition while the two of you sit there stuffing your faces with celery!" she told them, but they only bleeked more loudly, and Karl shook his head.

"I think you'll survive just fine. In fact, I'm starting to be a little suspicious about just how critically necessary it is to stoke your metabolism and how much of this is that you just have the Star Kingdom' worst sweet tooth."

"Could be both, I guess," Stephanie said in the judicious tone of someone trying to be completely fair. "I mean, both of them are true, after all."

Karl shook his head again and poured her another glass of milk.

"Here. Stave off starvation."

"Oh, thank you! My hero!"

"Yeah, sure!"

"Well—"

"Your dad's home!" Marjorie called from the living

room, and Karl and Stephanie climbed off their kitchen stools and trotted across the house to join her. A minute or two later, the snow porch's outer door opened and closed, and then the front door swung open.

"What's all the mystery, Richard?" Marjorie demanded, her tone just a tad suspicious, as her husband walked through the door without bothering to close it behind him.

"No mystery," he said innocently. "I just thought you and Steph would like to know we've got a visitor."

"A visitor?" Marjorie repeated in an even more suspicious tone.

"Of course!" Richard stood beside her and turned to face the door. "I think it's safe now!" he called.

"If you're sure," a deep voice replied, and Marjorie's eyes widened in delight as someone else stepped through the door.

He looked, Stephanie realized, a great deal like her father. In fact, he could have been Richard Harrington's taller brother, except for the beard. He was at least a centimeter or two taller even than Karl, and if she imagined him *without* the beard—

"Duncan?!"

It came out in something far more like a squeal than Stephanie was accustomed to hearing from her mother, and Marjorie flung herself forward, wrapping her arms around the newcomer.

Stephanie blinked, taken aback by her mother's reaction, but only until her own memories overcame the sheer surprise of seeing someone who couldn't possibly be here.

"Uncle Duncan?" she said suddenly. "What're *you* doing here?!"

"At the moment, trying to survive your mother's welcome, Peanut," he told her with a laugh, freeing one arm to hold out a hand to her, and Stephanie grinned as she scampered toward him. "I'm a little surprised you remember me," he continued. "You were only—what? Nine?"

"Ten," she corrected him severely.

"Oh, forgive me! One of the first things to go when you get to be my age is your memory. Especially for things like numbers."

"Yeah, sure!"

Stephanie smiled up at him, and he squeezed her hand, then tucked her in at his side with her mother. He was tall enough he could hug both of them, and she shook her head in wonder.

Duncan Harrington was actually her first cousin once removed, but given the difference in their ages, she'd always called him "Uncle."And he'd been the only person on all of Meyerdahl who called *her* "Peanut," because—as he had explained to her *very* seriously when she was about five—she was no bigger than a peanut and unlikely to make it to walnut size. He was also quite possibly the most brilliant man she'd ever met *and* the xeno-anthropologist who'd powerfully nourished her need to understand other creatures and other societies.

She leaned against him, beaming up at him, and as the sheer surprise faded, she realized that if there was one person in the entire galaxy she could have transported to Sphinx on the wings of a wish, she was hugging him at that very instant.

"So when the Prometheus Foundation approached the University with the suggestion we offer our assistance to the Star Kingdom, they decided that since I was related to the treecats' discoverer, I was the logical choice. Needless to say, I explained to them at length why it would be totally inconvenient and out of the question."

Duncan smiled wickedly across the table at Marjorie as

she shook her fist at him. The remnants of a Harrington-sized dinner lay strewn across that table like a vanquished army, and all three Harringtons and Karl sat nursing after-dinner coffee.

"Seriously," Duncan continued, "I jumped at the chance, for obvious reasons. I'd read everything you sent me, Richard, and it was fascinating. But I didn't see any way I'd be able to get out here on my own. Until Portnoy at the Foundation—you remember him, don't you?"

"Abner Portnoy?"

"That's him. Apparently, the Foundation picked up on the Star Kingdom's request for assistance. I know the Whitaker Expedition did some pretty heavy lifting, but from a couple of the things you had to say, Richard, and given my own ineffable paranoia, I sort of suspect that recognizing treecats as fully sapient won't be entirely welcome in some quarters. I'm not trying to insult your new star nation when I say that, either. But humans are humans, and, unfortunately, we don't have the universe's best record for dealing equitably with indigenous peoples or species. From what I know of the Star Kingdom, I wouldn't expect a repeat of the Amphors, but that doesn't mean a lot of less terrible but still bad things couldn't happen. So when Portnoy convinced the University to give me a three-T-year sabbatical and let the Foundation fund my travel expenses, I jumped at it. After all," he smiled across the table at Stephanie, "I can't let anything bad happen to the Peanut's discovery. Especially"—his eyes moved to the two treecats in their highchairs between Stephanie and Karl—"now that I've met them."

Stephanie looked at Karl, and her eyes were bright. Neither of them was about to bring Duncan fully into their confidence until they'd had a chance to talk it over with the other Conspirators. But the thought of how this might affect their plans sent ripples of excitement through her, and she recognized his matching eagerness.

She glanced at Lionheart. Of course, neither he nor Survivor could begin to visualize what a powerful ally someone with Duncan Harrington's credentials and towering academic reputation could be, but the 'cat's relaxed body language, the set of his ears, told her that he, too, approved of Duncan. And when she thought about how Dr. Hobbard would react to his arrival...

"The really hard part," Duncan continued, "was getting my tickets and planning my connections to get me here by the Peanut's birthday. For a while there, I didn't think I was going to make it, but here I am."

"Yes, you are," Stephanie told him. "And if my fairy godmother had given me one wish for a birthday present, you'd have been it, Uncle Duncan. I've never been so happy to see someone in my entire life. Well, except for Karl, but he's got an unfair advantage."

"And I am honored to come in second to such competition," Duncan told her. "But trust me, anything I can do to help you or your friends"—he twitched his head at the treecats—"is yours, Stephanie. Anything."

<I have seldom tasted such happiness from Death Fang's Bane,> Keen Eyes said as he and Climbs Quickly nibbled their after-dinner celery.

<Nor have I,> Climbs Quickly agreed. *<Clearly this is another elder of Death Fang's Bane's Clan. And from their surprise at his arrival, he must have come from very far away. It would seem there are even more worlds beyond ours than we had guessed!>*

<I suspect it will take us quite some time to learn all of the two-legs' surprises,> Keen Eyes said dryly, and Climbs Quickly bleeked a quiet laugh.

<No! Do you really? Why, I believed we would have them all figured out by next green leaf days!>

<Of course you did.> Keen Eyes flipped his ears at his friend, then looked back at the two-leg newcomer. <What do you think of Far Traveler's mind-glow?>

<A good name for him,> Climbs Quickly approved, and turned his own gaze upon the two-leg. <It is very strong, his mind-glow. Almost as bright as Death Fang's Bane's. And I can taste the depth of his joy at being here, with these two-legs he loves so much. It is very focused, too. I think he is a hunter who will run down any prey whose scent he catches. But there is something....>

His mind-voice trailed off, and Keen Eyes tasted the intensity of his thoughts. Several moments passed, and then Climbs Quickly flicked his ears again.

<There is some tiny edge of unhappiness in his mind-glow. It is very small—small enough I think, perhaps, it is hidden even from him. Yet it is there, and I think it is somehow bound up in his heart with Death Fang's Bane.>

<I had not considered that,> Keen Eyes replied. <I do not think I have seen as deeply into his mind-glow as you have—you are more sensitive to the two-legs' mind-glows in general than I—but I had tasted some trace of darkness. I had not thought of unhappiness, and certainly not because of Death Fang's Bane. His love for her—for all of her family—burns too brightly for that to have occurred to me.>

<I am not certain that it is,> Climbs Quickly acknowledged, <and even among the People it is sometimes difficult to determine—even for oneself—why one feels what one feels. But that is how it tastes to me.>

<But why should he feel unhappy now that he is here, with her?>

<If I could answer that question, we would know far more about the two-legs than we do, would we not?>

Climbs Quickly said wryly. <*Of course, we do not know how long he will be able to remain here on our world. Perhaps what he feels is regret because he knows he must eventually depart and once more leave the ones he loves so dearly?*>

<*I suppose that might explain it,*> Keen Eyes said. <*But if that is true, then I hope he and Death Fang's Bane take all the joy they can of one another while he is here!*>

27

THE MORNING OF STEPHANIE'S SEVENTEENTH BIRTHDAY
dawned clear and bright—and, for Karl, awash with terror. It turned out that *deciding* to propose on Stephanie's
birthday had been the easy part. He'd spent the last several
weeks anguishing over just the right moment to bring
out the ring and present his carefully prepared speech.

Before the party or after? Or during? He'd ditched
the last option pretty fast, after Stephanie made some
scathing comments about "public pressure proposals,"
when a popular sports star on Manticore had proposed
to his girlfriend in front of a live audience.

"What's she going to say? 'No?' 'I need time to think?'
That's a power play, not a marriage proposal."

But if Karl asked before the party, and Stephanie
turned him down, then that would put a damper on
the celebration. But if he asked before the party and she
said "Yes," then they could share the good news with the

couple dozen of their closest friends who were attending the party. On the other hand, they could share the news after the party, too. That would be useful in another way. After they told one or two people, the word would get out. Even the Great Treecat Conspirators weren't immune to the delight of happy gossip.

Once Karl had decided he would wait to propose after the party, he realized he'd need at least a little gift for Stephanie, or she was either going to feel hurt *or* start wondering if he had a surprise planned. More likely the latter, since she wasn't into self-aggrandizing drama, but was definitely alert to conspiracies. He'd commissioned a watercolor of Lionheart amid the celery from Zack Kemper, which—despite Zack's self-criticism on matters of perspective and worry he'd gotten the "hands" wrong—was actually terrific.

Karl neatly wrapped the picture and carried the package down to breakfast with the Harringtons on the morning of the Big Day. Stephanie was already in the kitchen, helping her mother set up trays for toasting one of the Harrington's super-secret snack mixes. Marjorie was up on a stool, digging through a cabinet.

"I can't believe I forgot the Rex Bites!"

"Mom, we can do without them," Stephanie reassured her. "It's not as if we haven't got tons of other snacks. And I outgrew my dinosaur thing back before we left Meyerdahl."

"We've had Rex Mix for every one of your birthdays," Marjorie protested. "It would be bad luck to not have it this year. But, sheesh, I would forget a key ingredient for something that has to be made in advance."

"We could get it," Karl offered.

"Would you?" Marjorie's relief seemed out of proportion. "Richard took Duncan in to tour the clinic this morning, but now they're both out on an emergency call in exactly the wrong direction, or I'd ask him to pick it up, since he's coming home for lunch—or that's the plan."

"If Dad's out," Stephanie countered, "I should stay and help you. Or maybe Jess could come out early and bring the Rex. Wait, she's at the hospital this morning. Maybe Cordelia..."

"We'll go," Karl interrupted, wondering if Marjorie might somehow have guessed about his own plans for the day, and Stephanie relented.

"Okay, Karl and I will go. After breakfast. We can stop at the Red Letter Café to pick up the cupcakes, too. Save Mr. Flint from needing to send a delivery."

"Wonderful! I'll screen Eric, then put the order in for the Rex. Try to be back for lunch, okay? I thought we'd have a little family celebration before tonight's bash."

After Marjorie had had bustled off, Karl extended his gift.

"Hey, want to open my present, or wait until we're back?"

"I'll open it now." Stephanie put down the carton of eggs and accepted the gift. "We did say 'no presents' on the invite, after all."

"But boyfriends are special."

"Mine certainly is," Stephanie replied solemnly.

Zack's painting was a complete success, and after breakfast the two piled into Karl's air car and headed toward Twin Forks. When they were out of sight of the Harrington house, Stephanie started laughing.

"My mom is so hopeless sometimes, isn't she?"

"What do you mean?"

"Well, she's got a daughter who's bonded to a telempath, but she still tries to fool me into believing she doesn't have an ulterior motive for getting me out of the way."

"To be fair," Karl said, "maybe she thought all you'd feel was her excitement."

"But you got it, too, didn't you? That sense she was planning something?"

"Well, sure," Karl said, "but it's a birthday. Surprises are part of the fun, even when the kid is nearly all grown up."

"I wonder what they're going to get me?" Stephanie speculated. "It has to be something that's hard to hide or they wouldn't have to chase me off while it's delivered."

She shook her head, thinking hard, then shrugged.

"I guess I'll find out when I find out," she said philosophically. "And I didn't have the heart to tell her I'd guessed she was planning something. Not when it was obviously so important to her. Seriously, though, it's *really* tough to surprise someone who's been adopted by a 'cat, isn't it?"

"We manage," Karl reminded her, and she grinned at him.

"We do," she agreed.

"And I bet I could even hide a secret from you," Karl dared her.

"Oh, yeah?"

Karl put the air car on hover. This wasn't how he'd planned it, but it felt right. He dipped his hand in his jacket pocket, turned her to face him.

"Stephanie Elizabeth Harrington, would you marry me?"

Her deep brown eyes widened, huge and dark with an emotion he couldn't quite parse. Excitement, yes. And genuine surprise. But something else, as well. Something that might have been doubt or even...fear. But surely it wasn't! It couldn't be...could it?

He wanted to look at Lionheart or Survivor, read her reaction in their body language, but he kept his eyes steadfastly on hers as he put a finger on her lips and got the ring box out with his free hand.

"Yes. I'm serious. I've never been more serious. You

don't need to answer right away. I haven't told anyone except my mom. She warned me not to pressure you, so I'm not. You can take your time. But I wanted you to know I'm serious. I want to be with you for now, for aways, for as much forever as we get."

Karl had been prepared for a lot of things. Excitement. Refusal. A request for time to think, because they'd hardly been dating at all yet. What he hadn't expected was for Stephanie to burst into tears. Not sad tears, the high, happy purr buzzing out of Lionheart told him that! No, this was a dam breaking.

Stephanie flung herself into his arms, the legendary Harrington strength knocking the wind out of him. Karl managed to get one arm around her, closing his fingers around the ring box. Dropping it would be seriously unromantic. There were several minutes of kisses and inarticulate not-quite words, then Stephanie pulled back so she could look into his face.

"You're serious. I know you are but...Now? I thought maybe..."

"I don't want to play pretend, Steph. I'd get married tomorrow, except that then everyone would probably think we're being impulsive, but you know my heart, and I think I know yours, and I don't want to waste time on games. I thought about a promise ring, but you don't break promises and neither do I, so I thought..."

He shrugged, all the words he'd been carefully planning these last several months washed away by the tears that still sparkled on her lashes. Stephanie grinned at him, all imp now.

"And if I said 'yes,' but I want to take it slow, not because I have doubts, but because I don't want to rush all the 'firsts,' what would you say?"

Karl tousled her hair just as he had since she was much smaller.

"I'd say that sounds like fun. Isn't there a saying about anticipation sweetening the meal or something? My only question is do you want to keep this between just us, or would you like this ring?" He managed to get the ring box open without letting go of her. "It was my grandmother's, but we had it resized, and cleaned."

It was a lovely ring, rose gold with a deep green emerald set low in the band. It fit perfectly...and looked very good on Stephanie's hand.

"I picked this ring," Karl said, "because the setting is nice and sturdy. Fit for my lady of adventure."

"And the stone is almost the color of Lionheart's eyes," Stephanie said, tilting her hand back and forth to admire the sparkle. "I'd like to have it now."

"That's terrific."

He closed her fingers around the ring and gave her—his fiancée!—a kiss.

<*I wonder if Death Fang's Bane truly needs the flying thing,*> Keen Eyes thought dryly as Shining Sunlight turned back to the task of directing it to its destination. <*I think she could fly all the way to Bright Water's nesting place without her folding flying thing!*>

<*It is so good to taste her happiness,*> Climbs Quickly replied. <*She cares so deeply and she gives so much, and she worries. Worries about us and all the People, even if we do not know exactly why. To see her so wrapped in joy fills my heart like sunlight. Indeed,*> Keen Eyes tasted his amusement, <*it is hard to keep my own true-feet upon the ground when she soars so high!*>

<*I am not surprised,*> Keen Eyes said. <*And from the taste of their mind-glows, I think they have taken another step in whatever it is two-legs do when they decide to mate. I wonder how much longer this will take?*>

<*They* are *rather . . . slow about it, aren't they?*> Climbs Quickly replied with a ripple of laughter. <*Walks from Shadow and Protector were far speedier than they!*>

<*Be patient,*> Keen Eyes mock-scolded. <*The poor things are mind-blind! They cannot simply taste one another's mind-glows and know they are meant to be bonded for life. Even though*>—his mind-voice was gentle—<*that is exactly what they are.*>

The rest of the flight to Twin Forks and back again was enveloped in a happy glow as Stephanie slid her seat as close to Karl's as its track allowed so that she could lean her head on his shoulder. The arm he wrapped around her felt incredibly good as she nestled against him, and from Survivor and Lionheart's quiet, endless purring they felt almost as happy for their people as she did.

It had truly been a week for surprises, she thought happily. She didn't know what her parents were up to, but she had a suspicion. If she was right, it was something she'd looked forward to for a long time, and she intended to be just as joyous about it as they deserved. But the truth was that Karl had just given her the only gift that could have been even better than Duncan's arrival just when she and the GTC needed him worst.

Sometimes, she thought, the world was very, very good.

28

AN ALREADY REMARKABLE BIRTHDAY JUST KEPT GET-
ting better, Stephanie thought. Her parents, once again
demonstrating what superior parents they were, had,
indeed, bought her an air car of her very own. It wasn't
brand-new, but the Tristram Aeronautics Sabre was in
excellent condition. It was also fast, nimble, and her
favorite deep royal blue in color. And to make it even
better, they'd installed a treecat-sized seat with its own
safety harness between the front bucket seats.

Her first flight had been little more than a circuit of
the freehold, but she'd been delighted with the Sabre's
agility and responsiveness. Of course she'd had to promise
she'd be careful with it, at least until she and it grew
accustomed to one another, but she was fine with that.

In fact—

"Stephanie!" Duncan Harrington called from the
front of the house. "Are you expecting a delivery? I think
there's a van pulling up out front."

Stephanie ran from the kitchen to look out the front door. There was, indeed, a van on the apron. Painted on the side was: "Heart of Cheese," the name of Cordelia's small company.

"Oh, she better not have..." Stephanie said, trailing off in dismay.

"Better not what?" Duncan asked, and Stephanie turned to him.

"Cordy said she was going to give me a pair of capri-cows for my birthday," she said. "I told her absolutely not. None of us are home enough to give dairy animals proper attention."

"Then she probably didn't," Duncan said with a smile. "Not if she's as good a friend as I think she is from the way you talked about her last night!"

Stephanie nodded to show she was listening, but her attention was fixed on the new arrivals. The doors of the passenger compartment had popped open, and people came spilling out like some sort of circus trick. There was Cordelia and her treecat, Athos; then her sister, Natalie; then the two Kemper boys. And lastly, wonder of wonders, especially emerging from such an essentially rural vehicle, there stepped the elegantly androgynous figure of Xadrian.

Xadrian was clad in formfitting violet trousers, a lavender ruffled shirt, and a bolero jacket the same color as the trousers. Those trousers were tucked in the high boots a few shades darker but the same hue as the lavender shirt. Her short hair was dyed peacock blue and swept back in what was doubtless the latest clubbing style. She walked around to join Cordelia at the back of the van, and when Cordelia popped the doors open, she stepped inside.

"Maybe it isn't capri-cows," Stephanie said with heartfelt relief.

Nor was it, and Stephanie's eyes widened as Xadrian

reemerged holding hands with what certainly looked like a sphinx the size of the pony.

It couldn't be, of course. Not really! But it moved smoothly, head cocked alertly, and its eyes were a bright, intense green. Its hair matched the tawny gold of its lion body, and its avian wings were tucked close to its flanks. Or, rather, to *her* flanks, because the Sphinx was bare breasted and very clearly female.

Stephanie flung the door open and raced across the snow porch to greet the new arrivals.

"You're the first to get here! And, wow! Xadrian, you said you were going to bring music and lights for the dancing, but this—?"

Xadrian swept Stephanie a deep bow and kissed her lightly on the cheek.

"This is my light show and musical equipment. She is called D.J., in memory of ancient lore. D.J., greet the birthday girl."

The robotic sphinx sat on her haunches, spread her wings, and began singing an upbeat, jazzy tune in which the words "Happy Birthday!" "Happy Stephanie!" and "Seventeen!!" were repeated several times in different combinations. As she sang, D.J.'s eyes flashed bright emerald and her wings glittered in silver and gold. Her tail lashed back and forth, and she danced in time to the music.

"Wow!" Stephanie repeated. "She's incredible! Is D.J. yours, does she belong to the Enigmatic Riddle?"

"She is a joint venture," Xadrian said. "Together, we venture out into the realm of home parties. When we do not, she is an ornament to the club. The arrangement works very well for us both."

Stephanie wasn't sure whether the "us" applied to the marvelous sphinx or to the nightclub, and decided she wasn't going to ask. Xadrian delighted in cryptic comments, but beneath the poseur exterior was as kind and thoughtful a person as anyone could wish to have by in a crisis, as Stephanie had reason to know.

"Come in!" Stephanie said. "Cordy? You can park your van right over there."

"Will do. We have a few things to unpack, though," Cordelia replied, and Stephanie narrowed her eyes in mock severity.

"I thought the invite said 'No Presents,'" she said, and Cordelia laughed.

"It didn't say anything about 'no samples,'" she pointed out. "I brought a selection of cheeses. And when he heard it was your birthday, Herman sent over an amazing selection of mushroom appetizers, including a new candy box assortment he and Glynis are really excited about."

"What's amazing," Mack Kemper, added as he hefted a crate with the mushroom growers' logo onto his shoulder, "is how good some of them are. They don't quite have chocolate right, but if you don't think 'chocolate,' but just sweet and rich, they work."

"Well, I can't be selfish and not support Sphinx's home growers' economy," Stephanie said. "But hurry. I've got news I'm dying to share!"

The day after her birthday, Stephanie didn't exactly feel let down. That was impossible, because all the really good things would continue into the future. But the house did feel very quiet the next morning. Karl had had to report to work, and her dad had flown Duncan back into Twin Forks that morning to pick up a rental vehicle, since Duncan had flown Stephanie's birthday present from the dealer in Yawata Crossing while Marjorie got Stephanie and Karl out of the way. He'd need an air car of his own while he was on Sphinx, of course. He'd be staying with the Harringtons as much as he could, but he'd obviously be spending a lot of his time with Dr. Hobbard and the other out-system xeno-anthropologists here to study the treecats. Although, as he'd pointed out with a chuckle, he was probably the only one of them who could "go to his room" and still have treecats *to* study!

Stephanie and Karl had taken advantage of the birthday party to discuss Duncan's arrival with most of the GTC's members, and they'd been as enthusiastic as she was about adding someone with his credentials to the conspirators. She hadn't yet found the opportunity to do that, but it was definitely on her list. In fact, she'd already invited Scott and Irina MacDallan and Fisher to drop by for a visit, and she was looking forward to Duncan's reaction to the notion that treecats were genuinely telepathic.

She'd overslept, which was unusual for her. Now she went down to the kitchen, yawning and scrubbing her eyes, and followed by Lionheart. Marjorie was already there, putting away some of the serving pieces that had been used for the truly heroic amount of food which had been prepared. Even after sending the Kemper boys home with leftovers and giving Jessica a box of extra cupcakes for her little brothers and sisters, they still had plentiful leftovers of their own, largely because most of the guests had brought something with them.

"Hey, Mom. Can I help?"

"If you'd hand me the blue and green platter, I'll be just about done until the load in the washer finishes."

Marjorie took the platter, put it away, then stepped down off the stepladder and gave Stephanie a quick hug.

"Quite a birthday," she said. "Marriage proposal. A new car. And topped off by a great party, if I do say so myself. Xadrian's D.J. was astonishing."

"It really was. Thanks so much for the Sabre. Is it

selfish to admit I'd been hoping? With both Karl and Jess working, it's been getting harder to hitch rides."

"I hope you don't mind secondhand," Marjorie said, "but given your tendency to hare off into the bush at a moment's notice, a new air car seemed like a bad idea."

"I don't mind one bit. I love it."

Lionheart jumped up onto his window ledge perch while Stephanie rooted around in the fridge. There was nothing wrong with having bean dip and cheese for breakfast, she decided. She'd handed Lionheart a leftover taquito—which he didn't mind at all wolfing down cold—and pulled out the containers and some flatbread to improvise a burrito, when she noticed her mom watching her.

"Want one? There's plenty."

"Oh, no." Marjorie waved her hand. "I had some of the nut bread Chet and Christine brought. It was too good to let go stale. Coffee?"

"Definitely."

Stephanie dove back into the fridge twice more, coming out with guacamole (Kemper boys) and goat cheese (Cordelia). She could tell her mom wanted to talk about something, but Marjorie seemed unusually hesitant for some reason. That wasn't like her, and Stephanie thought about asking her what was on her mind, then decided to give her time, instead. She was chewing her third bite when—

"So," Marjorie said with studied casualness, "now that you and Karl are engaged, is it going to be one bedroom or two?"

Stephanie nearly choked. Not that she hadn't been daydreaming about the someday when she'd wake up, maybe with her head pillowed on Karl's shoulder, maybe with him spooned around her, but this from her mom?! She finished swallowing her coffee and blinked tears from her eyes. Then she laughed.

"Thanks, for treating me like a grown-up, even if I'm still technically a minor for another year. I really do appreciate that."

"Well, age of consent and all that." Marjorie waved her coffee mug. "You're there. Anyhow, it's not like we haven't trusted you and Karl for a lot of years now. Not just tooling around in his air car or cruiser, but off on Manticore. If you were going to be having sex, it's not as if you haven't had ample opportunity. I thought about asking when you two started 'going steady,' back on Manticore, but that seemed to be pushing. Now though..."

Stephanie ate another bite of burrito while she organized her thoughts. Then she looked up at her mother.

"I know I have a reputation for rushing into things, but I've decided to take my time with sex. So, my impulsive decision is to be not impulsive."

"Karl's okay with that?" Marjorie asked. "Male egos are more fragile than you might think. He might worry you're having second thoughts or something."

"The great thing about both of us being adopted by treecats," Stephanie said, "is that neither of us have any doubts that we love each other."

"Do the treecats... Um..."

For the first time, Marjorie actually looked flustered, and Stephanie shook her head vehemently.

"Not a bit. They don't seem interested in the least. They're actually more likely to tune in if we're upset or distressed or something, because then they want to come help. But I guess they can tell the difference in types of emotional and physical intensity."

"Some future xeno-sociologist is probably going to get a paper out of that," Marjorie said with a chuckle. "So, still two rooms, at least for now. But since passion has been known to overwhelm even the most prudent of us, how about we make an appointment to get you a contraceptive implant? Unplanned sex is one thing, but unplanned babies..."

Stephanie's eyes widened, then she nodded vigorously.

"Absolutely! Let's do it," she said, and Marjorie grinned.

"Just consider it another birthday present."

29

IT TOOK A FEW DAYS FOR SCOTT AND IRINA TO CLEAR their calendar, but that worked out for the best, since it carried them clear to the weekend. Like any physician, Scott was always "on call" where patient emergencies were concerned, but he'd finally added a second doctor to his practice, and she'd volunteered to hold the fort while he and Irina spent Saturday night as Harrington houseguests.

Stephanie and Karl met them on the parking apron, and Lionheart and Survivor bleeked happily as Fisher leapt out of the passenger side door. The three 'cats bumped noses, then looked up at their humans, and Stephanie shook her head.

"Go!" she laughed, waving both arms at the surrounding picketwood. "But don't get lost! We're going to want you guys when we sit down to talk."

"Bleek!" Lionheart acknowledged, as if he'd actually understood her. Then all three of them headed for the trees.

"I don't think you really have to worry about rounding them up for show and tell," Karl said with a grin as all four humans watched them go. "I think treecats must have the Meyerdahl mods. I've never noticed them missing a meal, anyway!"

"Very funny." Stephanie poked him in the ribs with a stiff index finger, but even she had to smile, and MacDallan chuckled.

"Fisher never does, that's for sure," he agreed.

"Sort of like his two-footed partner, in that regard," Irina observed.

"What can I say? I married a magnificent cook!"

"Pay attention, Karl," Irina said. "This is how an old, stodgy married couple stays married."

"Actually, Karl's at least as good a cook as I am," Stephanie said. "I was a little surprised by how good he is, to be honest."

"Large families have that effect on older siblings," Irina said as she gave her nephew an affectionate hug. "Although, I have to admit he's a better cook than his dad!"

"Please." Karl shuddered. "I love my dad, but that's a pretty low bar, really."

Irina laughed, and the four of them started for the house.

"While we're admitting things," Scott said as they walked, "I have to admit, I'm a little nervous about laying this all out for your cousin, Steph. I've spent so long not being the 'weirdo' that the thought of coming out of the shadows for someone I haven't even met yet is a bit...disconcerting, let's say."

"I understand that—really, I do," Stephanie said seriously. "But this is absolutely the friendliest audience we're going to find, and Lionheart and Survivor both really like him. That's got to be a good sign."

"It's a good sign of where he is right now," Scott said

in his best devil's advocate tone. "Not even treecats can predict the future, though!"

Stephanie looked up at him, and he snorted.

"Don't mind me! I trust the 'cats' judgment, too. I think I'm just looking for a pretext to hang my opening-night nerves on."

<So, tell me of this new two-leg,> Swift Striker said as he settled between Climbs Quickly and Keen Eyes on the net-wood branch overlooking Death Fang's Bane Clan's nest place.

<We do not know Far Traveler yet as well as we do our own two-legs,> Climbs Quickly replied. <But he has a powerful mind-glow, and he is clearly of close kin to Death Fang's Bane. From his mind-glow, we believe he is Healer's brother, although he seems too old to be an actual litter mate. And there is great love between him, Healer, Plant Minder, and Death Fang's Bane. It is clear they did not expect his arrival, but their joy when he came was like the sun in green-leaf time.>

<And I believe Death Fang's Bane's joy may have been greater even than Healer's,> Keen Eyes put in. <There has been much discussion about him with the other two-legs of our new clan. We think he is . . . an elder who pursues new knowledge, much as Bleached Fur's sire. We do not know that for certain, but we taste the same sort of interest in him as in Answer Seeker.>

<True,> Climbs Quickly agreed. <Yet there is also an odd strand of . . . I would not call it unhappiness, but almost of regret woven into his mind-glow. We do not know what might cause it, but from the taste of all of their mind-glows, I suspect that it is that he cannot stay. That he must leave again when whatever has brought him to our world is accomplished.>

<The need to leave those whom one loves as dearly as you have tasted his love for Death Fang's Bane Clan would be ample cause for sorrow,> Fisher said.

<True,> Climbs Quickly repeated, then flirted his tail. <But come! Let us show you Death Fang's Bane's new flying thing before they summon us to eat!>

The Harringtons and their guests sat around a table littered with the aftermath of an inevitable Harrington repast. As the only two human members of the group who did not possess the Meyerdahl mods, the MacDallans had consumed merely mortal portions of it, but even the Harringtons' need for calories had been temporarily met.

"That was delicious," Scott sighed, sitting back and patting his stomach. "And I don't believe I've ever had chicken prepared quite that way. I'm not sure I would have thought mushrooms and tangerines would complement each other like that."

"It's one of Duncan's favorite dishes," Marjorie replied, smiling across the table at her husband's cousin. "And one reason—among many—I'm glad he came to visit us is that I'd forgotten how much *I* liked it. Richard taught me the recipe years ago, but somehow we'd just let it lie fallow."

"And I'm delighted to have helped resurrect it," Duncan said.

Marjorie snorted and Duncan grinned at her. But then he looked at the MacDallans and Fisher and cocked his head.

"Forgive me, Doctor MacDallan, but why do I suspect that there's a specific reason Richard and Marjorie—not to mention Stephanie and Karl—wanted me to meet you and your treecat friend?"

"Because you're a smart fellow," Richard said dryly

before Scott could reply, and Duncan chuckled. But his eyes never left the MacDallans, and Scott shrugged.

"I imagine that one reason is that Richard's obviously right about how smart you are, Doctor Harrington. And because you are, I suspect you've already figured out that the fact that you're one of the galaxy's most respected xeno-anthropologists has a little to do with the reason the entire Harrington clan wanted to introduce us to you."

"I might say I'm one of the galaxy's *more* respected xeno-anthropologists," Duncan replied. "I'm not so sure about 'most.' But you're right. I did dimly suspect that my area of study and what brings me to Sphinx—officially, at least—was involved. I understand from what little Steph's let drop about you and Fisher that your initial meeting had a certain similarity with hers and Lionheart's?"

"If you mean we basically saved each other's lives, it did," Scott said in a much more serious tone. "It was less traumatic, and no predatory wildlife was involved, but I'm pretty sure I would've drowned if he hadn't saved me."

He reached across, running a gentle hand down Fisher's spine.

"I've also read the official accounts of what happened with 'the Stray,'" Duncan said quietly. "I imagine that made up for some of the non-trauma of your original encounter with the treecats."

"You might say that." Scott nodded. "In fact, what happened when the Stray turned up is really the most fundamental reason all of us wanted me to talk to you."

"'All of us'?" Duncan arched one eyebrow.

"All of us," Stephanie replied, and Duncan looked at her. "Not just *us* 'us,'" she waved her hand around the dining room, "but all the rest of 'us.' The rest of the Great Treecat Conspiracy."

Duncan's other eyebrow rose, and she drew a deep breath.

"I know you came all the way out here with an open mind," she began, "and we hope you go on having an open mind while we explain to you. But the truth is, we really, really hope you can help us—*all* of us, humans and treecats. Because we need all the help we can get. You see—"

✧　　✧　　✧

"You weren't joking about hoping for 'open minds,' were you?" Duncan Harrington said, several hours later. The party had moved into the living room, and he leaned back in one of the comfortable armchairs, watching the treecats chew on after-dinner celery stalks. "You truly believe they're both telempaths *and* telepaths."

"I don't see any other explanation, really," Scott replied from the couch where Irina leaned against his shoulder. "That's the only way the 'cats could have shared those images with me. And it's also the only explanation I can see—that *any* of us can see—for the complex social interactions we've observed in a species with no *detectable* form of communication."

"The logic's irrefutable," Duncan said. "That doesn't necessarily mean the conclusion is correct, though. Logic and Occam's razor will only take us as far as our understanding of the actual parameters. Mind you," he leaned forward, bracing his elbows on his thighs, fingers interlaced, "I think you're onto something—all of you. I think"—his tone was touched with a sense of wonder—"that Stephanie really has discovered an intelligent, tool-using, *telepathic* species. And, God, Steph, do I *envy* you for that!"

Stephanie felt her cheeks heat slightly as he turned those glowing eyes upon her.

"I was just in the right place at the right time," she said.

"And had the guts to take on a hexapuma with a vibro-blade, you mean." Duncan shook his head. "I read that part of Richard's letters, but until I got out here, saw actual imagery of hexapumas, I didn't really understand. I thought," he shrugged in an almost embarrassed way, "that it was something the size of, maybe, an Old Earth cheetah. I mean, that would have been enough to terrify any sane human being! But now that I've seen what you—you and Lionheart—actually faced..."

He shook his head again, and looked at Karl.

"You've got a special one here, Karl. Treasure her."

"Oh, I do—I do," Karl replied, reaching out to take Stephanie's hand as she blinked suddenly burning eyes.

There was silence for a moment, and then Duncan sat back in his armchair and planted his forearms on the armrests.

"All right," he said in a brisk voice. "I think I've got the parameters of the problem and I understand why you call yourselves the Great Treecat Conspiracy. And I think you're right to go about demonstrating their sapiency as...circumspectly as you can. I've had a couple of conversations with Doctor Hobbard since I got out here. Obviously, I didn't know she was a 'conspirator' at the time, but what she was able to tell me without betraying any confidences confirmed me in my belief that the Star Kingdom's unlikely to do a repeat of Barstool. 'Unlikely' isn't the same thing as 'guaranteed not to,' though, and unless we can firmly establish their sapience, it *is* likely that they'll get shoved right out of humanity's way.

"The problem, of course, is the one you've already identified. How do we prove they communicate tele-pathically with one another when there's no way to prove telepathy actually exists?"

"If we could be positive *they* understand *us*, I could see a series of controlled experiments with bonded pairs in different rooms," Richard said. "If we could communi-cate clearly with them, tell them—I don't know. If Steph could tell Lionheart 'Roll the purple dice' in one room and Survivor turned around and rolled them in another room, we'd be well on our way. But Steph and Lionheart don't have that degree of . . . complex communication. For that matter, we can't demonstrate that he understands her in the first place, because—having watched them—he *doesn't* understand her, a lot of the time."

"He seems to track pretty well with her from what I've seen."

"We've been together a long time now, Uncle Duncan," Stephanie said. "I think he does *completely* understand my emotions. I'm not saying they don't confuse him sometimes, which shouldn't be too surprising when we're talking about two totally different species, but I'm positive he senses them, that he's *learned* to understand them when they differ from other treecats'. That's not the same as understanding what I'm thinking, or what I'm *saying*. He has learned to understand certain gestures, certain combinations of sounds, but to be brutally honest, I've known dogs—like Cordy's Barnaby—who've learned the same things. I'm sure the 'nonbelievers' would argue that that's all Lionheart and I have really accomplished. And it's hard to blame them, really."

Her frustration was evident, and Lionheart leaned back in her lap, reaching up to touch her cheek gently with his remaining true-hand. She captured his wrist and pressed her cheek more firmly against his true-hand, and her eyes were dark.

"I don't think we're going to be able to prove that they're telepathic," she said. "I'd love to be wrong about that, and if you or anyone else can come up with a way to do it, it would be the most wonderful thing I can imagine. But if we can't do that, then we need to at least be able to demonstrate—prove—they're intelligent. That they're true sapients. The *indigenous* sapients of their planet."

"I understand." Duncan nodded soberly. "I really do, Steph. But it's my job to be skeptical. You understand that, right? My job to demonstrate their intelligence to my own satisfaction from my own observations before I sign off on that in any official capacity?"

"Of course we do."

"All right, then. With that proviso, I want all of you to know I'm firmly in your corner. Or, maybe what I mean is that I'm in the *treecats'* corner. But I also think, for their sake, that it's absolutely essential we establish at the end of the day that I *did* my job—that I was truly skeptical, I examined the evidence for myself, and I reached conclusions I can support on the basis of that evidence—rather than simply signing onto my cousin's campaign. Are we all agreed on that?"

He looked around the living room, and every human nodded. All three treecats sat very still, looking back at him with grass-green eyes, and he drew a deep breath.

"In that case," he said, "I think tomorrow I'd better check in officially with Chief Shelton and Doctor Hobbard. It's time I got around to establishing those 'independent bona fides' with The Powers That Be."

30

JUST UNDER A MONTH AFTER STEPHANIE'S BIRTHDAY, she found a message on her uni-link from Chief Ranger Shelton.

"Contact Francine and make an appointment for you to meet with me and Karl. It's not an emergency, but sooner would be better than later."

Stephanie checked with Karl, but he didn't have any better idea than she did as to what the chief wanted.

"Since curiosity will doubtless eat you alive," he said, "get in touch with Francine. She has my schedule already, so it's doubtless yours that's the issue. And don't cut class."

"They're mostly virtual this term," Stephanie protested. "I can screen later."

"Doesn't look as good on your record," Karl said. "You need to show you know how to manage your time."

"Fair enough," Stephanie sighed. "Probably the day after tomorrow then."

"You'll live."

The next fifty-two hours gave Stephanie far too much time to speculate. Her mind was still spinning like a chipmunk on an exercise wheel when she and Karl parked her new car in the lot at the SFS office in Yawata Crossing.

"Relax, Steph," Karl said, giving her hand a squeeze. "You worry too much. What's the worst that could happen? He's not going to fire you, not without reason. You've *given* him reason, a time or two, and he didn't fire you or demote you. Of course, it's hard to demote the most junior ranger. So I guess he would have to fire you."

"Do you have any idea what this is about?"

"Not the least idea," Karl replied with a lopsided grin. He released her hand. "Let's go find out."

"He's in," Francine said, waving them toward Chief Shelton's office. "There's even a snack tray."

She apparently meant this as reassurance, but Stephanie couldn't help but think, *I hope this isn't the condemned's final meal.* Lionheart's reaction was no help at all. He liked Francine and apparently found no reason to change his mind. She could hear his nose near her ear, slightly whuffling as he tracked an elusive scent.

Chief Shelton rose from behind his desk as they came in, waving them to the chairs with the wide upper backs that Stephanie suspected had been acquired specifically to make the treecats comfortable. His selection of snacks reflected that, too. While most people had celery, because they were fascinated by the weirdness of a felid that ate rabbit food, Chief Shelton remembered that the 'cats, and their humans, paid for the treat in the need to dose the treecats against constipation. Instead, he had a container of raw farmed shrimp for the treecats, already shelled, out of consideration for his cleaning staff.

Greetings were exchanged, beverages of choice were poured, and the tray of sweet and savory puff pastries shoved to where it would be in easy reach. Then, with a glance at the time and a swig of his coffee, Chief Shelton began.

"Stephanie, I realize that some may feel I'm pushing you toward a career path, but those are the people who don't know you. I believe you're not likely to give up your dream of being an SFS ranger once you get older and discover that there are a lot of professions open to someone as intelligent and talented as yourself, professions that aren't nearly as uncomfortable as being a ranger and are, quite frankly, a lot better paid."

Stephanie was momentarily speechless. Then she thought about other kids she knew. Through high school, even college, they were fanatically devoted to something: art, theater, sports. They took classes, spent hours practicing, and then, faced with earning a living, or just a desire to live somewhat better than hand to mouth, they put these their passions aside. They even called it "growing up." The idea that anyone could think her devotion to Sphinx wildlife, animal and vegetable, as well as the larger ecosystem that sustained it, fell into the hobby category made her feel as if the floor had been pulled out from under her feet.

"I do want to be a ranger. Seriously!" She forced a version of her usual grin, but was pretty sure her dismay still showed. "Heck, I even want to have your job someday!"

Chief Shelton waved a warning finger at her.

"I told the naysayers that would be your reaction. You've never thought of doing anything else, and you've been doing a ranger's job with as much time as you can spare from your studies. Don't think I haven't noticed. I've even had Francine keep a record of your estimated hours with this meeting in mind. Despite some protests, I've gotten clearance to hire you as a full ranger, with all the duties and responsibilities that entails. With a starting salary, too, but no vehicle."

"Sir!" was all Stephanie could manage, but she sat straighter, her eyes round.

"You'd be expected to finish the credits needed for your high school diploma," Shelton went on. "However, given that you've been taking advanced coursework in most subjects since you arrived on planet at ten, that really isn't an issue. In some subjects, you're actually partway to an undergraduate college degree. We'd like you to get that college degree, as well. I fear that's going to be—as it is for Karl—extra study on your own time. I realize this isn't a very tempting offer..."

Stephanie shook her head vigorously, then nodded. Then managed, "Permission to speak, Chief Shelton?"

"Go ahead." His eyes were creased at the corners with laughter, but he managed to hide what Stephanie was pretty sure was a grin with his coffee mug.

"I'd love it! I really would. I'd need to ask my parents. I mean, I'm still a minor, but I can't see them complaining about my wanting to work harder. They both work really hard. Plants don't go by human schedules, and neither do sick animals."

"I haven't asked Richard and Marjorie what they think," Chief Shelton said. "You'll need to speak with them yourself. However, I think they have no doubt of your future career, including the drawbacks—maybe even especially the drawbacks."

"Now, Karl," Chief Shelton began. His comm buzzed, and Francine's voice said, "Minor emergency, Chief. Sending it to your terminal."

"Excuse me," Shelton said. He turned on his privacy screen.

While politely not trying to read his lips, Stephanie found herself wondering for the first time why Karl had been asked to attend this meeting. Was it because they were engaged, and Chief Shelton thought Karl should have a say? That wasn't a pleasant thought. She wasn't trading her parents' authority for Karl's, no matter how much she loved him.

Chief Shelton turned off the privacy screen as he was finishing up his call.

"Use your discretion, Ainsley. We don't need another bad tourist review. Let me know how they do. The tuskalope is all right?"

"Hale and hearty," came Ainsley Jedrusinski's voice, "if annoyed. Later."

Chief Shelton turned to Karl and Stephanie.

"As I was about to say, Karl, the reason I asked you to join us is not only are we planning to hire Stephanie, we want to create a new position for the both of you. Like most SFS jobs, this means more work, not necessarily more pay, and you'll be pulled off it as needed for other jobs."

"I can hardly wait to hear," Karl replied.

Stephanie nodded agreement. The elaborate calisthenics her brain and stomach had been doing a few moments before slowed. She always had dealt better with the definite than the possible. A new job. A new position. Shelton's pleased expression.

"We want to designate the two of you as our official treecat specialists. This won't mean doing 'our friend the treecat' presentations for the tourists. Let me reassure you on that before Stephanie can blow a seal. In fact, most people aren't going to know what you're doing. I don't need to remind you that the Governor's protection order is only a first step... or that it could still be overturned after parliamentary review. Your cousin looks like being a big help in that regard, Steph, but we need to build up the deepest database we can if it comes time to defend it. Right now we're still really short on the kinds of information we'd need to make fact-based, verifiable arguments about population sizes, the amount of range a given community requires, or even how many communities of them there are. Thanks to Stephanie, we know quite a lot about Lionheart's community. Then there's the community you helped relocate before last winter, the one Survivor comes from. And, of course, there's the group we relocated back after that very unfortunate incident with Dr. Ubel. But we need to know more."

"Will the information be secure?" Karl asked. "We don't want it leaking to the tour groups. Even the best, most ecologically sensitive visitors would be a problem."

"The information would be as locked down as I can make it," Chief Shelton promised. He went into details, and even as Stephanie listened in growing delight, her imagination was full of images of long hours spent out in the bush with Karl visiting treecats. It really didn't get much better than that.

"We also," Chief Shelton said, "want you two to do what 'leadership' you can with the treecats—although I suspect that will be Lionheart and Survivor's job. If, as you've proposed, the treecats are indeed telepaths, then Lionheart and Survivor will be able to share a great deal of information with other 'cats. Even if the treecats are 'only' telempaths, the opportunity to share that some humans are friends would still be a good thing."

He glanced at his chrono again.

"Now, I need to get ready for my next meeting. Stephanie, you'll find the details of your job offer on your uni-link. Review them and discuss them with anyone you like. This is a job offer, not a conspiracy."

"Thank you, sir!" Stephanie beamed. "I'll do my very best not to ever give you reason to regret this."

Karl nodded.

"And thank you on my behalf, as well. I've wanted to be a ranger ever since Ainsley and Frank got me interested in the SFS, but I never imagined I'd be lucky enough to be a sort of ambassador to another intelligent species. I'm absolutely blown away by your trust."

Chief Shelton laughed and inclined his head to Lionheart and Survivor.

"They're the ones who nominated you by choosing to bond with you. I know you won't disappoint either them or me. Now, out of here! Take the rest of the shrimp and pastries with you."

"Bleek!" Lionheart said to Shelton as they rose to leave. Stephanie had no idea what he meant, but she liked to imagine it might be "thank you."

31

"GWEN! I'M GLAD YOU WERE IN TOWN. I HAVE SOMEone I want you to meet."

George Lebedyenko beamed at his cousin as his secretary ushered her into his office. Bright morning sunlight streamed through floor-to-ceiling crystoplast windows that looked out over downtown Landing, and a coffee cup and a half-eaten Danish sat on Earl Adair Hollow's desk. Both of the people seated in two of the large, comfortable armchairs in his office held cups of their own. Gwendolyn Adair recognized Sanura Hobbard, but she had no idea who the tall, dark-haired man sitting beside her was. Although, she thought, he *did* look vaguely familiar somehow.

"I was actually headed out the door on my way to White Haven when you pinged me, George," she replied. "The Countess and I were supposed to tour the area where she plans to set up the arboretum. It's not exactly urgent, though, so we rescheduled for this afternoon."

"Julia was okay with that?"

"She's one of the Foundation's charter members, George," Gwendolyn reminded him with a smile. "In fact, I think she may be one of the very few members of the board who're more...enthusiastic then *you* are." She shook her head. "She was fine."

"Good—good! In that case, let me introduce you to our visitor."

"Of course," Gwendolyn said, turning toward the other two people and nodding to Hobbard.

"You and Sanura are old friends, of course," Adair Hollow went on, "but we're incredibly fortunate to have another visitor on hand. Gwendolyn, this is Doctor Duncan Harrington. Doctor, my cousin, Gwendolyn Adair, the associate director of the Adair Foundation. To be honest, in many ways, Gwen should be the CEO, but she's far more useful actually running things than she is cutting ribbons and giving speeches."

Gwendolyn's eyes flared before she could stop them. Harrington—*Duncan* Harrington?!

She stood there for an instant, unable to speak, and self-anger burned through her as she realized how stupid she must look. And reminded herself how important it was that she not allow her sudden spike of dismay to show. Then Adair Hollow chuckled.

"I don't blame you one bit!" he told her. "I never imagined we might be lucky enough to get someone with Duncan's stature involved in this."

"No." Gwendolyn shook herself, grateful for her cousin's misinterpretation of her stunned reaction. "No, I wouldn't have either!" She held out her hand. "It's very good—and an honor—to meet you, Doctor. Your reputation precedes you."

"Please, it's just Duncan," Harrington replied. He shook her hand, his grip the same carefully metered power she'd felt from Stephanie and her parents. "And I hope if my reputation preceded me that it was thoroughly dishonest and failed to mention what a completely *dis*reputable sort I actually am."

"I assure you, it did," Gwendolyn said with a smile. "And I must say you have the 'Harrington look,' Duncan. You and Richard might almost be brothers."

"Cousins, actually," he told her as he released her hand and Adair Hollow waved all of his guests back into chairs. "And if my infinitely precocious cousin Stephanie hadn't discovered treecats, I doubt I'd ever have gotten all the way out here to visit the three of them. Which is another reason for me to be profoundly grateful to the little critters."

"Should I assume, then, that you're here specifically to study them?" Gwendolyn asked as she seated herself, half-praying he'd say no, but dismayingly certain she already knew the answer.

"You should," he confirmed. "The Prometheus Foundation—it's a Meyerdahl think tank and research association that funds interdisciplinary studies in every conceivable field—picked up on the treecats. I'm not certain how they came to Prometheus's attention. If I'd had an IQ higher than my shoe size, *I'd* have mentioned them, because this is exactly the sort of thing they were chartered to investigate. Fortunately, someone else did, and they arranged a grant to send me out here to assist the Star Kingdom in studying and evaluating them. And the University was kind enough to grant me a sabbatical to make the trip...on the understanding that *they* get to publish my findings first, of course." He rolled his eyes. "When I called on Minister Vásquez at the Ministry of the Interior with the Foundation's letter of introduction in hand, she introduced me to Dr. Hobbard, who happened to be here in Landing at the time, and Dr. Hobbard immediately introduced me to your cousin."

"I see." Gwendolyn nodded with a pleasant smile. "And how long are you likely to be with us?"

"My original sabbatical was for two and a half T-years,

which would've given me about nine T-months here in Manticore, but I was preapproved for a six-T-month extension. I've already sent word I'm going to take it and warned them I might extend even that."

"I'm delighted to hear it!" Gwendolyn lied through her teeth. "And I imagine Stephanie and her parents were ecstatic to see you."

"'Ecstatic' might be putting it a little too strongly," Duncan chuckled, "but I think you can assume there were happy tears all around. And it gave me an opportunity to meet Lionheart and Survivor under completely informal and natural conditions."

"I'm afraid some of our critics here in the Star Kingdom might question just how 'natural' the conditions were." Gwendolyn shook her head sadly. "There's a very persistent element that insists the 'cats are simply well-trained performing animals."

"That's scarcely surprising. I didn't know that until I got here, but it wasn't unexpected when Stephanie and Karl told me about it. Thankfully, as far as I can tell, no one's discussing them in the same terms the Amphors were discussed."

"That much, at least, I can guarantee won't happen here," Hobbard put in. Duncan looked at her, and she grimaced. "Gwen's absolutely right about the persistence of efforts to deny their sapiency, but Minister Vásquez has assured me neither the Crown nor Parliament has any intention of overturning Governor Donaldson's protected species order. Which isn't to say plenty of unfortunate things couldn't happen to them anyway, but at least nobody's going to sign off on any sort of species genocide."

"I'm relieved to hear that," Duncan said. "From my conversations with Steph and Karl, I know they were worried about the possibility it might be overruled. May I pass on what you've told me, Sanura?"

"Of course you can. I was going to tell them myself as soon as I got back to Sphinx, but I'm pretty sure you'll be back before I am."

"That's really good news, too," Gwendolyn said brightly as the hits kept on coming.

She could already imagine how Countess Frampton would react to that tidbit of information! But she made herself smile and looked back and forth between Harrington and Hobbard.

"May I ask if you've decided how best to incorporate Doctor Harrington—forgive me, Duncan—into your efforts, Sanura?"

"He'll be joining our group as one of its directors," Hobbard replied, "but he'll also be one of our primary field investigators. I've asked Doctor Mulvaney to share his files with Duncan, and I've already made all of the official database available to him. It'll take him several days, probably a week or two, to get fully up to speed on that, but then I very much want him back on Sphinx, directly interacting with the 'cats and liaising with the Forestry Service. Chief Shelton's very excited about having someone of his stature and proven expertise available."

"I'm certain he is. And I imagine Stephanie and Karl will be overjoyed to show you around, Duncan."

"I'm sure they will." Harrington nodded. "On the other hand, as I understand it, Chief Shelton intends to make the two of them his primary field team. As you know, the Forestry Service wants, above all, to protect the 'cats from human intrusion into their territory. With Lionheart and Survivor as 'ambassadors,' Steph and Karl will probably be the least intrusive team we could send out. Chief Shelton will share all their data with me, and of course I'll have direct access to them whenever Steph is home, not out in the field. But we don't want a batch of uninvited humans trampling all over their ranges, so

I probably won't go into the field myself for at least the first couple of T-months. I will have input into where they go and how they conduct their studies, however, and if anything extraordinarily interesting comes up, I very probably will go out to take a look at it myself. I don't expect that to happen but then, no one *expected* to discover the treecats in the first place."

"No, I think we can all take that as a given," Gwendolyn agreed, then quirked a thoughtful eyebrow. "On the other hand, what you've just said, brings a potentially unpleasant thought to mind where the people who don't want the treecats to be ruled true sapients are concerned."

"Nepotism and bias on my part?" Duncan smiled thinly.

"No one who's read your work the way we have here at the Foundation would think that for an instant." Gwendolyn shook her head quickly. "But people with a vested interest in proving they *aren't* sapient are unlikely to be overly scrupulous in the way they attack any argument that they may be."

"I'm afraid that's a fair observation," Adair Hollow put in, and grimaced. "There are enough people here in the Star Kingdom who think I'm some kind of gooey-hearted, softheaded do-gooder with a messianic complex. And then there are the ones who think I'm simply an idiot to be worrying about planetary ecospheres when there are still fewer people in the entire Star Kingdom than in a single mega-urb back on Old Terra. After all, plenty of time to worry about that later, isn't there? And then there are the ones with a powerful vested interest in making sure there are no inconvenient native sapients getting in the way of their own ambitions. Between them, there aren't very many arguments or tactics I'd put past them."

Harrington nodded soberly, then shrugged.

"I've already thought about that, and I've discussed it with Stephanie and her parents, for that matter. All of them understand why it's essential that anything *I* say about the treecats absolutely has to be backed up in triplicate by the data. Frankly, I'm afraid that's only too likely to limit how high on the sapience scale I can successfully argue for placing them."

"Really?" Adair Hollow cocked his head. "Why?"

"Because while I disagree with Cleonora Radzinsky's argument that the treecats have no form of complex communication, and as such cannot be considered truly sapient, she has a point that much of the galaxy's xeno-anthropology community will agree with. One I'm afraid even Clifford Mulvaney's increasingly inclined to endorse—which, frankly, surprised me a bit. And the problem is that so far they *don't* have any *observable*, quantifiable form of communication. It's obvious to me that they must have one, based simply on what I've already seen of their social organization and Lionheart and Survivor's interaction both between each other and with Stephanie and Karl. But if we can't demonstrate it, there's going to be a lot of pressure to rank them no higher than, say, Old Earth dolphins, who rank zero-point-six-five. On the one hand, we can point to the fact that unlike dolphins, the 'cats make use of at least Paleolithic tools and the dolphins don't. Critics will respond that dolphins *can't* make tools because they have no hands, but that unlike treecats, we've been able to communicate with them for literally millennia. And the conversations we've had with them have pretty amply demonstrated that while they *are* sapients, they simply can't process the complicated concepts humans do. So if the treecats can't even talk to *each other*, far less to us, how intelligent can they really be?"

"And you're afraid that if you disagree too strongly with that argument, someone will point out that you're Stephanie's cousin," Adair Hollow said, nodding with a disgusted expression.

"Exactly, and those people who don't want them to be sapients will get behind that and push." Harrington shrugged. "Trust me, if I do determine—on the basis of the evidence, not just how much I love Stephanie—that they're as intelligent as I already think they are—as intelligent as I'm telling myself I have to reserve judgment on—that's exactly what I'll tell academia and the galaxy at large. The problem is that I'm only one of the people who'll end up making that judgment, and when it's finally—officially—made for people here in the Star Kingdom, my relationship with Stephanie is one of the factors I assure you will be taken into consideration by those who disagree with me."

"Wonderful."

Adair Hollow puffed his lips, then straightened in his chair.

"I promise you the Adair Foundation will support you in any way we can, Duncan. Won't we, Gwen?"

"Absolutely!" Gwendolyn nodded firmly.

"That said, however," Adair Hollow continued, "would you be willing to put any preliminary rating on the table for us? I promise we won't hold you to it, and that it won't go anywhere outside this office until and unless you sign off on it."

Harrington gazed at him for several seconds, then shrugged again.

"To be honest, at the moment I'm strongly tempted to rate them at a solid one-point-oh on the sapience scale," he said flatly, and Adair Hollow sat back abruptly in his chair. Even Sanura Hobard's eyes widened in surprise, and Gwendolyn hoped her own flash of deep dismay would be put down to the same surprise. Homo sapiens rated 1.0 on sapience scale.

"That high?" Adair Hollow asked after a moment.

"That high," Duncan confirmed. "Which is one of

the reasons I'm telling myself I need to reserve judgment, even in my own mind, until I've had time to
study a much larger sample than just the treecats who
have bonded with Stephanie and her friends. I need a
lot more observational data of the 'wild' 'cats before I
could even remotely justify committing to something
like that in any official context, and any conscientious,
honest scholar knows the danger of prejudgment when it
comes to something like this. And, as I say, if we can't
demonstrate how they communicate with one another,
it's unfortunately likely xeno-anthropologists in general
won't sign off on that conclusion even if it's the one I
believe is ultimately sustained by the data."

Gwendolyn Adair managed to keep her seething
fury out of her expression as she stalked into Vidoslav
Karadzic's private club, but she couldn't keep it out of
her quick, angry stride. Not only had she been forced to
demonstrate her own joy at Duncan Harrington's arrival,
she'd also been tasked to show him around the Foundation's headquarters when what she'd really wanted to do
was shoot him.

Duncan Harrington. One of the dozen or so top
people in his field, and he was that never-to-be-suffi-
ciently-damned Stephanie's *cousin*. The tiny, isolated Star
Kingdom of Manticore was scarcely at the cutting edge
of academia in any field, especially not after surviving
the Plague. But Interior Minister Vásquez and Sanura
Hobbard's team had been doing their damnedest to correct that fact, at least in the field of xeno-anthropology,
and Duncan's work had figured prominently in its recent
scholarship. Somehow Gwendolyn had missed the last
name. Or, rather, she'd assumed the universe couldn't
be perverse enough to make Duncan a member of the

same Harrington clan. He might be from Meyerdahl, but surely there were hundreds—thousands!—of Harringtons on Meyerdahl.

And now this.

Any chance I ever really had of "proving" the little demons are only animals just went right out the window, she thought bitterly. *I was always afraid it would, but with* him *in their corner, it's damned well certain. And from there, it's only a hop, skip, and a jump to ruling them not simply sapient but Sphinx's indigenous sapients, with all the rights pertaining thereunto. Angelique's going to be royally pissed when she hears about this, and if she decides she has to pull out all the stops and things start splashing—*

That angry stride carried her across the foyer to the concierge's desk, and the attractive young woman behind it looked up at her.

"Ms. Adair! We haven't seen you in a while."

"Good evening, Trish." Gwendolyn made herself smile pleasantly. "I've been far too busy to do a lot of things I should have been doing, but tonight I plan to mix at least a little pleasure with business. I have several things I need to discuss with Mr. Karadzic for my cousin, and your kitchen's okroshka and shashlik are to die for. So—"

She shrugged whimsically, and Trish chuckled.

"I can't—and won't—argue with that, ma'am. My personal favorite's the stroganoff, though. And Mr. Karadzic did mention you'd be joining him." She tapped the smart surface of her desk and a liveried club steward appeared as if by magic. "Clifton will escort you to him."

"Thank you," Gwendolyn said graciously, and followed Clifton deeper into the club.

After several minutes' walk, they arrived outside one of the small dining rooms. The privacy light beside the door glowed, and Clifton touched the com pad below it.

"Yes?"

"Ms. Adair is here, sir."

"Ah! Excellent. Excellent!"

The door opened, and Vidoslav Karadzic smiled out at Gwen.

"It's so good to see you, my dear!" He extended a hand to shake hers, then looked at the steward. "I'm sure we'll be ordering sometime soon, Clifton. We do have several dreary business details to discuss first, however. I'll ring when we're ready."

"Of course, sir."

Clifton inclined his head in an abbreviated, respectful bow, and Gwendolyn gave him another smile as she stepped past him into the dining room. Karadzic closed the door behind her, then turned and leaned back against it with folded arms.

"I must say your message was rather...abrupt, my dear," he observed in a whimsical tone.

"I'd had rather an abrupt and unpleasant shock before I sent it to you."

Gwendolyn crossed to the table and dropped her briefcase into one of the unoccupied chairs, then looked at the two men already seated at it. She was less than enthralled to see them in person, since that might make deniability hard to come by if this little operation went south on her. On the other hand, she'd always known she'd have to meet with them eventually. And at least the club was a sufficiently secure venue to make it unlikely anyone would connect her directly with them.

"I believe you know Doctor Bronstein and Doctor Muñoz," Karadzic said.

"No, not personally," Gwendolyn replied. "I do know both of them—especially, if you'll forgive me, Doctor Bronstein, you—by reputation, however."

Bronstein was only a centimeter or two taller than

Gwendolyn herself, with a slim build, fair, receding hair, blue eyes, and a pale complexion. Blue eyes which turned remarkably hard and a complexion which flushed angrily as she nodded to him. Not surprisingly, she thought. A former senior employee of BioNeering, he'd been an associate of Muriel Ubel. He hadn't been directly involved in her catastrophic implosion on Sphinx, but the in-house investigation that followed her death had uncovered... irregularities in his own research. The investigators' findings had never been publicly disclosed, but he'd been promptly terminated "for cause," which had made him anathema to most of Manticore's other R&D firms. And while he might not be aware of it, Gwendolyn—courtesy of Karadzic—knew exactly what those investigators had found. Including the fact that his "irregularities" could easily have led to a similar disaster with *human* subjects.

She wasn't especially worried about any scruples that might have gotten in the way of his participation in the project.

She knew much less about Joshua Muñoz, however. Physically, he was almost Bronstein's antithesis, heavyset with dark brown eyes and an unruly thatch of thick, brown hair. He was a physician—a rheumatologist, if she remembered correctly—and not a researcher, but he was no longer in practice. Instead, he'd become the CEO and majority stockholder of the Urquhart Group, one of the bio research firms which had been heavily involved in fighting the Plague. Its reputation at that time had been enviable—and well-earned. Unfortunately, at least from a profit-and-loss perspective, Urquhart and its fellow researchers had succeeded in their task.

In the course of surviving the Plague, the Star Kingdom had been forced to build a medical infrastructure vastly in excess of the normal needs of a star nation with its population. Once the threat receded, there simply wasn't enough demand to keep all those R&D firms, all those specialists, employed. Quite a few of the actual physicians had moved on to open private practices on Sphinx as that planet's population began expanding once more, and others had emigrated to star systems where their services were far more urgently required. Many of the researchers had moved on, as well, and the firms which had employed them had undergone a rapid—and sharp—downsizing.

As the Urquhart Group shed value, Muñoz had picked up its shares for a song, and under his direction, Urquhart had made a modest recovery. In fact, its legitimate business probably covered as much as eighty percent of its operating costs these days. Which was especially interesting because it had posted a steady, slowly increasing profit for the last ten T-years or so.

Until recently, Gwendolyn hadn't been aware of that minor fact. Now, courtesy of Karadzic, she was one of the people who knew how it worked.

"May I assume you've briefed Doctor Bronstein and Doctor Muñoz on what it is we need to accomplish?" she asked Karadzic now.

"I had to at least sketch out the parameters for them in order to determine the practicality of your requirements," he replied.

"And dare I hope you gentlemen have determined that there *is* a practical solution to the problem?"

"Actually, Conrad and I believe we may have found an approach that would accomplish most—possibly all—of the objectives Vidoslav laid out for us," Muñoz said after a moment. "It won't be cheap, assuming it's practical at all, but if it works, it should do just about everything you want done."

"Define 'not cheap,' please," Gwendolyn said.

"It's impossible to define costs precisely at this point,"

Bronstein put in. "I'm confident it's possible to design the...tool I have in mind, but exactly how long that will take and exactly how much it will cost is impossible to pin down with any degree of exactitude."

"Can you at least give me a probable price range?"

"Assuming Conrad is able to retrieve and reconstitute his notes and data on a project upon which he and Doctor Ubel collaborated before that...unfortunate business on Sphinx, we're probably looking at no more than twenty to twenty-five million for the basic research. Assuming it's practical, the deployment mechanism would add another eight to ten to the price tag. So, on that basis, a low-end of twenty-eight million and a high-end of thirty-five."

"And if he's not 'able to retrieve and reconstitute' his and Doctor Ubel's notes?"

"If I can't, then I'll have to rebuild the database in the lab," Bronstein said. "The good news in that case would be that I already know what I'd have to do to get there. The bad news is that actually doing it would take time and it would drive up the R&D costs by a minimum of ten million. I doubt it would run as high as fifteen, but I can't completely rule that out."

"So, best case, everything works perfectly, we're looking at twenty-eight million dollars. *Worst* case, it's still possible, but you have to rebuild your research first, and we could be looking at fifty million."

"Exactly." Muñoz nodded. "Having worked with Conrad for some time, I feel confident he'll succeed, and I strongly suspect he's overestimating the required lab time even in a worst-case scenario. I can't—and won't—guarantee that, you understand."

Gwendolyn nodded, sitting back and rubbing her chin as she pondered the numbers. Even the low-end figure was considerably more than Countess Frampton would be happy to see. On the other hand, the treecats' persistent refusal to be "solved" by lesser means had become increasingly infuriating to her. That was likely to loosen her checkbook a bit. For that matter, Gwendolyn knew of a dozen other well-heeled Manticorans who stood to lose at least as heavily as Frampton did. If the Countess approached them discreetly, some of them would probably agree to kick some additional cash into the kitty.

And the notion that a probable solution to the problem was in the works might just soothe some of the fury Gwendolyn anticipated when she finally had to tell Frampton about Duncan Harrington's arrival.

"That's pricey," she said finally. "Assuming you do have to reconstruct your data the hard way, what probability of success are we talking about here? I know you said you can't guarantee success. But you need to understand that if you don't succeed in the end, you also won't be paid in the end. And that there will have to be agreed-upon benchmarks before each increment of funding is released."

"I would say," Muñoz said slowly and thoughtfully, "that the ultimate probability of success would be in excess of eighty-five percent. Assuming we don't have to repeat all of Conrad and Doctor Ubel's original research, that would go up to ninety."

Gwendolyn looked at him, impressed despite herself by his confidence. Of course, confidence was easy at this point, wasn't it?

"And the odds of its being recognized as a deliberate action on someone's part?"

"Given our current projections and the dispersal method Conrad's proposing, very, very low. Indeed, the odds are high that no one will even realize what's happening for at least fifteen or twenty T-years. And when they do realize, I think the odds are excellent that it will be dismissed as a natural mutation."

"I see."

Gwendolyn leaned back in her chair in silent thought for a full minute, then inhaled sharply.

"All right. I can't commit my principal tonight, but I will recommend that your proposal be very carefully looked at. I'll want a written précis a little more comprehensive and detailed than what you've just sketched out for me before I can do that, of course. How soon can you have one for me?"

"Give me a day or two, and I should have a fairly detailed brief on what we hope to accomplish and how," Muñoz said. "I want the extra time so we can build best-case and worst-case timelines into it."

"I think that would be a very good idea," Gwendolyn agreed. Then she smiled and looked at Karadzic.

"Why don't you get someone in here to take our orders, Vidoslav? I find I suddenly have a much better appetite than I'd expected."

32

"WE'LL START WITH THE GROUPS WE KNOW SOMETHING about," Stephanie explained to Chief Shelton. "Duncan agrees we'll probably be a lot less 'intrusive' to them, and we're hoping Lionheart and Survivor will figure out what we're doing when we visit them. If they do, then they're a lot more likely to be able to explain what the heck we're up to when we drop in on a clan that doesn't know a thing about us."

"Is the weather going to cooperate for Lionheart's clan?" Shelton asked, and Karl nodded.

"We're pretty sure it'll work. The weather sats say we should have at least three days, maybe even five, of clear weather. And even if this time of year is still cold, soggy, and not much fun to be out in, there are advantages. For instance, we should be able to spot and record individual treecat nests. And coupled with the lack of leaf cover, the colder background should help us spot infrared signatures when we go 'cat hunting."

"Exactly," Stephanie agreed. "And maybe we can find indications of how the treecats manage when the weather is less conducive to the sort of hand-to-mouth subsistence hunter-gather communities are supposed to employ. That would mean that later, when we locate new-to-us treecat communities, we'll have some idea of how to judge how much area they're using, which should have a lot of future applications, especially when the SFS is asked to give advice on human settlement."

"Sounds like a good start," Shelton said. "Eventually, we'll probably designate each group by their grid locations on a map but, just in case our records get illegally accessed—or even someone who does have legal access talks too much—why don't we assign them codes? Lionheart's group can be One, since you located him first. Two can be Fisher's clan. Three will be the group we relocated after that debacle with Ubel. Four can be that group who lives near the swamp, the ones whose leavings Dr. Whittaker was so excited about. I believe you said they'd moved back to their old stomping grounds?"

"That's right," Stephanie said. "The area's so well-watered that it's recovered pretty rapidly from the fire damage. Jessica's been taking Valiant there from time to time. We thought at first that Dulcinea probably came from that clan as well, since it's the closest we know of to the Franchitti barony. It doesn't look like it was, but Dulcinea can possibly direct us 'back home' from there, if we take her in the right general direction. She and her late husband came to the Franchitti property without using an air car, after all."

"True," Shelton said. "Very logical."

"We'll call Survivor's clan 'Five,' then," Karl said. "We know where they are, since we helped relocate them. I've gone visiting with Survivor and I'm happy to report that they're adjusting well to their new location."

Stephanie made a note. "Six could be the clan that

wasn't thrilled when Survivor's clan was forced into their area. We can probably track them down, and certainly should, since they're probably at risk of being impinged upon by humans. Or as the humans would see it, of imping- ing on human claims. Those treecats may be at risk."

"Unless," Karl said, "as the hunting gets better, they move away from where they border on humans into ter- ritory Survivor's family once used. The sort of hunter- gatherer lifestyle we're assuming the treecats depend on will be easier when the rivers aren't frozen and the small game isn't living in tunnels under the snow."

Shelton nodded.

"A key word there is 'assumption.' We really don't know enough. It'd been only one full Sphinxian year since Stephanie first made contact with Lionheart. It's a long time in one sense, but hardly anything in learning how a specific species manages to survive."

Karl stiffened.

"I'm sorry. I stand corrected, sir."

"Oh, relax." Shelton waved a hand at him. "I'm not saying you're wrong. In fact, based on what the xeno- anthropologists have come up with, I think you're right, but it'll be nice to have more hard data. By the way, any idea where the treecat who adopted Cordelia came from? You might want to look for a group in her general area."

"We really don't know where Athos came from," Stephanie said. "Cordelia's scouted around a bit with him, but even though he's caught on to pointing as a way of giving directions to humans, he hasn't tried to steer her to any specific group. We're wondering if he might be solitary by nature or something. He gets along with Lionheart and Survivor well when we're all together, but he has different body language somehow." She shrugged. "There's so much we don't know, so much we may never know. But you're right," she made a note on her uni-link.

"We should look in the area near the Schardt-Cordova and Kemper baronies, too."

"This is going to have me and Karl in the field a lot, sir." She stopped herself before she said, "Can you do without us?" but Shelton seemed to guess.

"I'm hardly used to having you on my staff, Ranger Harrington. While Karl's proven himself calm and ordered in a crisis—actually, you've both done that, now that I think about it—I think we can spare him now and then. This is a good time of year for sending you into the field for more reasons than the lack of foliage and the end of the worst of the winter weather. The winter tourists are gone, and the 'nice weather' tourists and prospective colonists won't be overburdening us for T-months yet. Don't waste the time we have, because when the tourists do arrive, I'll definitely need you to take up more usual duties."

As planned, they started with Lionheart's family. After Stephanie's incident with little Tarzan, whenever she and Lionheart had visited, the clan seemed very eager to be extra welcoming to their human guests. Stephanie took advantage of this to get a look at some of the arboreal shelters the treecats made for themselves in a different light.

"I don't usually think about this," she said to Karl, "but the way the treecats build most of their nests in crown oaks for cover from aerial hunters, like mountain eagles and condor owls, also works in their favor for staying concealed from humans. Otherwise, someone would surely have noticed them. These nests aren't exactly small."

"Though some of them are smaller than similar structures would be for humans," Karl commented, "even at a similar tech level. I'd say that those nests are mainly for sleeping, storage, and maybe shelter in extreme weather conditions. They're not dwellings, as we think of them."

"That makes sense," Stephanie agreed, taking reference images. "And it's probably more proof that they actually plan their communities."

Next up was the home of the Swamp Cats, as Jessica had dubbed the clan Valiant, her bondmate, had come from.

"Let's see if Nosey wants to bring Dulcinea out, too," Jessica suggested when Stephanie screened to ask if she'd be free to go with them. "I know she's getting close to dropping her kittens, but this would probably be the best time to find out if she really is a Swamp Cat."

"I'm all for asking them to join us," Stephanie agreed. "We'll need to take more than one vehicle, though."

"How about I ride with Nosey, Trudy, and Dulcinea? I know the way, and that way Valiant will be available if this is her clan and the trip proves stressful."

"Great! We'll pack a picnic."

On the day of their expedition, the weather was bright and clear, and much of the snow had melted away in the swampy lowlands. Pale spring foliage shaded the canopy that, only a few weeks earlier, had been mostly grays and browns. In the roughly two T-years since the fires had driven the treecats from their home, the forest bordering the Swamp had done a great deal of recovering. The towering, heavy-trunked crown oaks had simply shrugged off the fire damage, and the lighter picketwood had adapted by sending up new nodes wherever they were needed. Even in the extremely dry conditions that had made that fire season so much worse, the higher water table of the area had helped preserve much of the plant life.

Jessica directed them to the flat area where she typically parked her air car when she came for a family visit with Valiant. This was a polite distance from the crown oaks used by the treecats, and the humans made certain to give the swamp that had nearly meant the end of the Whitaker Expedition a very healthy margin, especially since this year's snowmelt was likely to have expanded the soggy areas.

When they got out of their vehicles, Stephanie walked over to where Nosey carried a very pregnant Dulcinea. She and Karl had given Nosey a jacket adapted to make it easier for a treecat to ride a human's shoulder with its true-feet on a built-in support near belt level and its true-hands on the human's shoulder. Dulcinea was peering over Nosey's shoulder, and her green eyes looked intent.

"How's she doing?" Stephanie asked.

"I'm not sure," Nosey admitted. "She doesn't seem tense or wary, but she doesn't exactly seem to be quivering with eagerness, either. We've shown her that she can get back in the air car whenever she needs to—she picked up on how to open the canopy release incredibly quickly—but she doesn't seem inclined to go."

"Well, she's not running ahead or away, so let's see what happens," Stephanie said.

After Lionheart's family, the Swamp Cats were the treecat community Stephanie knew best. Two of the younger members, mirror twins her family had dubbed Right-Striped and Left-Striped for the reverse match of the markings within their gray coats, had lived with the Harringtons while they recovered from smoke and fire damage before returning to the wild. Valiant had been part of this clan originally, as well, although Stephanie suspected he'd been a bit of an oddity among them, what with his very un-treecat interest in things botanical.

Today, the visitors were met by a small group of treecats, led by the portly senior female Stephanie thought was important in the way Lionheart's sister, Morgana, was to Clan One. Jessica had dubbed her Queenie.

"Not because I think she's necessarily in charge or

anything," Jessica had explained, "because she acts like one of those pompous royals in the historical vids. I keep expecting her to say something like 'We are not amused.'"

Now, watching her, Stephanie had to smother a giggle at the appropriateness of her friend's observation. From the look Queenie gave her, the 'cat had sensed her amusement anyway, but she couldn't help that.

Nosey went to one knee, gently lifting Dulcinea down to the ground, and Queenie approached her carefully.

<You are Still Water,> Brilliant Images said as Still Water's two-leg set her on the ground. *<Dirt Grubber has told us of how your mate died, but I had not realized you were so close to your kittens' birth!>*

<I wish Leaf Racer were here to see them, Senior Memory Singer,> Still Water said, recognizing the power of the other's mind-voice.

<The two-legs are far more . . . different among themselves than the People are,> Brilliant Images said. *<I think their mind-blindness makes it easier for their evildoers to hide who and what they are than it is among the People. But these two-legs, and especially Windswept's friends, have always done good for Damp Ground. Indeed, we would all have perished in the last fire season if not for them.>*

<Climbs Quickly and Dirt Grubber have shared their own memories of that day with me,> Still Water replied. *<And even if they had not, I could not taste the mind-glow of my two-leg, Protector, or of Walks from Shadow and not know that there are those among the two-legs who would protect the People with their own lives.>*

<That is true.> Brilliant Images reached out and touched Still Water's belly with a gentle true-hand. *<And I imagine Healer has taken excellent care of you.>* Amusement colored her mind-voice and she threw Still Water

the mental picture of two far younger males who were obviously twins. *<It is what he does!>*

<Indeed it is!> Still Water bleeked a quiet laugh.

<Do you know what it is that brings them here today?> Brilliant Images asked. *<We are always happy to see Windswept and Dirt Grubber, but they do not usually come accompanied by friends.>*

<I do not,> Still Water admitted, and looked over her shoulder and raised her mind-voice. *<Climbs Quickly?>*

Lionheart leapt lightly down from Stephanie's shoulder and flowed across to Dulcinea and Queenie.

"Somehow that doesn't look like welcoming home a missing family member," Stephanie said, and Nosey shook his head.

"I'm pretty sure it isn't. I think I've gotten pretty good at reading her body language, and she certainly looks relaxed, but there's no ... eagerness that I can see. Happiness, yes, but if this was really her family, I think she'd be at least as excited to see them as she is to see celery!"

"Given treecats and celery, I wouldn't be too sure of that, if I were you," Stephanie said dryly. "Still, I take your point. And it looks like they've called Lionheart over to explain what she's doing here." She snorted a quiet laugh. "I bet they give him a hard time!"

<It has been a long time since your last visit, Climbs Quickly,> Brilliant Images observed as the Bright Water scout reached her. *<How is your sister?>*

<Sings Truly is well, Memory Singer,> Climbs Quickly told her.

<Good. Then now that the courteous question is dealt with, can you tell us what brings your two-legs here today?

This is not simply one of Windswept and Dirt Grubber's visits home.>

<It is always impossible to know all that a two-leg, even my own Death Fang's Bane, is up to,> Climbs Quickly admitted. *<I sometimes—often—think that even they are not always certain, in their mind-blindness. But I believe Death Fang's Bane and Shining Sunlight are here for at least two reasons.>*

<And those are?>

<I believe the two of them are studying the People for the two-leg elders. Before we came here, Death Fang's Bane took Shining Sunlight to Bright Water's central nesting place. He had been there before, although not nearly so often as she has, but this time they used their image-makers to make many images of our nest places and our storage areas. From the taste of their mind-glows, I believe this is at least partly because of what happened to Leaf Racer. The good two-legs have punished the one who slew him, and from Death Fang's Bane's mind-glow, especially, I believe that their study of the People is intended to help protect us against others like Mind Canker.>

<And how will studying us help them do that?> Brilliant Images asked doubtfully.

<That I do not know,> Climbs Quickly acknowledged. *<But I have spent too long bonded to Death Fang's Bane to not recognize when she is fighting to protect the People. I suspect that the two-leg elders need fuller knowledge of the People in order to go to their own higher elders and enlist their aid in our protection. After all, if they do not even know how many of us there are, or where our clans dwell, then it will be difficult to prevent their own evildoers from doing us harm.>*

<There is reason in that,> Brilliant Images decided. *<And we will do what we can to aid in that project. But you said you believed there were two reasons for today's visit?>*

<I cannot be certain of this, either, but I believe they are seeking Golden-Leaf Clan. They do not know the clan from which Leaf Racer and Still Water came, and there is no way we can tell them that. But your range is not that far distant from Golden-Leaf's. I think it possible that they believe she is of Damp Ground.>

<We would be honored and pleased to have one strong enough to survive her mate's death for the sake of her unborn kittens,> Brilliant Images said, *<but obviously, she is not.>*

<Of course not,> Climbs Quickly said, *<and from the taste of Death Fang's Bane's mind-glow, they are beginning to realize that. Even if they are mind-blind, they are also very clever.>* He laughed softly. *<So I believe that when we leave here, they will understand if Still Water seeks to guide them to her own clan.>*

<I would like that,> Still Water said wistfully. *<I miss my clan's mind-glows, and I must prove to them that I am well.>*

<Well, in that case,> Brilliant Images said, turning to trot sedately toward the watching two-legs, *<we had best be about helping these poor mind-blind two-legs accomplish their mission as swiftly as possible so that you may be on your way.>*

"Nope, definitely not her clan," Stephanie said as Queenie came towards them, followed by the other 'cats. "I've seen Lionheart making introductions before."

"Where *is* it, then?" Trudy asked. "This is the only clan near the house, isn't it?"

"It's the only one we've located so far." Stephanie shrugged. "The whole reason Chief Shelton sent us out, though, is that there's so much more we *don't* know about the treecats than we *do* know. And we don't know exactly what direction Fuzzy Friend and Dulcinea came from. So we're really just checking the Swamp Cats first because we knew where they were. It's kind of frustrating that we can't just ask Dulcinea!"

"I'm sure she'd tell us if she could," Nosey said. He sounded just a bit protective of Dulcinea, and Stephanie shook her head.

"Of course she would! Don't forget, I've probably had more experience with one-way conversation frustration than anyone else on Sphinx! And it's never been because Lionheart didn't want to help."

Nosey nodded as Queenie reached the humans. She looked up at Jessica with a bleek of welcome, but then she turned back to Stephanie. She rose high on her haunches and patted Stephanie's knee. Then she pointed at Karl—no, Stephanie realized. Not at Karl, but at the camera hanging from his shoulder.

Stephanie felt her eyebrows rising as Queenie finished pointing at the camera, and then pointed back the way she'd come with what certainly looked like an air of welcome.

"Golly," she said. "Maybe Lionheart and Survivor have figured out more about our new assignment than we thought, Karl. That sure looks like an invitation to come take pictures of the family and kids!"

"It certainly does," Karl agreed. "So what are we waiting for?"

33

IT WAS DISAPPOINTING THAT DULCINEA CLEARLY WASN'T a member of the Swamp Cats, but the visit to Valiant's clan went much more quickly and smoothly than anyone had expected. Clearly, Lionheart had grasped what Stephanie and Karl were doing, even if he might not have a clue as to *why* they were doing it, and Queenie and the other senior 'cats organized the day's operations far more expeditiously than she and Karl ever could have managed without that. In fact, they finished their preliminary survey—they intended to make follow-up visits to each of the clans they identified on a regular basis—well before lunchtime.

Stephanie, as a daughter of Meyerdahl, was totally in favor of going ahead and eating early, but, surprisingly, the *treecats* weren't.

"What in the world's gotten into them?" Trudy wondered as a wavefront of furry arboreals flowed about the humans' ankles and headed back for the parked air cars.

"I don't have the least idea," Stephanie admitted. "I've never seen them act this way before! It's almost like they're trying to get rid of us!"

"If that was what they wanted, they wouldn't have cooperated so enthusiastically while we took pictures and measured things," Karl pointed out.

"Okay, Mr. Brilliant. What do *you* think they're doing?" his fiancée demanded.

"I'm not sure, but if you'll notice who's taking point—"

He pointed with his chin, and Stephanie's eyes narrowed as she saw Dulcinea scampering towards Nosey and Trudy's air car. As Karl had suggested, she was well out in front of the crowd, despite her gravid condition, and as Stephanie watched, she hopped up and hit the lever to open the canopy. She jumped up into the cockpit and looked back down at Nosey.

"Bleek," she said. "Bleek!"

"Well, *somebody's* ready to go," Nosey said, and then the canopy of Karl and Stephanie's Forestry Service cruiser opened, as well.

Stephanie looked across and saw Lionheart perched on the running board, looking back at her with undeniably smug ears, and shook her head.

"I wish the people who don't think 'cats are intelligent could be here to see *this*," she said. "I don't know what they're up to, but it's clearly a mass conspiracy."

"Then I guess we should see what, exactly, they have in mind," Karl said.

"Oh, definitely. But we need to drop off the Swamp Cats' celery, first! It'd be rude not to."

"Agreed," Karl said, opening the cargo bin to pull out the bagged celery from Marjorie Harrington's greenhouse. "On the other hand, it might be a good idea to only drop off half of it."

"Do you think?"

"I dunno, but from the looks of things, we might need some of it in a little bit."

"That would be fantastic."

"Yes, it would," Karl agreed, and looked at Jessica as the ecstatic Swamp Cats flowed forward and took one of the celery bags into custody. "Jess, you still have free time to spend on the mystery?"

"I cleared the whole day," Jessica replied. "And you know me. I'm always in favor of mysteries!"

"I knew there was a reason you and Steph got along so well." Karl shook his head and waved Stephanie ahead of him. "Go ahead, Lionheart's chariot awaits us."

Even as he spoke, Survivor leapt gracefully into the cruiser, as well, and Stephanie stuck her tongue out at her fiancé before she followed.

Both vehicles rose in the silence counter-grav allowed, and Karl looked at Lionheart as he perched between the two front seats.

"Okay, Navigator. Where to?"

Lionheart only looked back up at him, and Karl frowned. Most of the cats who'd adopted had figured out how to direct their humans once they were in the air, but apparently Lionheart had forgotten.

Then his com pinged.

"Yes, Nosey?" he said as he accepted the call.

"Jess said I should com you and tell you Dulcinea is pointing almost due north."

"*Dulcinea* is pointing?"

"Definitely. And she's looking at me a bit impatiently, too."

"Hmm." Karl glanced at Stephanie, then back at the com display. "It looks like they may have figured out even more than we thought. This obviously wasn't her family, but if she's pointing, then maybe that's where she wants us to go next."

"That's what I figured, too," Nosey said, and Stephanie felt a pang of sympathy as she heard the note of worry buried deep in his voice. "And from her body language, it looks like she wants to see them pretty badly."

"In that case, take the lead and we'll follow."

Karl slowed and allowed Nosey to pass the cruiser, then turned to follow in the other air car's wake.

"We have to tell Uncle Duncan about this," Stephanie said beside him as the still-bare treetops flowed away below them. "This is obviously a group effort, and they must've organized it only after we got here. Otherwise, Dulcinea would've been pointing by the time we left home."

"Which clearly demonstrates the ability to communicate complex ideas." Karl nodded. "But we still don't have any proof of *how* they do it."

"No, but I think we're collecting more and more circumstantial evidence in favor of telepathy."

"Which people like the Franchittis and their sympathizers will laugh out of court," Karl replied grimly.

"We're never going to convince *them*," Stephanie pointed out. "But we won't have to if we can convince enough people whose brains actually work."

"There's that," Karl agreed, reaching across to lay one hand on her knee. "There's that."

"I think we're getting close," Nosey announced about forty-five minutes later. "She seems awfully excited about something, anyway."

"I'm looking for a break in the canopy big enough to get in through," Karl replied, studying the feed from one of the SFS's satellites on a window in his HUD. "Doesn't look all that promising, but we *might* be able to squeeze in through that opening to the west. Looks like there's a pretty good-sized stream down there, and I don't see a lot of undergrowth along the banks. Not yet, anyway."

"I think you're probably right," Nosey agreed, but his tone was dubious, and Karl flashed a smile at Stephanie.

"We'll take the lead on this one," he said. "This cruiser's designed to bull through pretty dense growth. It's stout enough to handle some serious branch impacts, it doesn't mind rough terrain landing spots, and it's bigger than your car, too. If we can get down there and sort of clear the way, we'll find the best landing spot we can and then coach you down."

"Sounds good," Nosey replied, and Karl began easing the cruiser down through the treetops.

It would have been impossible to get into the narrow opening without counter-grav, and the sound of branches dragging across the hull and canopy was accompanied by more than one sharp-edged "crack!" as some of those branches snapped completely. But this was scarcely the first time Karl had inserted a cruiser into narrow quarters, and his hands were gentle on the controls. The stream itself was more of a narrow, shallow river than they'd thought from above, and its banks showed clear evidence of how high and wide it had flowed with snowmelt. It was still at least several meters wider than it normally was, judging by the flow patterns and flotsam, but there was enough room between it and the denser undergrowth above the floodplain line, and Karl brought the cruiser in for an almost perfect landing.

"Not too shabby," Stephanie congratulated him, and he gave her another smile. Then he toggled the com.

"We're down, Nosey. I think you could probably get in here on the bank, but it would be tight and the ground's kinda soft. On the other hand, this river may still be a little wider than usual, but it's pretty shallow, too. Let me check to be sure, but I think there's a big enough, firm enough 'sandbar' out there to support your landing skids."

"Copy," Nosey replied, and Karl popped the canopy.

He and Stephanie climbed down from the cockpit, followed by their companions, and Karl waded cautiously out into the icy, fast-running stream. It never came above his boot tops, although it got close on more than one occasion, and he raised his uni-link as he got to the middle of the stream.

"I was wrong, Nosey. It's not a 'sandbar' at all. This part of the river—well, anyway, big creek—has a bottom that's pretty much solid rock. Let me get out of the way, and you can set it down. Might want to use your personal counter-grav to keep your feet out of the water when you climb out, though. It's still mighty cold."

"Soon as you're clear," Nosey acknowledged, and Karl waded back across to join Stephanie, Lionheart, and Survivor.

Nosey landed neatly in the exact center of the stream-bed as soon as Karl was out of the way. The canopy opened, and the humans disembarked. Jessica and Trudy had both worn knee-high thermal boots when they set out, and they splashed cheerfully down into the water, with a chittering Valiant on Jess's shoulder. Nosey, who *hadn't* worn thermal boots, took Karl's advice and adjusted his counter-grav until he floated in mid-air with Dulcinea cradled in his arms. Then he pushed firmly against the air car with one foot and drifted toward the bank.

He came up about a meter short, and the other four humans looked up at him.

"Plan on hanging around out there long?" Stephanie asked innocently.

"I could use a hand."

"You seem to be doing fine so far. What's the problem?"

Butter would not have melted in Stephanie's mouth.

"Look, I took your boyfriend's advice. That's why I'm stuck out here. So the least you could do would be to give me a tow. It's only a meter, for goodness' sake! Just lean out and grab an ankle or something!"

"I don't know...." Stephanie's voice trailed off, and she looked up at Karl. "What do you think?"

"I think I'm engaged to a cruel, cruel woman," he replied gravely, and reached out to pull Nosey the rest of the way to the bank.

"Yeah, and you love it!" Jessica told him.

"Never said I didn't," Karl agreed with a grin, steadying Nosey as he dialed back the counter-grav. "Feisty little thing, isn't she?"

"Dead man walking," Trudy said somberly.

"Oh, I *might* let him live," Stephanie replied, and watched Nosey set Dulcinea gently on the ground.

The treecat looked around, then up at him, and pointed again, deeper into the bush. Given that they knew absolutely nothing about this area or its wildlife, Stephanie checked her sidearm and Karl collected his rifle from the cruiser's gun rack, chambered a round, and set the safety before they nodded to the other two.

"Not likely anything's going to sneak up on us with four treecats keeping an eye out," Stephanie observed dryly. "Never hurts to be sure, though."

"Oh, I can get behind that idea," Nosey assured her, then looked down at his companion. "Okay, Dulcinea. Lead the way."

Dulcinea looked up again, bleeked softly, and headed away from the stream, flanked by Valiant and Survivor while Lionheart took point ahead of her.

<*Still Water?!*> Still Water paused as the mind-voice called out to her. <*You are well? We thought the evildoers had slain you, as well!*>

<*I am, indeed, well, Ground Runner's Bane,*> Still Water replied as she recognized the hunter's mind-voice. <*As Bright Water's songs told us, not all two-legs are evildoers, and the good two-legs have punished Leaf Racer's killer.*>

<*Sharp Scent was near enough to taste Leaf Racer's mind-glow when it was ripped away,*> Ground Runner's Bane said. <*But he could not taste your mind-glow after that. We believed you had followed Leaf Racer.*>

<*And so I would have, if not for the two-leg who saved me. He used his own thunder-barker to stop the evildoer who had murdered Leaf Racer from murdering me as well. And then his mind-glow held me, when I would have followed. He would not let me go—he and my kittens' mind-glows. It took hands of days for my own mind-glow to heal, but it has done so.*>

<*So I taste,*> Ground Runner's Bane replied, blending out of the branches on a net-wood branch. <*But I did not expect to see you here with two-legs.*>

An edge of disapproval colored his mind-voice, but Still Water half-flattened her ears.

<*These are my* friends,> she said sternly. <*And among them are Death Fang's Bane and Shining Sunlight. All the People know they have been our friends and our protectors from the moment she met Climbs Quickly! I would not bring evildoers here to our central nesting place.*>

<*Forgive me.*> Ground Runner's Bane might not be fully convinced of the wisdom of her actions, but his apology was genuine. <*May I ask why* you *have brought them?*>

<*As I explained to Damp Ground Clan earlier today,*> Climbs Quickly said, entering the conversation, <*I believe Death Fang's Bane and Shining Sunlight have been assigned by their elders to learn all they may about the People in*

order that they and the other two-legs who would protect us will have a better idea of the task which confronts them.>

<And that is what I believe, as well,> Still Water said firmly.

<In that case, please remain here while I return to our nesting place and...warn our elders Still Water has returned.>

Stephanie watched the treecats conferring, then shook her head as the male 'cat on the picketwood branch turned and disappeared once more.

"Going home to check in before they welcome us for a visit," she said.

"Yeah, and from the look of things Dulcinea had to give him a piece of her mind before he did," Nosey agreed.

"Something I'm already learning. Never argue with a female," Karl said solemnly.

"My goodness!" Trudy widened her eyes at him. "I hadn't realized you were a man of such wisdom, Karl!"

"Believe me, Ranger Harrington is keeping me firmly in line."

"Hey! Don't go picking on me," Stephanie said.

"I wouldn't dare," Karl assured her, wrapping an arm around her.

They stood waiting for perhaps fifteen minutes, and then the other treecat—or another male the same size, at any rate—reappeared. He looked down at their four companions, then flirted his tail, and Lionheart looked back at the humans and made an unmistakable "follow me" gesture.

"Guess we passed muster," Karl said, pulling out his vibro-blade bush knife as he eyed the undergrowth. "This way, ladies and gentlemen."

They needed Karl's bush knife to create a human-sized hole in the thick underbrush fringing the top of the river's floodplain. Once they were ten or fifteen meters in, though, the upper story canopy had blocked enough sunlight to choke out most of the undergrowth and the going was much easier.

All of the male treecats had taken to the picketwood, with Lionheart, Valiant, and Survivor following the stranger, but Dulcinea had returned to Nosey and patted his knee until he scooped her up in his arms once more. Now she rode in the crook of his right arm, her muzzle pressed against his cheek while she buzzed a deep purr.

"I think she's glad to get home," he said, and Stephanie nodded, pretending she hadn't heard the worry that still edged his voice.

Trudy only reached out and took his free hand, squeezing it firmly. He looked down at her with a quick smile and squeezed back.

After about another five hundred meters, they reached a stand of crown oak and found themselves looking up at scores of treecats. The branches were lined with them, some of them clung head down to the tree trunks, like Old Earth squirrels, and a few hung from their tails, high overhead. The one thing all of them had in common were the sharp, unwavering gazes with which they examined their unexpected visitors.

The humans paused, waiting, and then a quartet of treecats dropped lightly to the ground and came toward them. A female, larger and (Stephanie suspected) older than almost any of the females she'd yet met was at the center of the group. She lacked Queenie's stoutness. Indeed, she was lean and rangy and she moved with what could almost have been an edge of fragility that Stephanie was unaccustomed to seeing in treecats.

She and her escorts—all of them male—came to a

halt two or three meters from the humans and sat very upright, their tails curled around their feet.

<It gives me great joy to see you, Still Water.> Wind of Memory's mind-voice was soft, but her mind-glow blazed. *<We believed you were dead.>*

<And so I would have been, if not for Protector, my two-leg, grandmother,> Still Water replied, gazing at Golden-Leaf Clan's senior memory singer.

<So Ground Runner's Bane has told us. This>—she looked up at Protector—*<is "your" two-leg, granddaughter?>*

<He is.>

<I see.>

Stephanie glanced at Nosey as the elderly female gave him a very searching look.

"And who," she muttered sotto voce, "is this young man you brought home with you?"

Nosey gave her a look of his own, then stepped cautiously forward and went to his knees behind Dulcinea. He let the treecats get a good look at him, while keeping his hands to himself, and the female rose to stalk around him. She looked back at Dulcinea, then glanced up at Trudy, and made a final circuit around Nosey. She parked herself beside Dulcinea and looked over her shoulder at the male 'cats of her escort, then back up at Nosey.

Then she gave a single sharp, clear "Bleek!"

"Well, you'll do, young man," Stephanie continued her soft-voiced "translation" at Nosey's side. "You and your woman. You just make sure you take good care of our girl, now. She's had a hard time."

"I'll take care of her, ma'am," Nosey told the treecat.

"I just wish we could've saved her husband. We should never have let that happen."

"No, we shouldn't have," Trudy said, and her eyes filled with tears. "I really miss Fuzzy Friend, and I'm sorry our making friends led to this." She turned to Stephanie, Karl, and Jessica. "I know they can't understand the words, that they might not even understand we're making sense, but you told me the Swamp Cats used sound to chase off the swamp siren, so maybe they'll get the 'melody' even if they don't get the meaning."

"I talk to Lionheart all the time," Stephanie told her with a smile. "And this fine lady—I think we should call her Victoria—doesn't seem offended."

Indeed, Victoria had risen onto her tree feet and was pointing back toward the heart of the clan's central nesting space.

"Apparently, they've communicated the notion of pointing to *her*, too," Stephanie observed wryly. "Come on, Nosey. Let's go meet your extended family."

The rest of the visit went remarkably well, really. Stephanie and Karl's suspicion that Lionheart had explained to the Swamp Cats what Chief Shelton had assigned them to do appeared vindicated when after an obvious confab between him and Victoria, she and the rest of what must be the senior members of what had just become Clan Seven actually marshaled the clan's members to be counted. And they seemed remarkably unperturbed as she and Karl recorded imagery of their nests and their storage areas. Stephanie was intrigued when she realized that Clan Seven's pottery makers had a considerably larger work area than Lionheart's clan did. In fact, she suspected that it was much bigger than it needed to be to meet Seven's own needs.

"Look at this," she said to Karl. "Do you know, I

think Dulcinea's clan may make pots for other clans. I never thought about that possibility!"

"Me neither, but if you're right, I'd say that's even more evidence of their intelligence. I wonder what they get back in trade?"

"Me, too. Which makes it even more frustrating that I can't just ask Lionheart."

"I expect we're going to think that pretty often in this assignment," Karl said philosophically, and she snorted.

While they worked, Dulcinea was the center of attention. It seemed that every single member of her enormous family came by to rub muzzles with her, wrap arms and tail around her, and croon softly to her. Victoria, especially, stayed close beside her, the very tip of her tail tucked around her, and Nosey's eyes prickled. He wasn't a treecat, but even so he could almost literally taste the welcome and the love flowing over her, and his heart ached with joy for her. But he held tightly to Trudy's hand, because the more of that joy he saw, the more uncertainty colored his own happiness.

By the time Karl and Stephanie had finished making their records the long Sphinx day had shifted well into afternoon, so they brought out the picnic lunch they'd packed expecting to dine with the Swamp Cats. A circle of 'cats gathered around them, watching alertly as the humans unloaded the food...and especially the kilo or so of celery they still had left. They sampled several of the other human foods, and Victoria dispatched one of the younger males to return with a carry net filled with near-pine seed pods as their contribution to the meal. Stephanie was glad she actually liked the seeds' strong, nutty flavor, although she would have eaten them anyway, to be polite.

Finally, though, the daylight began to fade, and it was time for the humans to go. Stephanie found Nosey standing beside her, and he shifted uneasily, then looked down at her.

"I wonder if Dulcinea wants to stay here with her family," he said softly. "She's obviously enjoyed being with them, and certainly she should have the right to choose where she's going to live. When she reached out to me, she was in shock and pain. It doesn't...it doesn't seem *right* that she should be bound by a decision made under so much stress. Can the link be unlinked?"

His question made Stephanie uneasy. What would she do if Lionheart decided to dissolve his bond with *her*? As much as she loved Karl, her relationship with Lionheart was closer, tighter. It really felt like "till death do us part," but what if that had been just her eleven-year-old self's way of interpreting the feeling? Much as she loved him, she couldn't really know what *he* felt; she could know only what *she* felt.

Worse, she'd learned so much these last few years about how her feelings weren't the most reliable guide. She'd thought Anders was her One True Love; now he was just a very long-distance pen pal. She was going to marry Karl, and she knew she loved him far more deeply than she'd thought she loved Anders. Yet there was a reason "divorce" was in the human vocabulary, written into the legal system. Humans weren't always good judges of emotional ties. Were treecats truly better? Might Lionheart "divorce" her one day?

Lionheart leapt from the upper limbs of a crown oak where he'd been relaxing with some of the other cats. He flowed across to her, and she held out her arms, lifting him to her shoulder.

"Bleek?" he said.

But I'm the one who put the question mark there, Stephanie thought. *It's the same sound he makes* whenever *he needs to get my attention, really.*

Isn't it?

Her panic was rising but, with Lionheart warm against her back, his whiskers tickling her cheek, she could pretend to be calm.

"I don't know, Nosey. So far, all the human-treecat bonds have remained intact. But, really, is less than a decade a big enough data set to make sweeping judgments? Why don't we try a test? Head back for your air car. See if Dulcinea follows."

"Right!" Nosey grasped Trudy's hand, drew a deep breath, squared his shoulders, and started back towards the stream.

He didn't look back, but Trudy did. Even in the failing light, Stephanie saw her perfect teeth bite anxiously into her lower lip. It was obvious she wanted to call Dulcinea as she might have called to a pet dog, and equally obvious that she would rather bite hard enough to draw blood before she did.

She and Nosey had half-vanished under the trees, and Dulcinea had made no move to follow. But they were still well within the "safe" range, even for new adoptees, Stephanie thought.

"We should take our leave," she said.

"Right." Jessica nodded, gathering up her pocket med scanner and a few other odds and ends she'd used to examine Clan Seven's members.

She didn't glance to where Valiant had his head together with a 'cat she'd tentatively named "Farmer." He and Valiant had spent their time happily poring over a collection of dried lichen which had obviously provided a significant portion of Clan Seven's winter diet. Now, although she'd given no signal, Valiant shook himself, touched noses briefly with Farmer, and loped after her.

"Time for us to go, too, Steph," Karl said gently.

"Right."

They started toward the river in Jessica's wake, and Lionheart and Survivor raced ahead of them, tussling with each other in the leaves.

They'd gotten nearly halfway back to the river, almost completely out of sight of Clan Seven's nest place, before Dulcinea detached herself from Victoria and the other female 'cats with whom she'd spent the entire visit. She gave Victoria a quick nose touch, then hurried after Nosey. He stopped and turned, and she patted his knee and held her arms up to him.

He scooped her up, holding her to his chest, and walked swiftly, without a word, back to the river. He didn't bother with counter-grav; he just waded through the icy water to his air car, set Dulcinea gently into the cockpit, then waited for Jessica and Trudy to climb aboard with Valiant before he followed.

The canopy closed, and Stephanie looked at Karl, one eyebrow raised.

"Let's go," he said, and they climbed into the cruiser with their companions, then lifted carefully through the branches.

Stephanie watched the display from the rear camera as Nosey's air car rose behind them. There was just enough light that she could see through the canopy, and she realized Trudy was driving.

"Com Nosey," she told the cruiser's computer, and waited a moment until the com pinged to indicate a completed link.

"How did that go?" she asked gently. "Do you feel like Dulcinea was comfortable leaving?"

She paused, waiting for his response, but the display remained blank, and it was Trudy's voice that answered, a little tight and anxious.

"Nosey's crying. Just a minute. I think it's okay."

There was another brief silence, and then Nosey's voice came, choked with tears.

"Just a sec...."

The display blinked alive, and Stephanie saw him tucking away his handkerchief and scrubbing at his eyes.

"It's fine. I'm still learning how to read Dulcinea's feelings, but she's rumbling at me. I get the feeling she wonders how I could've been unsure. I know *she* was sure, anyway, or she wouldn't have done whatever it was she did back there."

The tension Stephanie had been holding in her shoulders melted away. If Dulcinea had let Nosey leave, had broken the bond, that would have had such incredible implications.

Not that the bond between human and treecat doesn't already have incredible implications, she told herself, *but I'm so much more prepared to deal with* those.

34

"THIS IS TRULY MARVELOUS," DUNCAN HARRINGTON said, sitting beside Stephanie and Karl as he watched the imagery they'd brought back from Dulcinea's home clan.

Stephanie nodded in agreement, eyes sparkling as she watched the recorded Victoria marshaling the troops to cooperate with them. She hadn't understood why Nosey had insisted on dubbing them the Clan of La Mancha, but Duncan had enjoyed a hearty laugh when he heard the name, and she'd demanded to know what was so funny. But he'd only chuckled again, then pointed at her computer terminal with the suggestion that she research it herself.

Now he leaned back in his chair, folded his arms, looked at her and Karl, and shook his head.

"I never imagined something like this happening so quickly," he told them approvingly. "Watching the imagery, I think you're absolutely right. Lionheart and Survivor"— he looked equally approvingly at the 'cats stretched across the backs of Stephanie's and Karl's chairs—"clearly do understand what you're after. I can't begin to judge whether or not they understand *why* you're after it, of course. In fact, I rather doubt they do. But that doesn't detract anything from the evidence—the *obvious* evidence, in my opinion—that they explained to Queenie and then to Victoria what it was you wanted. And in both cases, the clans organized themselves to help you do it from a completely cold start. More than that, it seems to me, although I can't be certain, that La Mancha was actually better organized than the Swamp Cats. Things went even more smoothly, despite the fact that La Mancha had no previous contact with humans at all. And if that's true, Peanut," he turned back from the 'cats to beam at Stephanie, "it indicates that Lionheart and Survivor—and quite probably Valiant and Dulcinea—all learned from watching you with the Swamp Cats, recognizing what worked well and what didn't, and were able to suggest improvements to streamline the process to La Mancha. And if it turns out they truly are exporting pottery outside their own clan group, you've turned up significant objective, physical evidence that they *must* be capable of communication with one another. It's difficult to imagine how they might engage in even a simple barter economy without one!"

"I never expected La Mancha, either," Stephanie said. "And I think you're absolutely right about what our 'ambassadors' did." She reached up to caress Lionheart's ears, and the 'cat pushed back against her fingers with a buzzing purr. "I've tried—I've really tried—to be skeptical about that, but—"

She shrugged, and Duncan unfolded his right arm to give her shoulder a squeeze.

"I have to do that, too, of course," he said. "In fact, that was a point Sanura and I made with Earl Adair Hollow and Gwen. Not just because it's never permissible for a scholar or a researcher to allow preconceptions or personal desire to corrupt his observations and conclusions, but because of our shared last name."

She looked back at him and nodded with a wry expression.

"That said, though, and understanding that I'm not going to allow myself to draw any ironclad conclusions for a while yet, at this point, I genuinely don't see any way to deny the treecats' sapiency. I'm pretty sure all we really need to establish is how high on the scale we place them, not whether or not they belong on it in the first place. Unfortunately, to be honest, I think there's a certain species-based chauvinism in the way the scale is structured. I've said that for a long time, but I'm afraid the 'cats are likely to prove my point."

"Afraid?" Karl repeated, and Duncan grimaced.

"It comes back to that whole communication thing, and not just because the absence of an observable, provable form of communication will make it so much easier for the skeptics to place them lower than they deserve to be ranked. How much thought have the two of you given to how differently a telepath must process information and think?"

"We've thought about it a lot, actually," Stephanie replied. "We know it would have to have a major impact on how they *communicate* information to one another, but we don't see any way to get a handle on how that would affect the way they process it once they've shared it."

"One thing Steph suggested to me a while back," Karl put in, "is that however they communicate, they almost certainly don't do it in what we might think of as discrete data bytes."

"Ah?" Duncan raised an eyebrow at him.

"She said—and I agreed with her, after she pointed it out—that if they used discrete, separable 'data packets' they'd probably have a better window into the way we use spoken language. They might not break their communication down into such small packets, but they'd have at least the notion of building communication out of separately transmitted pieces. We haven't seen any sign that they do have it, though. That doesn't *prove* anything, of course, but I think she's onto something when she suggests that what they're really sharing is more of a gestalt. A data stream with so much bandwidth, so much...connectivity, that they probably don't even have a concept that it would be *possible* to break it down the way we have to."

"You came up with that on your own, did you?" Duncan asked, looking at Stephanie, and she shrugged with an unusual air of embarrassment as she heard the approval in his voice.

"In a way, I hope I'm wrong," she said. "Because if I'm not, it'll be really hard for them to ever understand what noises we make mean. And if we can't get that across to them, we'll never be able to truly communicate with them, which'll be another brick for people who don't want to acknowledge how smart they really are."

"That's precisely what I was thinking," Duncan agreed. "It is also why I've been arguing for so long that we need to reevaluate the human-centric prejudices built into the way we've structured the sentience scale. It's biased in favor of species—*people*—who think the same way we do. I'm not talking about prejudices, or ideologies, or philosophies, or anything like that. I'm talking about the *mechanics* of the way we think. Of the way we perceive and process information, communicate with each other. If the 'cats' minds work as differently from human minds as I think all three of us now suspect they do, it's going to work against their sapience rating because of those built-in biases."

"I wish just *something* about the treecats could be

so simple, so straightforward, no one could *argue* with it!" Stephanie's tone was suddenly fierce, and so were her eyes. "You're right, Uncle Duncan—they're not the same species we are, but they're just as much *people*! And this is *their* planet! It's not *right* for someone like... like the Franchittis to just move in and treat them like animals—not even *protected* animals!"

Lionheart shifted on the back of her chair to press his chin against the top of her head and croon to her, and Duncan tucked an arm around her and hugged her tightly.

"Have I mentioned lately how proud of you I am, Peanut? I know people four times your age, people who call themselves xeno-anthropologists, put all kinds of letters after their names to prove how educated and erudite they are, who don't grasp what this is all about *remotely* as well as you do. Lionheart and Survivor *are* people, and it's up to us to demonstrate that to the rest of the human race. Especially to the part of the human race that most wants to deny it. And you—you and Karl, and all of your friends—have made one heck of a start on doing just that."

Later that evening, as Duncan sat at his bedroom terminal, updating his own notes, he thought about that conversation. And how much he'd meant every word of it.

He paused in his dictation and frowned.

When he'd told her how proud he was of her, it had reminded him of what had drawn him to xeno-anthropology in the first place. He saw so much of himself in her—that need to understand, that drive to explore the ways in which other species' minds might work, to appreciate the things of which they were capable. Yet she brought her own fiery need to protect and preserve to the quest, as well. That soul-deep passion to fight for the entire natural world. Not to bar humanity from any access to it, but to insist that humans respect it, take care of it. *Cherish* it. She'd been that way since she was a little girl, unable to articulate her needs and desires clearly even to herself, and she'd grown so *much* here on Sphinx.

Some of that might be due to the tweaks the Alignment had inserted into the Harrington genotype in her great-grandparents' generation. But he had those same tweaks in his own genes, and while they undoubtedly did contribute to her determination, that iron will to succeed, and while they might help to explain the sheer brilliance of her intellect, they hadn't defined what her drives would be. That was all her. The Alignment had contributed to *what* she was, but that need to protect, to revere and nurture...that had nothing to do with her DNA. No, it stemmed from the wellsprings which made her *who* she was. She'd found the task to which she would joyously devote her entire life, and if she had this much passion, this much fiery commitment when she was only seventeen...

As he sat there, looking at the display, the words he'd dictated, he realized how deeply he shared her determination to protect the treecats and preserve their claim to their world. And how glad he was that there was nothing in his mission for the Alignment which would have precluded that. How deeply, deeply glad he was that he could help the cousin he loved accomplish the great, lifelong goal she'd set for herself.

Yet that gladness *was* shadowed by the Alignment, he admitted to himself. He had no idea who the "specialist" the Alignment's intelligence directorate had sent along might be. Whoever it was, he—or she—probably wasn't from Meyerdahl, because Duncan had been the only passenger bound all the way to Manticore when he boarded ship for the first leg of his journey. He would have preferred to think that meant Abner Portnoy had been wrong, that no specialist had been sent after all, but he didn't believe that for a moment. That wasn't the way the Alignment worked.

He drew a deep, unhappy breath, then exhaled it.

He'd realized long ago that something like the Alignment, an organization which had dedicated itself to a centuries-long task that had to remain covert—hidden—because of the prejudices built into the Beowulf code, would inevitably find itself forced to compromise its own principles at times. That was, unfortunately, the way the galaxy—or the human race, at least—was wired. When discovery meant the automatic failure of their goal, they literally could not risk allowing the rest of the galaxy to learn of their existence. And that meant they must maintain ironbound, inflexible security...and that there would be times when they needed a more *proactive* response to threats. The ability to...neutralize threats which couldn't simply be eluded.

He didn't like that, and he never had, but likes and dislikes didn't change reality. And so he understood why the intelligence directorate had "specialists," and that some of those specialists didn't exist solely to gather intelligence.

Yet what truly bothered him at this moment was what Portnoy had said about needing live treecats if, indeed, they proved to be telepathic. Because what he hadn't considered when Portnoy explained the mission to him—what he hadn't bothered, or possibly *allowed*, himself to consider—was that Stephanie was right. Treecats *were* people. Not only that, she was almost certainly right that they were telepaths, as well, and he'd seen what the loss of Dulcinea's mate had done to her. Which meant the notion of kidnapping intelligent telepaths, ripping them away from all the soul-deep interconnectedness with their own kind telepathy *had* to imply, no matter how noble the avowed purpose, was an act of unconscionable evil that sent a wave of nausea rippling through him.

But what could he do about it? If he didn't even know which of his fellow passengers to Manticore was associated with the Alignment, how did he get any sort of "stand down" message to him? And why should whoever it was listen to him, even if he did?

He couldn't, but as that thought rolled through him, he realized it didn't mean he was automatically helpless, now did it?

If treecats truly were the telepaths and telempaths he was increasingly certain they were, they'd be extraordinarily difficult to trap, as Tennessee Bolgeo had discovered. By the same token, though, Bolgeo had demonstrated that they *could* be trapped if one went about it properly. And Duncan's position as a member of Sanura Hobbard's team, a member of the Great Treecat Conspiracy, and a trusted advisor of the Adair Foundation left him perfectly placed to remind everyone of that fact and emphasize the need to protect the 'cats from other trappers who might mean the species ill.

He was certain at least one of the native Manticorans opposed to recognizing any treecat claim to Sphinx would inevitably look for a way to eliminate the problem by eliminating the 'cats themselves. It was probable they hadn't yet reached the point of actively working on it, but from what he knew of human nature and the briefings George Lebedyenko had arranged for him, he was grimly certain it was only a matter of time until someone did. And it might be his own membership in Alignment which suggested it to him, but the possibility of some sort of bioweapon struck him as the most likely, most cost-effective way for some sick bastard to go about it.

Which meant, if his darker fears were justified, that *they'd* need treecats for experimental purposes.

And if protecting the 'cats from vermin like that just happened to protect them from the Alignment, as well, Duncan Harrington, loyal son of the Alignment though he was, would shed not a single tear.

AFTER STEPHANIE AND KARL SHARED THEIR PRELIMI-
nary survey with Duncan, he had several suggestions
for ways they might refine their techniques. He'd also
requested a more detailed survey of the environment
around each clan's central range, which required multiple
additional visits to each of them. The 'cats greeted them
enthusiastically each time—and *not* as Stephanie had told
Karl, just because they brought celery each time—and
the fact that Lionheart's community, the Swamp Cats,
and La Mancha were all relatively easy flights from the
Harrington freehold, meant they could return "home"
to share each day's results with Duncan and refine their
studies' parameters still further.

After they'd finished with La Mancha, though, it was
time to move farther afield, and they debated which of
the other three known clans—the Ubel Disaster's relocated refugees, Survivor's clan, or Fisher's clan—they
should visit next.

"We already know where the Refugees and Survivor's clan are located, and they already know both of us," Stephanie said, looking across the breakfast table at Karl and Duncan.

"That's true." Karl nodded. "On the other hand, we already have more data on the Refugees than we had on anyone else—including Lionheart's clan, really, Steph. And I'm sure both of those are still pretty badly stressed by what's happened to them."

"Which would 'contaminate the data' in terms of 'cats in the wild," she agreed, nodding even more vigorously than he had.

"Actually, that might be an argument in favor of surveying them." Duncan set down his coffee cup with a thoughtful frown. "Eventually, we'll want a meterstick for how interaction with humans and with our technology affects the 'aboriginal' treecat template. From what I've seen so far of the Refugees, I suspect they'll be the best example of that we'll see for a long time. I certainly hope so, anyway. I devoutly hope no one ever has to rescue another clan from that sort of human-generated catastrophe!"

His eyes darkened grimly for a moment. Then he shook himself.

"Survivor's people—like the Swamp Cats—represent a more intermediate step than the Refugees do. But your excellent work with the Swamp Cats is already in the database, and I'd suggest waiting until Survivor's clan's had more time to settle into their new range under less severe weather conditions before we take a closer look at them. I do want to chart the fashion in which they go about establishing their new range with minimal human intervention so that we can compare it to how the Refugees have done the same thing, but that's another reason to wait until later in the spring before you two drop in on them."

"Makes sense to me," Stephanie said after a moment.

"Yeah, and even if we don't know exactly where Fisher's clan is, we know it has to be somewhere near my folks' place," Karl put in. "That would give us a base of operations close to them."

"In that case, we should probably screen Scott and Irina and tell them we're coming."

"Karl! Stephanie!"

Stephanie looked up from the bag she'd just hoisted out of the SFS cruiser as Karl's oldest sister, Nadia, called their names from the sprawling Zivonik farmhouse's snow porch.

"Hi, Nadia!" she replied.

"What're you doing here?" Karl asked as he set his own bag down beside hers. "I thought you and Staysa were supposed to be in town this morning."

"When we found out you guys were coming, we decided to move that to the afternoon," Nadia said, walking across to them. "Someone"—she rolled her eyes—"wants to stuff Lionheart and Survivor with celery."

The treecats bleeked at her from the cruiser's opened canopy, and she shook her head, then laughed and gave each of the humans a hug.

"It's good to see both of you. Got anything else in there you need somebody to carry?"

"No, I think we're good," Stephanie replied as Lionheart leapt down beside her. Survivor followed, and all five of them headed for the house.

To her own considerable surprise, Stephanie had discovered she felt almost...shy about staying with the Zivoniks. She'd visited several times before her birthday, and both of them had visited together since their official engagement, but they hadn't stayed over, and as they walked toward the house with Nadia, she found herself looking at it through different eyes.

I never really thought about it until Jessica teased me, but now I can't get out of my head. The Zivoniks' claim is huge compared to Mom and Dad's. It's bigger than Cordelia's mom's, and a lot bigger than the Franchitti place—almost big enough it turned into an earldom, instead of a barony. And legally, Karl's the next Baron Zivonik. When that happens—when he inherits—will he have to give up working for the SFS and turn into a farmer and landholder? That doesn't seem like him, somehow. And would I still know Karl like I do if he suddenly started fussing over crop yields and timber management?

Evelina Zivonik was waiting to welcome them as they headed inside, and Stephanie tried to put that particular future out of her head as her future mother-in-law embraced her firmly. Karl's parents were still young. They were raising a toddler. From a passing quip about whether or not they should give the highchair away, the idea that Lev might have a little sibling one of these days was not to be dismissed. And Karl must have told his mother that they weren't "sleeping" together, because Stephanie was given her usual berth in the guest room, which was something of a relief.

Later, after a boisterous family meal, Stephanie used the excuse of having to get up really early the next day to go up to her room. Once there, she lay awake, listening to the sounds of the Zivonik family slowly winding down, trying to work out how she'd feel if she was expected to think of this place as "home," the way Karl obviously still did.

It's so weird. I've been thinking about him and me, but getting married means accepting a relationship with all the Zivoniks, and there are so many of them! I bet Sumiko wouldn't have had this problem. She'd lived with the family since she was a kid. For her, marrying Karl would have firmed up her relationship, reassured her that the Zivoniks weren't going to ditch her just because she was "grown up." They wouldn't have anyway—I know them too well to think that for a minute!—but, at her age, would she have known that?

Uneasily, Stephanie wondered if she'd really considered what it meant to get married. Guiltily, she realized she felt immeasurable relief that she and Karl hadn't set a wedding date. She was pretty sure she wanted Karl to be her one and only, but all the rest—becoming a Zivonik with all that should entail if she took it seriously? No, she definitely wasn't as ready for that as she'd thought she would be . . . when she'd thought about it at all. And she needed to be certain about what all that meant and how she'd handle it. She owed that to both of them. And to the rest of the Zivoniks, for that matter!

Early the next morning, Stephanie and Karl grabbed coffee and thick slices of fruit bread and butter to eat in the air car, then flew over to Scott and Irina's. They'd been invited to have breakfast there, so Scott could brief them about the treecat community Fisher belonged to. On the way over, Karl was, for him, unusually chatty. He and his dad had sat up late, talking about "everything and nothing," as Karl put it. Stephanie did her best to ask questions and figured she'd hidden her unease pretty well, but when they were circling in to land, Karl turned to her.

"Are you feeling okay, Steph? You seem a bit off."

Stephanie was very careful not to lie, because she suspected Karl would pick up on it. Neither of them had the fine-tuned empathy of a treecat, but he'd always had more "people sense" than Stephanie had been issued pre-Lionheart, and both of them had become far better at "reading" the people around them—especially those close to them—since they'd been adopted.

"I am a bit off," she admitted. "Maybe I ate something that didn't quite agree with me. I feel a bit detached."

"Mom does cook differently than your family does," he said. "Should we have Scott look you over?"

"If breakfast doesn't settle my gut, I'll ask," she promised.

"Sounds good. Maybe the famous Stephanie appetite wasn't satisfied with starting off the day with a mere thousand calorie snack."

"It wasn't a thousand calories!" she protested, laughing.

"With all that butter? You might be surprised."

They walked to the house and were letting the auto-vac suck the mud off their boots when Irina opened the snow porch door and greeted them.

"Leave your boots out here if you want," she said. "There are scuffs in all sizes on the rack. This time of year, it's almost impossible to avoid the mud, and it's hardly worth your getting your boots clean since you'll be going out in such a short while."

They accepted her offer, then joined her in the kitchen.

"Where's Scott?" Karl asked, when it became evident the redhead wasn't in the house, and Irina sighed.

"He got an early call from old Mrs. Chambers. Sounds as if she's broken an ankle. He'd arranged cover for today, so he could go out with you, but he didn't want to leave her waiting. She's alone while her son is off on a business trip to Manticore. Scott pinged me just before you landed and said we should start eating. Mrs. Chambers insisted he eat something there."

"It's not easy being married to a doctor, is it?" Stephanie said. "My dad is the same way. Mom's pretty resigned to making plans that assume he'll cancel at the last minute because some animal emergency comes up."

"It's certainly harder to be married to a doctor than it would be to be married to, say, a potter." Irina made a vague gesture in the direction of her pottery studio. "But, really, most jobs that involve living creatures have a degree of unpredictability. Now that you and Karl are both working full time for the SFS, I'm guessing you'll join the ranks of the 'on call.'"

"True enough," Karl said. "We're lucky Chief Shelton put us on this treecat survey, but it won't always be like this."

Irina served up breakfast: buttery cheese and mushroom omelets, very fluffy biscuits topped with more butter and honey, accompanied by fresh citrus from the trees in her own greenhouse. Stephanie was careful to eat heartily to assuage any worries Karl might have. In truth, her unease had let up once they were away from the Zivonik house. She was determined not to let it come creeping back.

"Do you grow your own mushrooms?" she asked Irina.

"I do," Irina said, evidently pleased. "Your mom and Glynnis Bonaventure were looking for people to help them test some home-growing kits. Scott and I signed up right away. The cheese is made from milk from Cordelia's capri-cows. She doesn't produce enough to go full commercial, but she has a very reasonable subscription service."

"She gave me some of her cheese for my birthday," Stephanie said. "I don't think it lasted to the end of the party."

After that, conversation segued to mutual friends and their ventures. Irina and Scott were particularly interested in Jessica, who Scott was mentoring in her quest to build a substantial resume to get every possible scholarship for med school.

Scott arrived as they were helping Irina wash up,

and Fisher immediately trotted over to touch noses with Lionheart and Survivor. Stephanie sometimes wished a treecat would adopt Irina. It had to be hard for Fisher to not have other treecats around.

"Do you think Fisher gets lonely?" she asked Scott.

Scott paused in the middle of smearing butter on a leftover biscuit.

"You know, I don't think he does. We're out and about a lot, and he gets fussed over pretty much everywhere we go. I had to put a moratorium on giving him celery, because he has absolutely no self-restraint in that department."

"I've yet to meet a treecat who does," Karl said with a laugh.

"But how about lonely for other treecats?" Stephanie persisted, and Scott raised and lowered his shoulders in a shrug.

"I don't think so, but I don't think Fisher is doing without other treecats. Especially out here where humans are spread pretty thin, I wouldn't be surprised if some of Fisher's family comes within range for them to talk. I bet Lionheart's family does, too, since the Harrington freehold was definitely on their radar well before you two bonded."

"But you do take Fisher to see his family, right?" Karl asked.

"I do," Scott said, "and sometimes Irina comes as well."

"I'm coming today," Irina said firmly. "Scott doesn't take enough time off as it is. I'm not going to waste this opportunity to spend time with him and Fisher. Let's get a move on before someone else has a problem Scott thinks no one but he can solve."

36

<I THOUGHT THIS MIGHT BE WHERE WE WERE GOING,>
Climbs Quickly commented as the flying thing began its descent at the outer perimeter of the central nesting place of Fisher's family, Laughing River Clan. <I think they are going first to those clans that are near to where they can nest with their own kind. Not a bad idea, given how cold the nights still can be, and how the two-legs are not as well adapted for the cold as we People are.>

<As People usually are,> Keen Eyes amended. <My coat does not know whether to re-grow its ice-time thickness or to stay lighter in response to the unfurling of the leaves. We both shed as if it were green-leaf time when we were in the Hot Lands. I have been glad for the false fur at night since our return, I will admit.>

<Today is bright. The sun is warm,> Swift Striker put in. <And it is less cold here than in the higher reaches where Bright Water Clan nests. Even if we stay out late, you should be fine.>

<We will not stay late,> Climbs Quickly predicted. <We will leave while it is still daylight, because your Darkness Foe does not like being away from those for whom he cares for very long. This visit is for introductions. If Laughing River does not demonstrate that it objects to the two-legs, we will make a longer visit tomorrow so they may begin their study here.>

<Darkness Foe is welcome at our central nesting place.> A new mind-voice entered the discussion, that of Intertwined Harmonies, the senior memory singer of Laughing River. <Yet my clan has never met so many two-legs, so I and a few of the elders have decided to make the first contact.>

So it was that when the travelers emerged from the flying thing, they were met by a delegation of five People, all of whom politely approached on the ground, so as not to seem to be threatening the two-legs from above. The two-legs made what were, based on the taste of their mind-glows, delighted mouth noises. Darkness Foe in particular seemed pleased. No doubt he had been concerned that bringing additional two-legs to Laughing River's territory might be taken as impolite.

Clusterstalk was offered and accepted. The People then offered a selection of bright green snowberries, so called because they were among the first sweet fruits available in the spring. The two-legs were evidently pleased, and ate them after Darkness Foe examined them with one of the made things he kept in his healer's bag.

<I think snowberries are not usually eaten by the two-legs,> Climbs Quickly said. <Possibly because the two-legs do not go foraging while there is still snow on the ground. By late new-leaf time, the snowberries have shifted to building next season's roots. See how Death Fang's Bane is carefully putting some away? I will bet my next five helpings of clusterstalk that she plans to give them to Plant Minder.>

<None of us will take that bet,> Swift Striker replied with false solemnity. <We have all seen the plant growing places Plant Minder maintains. Other two-legs have larger such places, but Plant Minder's have a tremendous variety of all manner of growing things.>

<As well as the best clusterstalk,> Keen Eyes added.

The visit progressed very nicely. After the exchange of edibles, Death Fang's Bane and Shining Sunlight began a slow tour of the area with their making images things. They took great care not to get too close to any individual nests, but they did use their making lighter things to rise into the air and take images from their level, and even from above.

As he usually did when he came to visit Laughing River, Darkness Foe had brought his carry bag containing the tools he used when treating the sick and injured. This had become a ritual all the clan understood. Soon People with minor injuries, as well as a few who were just curious about the shining not-rock tools and interesting-smelling ointments gathered near him.

<Darkness Foe has studied with Healer,> Swift Striker commented. <Sometimes, when Darkness Foe encounters an illness or injury he is uncertain about, he will consult Healer using those things the two-legs use to share mouth noises. Darkness Foe is very devoted to his craft and wants to make certain that what he knows about healing two-legs will transfer to helping People.>

Darkness Foe's mate, Embracing Risk, was drawn off by Delver, the elder who was in charge of working in clay. Although two-leg mind-blindness blocked direct communication, a shared passion for their craft bridged the gap. Climbs Quickly noted that Embracing Risk did not bring out any of the elaborate tools he had seen her use in her own workplace, but worked with what the People used with evident enthusiasm. Today the pair seemed to be comparing different additives and how they affected the clay.

<Perhaps we should tell them about Embracing Risk and her *clay shapes*,> Climbs Quickly said, directing his mind-voice so that only Swift Striker would hear. <I think Delver would love the turning thing that lets her make them so quickly!>

<I am sure he would, if there were only some way for him to make a turning thing of his own,> Swift Striker replied drily.

<Well, perhaps not that *part*,> Climbs Quickly agreed with a laugh. <But I think he might well like to know more of the way she heats them to make them harder and even able to hold water.>

<What works for two-legs and their made things may not work for People,> Swift Striker replied. <I think this is matter for the elders to decide. Also, while we can show images of her heating the things she has made from clay, we cannot explain why she does what she does or why problems can be caused by too much or too little heat. I have heard Embracing Risk make some very loud, very angry noises when her clay shapes break in the fire.>

<Hmm . . . I hadn't considered that there might be complications like that.> Climbs Quickly bleeked laughter. <Best to keep my nose out of trouble.>

<I think of her as Embracing Risk,> Swift Striker said, <because her clay making is something she does with a full knowledge that what she has spent so much time with may not survive the test of the fire's heat. She brought that same courage to her bond with Darkness Foe. I was already bonded to him when they began to spend more time with each other. I could taste that—like Shining Sunlight, who was Shadowed Sunlight before Keen Eyes came into his life—something had caused great grief to Embracing Risk, and that she knew full well that if she let herself come to love Darkness Foe, she was accepting that something similar could happen again. But she embraced

the risk along with her new mate, and brings that courage to everything she does.>

<*She is much to be admired,*> Climbs Quickly agreed.

Intertwined Harmonies was very interested in Climbs Quickly's and Keen Eyes's recent travels to what the People were beginning to accept might indeed be lights in the sky.

<*I would like you to share your visits yourself,*> the senior memory singer said. <*The strongest memory songs are those of the People whose memories they are, and different perspectives often reveal new details.*>

As Climbs Quickly had predicted, well before the daylight had begun to fade, the two-legs gave signs they were preparing to depart. Death Fang's Bane knelt down so she could be closer to eye-to-eye with the clan elders. Then she made mouth noises and waved her right upper limb first to encompass the golden-leaf trees that cradled and concealed the People's nests, then the surrounding forest.

<*She is asking if she may return,*> Climbs Quickly translated. <*I cannot tell for certain if she means someday or tomorrow, but if the fine weather holds I am certain we will visit again soon so she and Shining Sunlight may continue their study.*>

<*There are head gestures you use to indicate "yes" or "no,"*> Intertwined Harmonies said. <*I have tasted them in the memory songs. Let me try.*>

Very carefully, and a little stiffly, she nodded, and Death Fang's Bane made noises that even the mind-blind could have told indicated pleasure. As he turned to accompany his two-leg to the flying thing, Climbs Quickly could taste heated discussion among the elders. He was tempted to ask if he could help by clarifying some point, then decided he would wait. He'd often been chided for being too impulsive. This time, he sensed, prudence would be better.

✧   ✧   ✧

Karl couldn't help but notice the way Stephanie's mood kept shifting. At first, he thought her increasing quiet and tendency to dive into her datapad were because this was the most challenging site they'd visited. Like all treecats, Fisher's family used picketwood as a natural highway. In this case, their community's nests spanned both sides of several of the smaller waterways that fed into the rocky and fast-moving Thunder River that gave the area its name.

Combine the tangle of picketwood with the crown oaks that were the treecats' favorite nesting place, and you had a territory that needed to be surveyed largely on foot. The images they'd collected during their visits to Lionheart's family, the Swamp Cats, and La Mancha helped them pick out indications of where the treecats were using the area. In the interests of creating a database that would help the SFS to eventually understand just how much land it took to support a thriving treecat community, Karl and Stephanie searched not only for trees and foods they already associated with treecats' lifeways, but also tried to add new elements. One of the most interesting had been a "quarry" for the flint the treecats used to make their stone tools, but they'd also found some semi-tended food plants.

Stephanie had taken to going into her room at the Zivoniks' rambling residence soon after dinner. After she finished her homework, she reviewed images from their other visits to treecat communities to see if these new elements were there as well and they'd just missed them.

"Anders gave me some Old Earth anthropology to read before he left," she told Karl when he protested that after working so very hard all day, she deserved some time off in the evening. "I've been comparing them to the texts Duncan brought with him, and one of the fascinating things was the way a lot of early Old Earth anthropological assumptions about how wide-ranging trade networks were overturned once it was possible for geologists to use x-ray refraction to source specific types of stone. Suddenly, those 'primitive' stone tools showed that resources were being traded, sometimes across an entire continent. La Mancha's pottery production suggests that might be true, but think what it will mean to assessment of treecat culture if we can *prove* it. Demonstrate, say, that Lionheart's clan really is getting its flint from Fisher's or that the Swamp Cats are getting pottery from La Mancha, or something like that. Duncan's right about what a phenomenal way to show treecats should be placed higher on the sapience scale proof of trade would be."

"I see your point," Karl said, catching some of her enthusiasm, "but I really don't think a couple days one way or another would make a difference."

"But I'm a lot more interested in this," Stephanie said with a stiff, forced patience, "than I am in watching Lev build things with his blocks or hearing Dia tell about her latest date with Loon. This is *my* idea of a great way to relax."

Karl wanted to ask Stephanie if she didn't like his family, but he knew that was unfair. He just hoped his parents didn't get the wrong impression about her.

Or maybe I'm the one who's getting the wrong impression. Would I have cared before if Steph pulled into herself? At her parent's house, we all often end up with her doing her homework, while I work on my reports or my remote college courses. Before, I would have just thought, "Hey, that's Steph. An only child, a bit of an introvert." But now that she's going to be my wife, and part of my family, my expectations are changing. Maybe not for the good.

Karl decided that, as much as he'd enjoyed being back in the middle of his familiar family chaos, he was relieved they'd soon be moving on. First they'd report into Chief Shelton—and Duncan—then go visit Survivor's family.

Stephanie brightened up almost as soon as they were away from Thunder River. As she did, Karl felt a wash of contradictory emotions. On the one hand, he was pleased she was feeling more cheerful. On the other, he was... annoyed? Uncertain? Unhappy?

He couldn't quite pin down his emotions, but he was definitely less than thrilled that Stephanie hadn't confided whatever was bugging her to him. He had a perverse desire to not stay at the Harrington house when they got back, to make an excuse to go see Cordelia or Nosey or someone. Or just to stay in the "bunkhouse" the SFS maintained because rangers didn't always end their days close to home. Karl was aware when Survivor slipped into his emotions, calming him, letting him think more clearly. Like Stephanie, he was never able to describe, even to himself, how Survivor did it, but also like Stephanie, he was certain the 'cat *did* do it. And that was one of the great things about being bonded to a treecat. Survivor wasn't shutting his emotions down, like some drugs did, but whatever he was doing somehow managed to quiet emotional surges, so it was possible to think without emotional waves beating thought to pieces.

Karl had seen Lionheart's influence on Stephanie. She was a lot less likely to fly off the handle than she'd once been. Somehow, though, he'd never thought of himself as needing that sort of moderating influence. He was, after all, the quiet one, the calm and cool-headed one.

Shows what I know, he thought wryly. *These days, I seem to be the flustered one, the uncertain one, the can't-start-the-conversation one.*

He did calm down enough to realize that staying somewhere other than the Harrington house would be the absolutely worst thing he could do, but when Stephanie locked herself in her room to take an exam on the data net for one of her classes, he found himself restless.

Marjorie and Richard were both out, but Duncan was in the living room browsing the report they'd brought back from Fisher's clan.

"What's up, Karl? Did you and Stephanie have a fight? You've both been prickly since you got back from your trip. And it's not like the Peanut to not spend the odd hour or three enthusing over your latest 'cat findings."

Karl sank down into a chair. Survivor bounced up onto the chair back, then apparently decided this wasn't close enough and flowed down into Karl's lap.

"Is it that obvious? I mean the prickly bit. We didn't get into a fight. I almost wish we had, because this feels like a storm waiting to break."

Duncan set aside his datapad, and leaned back in his chair, folding his hands across his middle. He made a slight, prompting, "I'm listening" sound.

"I *think*—I'm pretty sure, actually—that whatever is bugging Stephanie has to do with my family. It's weird. She's known them forever, stayed with us before. No problems then, as far as I could tell, but this time, Steph got moody practically as soon as the cruiser set down."

"Did you ask her why?"

"I asked her why she was shutting herself up in her room. She reminded me that she had homework to do. She also said she found, well, I got the impression that my family bored her. She didn't want to watch Lev play or listen to Dia or . . ." He raised his shoulders and let them drop, unwilling to put words in Stephanie's mouth, but also feeling that Stephanie had been objecting to more than she'd actually said.

"How much did you two discuss what getting married would mean to your futures?" Duncan asked.

"We discussed that we wanted this to be forever," Karl answered, confused. "Is that what you mean?"

"Not really. 'Forever' is very nice, very romantic,

and very determined. But it doesn't really address that marriage involves a lot more than two people. You come from a big family and probably take that for granted. Stephanie, though, she's a seventeen-year-old only child. Marjorie and Richard have done a very good job keeping her from thinking she's the center of the universe, but I doubt she'd really thought about how accepting you meant accepting an entire family group, and a large one at that."

Karl nodded. "I have three sisters and two brothers. I'm the oldest. And I have aunts and uncles and cousins and in-laws. The plague thinned out our family, the way it did so many, but even if there are fewer twigs, the tree has a lot of branches."

"And there will be more," Duncan prompted, "unless you think all of your siblings plan to remain childless."

"Hardly..." Karl forced a laugh. "I'm not even certain my parents are done."

"What about your own children?" Duncan pressed. "Have you and Stephanie discussed whether you want children and when?"

"Not really." Karl frowned. "I mean, jokes, but not really. We haven't even set a date for the wedding."

"So, as I see it," Duncan replied, much the way he might have set forth points in an anthropological discussion, "Stephanie is suddenly facing not only a future as your wife, but going from being a basically solitary person to being grafted onto a wildly growing tree. Moreover, she's probably getting little hints that you aren't, about when will there be little Karl-Stephanies."

"I haven't heard any!" Karl objected.

"You might not notice, because they're not direct," Duncan said. "I heard one the other day. Marjorie and Richard have always meant to have more children, but they haven't quite gotten around to it. The other day,

Marjorie said something along the lines of, 'If we don't want our next kid to have nieces and nephews older than it, maybe we should seriously consider the next baby.'"

Karl felt himself nodding.

"I did hear the comment about how quiet the house would be if Stephanie and I set up our own place, but that was followed almost immediately by 'There's plenty of room for you and your kids here, if you want to stay.' I get it. And you think Stephanie feels pressure?'"

"Not pressure so much as an awareness of a whole new set of expectations. Have you ever heard Stephanie voice any goal other than wanting to be a ranger?"

"Not really." Karl felt uneasy.

"Well, as of a few months ago, Stephanie made that goal. What's next?"

"Head of SFS," Karl said promptly, then nodded. "I get it. Do you think she's really thinking all of this?"

"Honestly, I don't know. She hasn't said anything about it to me, if that's what you're wondering."

Karl laughed, then shoved his hand back through his hair.

"I know *I* really didn't think about any of this. I just knew I love her and I wanted to have her part of my life, no matter what. I didn't think about what 'my life' meant, how it means more than just me, it means my family, my family's expectations for me—as eldest son, I'm slated to be the next baron. I wonder if Stephanie's thought of that."

"I bet she has," Duncan said. "If she didn't think about it on her own, one of her friends is sure to have teased her about marrying into the nobility."

"It's a pretty meaningless title," Karl mumbled. "Cheap compensation for a lot of pain and suffering."

"Maybe...but it's still there."

"Should I talk to Steph about this?" Karl really didn't

want to. It wasn't as if he could change any of it so it would be pretty pointless. He didn't think Stephanie expected him to give up his family. "Or should I let it go for now, give her a chance to work it out?"

"That," Duncan said, rising to his feet, "is a question only you can answer. Now, I hear the pitter-patter of little feet on the stairs. I'm guessing Stephanie's done with her test. Richard and Marjorie should be home soon, too. How about we pull out the makings for hot fudge cake? And after dinner, we can talk about Survivor's clan. I think it's time you two did a quick survey we can use as a datapoint on their recovery."

37

THE VISIT TO SURVIVOR'S CLAN WAS POSTPONED, however.

The Harringtons and Karl had just sat down to a Meyerdahl-scale meal when Richard's uni-link beeped with the urgent tone of an emergency call. He tapped the display immediately, and Trudy appeared on it.

"I know it's dinner time," she said quickly, her tone apologetic, "but we really need you, Doctor Harrington!"

"Let me guess." Richard's tone mingled resignation and humor. "Somebody's gone into labor?"

"We're pretty sure, yes." Trudy shook her head. "I don't know if she's having actual contractions yet, but I've seen too many births now not to recognize when a mother-to-be's ready to deliver. She's built a nest out of Nosey's softest, fuzziest sweaters, and she's parked in it just inside the bedroom closet. And she's making a lot of soft little sounds we've never heard out of her before."

"Is she showing any sign of distress?"

"Not of *acute* distress," Trudy said. "Nothing at all like right after Ralph killed her husband, anyway! But I wouldn't say she looks entirely happy, either. Of course, if this is her first litter, that could explain a lot. Only—"

"Only treecats are telepaths," Richard interrupted, looking across the table at Stephanie and Karl. "And that means treecat moms are accustomed to a support team she simply doesn't have."

"Exactly," Trudy said gratefully.

"Well, let us throw some sandwiches together so we don't starve on the way, and Steph, Karl, the boys, and I will be there as quick as we can."

"Thank you, thank you! I'll tell Nosey you're coming. Clear!"

The display blanked, and Richard looked at Duncan. He opened his mouth, but Duncan shook his head before he could speak.

"I'd love to be there, but the last thing Dulcinea needs if she's already stressed is another gargantuan, lumbering human hanging around. I think you're absolutely right to take Steph and Karl and the guys, but much as it grieves me, it'll be better all around if I just stay home and keep Marjorie company. And, of course," he grinned impishly, "help eat this lovely dinner you three won't have an opportunity to share!"

"I'm so happy your cloud has a silver lining," Richard told him dryly, then looked back at his daughter. "You guys throw the sandwiches together. Lots of mayo and mustard on mine, please! I'll go get the air car out of the garage."

"I am *so* glad to see you—all of you!" Trudy said fervently as she opened the front door. "After this long with Wild and Free, I should be taking this right in stride, and instead I'm a nervous wreck! Which probably isn't exactly what Dulcinea needs right this minute."

Richard chuckled and patted her on the shoulder. They'd maintained an open com link all the way from the Harrington freehold into town, and Trudy had sent them real-time video of their patient, so he was as well briefed as any veterinarian could possibly have been.

"If it had looked to me like she was in any sort of trouble, I'd have had you bring her into the clinic," he said now, reassuringly. "As it is, as calm as she seems—whatever *your* mental state may be—it's far better to leave her where she is with her person in the nest she's built. The truth is, Trudy, I'll be very surprised if I'm much more than an observer for this particular delivery."

"I know. I know!" Trudy flashed a smile. "And I know you've monitored every stage of the pregnancy since she adopted Nosey. But—"

"But you're about to become the first human treecat stepmom in history." Stephanie gave her a quick hug. "And Dulcinea's already been through enough for a dozen 'cats. Of course Daddy's going to be here for you and her."

Trudy hugged her back, then led the way to the master bedroom.

Nosey sat on a pillow just outside the closet, one hand stretched through the open door so his fingers could gently caress Dulcinea's ears. Trudy hadn't exaggerated about the nest the treecat had built, either. At least half a dozen of Nosey's sweaters had been heaped into a luxuriant pile deep enough for her to settle into its soft, soothing warmth with only her head and ears showing. The clothing hanging from the closet pole above her was like a roof, turning the floor of the closet into something very like a cave. Or, Stephanie thought as she un-cased her camera and set it to record, like a treecat nest high in the angle of a crown oak's branches.

She'd been a little leery of bringing Lionheart and Survivor along. On the one hand, they should be soothing presences for Dulcinea. But so far, the SFS knew very little about treecat birthing customs, and she'd been half afraid males were unwelcome in the process. That worry, at least, disappeared the instant Lionheart and Survivor went scampering across the bedroom's colorful throw rugs to the closet. Dulcinea's head rose clear of her nest when she saw them, and the ears that had been half-flattened pricked sharply.

The two males stopped just outside the closet, and Lionheart leaned in to touch noses with her very, very gently.

<I am glad you are here!> Still Water said. *<Protector and Walks from Shadow could not love me more, but they cannot hear my mind-voice and I cannot hear theirs.>*

<It is true there are times when the People need to taste one another, and never more than a moment like this,> Climbs Quickly told her. *<And I am glad we are able to be here.>*

Keen Eyes radiated agreement, and his ears flickered in mingled amusement and respect as he tasted the mind-glows of her kittens.

<They are even stronger than the last time we visited,> he said. *<I would not be surprised if Sunlight proves a memory singer!>*

<There have been many memory singers in my line, and in Leaf Racer's. Wind of Memory is the strongest in many turnings, but my own dam was also a memory singer before the gray death claimed her.>

Both males sent a wave of comfort and understanding to her, and she pressed her head more firmly against Protector's fingers as a fresh contraction rippled through her.

<I wish one of Golden-Leaf Clan's birth-healers were here, though,> she said a bit fretfully. <I know Healer will care for me and the kittens, but they cannot hear his mind-voice.>

Lionheart touched noses with her once more, this time as much in understanding as in comfort. He and Keen Eyes were looking forward—not without some trepidation—to experiencing the birth of Death Fang's Bane's and Shining Sunlight's first kitten. They had discussed it at some length and decided that the only thing they truly knew was that they could not imagine how someone who was mind-blind coped with birth.

Bizarre as it seemed to any of the People, Death Fang's Bane and Shining Sunlight could not share mind-glows when the time came. It seemed likely that the best they could do would be to hold hands, and that could be only a pale substitute for embracing one another mind-to-mind in that most magical of moments. Even stranger, perhaps, was that they would never be able to taste their child's mind-glow as it came into being. Any child of theirs would be born with no name, without ever having touched their minds or being touched by them in return. Never knowing that loving caress as they grew into being. For all the marvelous made-things, all the miraculous tools the two-legs possessed, there were times—especially at moments like this—when he could only pity them and marvel at the courage it must take for each of them to live their lives in such isolation from one another.

But Still Water was right, there was no birth-healer to aid her kittens as they emerged from the warmth of her womb into the world in which they must live. No one could possibly explain what was happening to a kitten. Their mind-glows were too new, with too few memories and too little experience to comprehend complex ideas. They had come to know their mother's mind-glow, to taste and embrace its loving welcome, but their world was now in turmoil, and birth was a traumatic experience. Still Water would radiate love and reassurance, but they really needed more than just *her* mind-voice. And that was one of the things birth-healers were trained to do. To be that second mind-voice, the one her kittens did not know, calming them and telling them all would, indeed, be well.

<We are no birth-healers, heart-sister,> he told her. <We are merely males, good for hunting and scouting but not to be trusted with any truly important task.> He treasured the ripple of amusement he tasted in her mind-glow, and his mind-voice softened. <Yet males that we may be, we are here, and we will help your children into the world.>

Obviously, it was *a good idea to bring them,* Stephanie thought, turning to smile up at Karl as Lionheart and Survivor lay down on the carpet on either side of Nosey, just outside the closet door, crooning softly, and Dulcinea began to purr.

"I have the feeling I may turn out to be completely superfluous," Richard said, watching the same interaction. "On the other hand, I should probably examine my patient. Just to bolster my own sense of importance, you understand."

"I'll certainly feel better if you do, Doctor," Nosey said. "Although you're right about how happy she is to see the boys. To be honest, that was what worried me most all along when she chose to stay with me. I hated the thought of that keeping her from having her family around her when the babies came."

"I believe this young lady has plenty of family, Nosey," Richard told him, going down on one knee and opening his bag to remove his diagnostic scanner. "There's you, there's Trudy, both of the boys, Stephanie, Karl—even me. We may not be telempaths, but I'll guarantee you she knows how much love there is in this bedroom right this minute. Now, excuse me while I take a moment with my patient."

Two hours later, Dulcinea was no longer alone in her nest of sweaters.

Those sweaters would require some serious attention from the laundry, Stephanie reflected, and the scent of afterbirth was strong enough it would take the environmental system a while to filter it out again. But watching Nosey and Trudy as they sat side-by-side on the floor like Old Earth tailors, she knew neither of them could have cared less about that.

The four treekittens crowded against Dulcinea, tiny true-hands kneading the soft warmth of her belly fur as they nursed, were incredibly small. Stephanie could have held all four of them in the palms of her two hands without crowding. They would have been lost in hands the size of Karl's! But there was nothing wrong with their purring mechanism, she thought wryly, listening to the powerful buzz rising from those tiny bodies.

Dulcinea lay on her back, obviously weary, but buzzing a soft, gentle purr of her own as true-hands and hand-feet caressed her children. There were what might have been tears in Nosey's eyes as he looked down at her, and Trudy leaned her head against his shoulder, holding his left hand in both of hers.

"I make that one little girl and three boys," Richard said. "And it looks to me like mother and children are doing quite well."

"I know. And thank you for coming!" Nosey looked up at him with a slightly off-center smile. "And now that they're here and they're safe, I can start worrying about the *next* item on my list."

"You know I love you, Nosey," Trudy said without ever taking her head from his shoulder, "but there *are* times I could strangle you."

"I know." He kissed the part of her hair. "Still—"

"You're worried about her having to raise them on her own," Stephanie said, and he looked up at her with a quick nod.

"Well, maybe you're right to," she continued, "but that's one smart little lady in your closet, Mr. Jones. If she needs help—if she needs to take them back to her family for regular visits, or even to foster them—she'll let you know. But one thing I can tell you right now, just looking at her, is that she doesn't want to take them anywhere *you* aren't one second sooner than she has to."

"You think so?" Nosey's tone was the tiniest bit tremulous. "I mean, I don't want her to think she can't do whatever—"

He broke off as Dulcinea braced herself on her mid-limb elbows, raising her head and shoulders from her nest. As he looked down at her, she gathered the tiny, dappled female kitten in her true hands, then raised them, holding her daughter up to Nosey.

He froze, looking down at her, and then gently, gently held out his own hand for her to lay that tiny, fragile body in his palm. He raised the baby carefully, cradling her in both hands, to his cheek. Her head quested from side to side, eyes still closed, tiny nose quivering as she inhaled his scent. And then she buzzed softly and touched that nose to his cheek in a moth wing caress, and a tear trickled down his face while Dulcinea crooned to him.

❖   ❖   ❖

<That is good,> Keen Eyes said softly. <I only wish Protector could taste what we taste!>

<I agree,> Climbs Quickly replied. <Yet even though he is mind-blind, the joy and welcome in his mind-glow fills him like the summer sun.>

<And that fills me with joy,> Dulcinea said, yet there was a trace of sorrow in her mind-glow even as she said it. <I wish with all my heart that Leaf Racer were here, that he could taste Sunlight as I do, and that she could taste him. That he could mind-speak to her on this very first day. But that cannot be, and even if Protector's mind-blindness means he will never taste her mind-glow, she will never forget the taste of his. Of the welcome and the joy, and that fierce determination to protect her against all the world. I have lost Leaf Racer, but I know what happiness he would feel if he knew how safe his kittens and I are in the fortress of Protector's heart.>

KARL AND STEPHANIE WOULD HAVE PREFERRED TO stay closer to home while Dulcinea's kittens took their first steps into their new and wider world. Unfortunately, the weather sats promised almost a solid week of clear skies over the area in which Survivor's clan had been resettled. Given typical Sphinx spring weather, that was an opportunity they couldn't afford to miss.

Studying what the treecats had done with their new territory in something over a T-year added terrifically to their database. As Duncan had pointed out, both Survivor's clan and the Refugees constituted what Gary Hidalgo would, with reason, have described as "contaminated samples," given the part humanity had played in their rescue. On the other hand, one major goal of their study was to evaluate humans' impact on the 'cats, and one unique advantage of this data set was that they had numerous images of the area from before what had become Community Five in their notes had been relocated here. That gave them a wealth of opportunities to make "before and after" comparisons, and they spent extra days doing just that.

The days were getting longer with the advancing of spring, so there was ample time for them to make the somewhat longer flight between the treecat community and the Harrington freehold. They split the travel time between creating their search plan for the next day and catching up on schoolwork. Stephanie was still processing her not-quite-panic during their stay with the Zivoniks and felt very grateful that Karl didn't press her.

I just might get defensive and say the wrong thing. I've already come pretty close a couple of times.

They were on the way back from a day of survey, trying to decide if they needed one more day, or if that would be overkill, when their conference was interrupted by a com message from Scott MacDallan. Karl brought the image up on the cruiser's HUD.

"What's up, Scott? Nothing wrong, I hope."

Scott shook his head vehemently. "Nothing wrong. In fact, depending on if you're still freed up to work on your treecat survey, it could be very right."

"That's still our major focus," Karl confirmed. "Did you get a line on another treecat clan?"

"Well," Scott's brow crinkled, "I didn't precisely, but I think Fisher has. I had a case that took me out near one of the boundaries of his clan's territory. He frolicked off to go visiting, as he often does. He seems to have a sense when a case is going to take a while. When he came back, he was very excited. After a while, I got the idea he was trying to tell me his clan had been in touch with another clan, and that clan might be open to a visit."

Knowing how difficult it sometimes could be to figure out what a treecat was trying to explain, Stephanie didn't press Scott for details. She was impressed though that Scott had been able to figure out such a complicated idea.

Then again, after me, Scott has been adopted the longest, and he's a doctor. He has a lot of experience guessing what people who can't communicate clearly because they're in pain or just kids or whatever. And he has that "sight" thing, too.

She glanced over at Karl.

"We were trying to decide if we needed more time with Survivor's clan. I'd love to see what Fisher has to show us, but you're the senior project director."

"I'd like to see, too," Karl replied. "The sooner the better. I doubt it's an emergency, or Fisher would have gotten Scott out there already, but it's possible that treecats are like humans, and might change their minds. Can you and Fisher make time for us tomorrow, Scott?"

"Absolutely," Scott said. "I'm due for a break, and I'll start arranging coverage as soon as I'm off the call with you."

"Excellent," Karl said. "Look for us mid-morning."

When he broke the call, Stephanie said with what she hoped was convincing casualness. "If you want, we could grab overnight bags and spend the night with your family."

Karl grinned at her. "Thanks, but waiting to fly out will work better for Scott. He'll be able to handle his morning calls and leave with a clear conscience. Maybe, if we end up in the area, we could stop by my folks' for dinner."

"Let's plan on it," Stephanie said. "I'll see what I can raid from the greenhouses, so we don't show up emptyhanded."

Climbs Quickly and Keen Eyes had enjoyed their visit with Swaying Fronds Clan, but they were pleased when the next long trip in the flying thing took them in a different direction. They were both scouts, and had learned to recognize some aspects of the rise and fall of the terrain from their high perch, especially when they could see mountains or large bodies of water.

<We are going to see either Shining Sunlight's clan or Darkness Foe and Swift Striker,> Climbs Quickly guessed. <Or both. They are close enough we often visit both on the same journey.>

<I would guess both,> Keen Eyes said. <When we stopped in the place where many two-legs have their nests, Shining Sunlight stopped and bought a treat that his mother likes nearly as much as we People do clusterstalk.>

Climbs Quickly nodded agreement, radiating pleasure. He was doubly pleased, for while Death Fang's Bane still retained a touch of her ongoing edginess, she had overlaid it with a very familiar determination. Whatever was troubling her, she was determined to face it, as a much younger version of herself had faced the death fang and won her name for her valor.

Their first stop was Darkness Foe's nesting place. Embracing Risk welcomed them with a meal, which included freshly caught fish for the People. Swift Striker and his two-leg were not there but arrived very soon thereafter. Time must be important, for Darkness Foe took his treats with him. This time Embracing Risk didn't come with them. The odor of baking clay from her studio testified as to why she had chosen to remain behind.

When they climbed aboard the flying thing, Darkness Foe sat in the front seat beside Shining Sunlight, with Swift Striker on his lap. Death Fang's Bane seated herself in the middle of the back seat, so that Climbs Quickly and Keen Eyes could each sit where they could look out.

Once the flying thing was aloft, Swift Striker angled

himself very precisely, then balanced on his hand-feet and true-feet so he could point. Shining Sunlight made a series of mouth noises, then adjusted the nose of the flying thing so that it would move along the course Swift Striker had indicated. Once this was done Swift Striker hunkered down in Darkness Foe's lap and accepted a piece of fish.

<We have a distance to go before I need to point again. We are going to see the Hanging Berries Clan,> he told the other two People. <After you made your visit to Laughing River, Intertwined Harmonies shared the song with our neighbors. Hanging Berries Clan was conflicted about having two-legs visit, but those who wanted a closer look at two-legs themselves, as well as a chance to watch them at work, won out. I was uncertain if I could explain to Darkness Foe what I wanted, but he has always been very good at understanding me.>

<Better even,> Climbs Quickly agreed, <than Death Fang's Bane is at understanding me. Her mind-glow is brilliant, but in Darkness Foe there is a glimmer of something that sets him apart from the other two-legs. We know too few two-legs to know if this quality is unique to him, or simply his own special light.>

<Will you be able to find where we are going from above?> Keen Eyes asked.

<Easily,> Swift Striker reassured him. <There are several landmarks that will be visible from here.> He stood, his partially eaten piece of fish clasped between his true-hands. <The first is that river. When we reach it, I will indicate that we should turn and follow its course.>

Shining Sunlight followed Swift Striker's directions with relatively little backing and forthing, but that did not mean there were no problems. One of them was that Swift Striker had no way to indicate whether the flying thing should move at a fast run or a slow jog or even a walk, so they overshot their target the first few times. Eventually, they stopped and hovered, while the two-legs consulted the big makes images thing that lived in the flying thing. The images were very realistic, and Climbs Quickly realized from watching the two-legs trace their fingers along the images that they were looking for places where net-wood and golden-leaf met.

Meanwhile, Swift Striker was doing his best to get Darkness Foe to understand that they were close, that flying more slowly would help. Darkness Foe must have understood, because when they finally started moving once more, the flying thing moved slowly enough that the passengers could distinguish the individual leaves on the trees. Shining Sunlight lowered the flying thing down, closer to the canopy, which enabled the three People to taste the mind-glows of the Hanging Berries Clan.

The clan's senior memory singer, a strong-voiced female who identified herself as Yells Fiercely, a name that was undoubtedly the result of some long-ago conflict, took the lead.

<Bring that flying thing down to roost in the meadow at the edge of the net-wood grove. The two-legs can walk over from there. Our clan elders will come to greet them.>

Shining Sunlight brought down the flying thing where indicated, but then drifted it over to where overhanging tree limbs would hide it from view from above. Swift Striker once again took point, guiding the two-legs to meet their hosts.

The visit began stiffly. Death Fang's Bane had brought clusterstalk, as had been the custom in such meetings, and the members of Hanging Berries Clan were eager to sample the new delight which had been celebrated in several memory songs. But—

<Why are the portions so small?> Yells Fiercely asked, turning one of the stalks in her true-hands to examine

it. <*They are much larger in the memory songs Bright Water shared when the two-legs first gifted them with it.*>

<*Since then,*> Climbs Quickly replied, <*we have learned from painful experience that too much clusterstalk can cause digestive upset. These days, Death Fang's Bane is careful that her gift does not come with a hidden price.*>

<*I see,*> Yells Fiercely said as Climbs Quickly shared a memory of precisely what he meant. <*I could wish we had received more memory songs of the two-legs. We know very little about them even now, which is why so many members of our clan were originally against inviting them here.*>

<*Hanging Berries is scarcely alone in that,*> Keen Eyes said. <*And it is the path of wisdom to be cautious about that which one does not already know. But Swift Striker said that the memory song of our visit to Laughing River had been shared with you.*>

<*It was, but even if Intertwined Harmonies and Laughing River's other elders understood the two-legs' purpose, that does not mean that they understood it correctly. And we have heard also the memory songs of Bright Heart Clan and the evil the two-legs wrought upon their range. There was much fear and uncertainty before our decision was made.*>

<*There are evildoers among the two-legs,*> Climbs Quickly acknowledged. <*In my experience, they are greatly outnumbered by the good two-legs, and some of the two-legs—like my own Death Fang's Bane and Shining Sunlight—are fiercely dedicated to protecting not just their own kind but the People from the evildoers.*>

<*That is true,*> Keen Eyes said firmly. <*Bright Heart would surely have perished to the last kitten had not the good two-legs saved them. The Damp Ground Clan would have perished in the last fire season had the good two-legs not saved them. And my own Swaying Fronds was*>

in desperate straits until the good two-legs transported us to our new range and helped provide us with the food we needed to survive until we had regained our strength and could hunt for ourselves once more.>

<*I wish we could get your memory singers here to sing those memories to us,*> Yells Fiercely said.

<*It is difficult enough to communicate even the simplest things to one who is mind-blind,*> Climbs Quickly said wryly. <*Death Fang's Bane is very clever, yet explaining to her why I must bring Sings Truly to visit you—even assuming the others of Bright Water would risk their senior memory singer so far from home—would be much worse than merely "difficult," I fear.*>

<*They are truly very strange, the two-legs, are they not?*> Yells Fiercely mused.

<*Indeed they are,*> Climbs Quickly said. <*Yet they are also here, and they are not leaving. Sings Truly had the right of that. And if we must share our world with them, then does it not make sense to be on the best terms we can be with the good two-legs?*>

<*It does,*> Yells Fiercely acknowledged, nibbling on her clusterstalk. <*And that does not even consider this!*> she added as the marvelous taste flowed through her.

<*No, it does not,*> Climbs Quickly agreed with a laugh.

<*In that case, I suppose you had best explain to the clan how this study by your two-legs is supposed to work.*>

Late afternoon came all too quickly, but Stephanie felt she should be the one to call it quits for the day, especially since she didn't want Karl to think she was avoiding going to the Zivoniks' for dinner. Irina had commed earlier, saying that she and Scott had been invited to join the family party that night, and she'd accepted for them both.

"We probably should pack up," Karl admitted. "I really wish there was a way to ask if we could come back tomorrow. Doctor Hobbard's suggestion that we take core samples that she could analyze in an attempt to get an idea how long groups of treecats have been in an area is terrific, but it does add to the workload."

"I guess the best idea," Stephanie said, "is to show up tomorrow. If that particularly elegant female starts shaking her head at us and growling, we'll know we've over-extended our welcome."

"This is farther out from the other communities we've investigated so far," Karl said. "What do you think about putting some camping gear in the trunk and staying overnight? We'll save a lot of commuting time. If the treecats look unhappy at our staying close by, we can move a couple kilometers outside where we guess their boundaries are and set up there."

Stephanie grinned. "That would be terrific. Spring is far enough along now that camping will be chilly, but at least we won't be dealing with snow."

"I wish I could stay with you," Scott said, almost wistfully. "But Irina would have something to say about that, as would my patients. Still, it's been good to get away from work—if not from Irina."

Maybe because their engagement was no longer new news, maybe because Stephanie herself was determined not to let her own thoughts overwhelm her, the overnight visit went well. Karl's brother Gregor and sister Larisa had been sorting through the camping gear already, because the SFS Explorers had late spring camping trips planned, and they'd offered to do a demonstration on how to set up a campsite. There was far more gear than they needed, so Karl and Stephanie could choose what they wanted to make a comfortable camp, even bags for heating water using passive solar, so they wouldn't need to do without showers. There was a moment of awkwardness on the subject of "one tent or two" but the limited space available in the cruiser's trunk decided in favor of one tent without too much discussion.

The next day, they arrived to find that they hadn't exhausted Community Seven's welcome. Most of the treecats went about what was probably their usual routine, but a small contingent whose membership constantly shifted accompanied them, watching intently while the humans did even the most routine tasks.

"They're probably wondering if we eat dirt or something," Karl quipped as he took yet another core sample, "and are looking for tasty samples."

The exceptions to their escort, interestingly enough, were their own bondmates. Survivor and Lionheart spent most of their time with what Stephanie had decided must be the community leaders. Most of the males had tails with numerous rings, which indicated they were quite mature, at any rate. It was harder to judge with the females, of course.

When Karl and Stephanie had begun their ambassadorial leadership and survey earlier in the spring, they'd had to guess at whether some of the females were pregnant. Now, in late spring, their condition was more evident. The way Richard Harrington had been able to track at least the later stages of Dulcinea's pregnancy with weekly scans had been a very useful addition to their database, and they were careful to add their own field observations to it.

"Pretty soon," Stephanie said, "the treecats will have kittens. Lionheart's clan didn't seem to mind me being around, and Dulcinea certainly seemed happy to see us! But we should still be careful. We don't have nearly enough data on the 'wild 'cats' to go on."

"When the kittens come will probably vary according

to microclimate," Karl added. "And we don't really know how precocious they'll be. Judging from Dulcinea's kids, they'll be blind and fairly helpless for a while, but we don't even know how many weeks it will be before they're up to eating solid food."

"We have so much to learn," Stephanie agreed contentedly. "It's going to be fun."

Uncertain as they were as to just how long this group of treecats would put up with them, Karl and Stephanie took only a short break for lunch and another for the high-calorie snacks Stephanie's metabolism required. They planned to push on working until the amount of light filtering through the brilliant spring green leaf cover would necessitate artificial lighting.

"These treecats might not appreciate our messing up their day/night cycle," Karl said. "So let's be polite."

"We can always do analysis in our tent," Stephanie put in.

"If we can't find something else to do," Karl answered with a grin that made her heart start pounding very fast.

When they'd set up camp, they'd carefully placed their sleeping bags on opposite sides of the tent, placing the chest in which they'd put extra clothing and suchlike in the middle, where it could serve as a nightstand. Most of the food they'd brought they were keeping locked in the cruiser, where it should be safe from any curious wildlife, up to and including their treecat hosts.

"Things to do," Stephanie replied, trying for deadpan, but not quite able to stifle a grin, "like homework."

"Or research," Karl added.

Working as the natural light was failing turned out to not be the best of ideas. Afterwards, Stephanie wondered if their mutual awareness of that cozy tent and the somehow special sense of being alone together didn't have a part to play in the accident. However, at the time, she was focused on an area near one of the quieter feeder streams, carefully cutting away at the bases of reeds that looked as if they'd been trimmed, possibly for making baskets or cushioning sleeping platforms. The plan was to turn the reeds over to Duncan and Dr. Hobbard's team, so they could determine if they'd been cut by one of the treecats' stone tools, bitten, or, perhaps, sliced with the edge of a claw. Why creatures naturally equipped with cutting tools would go to the trouble of making stone tools was one of the ongoing questions, and figuring that out might give some insight into the complexity of the thought processes involved.

"Let's take a sample of some untouched reeds as well," Stephanie suggested. "It's possible the sap is bitter or caustic or something that might make the treecats want to use something else to cut them with."

"Maybe, they just don't like getting grit in their mouths," Karl suggested, but he flipped on his vibroblade and hunkered down to cut some of the pristine reeds, down below where they joined into a single plant.

As he did so, he missed a patch of slick clay. His feet went out from under him, and he went down on his butt. Mud and reeds combined to make a slippery track along which he plunged down the bank, toward the water. Stephanie flipped on her counter-grav and kicked off to grab him, hoping to keep him from falling into the snowmelt-icy water.

Because he lacked Stephanie's Meyerdahl mods, Karl's counter-grav had already been on, so his fall had been at a standard grav, enough to startle him, but probably not enough to break any bones. By the time Stephanie had grabbed under his arms and planted her feet, Karl had dropped his bundle of reeds, thumbed off his vibroblade, and was fumbling to reset his counter-grav unit for a lighter setting.

Knowing perfectly well how strong Stephanie was, even

without the counter-grav assist, he hung limp and let her haul him onto the comparatively dry forest floor. Their treecat escort was bleeking in alarm, bringing Lionheart and Survivor streaking through the trees, silvery grey blurs that slowed as soon as they confirmed that their humans were in no immediate danger.

"You okay, Karl?" Stephanie asked, aware as she inspected him how much the ambient light level had dimmed without her noticing. Sometime while they were engrossed in their project, it had crossed the nebulous line between late afternoon and twilight.

"I'm going to need some quick heal," Karl said, "or I'm going to have some nasty bruises, but my field uniform kept me from getting torn up on the reed stumps. My boots are soaked, and I'm all over mud."

"Me, too," Stephanie said, glancing down at herself. She realized that she was still holding Karl, which accounted for much of the mud.

"I guess," Karl said, "it's quitting time."

"Yeah."

They collected the dropped sample bags. As they were making their way back to their camp, a slightly damp Survivor came loping through the trees, something in a carry net across his back. He paced them until they reached their camp, then came down and triumphantly presented Karl with the bundle of freshly cut reeds that had caused all the trouble.

"Thank you," Karl said solemnly, accepting the prize. "We'll need to cut a fresh sample, since these have been rinsed, but I appreciate the thought."

Survivor bleeked satisfaction, backed up, shook water from his fur, and was nearly dry. Richard Harrington had long ago noted that a treecat's coat shed water very well, a near necessity for survival during the long cold seasons, when sodden fur could lead to hypothermia and death.

"I wish getting clean and dry was going to be as easy for us," Karl said. "At least we'll have hot water."

They'd packed two bags for heating water, but only one shower tent. Stephanie insisted Karl go first, since he'd gotten chilled by his partial immersion in the river.

"As you wish, milady," he said.

He started to bend to unlace his boots, then stopped short.

"What's wrong?"

"I can't bend to get to my boots." Karl made a sound between a laugh and a gasp of pain. "I think I'm more seriously banged up than I thought."

"Can you sit down?"

"I don't think that's a really good idea, actually."

"Oh, you landed on your backside, right?"

"Yeah."

"Let me get those boots off of you, then," Stephanie said. She knelt in front of him, very conscious of his nearness. "Lift your foot."

"Let me move to where I can lean against a tree," Karl said.

"Maybe we should just get in the cruiser," Stephanie said, worried. "You might have broken your tailbone or something. You could lie down in the back, and I could drive us to Scott's."

"I don't think I could have hiked back here if I'd broken something," Karl said. "Quick heal will fix up the bruising. I'll be good as new in a few hours."

Stephanie mentally reviewed her first aid courses and reluctantly agreed. She followed anxiously as Karl moved to where he could use a young picketwood for support while she pulled his boots off.

"Ready?"

"Ready, steady," he said.

Karl's boots had kept most of the wet out, but the

upper parts of his socks were sodden. Stephanie got those off, then stood to unfasten Karl's belt and the control panel for his counter grav. He shivered.

"Getting cold? Maybe shocky?" she asked, pulling away, and working his counter-grav unit off his back and onto the ground.

"Uh, I should be cold, but I'm not." He wrapped his arms around her and pulled her close, kissed the top of her head, then tilted her face up so he could kiss her mouth.

"I'm getting mud on you," Stephanie said after a long interval.

"There's a solution for the mud," Karl said. "We get these uniforms off and us both into the shower. It'll be a tight fit, but without my counter-grav, I'll probably need your help to make sure I have the mud off everything."

Stephanie's brain understood perfectly that it was unlikely Karl would have much mud left on him once the muddy clothes were off. But her brain was losing ground to the rest of her...which thought a shower with Karl sounded wonderful. He was helping her unbuckle her own counter-grav unit. Weirdly, once the bulky thing was gone, she felt much lighter.

They helped each other get their dirty uniforms off, a process that involved a lot of kisses and a certain amount of giggling. They parted only long enough for Stephanie to rig both shower bags to feed into the tent. There really wasn't a lot of spare room, but they both fit, and even managed to get soaped and rinsed before the hot water ran out.

Dripping, they hustled back to their tent through the increasingly chill evening air. If it had seemed a little close when they were setting up, after the shower, it was positively roomy.

"Wow!" Stephanie said, as she dried Karl's muscular

back. "You are amazing...ly bruised back here. Let me get some quick-heal on that or you're going to stiffen up, and not in a good way."

Karl gave an abrupt laugh. "Be grateful for those bruises, my dear, or something would have happened far too fast in that shower."

Stephanie felt relieved. She hadn't felt any desire to stop, cramped shower or not. She hadn't known it was possible to be simultaneously acutely aware of another person, and yet feel as if that other was somehow an extension of oneself. Her head was still muzzy from the rush of new sensations, and yet she was definitely hungry for more, so it was nice to know Karl had a good reason for his restraint.

The first aid kit yielded what they needed. While Karl stretched on his stomach to give the medications a chance to take hold, Stephanie got dressed and went out to hang their muddy uniforms up where they could dry. She finished off by getting food from the cruiser and carrying it back. Lionheart and Survivor hadn't come back to scrounge, but she could feel Lionheart at the edge of her senses, content and relaxed.

"Feeling better?" she asked Karl as she re-entered the tent, and he moved to carefully prop himself up on one arm and look up at her, his grey eyes alight.

"Much. How could I not? A jug of wine, a loaf of bread, and thou," he recited in that voice people use when they're quoting. "Beside me, singing in the wilderness. O, Stephanie, were Paradise enow!"

"No wine," she replied, "but there is bread. Your mom's good dark rye. And some of the stew from last night. She very kindly put it in flash-heat trays. And there's salad, cheese, and winter apples. Accompanied by your choice of teas or coffee. Hungry?"

"Food would probably be a good idea," Karl admitted.

"I don't want to collapse on you. If you don't mind, I'll eat like a Roman, reclining on one arm, while the last of the posterior twinges fade."

"I'll excuse eccentric table manners this once," Stephanie said mock sternly. "I seem to recall Roman men ate reclining, but the women ate sitting up. It's so weird what bits of history and culture survive."

"Probably that did because of all the dramas set in Rome," Karl said. "We probably have most of it wrong, that far back."

After an interval in which the main course was demolished, and they'd moved to the cheese and apples, Karl cleared his throat.

"Look, I don't want to ruin what's turning into a memorable evening, but I've got to ask something."

Stephanie inclined her head. "Go for it."

"You got really tense during our last visit with my family. We both know it, so can we move to why? I'm not pissed about it," he added quickly. "I guess what I am is . . . concerned, maybe. That's not exactly the right word either, though. I just don't want to worry every time we're visiting them, especially worry that you're beginning to have second thoughts about us. I absolutely don't want to be another of your youthful romances, something you'll look back at while you're with someone who didn't screw things up."

"You didn't screw anything up," Stephanie said, trying hard not to sound defensive. "I guess *I* did, sort of. I just didn't . . . I hadn't thought about anything or anyone but you. You come with a lot of things, people, obligations, I didn't consider. I've been considering. I still want you, and if that means figuring out how to deal with what comes with you, I'll learn."

"You're absolutely right," Karl said, "about not thinking. Me, either. You've been on my radar since you first hit the news, since I saw you facing down the old Trudy and her posse, the fierce little girl who was ready to take on the world. It took Anders showing up to make me realize I might not have all the time in the world, and how I'd lost my chance before I even knew how much I wanted it. I guess I rushed things proposing on your birthday. I should have given us time to talk about those silly things courting couples do, like where to live and 'our song,' and how many kids, and—"

"I'm glad you rushed," Stephanie interrupted. She wasn't sure how it had happened, but she'd moved across to Karl, and he'd slid over and they were snuggled up, him still propped on his arm, hovering over her so that kissing was the most natural thing in the world.

After a long while, Karl said, "I don't hurt at all now. We could move the chest over to make more room on this side, zip our sleeping bags together, get rid of a few of these clothes."

"It would be warmer," she agreed, sliding her hand around his back, reassuring herself that he really wasn't in pain. She let her hands wander. "Oh, a whole lot warmer, even without clothes."

After a while, it wasn't just warm. It was definitely hot.

39

THE NEXT SEVERAL WEEKS PASSED IN A DREAMLIKE idyll for Karl and Stephanie. They didn't abandon their planned itinerary entirely, but it seemed as if their visit to the treecat community Fisher had guided them to opened up the social registry for them. After their planned visit to the Refugees, now officially Community Three on their coded list, Lionheart hinted that a bright-eyed young male treecat wished them to follow him.

Stephanie had thought following their visitor might mean a long hike on foot, but Lionheart led them to the cruiser, then proceeded to sit upright on Stephanie's lap acting the part of a navigational compass. They already had a pretty good idea what constituted a comfortable travel speed for a treecat, especially if there was a convenient picketwood network for him to move through, so Karl set the autopilot slightly below this speed and contented himself with adjusting their course.

By now, they had developed a well-honed routine, and

from the way word of their activities had clearly spread, it was obvious the treecats' long range communication net was even better developed than they'd thought it might be. There was almost always a delegation waiting when their cruiser grounded in a new clan's range, Lionheart and Survivor hopped down to meet them, there was much touching of noses, and then the senior 'cat present—always a female—came over, patted Stephanie's knee in greeting, and led them back to their central nesting area. By the time they got there, the treecats had started bringing out their sick and injured and the entire clan had assembled for their introductory celery. Then it was off to take pictures, measure distances, map nest locations, take core samples, and all of the other survey tasks they'd worked out with Duncan.

Neither Stephanie nor Karl had anticipated the stream of sick or hurt 'cats they encountered, and both of them thought they certainly should have. At least as rangers, they'd already had extensive first aid training, and they both had worked with animals for most of their lives, but neither of them felt truly competent to deal with some of the more serious injuries, and they wanted to do their best for the 'cats. Once they realized the need, they asked Richard to give them further training in treecat first aid during one of their stays at the Harrington homestead, however, and their skillset improved rapidly. They felt far more comfortable at what Karl had dubbed "treecat sick call" after that, and it was quickly apparent that the gift of setting a broken bone or deep cleaning an infected wound was at least as much appreciated as the celery sticks they always brought with them. For other, more complicated cases, they could always video conference with Richard, or even transport the ailing 'cat to his clinic.

By the end of May Stephanie and Karl had almost tripled the initial list of known treecat communities.

Along the way, they'd collected enough data for them to build an augmented database, working with Duncan and the Interior Ministry's geologists and biologists, that they hoped would help them predict treecat-friendly terrains. That would not only assist them in finding other treecat communities, but also help the SFS recommend areas for human settlements that wouldn't impinge on those of the treecats. Only so much could be done to influence what private landholders could do on "their" land, but Ralph Franchitti's trial and twenty-T-year sentence, coupled with the treecats' protected species status (and the fact that it had been officially ratified by Parliament on an expedited basis), had demonstrated that the Star Kingdom's policy was not going to favor those who abused wildlife.

As terrific as it was meeting all these treecats and immersing themselves in the sort of work they'd both wanted to do since they were children, for Karl and Stephanie the long days that ended by camping out surrounded by increasingly warmer springtime weather were perfect in other ways. Uni-links meant they were seldom completely out of touch with their friends and families, but those people all had activities of their own. Even with reports to write and studying to do, there was a lot of time for talking, as well as for other activities that deepened their intimacy.

Stephanie had thought she might feel awkward when they returned to civilization, where she and Karl had always maintained separate rooms, but when she fell asleep in Karl's room one night only to wake when the house was still, it seemed much more natural to stay where she was. Only the slightest of conspiratorial winks from her mom the next morning gave away that Richard and Marjorie had noticed that their daughter's growing up had reached another stage.

As much as Karl and Stephanie might have wished

this sojourn to continue, they couldn't stay out in the wild forever, since they had other duties as rangers, in addition to visits to treecat communities. Stephanie's new car came in very handy when they were finally called in from the bush, since she and Karl weren't always teamed up for those "other duties." In fact, part of Stephanie's new SFS job was doing really boring office work, something she was pretty certain Chief Shelton had put on her roster to remind her that reports and public leadership and taking calls from concerned residents was also part of the job of being a ranger.

Duncan was spending most of his time on Manticore itself, working with the data they'd provided as he fully entered the fray to determine the 'cats' level of sapience. He got "home" to Sphinx whenever he could, but Karl and Stephanie missed their working sessions with him. On the other hand, being in the Twin Forks area had advantages of its own. One was their ability to get together with their friends more often, and they also went to SFS Explorers meetings when they could. Sometimes they just sat in and listened, but they did help Rozie and Moriah with programming.

"We're giving presentations to the Explorers about our visits off-planet," Stephanie told her parents and Duncan one night when all of them managed to be home at the same time. "We did Manticore first, and tomorrow we're doing Gryphon."

"Manticore?" Duncan said. "I thought many of the colony families came from Manticore. Surely the children have firsthand experience."

"Some do, some don't," Karl said. "The club has a lot of members who were born here on Sphinx, or whose parents immigrated when they were young. In any case, the emphasis is still on wildlife, ecology, and the like. Stephanie and I talked about the area around Jason Bay not as a vacation resort, but with an emphasis on the plants and animals. We talked about why so many of the plants there have foliage with that strong bluish cast, while here it's such a deep, dark green, things like that."

"Rozie and Moriah, the directors of the Explorers, believe kids actually learn best by teaching," Stephanie added. "So when we talked about Manticore, they encouraged those kids who'd lived there to contribute their own experiences, then cycled back around to comparing and contrasting these other worlds to Sphinx, so that everyone ended up more deeply appreciating what was unique and to be protected on their homeworld, rather than feeling that they were stuck on a backward planet and that the future was elsewhere."

"Jessica said Moriah and Rozie are encouraging the kids who've lived on other planets, outside of the Star Kingdom, to give presentations on those places as well," Karl said. "Since her family's moved around a lot, Jessica's siblings are very excited. In a way, by emphasizing that some of the club members were born here, and some of them came later, Moriah and Rozie are putting the elephant right in the room, countering the sort of elitism that idiots like Jordan Franchitti try to promote to the detriment of just about everything and everyone."

"How's Trudy doing?" Marjorie asked. "Your father sees her and Nosey regularly when they bring Dulcinea and her kits in for check-ups, but I don't think I've actually seen her since the trial. I know that whole mess was really rough on her. Are she and Nosey holding up all right?"

"They're doing great," Stephanie assured her. "He's been *so* good for her, Mom, and Dulcinea and the kittens all love her." Stephanie's eyes darkened for a moment. "She never got much of that when she was a kid, and she's soaking it up like a sponge. Or maybe like a snow lily when the ice melts. And what's even better in a way is that she and Jessica are hanging out again. They were friends when Jessica first moved here, but it wasn't at all a friendship of equals, given the way her father pushed Trudy to treat Jessica like some kind of vassal because her family rents from the Franchittis. That's over, bigtime. It's still a little awkward, since the Pherisses are still the Franchittis' tenants, but...I don't know." Stephanie frowned thoughtfully. "After all that's happened, I'd have expected someone like Trudy's father to evict them or something for daring to be her friend, but Jess says he hasn't said a peep about it. It's almost like he's scared of Trudy or something." She looked at Karl. "What do you think, Karl?"

"I'd say he's *definitely* scared of her." Karl's tone was grimly satisfied. "I think he was totally blindsided when she refused to drop the charges again Ralph. He was absolutely livid when Ralph was sentenced, and there's no way someone like him would back off punishing her somehow after that unless something *made* him."

"You think she has evidence of what he did to her when she was little?" Duncan asked quietly, and Karl nodded.

"I think that's exactly what she has, and after what happened to Ralph, he has to know she'll use it if he pushes her."

"Well, good for her!" Duncan said approvingly. "I don't know her nearly as well as the rest of you do, but from what I do know, it's amazing how well that young lady's turned out if even half of what we think happened to her is true."

Richard and Marjorie nodded in agreement, and Stephanie surprised them all with a sudden laugh. Her cousin looked at her with a raised eyebrow, and she shrugged.

"Oh, I agree with you completely, Uncle Duncan! I was just thinking how little I would have expected that when we first met. I remember the day it took everything Lionheart could do just to keep me from punching her in the nose! Now she and Jess are probably my two best friends. And getting back to your question, Mom, I think she's even closer to Jess than she is to me. I know Dulcinea's definitely always happy to have Valiant visit, and since Jessica's house is sort of overflowing with people, Trudy and Nosey invited her to use Nosey's spare room as a study. That gives the 'cats plenty of quality time, and Valiant's been planting bulbs. Jessica analyzed them, and they'll be ornamental, but also edible for Dulcinea and her kits."

"That sounds great," Marjorie said. "Trudy deserves to have good things happen to her for a change."

"She sure does," Stephanie agreed. "But speaking about deserving good things, one good thing I wish I'd get would be to figure out where Athos comes from."

"Still not a clue?" Richard asked, looking back and forth between her, Karl, and Duncan, and she shook her head.

She and Karl had known going in that there would be disappointments in their survey. That was inevitable. But the one they most regretted was that even after spending several days with Cordelia and Athos, they'd never succeeded in connecting Athos to any treecat community near the Schardt-Cordova and Kemper baronies. Despite their best efforts, the stone toolmaker remained a treecat of mystery.

"I could do a gene scan on him," Richard offered now. "Our treecat genetic database is even skimpier than you guys' anthropological database, but it's growing. If we can't link him to a known group now, there's a pretty good chance we'd be able to in another few T-years."

"I'll mention the option to Cordelia," Stephanie said hesitantly, "but in a weird way, it seems impolite. We wouldn't do a gene scan on a human without that human's permission—not without good reason at least. Since there's no longer any question that treecats are sapients, it doesn't seem right. We've had treecats invite us to visit, but if Athos has a reason for not taking us home, maybe his wishes should be honored."

"That's probably wise," Duncan said after a moment. "It's abundantly clear how close-knit the 'cats are, not just in their immediate genetic families but in their communities as a whole, and I can't begin to imagine how painful it must be for a telepath, especially, to be cut off from that. It would take something extraordinary to isolate an individual from that sort of community. Probably something very painful, as well."

"You're not saying you think he was . . . well, *banished* or something, are you?" Richard asked, and Duncan shook his head.

"It's still far too early to make any judgments about the 'cats' internal and societal matrices, but I've watched him with the other bonded 'cats. Steph's right that his body language—the way he communicates with them—is different from the ways in which the others interact, but they actually seem to show him more physical affection, not less. I'd doubt that could happen if he carried some sort of taint that would lead his own clan to exile him!"

"Why do you think their interactions are different with him?" Marjorie asked. And Duncan frowned.

"Obviously no one can say for certain," he said slowly, "but I'm actually coming to wonder if he might be the treecat equivalent of a deaf-mute."

"Really?" Stephanie's eyes narrowed. "I never considered that!"

"It's only a theory, and a very tentative one, at that,

Peanut," Duncan cautioned her. "But we all know his body language with Lionheart and Survivor is different from that of any of the other cats, and theirs is different with him. If he can't 'hear' them and they can't 'hear' him, they'd have to find an alternate way to communicate with him, wouldn't they?"

"That makes a lot of sense, actually," Karl said slowly. "And it would explain why Survivor and Lionheart couldn't get him onboard to introduce us to his clan. He couldn't hear them, and that's way too complex a concept to get across with just physical gestures and touch."

"I could see that," Richard agreed. "And speaking of introductions to clans, are you two back in the field again soon? I noticed the sleeping bags were being aired in the garage."

"Tomorrow," Karl replied. "We thought about staying and going with the Explorers on their next field trip. Rozie and Moriah are taking them to explore an abandoned near-beaver dam next week. Steph and I would really like to tag along, but given how many of my sibs are in the club, and given that this is the first big trip the Explorers have taken, we decided to stay away so the chain of command would be perfectly clear."

"Is it an overnight trip?" Marjorie asked.

"Oh, no, but it's a long daytrip. They're leaving Twin Forks at dawn and won't get back until well after dark. The kids can sleep in the air van each way, and a lot of them are staying in Twin Forks or nearby both the night before and then after they get back. My sibs are staying with Jessica's family. So is Cordelia's youngest sister."

Stephanie giggled, and Marjorie looked a question at her.

"Jessica's 'graciously' donated her room to the guests and gone to sleep over with Trudy and Nosey," she explained with a grin. "Poor Jess looked positively wild-eyed when the sleepover was first suggested and pleaded an upcoming exam to study for as her reason for escaping. Speaking of which, I have one myself. I'd better go lock myself in my room. Catch you all later!"

40

"YOU HAVE TO ADMIT, THE CHIEF DID US PROUD,"
Rozie said, examining the Silver Cloud VII van the SFS
had rented from Frontier Wilderness Tours for the SFS
Explorers' first big field trip. "This is one classy vehicle."

The Silver Cloud was fifteen meters long, painted in
Frontier Wilderness's red and white colors, with twin
turbines that gave a cruising speed of five hundred kilometers per hour but could push it up to six hundred in
an emergency. That was little more than a third of an
SFS cruiser's maximum speed, but the Silver Cloud wasn't
simply much larger, it was far more luxurious, with built-in
holo displays, deeply cushioned seats, and a central area
covered in carpet. Best of all, its floor plan was readily
configurable. Maximum passenger capacity was thirty-two,
but today it was configured for only twenty. The inner
two rows of modular seats had been removed, leaving two
ranks of single seats on either side of a double-wide aisle,
which meant no one got stuck with an "aisle seat," and

provided much better access to the narrow, five-meter-long roof hatch which was designed for open-air observation at lower speeds. An added—and unmentioned—advantage for this particular group was that the extra width would minimize kids' ability to poke each other, which both Moriah and Rozie felt made up for the fact that the seats were also very adjustable, a feature which the kids would find some way to abuse. There was ample space to stow all of their gear in the cargo compartments under the flooring, including a capacious refrigerated compartment at the rear that could be accessed from the interior. The flight deck—separated from the passenger compartment by a sliding crystoplast panel—was spacious, with seating for the pilot, a second console to control the sophisticated HD unit mounted at the front of the passenger compartment, and two additional seats: one for a tech to run the HD and one for the guide responsible for the running description of Sphinx's flora and fauna.

"I understand the *Silver Cloud* isn't even the top-of-the-line for Frontier Wilderness, either," Moriah said. "When I went to pick it up last night, I reminded Tina"—Tina Alba, the mother of one of their near-otter level Explorers, was Frontier Wilderness's CEO—"that we were taking out twenty kids, not a bunch of high-end eco-tourists. She laughed and told me this model was being phased out, so I shouldn't worry if the kids spill on the upholstery or manage to track mud past the hatch scrubbers and onto the carpet."

"I really like how the roof hatch is set up for observation," Rozie said. "We can let the kids take turns getting a view from there, as well as at ground level."

"Definitely," Moriah agreed. She was reviewing the weather report on her uni-link, and she looked up with a smile. "Meteorology's update still gives us clear weather today, but they've increased the probability of gusty winds later in the day. They're calling for peak gust speeds of thirty-five kilometers per hour, but less than a two percent chance of rain, so they should be able to enjoy it to the full!"

"Good. But keep an eye on that wind prediction. That's a—what? Ten KPH?—uptick to what they were calling for last night. If it gets higher than forty, we might have to rethink our hiking plans."

Moriah nodded. Sphinx winters were hard on more than just the human interlopers, and tree branches, especially in the upper story, could be badly weakened under burdens of snow and ice in a gravity 1.35 times that of Old Earth. They fell a lot *faster* on Sphinx, as well, when they broke, which had led to a revival of the old term "widow-maker" to describe them.

"The area around the dam itself is pretty clear of overhead limbs," she said. "They can splash around in the mud to their hearts' desire if the wind gets up too high. We can reschedule the leaf identification exercise if we have to. Although you *know* J.C. will pout if we do."

Rozie chuckled. Their eldest needed only four more plant IDs to complete his next award level, and he was really looking forward to it.

"He'll just have to deal," he said. "And I heard somewhere adversity builds character. Besides—"

He broke off and looked up at the sound of an approaching air car.

"Perfect! Right on schedule, here are our two junior assistants."

The arriving air car disgorged Natalie Schardt-Cordova, Anastasia "Staysa" Zivonik, and Staysa's younger sister, Larisa. Natalie and Staysa were among the older, but no less enthusiastic, Explorers. Today they were focused on earning points toward their "Leadership" badge by taking charge of organizing the other Explorers and their gear.

Although it wasn't nearly as exciting as badges for fire safety or identifying various animals by their scat and prints, Moriah and Rozie had made clear that "Leadership" was one of the hardest badges to earn, because in addition to a wide variety of skills it required adaptability.

Both young women had the sturdy build of the Sphinx native. Natalie's hair and eyes were nearly the same shade of cocoa brown. Staysa had shining black hair and pale grey eyes touched with the faintest hint of green. They wore their uniform vests, cargo pants, and boots. Their waists were encircled with utility belts hung with numerous useful devices; they wore heavier duty, field counter-grav units on their backs rather than the belt-mounted units most Sphinxians used when they didn't anticipate traveling through rough terrain.

Larisa Zivonik was ten (and more than a half, as she had taken to reminding everyone). In her club activities, she demonstrated the fierce focus children of that age bring to their first serious hobby. She'd jumped up the rankings in an astonishingly short period of time, and she today proudly wore a hexapuma hat, as well as a vest covered with badges for topics ranging from edible native plants to firearms safety. Larisa made no secret of the fact that she wanted to follow her big brother, Karl, into the SFS. Her dream was to be the youngest ever probationary ranger.

Larisa was so determined that she'd beaten out her twelve-year-old brother, Gregor, for a place on this trip. There was no official restriction on how many siblings made the trip, but Evelina Zivonik had chosen to limit the number of *her* children who'd be participating. The reason, as she'd privately confided to Moriah and Rozie, was that it would be sufficient burden to ask Staysa to act as a supervisor with just one of her siblings along. Two would be one-and-a-half too many, she'd said...

especially since Gregor and Larisa could be very com-
petitive.

Natalie and Staysa had already been briefed on their
duties, and they set about them without prompting. Staysa
moved to the landing apron and prepared to check in
each of the new arrivals, which included confirming that
each had brought the required supplies. Natalie's focus
was on herding the Explorers onto the van, showing
them how they could adjust their seats, handing out the
first of many rounds of snacks that would keep the kids
occupied, and supervising the inevitable bathroom visits.

Among the next to arrive were the thirteen-year-old
Pheriss twins, Archie and Melanie-Anne, dropped off by
their dad, Buddy. Buddy also delivered a crate of boxed
lunches, donated by the catering service he now worked
for. Moriah was stowing the lunches in the cooler when
Beacon Drystan's dad (also Beacon, but called Bird)
arrived, bringing with him Rozie and Moriah's two kids,
J.C. and Wade. Young Beacon was eight, like J.C., and
the two were good buddies. Wade, at age four, was the
youngest of today's group of explorers, an exception that
had been made when he promised to be on his absolute
"bestest" behavior.

After that, the arrivals came thick and fast, and the
kids and supplies were marshalled efficiently into place by
Natalie and Staysa. There were the inevitable screw-ups.
Vernon Simpson had forgotten his datapad. Skye Brooks
hadn't filled out the necessary permission forms for her
two kids, Rysard and Katarzyna. However, preparing for
things to go wrong was part of the drill, and the expedition actually departed on the earlier side of the margin
Rozie and Moriah had put on their schedule.

Moriah had drawn the first shift flying, so Rozie rode
in the main cabin and led a discussion on the impact of
human settlement on wildlands. This was the start of one

of the day's ongoing challenges, meant to stimulate discussion on responsible versus irresponsible use of natural resources. Aware that one of the perks of being on this trip was a chance to earn a special Successful Expedition badge, the Explorers settled down, or at least as much as one could expect of twenty enthusiastic young people between the ages of four and sixteen.

All and all, the day was off to an excellent start.

"LOOK! WHAT'S THAT DOWN THERE?" LARISA ZIVONIK
asked.

She stood on her seat, with her head and shoulders
through the Silver Cloud's roof hatch, pointing down.
They were almost to the near-beaver dam, and something
flashed back the late morning sunlight from the shallow
river north of the lake they'd come to visit.

"Well," Natalie Schardt-Cordova, whose turn it was
to keep an eye on the younger kids taking turns playing observer, said, "think about it. What do *you* think
it might be?"

Larisa frowned, obviously thinking hard, and Archie
Pheriss, standing beside her in the lee of the raised wind-
break at the front of the hatch, looked at her, then at Natalie
and arched his eyebrows. Natalie smiled but shook her
head, and Archie rubbed the tip of his nose for a minute.

"I'm trying to remember exactly where everything is
from the satellite pictures," he said.

"Oh. *Oh!* I remember—*I remember!*" Larisa half-squealed. "Those are those shiny rocks where the waterfall comes down, aren't they?"

Natalie gave Archie a fairly stern look, but he only gazed back innocently, and she shook her head. He hadn't *quite* given Larisa the answer, after all, only a very pointed hint. And one of the things she liked most about the thirteen-year-old was that, like his older sister, he was always looking out for the kids younger than him.

"Yes, that's probably exactly what they are," she said to Larisa. "Do you remember *why* they're shiny?"

"Because of the mica," Larisa said. "The cliffs there are . . . are . . . whatchamacallit . . ." She frowned, then smiled. "*Sedimentary*. They're sedimentary rocks with lots of mica in them!"

"Very good!" Natalie congratulated her. "Be sure you note that in your journal. It'll count toward the mineral identification award qualifications."

Larisa beamed, and Natalie smiled back. Then she checked her chrono.

"Shift change!" she announced. "Who's up next?"

Half-Tail was the first to realize the large flying thing wasn't merely traveling through the area. The two-legs' flying things did that, from time to time, but based on its circling path, how slowly it was moving, and the way it kept changing height, Sparkling Rocks Clan's senior scout decided it seemed to be scouting.

<*You might want to take your catch back to the central nesting place, and alert the others,*> he told Belly Filler, who was hunting nearby.

<*I would rather remain and hunt,*> Belly Filler protested. <*The small game will flee from the flying thing, and that makes for good hunting.*>

<You have a point,> Half-Tail conceded. <And they are flying very slowly. I think we can keep pace with them, and it would be well to learn more of what they are doing. Just do not get carried away in your enthusiasm for a packed carry net!>

<I promise.>

The flying thing was, indeed, moving slowly, and as Half-Tail gazed up at it, it slowed even further and he realized there was an opening in its upper surface. He watched in fascination as the hand of small two-legs in the opening poked their heads out and waved about some of their made things. Then they ducked back inside, and a second hand of younglings replaced them.

He reached out to touch the mind-voice of his mate, Sensitive Whiskers, taking advantage of the longer distance over which mated pairs could mind-speak one another. Sensitive Whiskers was heavy with kittens, and when he touched her mind-glow, he tasted her drowsy contentment as she lay stretched out along the limb just outside their nest, soaking up the sunlight.

<There is a large flying thing above the forest, near the lake where the lake builders abandoned their dam,> he told her. <There are at least several hands of two-legs within it, and many of them appear to be younglings.>

<I will tell the clan elders,> she replied. <Do you think these are Death Fang's Bane and Shining Sunlight? Remember the memory songs Deep Memory has shared from other clans where they have visited. Not simply because of whatever leads them to study the People so closely, but also to offer help to those in need.>

<I do not think so. This flying thing is much larger than any of the ones in which the memory songs say they have traveled on their visits to the People. And I think I would taste Climbs Quickly's and Keen Eyes' mind-glows if they were present. I have never met them, but their

*mind-glows are very powerful in the memory songs. And
I am close enough I should be able to taste any People
who might be within the flying thing.>*

<*I will tell the elders,*> she repeated.

He sensed her mind-speaking to others, although he
could not hear them. And then she spoke to him again,
her mind-voice no longer drowsy but alive with interest.

<*The elders wish you to keep an eye on the two-legs.
So far, no two-legs have attempted to establish one of their
nest places in our range, but it is possible these may be
looking for a new home.*>

<*I had not considered that. Interesting.*>

<*And not at all to the good,*> Sensitive Whiskers
added, her mind-voice fiercely protective of her kittens.

<*The two-legs have stayed in the flying thing to this
point,*> Half-Tail reassured her. <*They do not seem to be
coming closer to our central nesting place, nor have any of
them gotten out. Indeed, they have started moving again.
They are headed in the direction of the lake-builders' dam.
I will pace them and keep watch.*>

<*The elders are sending others to join you,*> Sensitive
Whiskers said. <*Deep Memory will be able to build a
better memory song of their actions if she has more than
one Person's memories to weave together.*>

Half-Tail acknowledged her message, and knew she
tasted the half-resigned amusement in his mind-voice.
He was among those who had desired to invite Death
Fang's Bane and Shining Sunlight to visit Sparkling Rocks
Clan if their travels brought them near. Not all of the
clan agreed with that notion. Sparkling Rocks was a very
old clan, one which had been founded hands of hands of
turnings ago, and, in Half-Tail's opinion, it had grown
more conservative than most with the passing of seasons.
He suspected Deep Memory, the clan's senior memory
singer, shared that opinion. She was clearly more in favor

of inviting the two-legs than not, but the memory song of Leaf Racer's murder had reached Sparkling Rocks from Golden-Leaf Clan. That was not something that could be overlooked, even by those most interested in experiencing firsthand contact with the two-legs.

<*Promise me you will stay out of sight!*> Sensitive Whiskers' mind-voice was so dark with worry that Half-Tail scolded himself for letting her taste his amusement. <*We know too little about what causes two-leg evildoers like Mind Canker to kill, and these two-legs have their young with them. Even two-legs who are not evildoers might strike out if they feel their younglings are threatened.*>

<*I will be careful,*> Half-Tail promised. <*As you say, the People know much too little about why the two-legs act as they do, yet this is a fine chance to learn more. We have not had many opportunities to observe their inter-actions with their young. Even the songs shared by those of the New Clan deal almost entirely with the families of their bondmates. Neither they nor their bondmates seem to spend a great deal of time with the younglings of other two-leg families.*>

<*That is true,*> Sensitive Whiskers conceded. <*Watch carefully, then. But remember—even a grass-runner can become ferocious if her little ones are threatened.*>

Both Moriah and Rozie had had ample opportunity to remember Rozie's quip about children being tiny sociopaths by the time the Explorers reached the abandoned near-beaver dam. The flight had lasted over three hours, and despite numerous treats and several stops (one unplanned but very necessary) to let the kids let off steam, Rozie had been forced to threaten to turn the van around and take the chosen Explorers back to Twin Forks before the more rambunctious kids calmed down. That had done the trick, though. Even fourteen-year-old Isa Manning, the overstimulated and over-indulged daughter of a city councilman, had believed he meant what he said.

Or maybe, Moriah thought, amused, *Isa believed Wade. She knows perfectly well that our youngest is a liter-sized chaos factor. When he quieted down after Rozie did his drill sergeant imitation, Isa probably realized enough was really enough. Natalie and Staysa have done great as kid wranglers, though. They're well on the way to earning their leadership badges after this expedition!*

Indeed they were, and because both of them had some experience in handling larger vehicles, Moriah and Rozie had been able to give them a break by letting them do some of the driving. That had freed the rangers to mingle with the kids, which had given them the opportunity to do a little laying-down of the law. And in addition to giving Natalie and Staysa some much-needed relief, it had demonstrated to the other Explorers that their authority as auxiliaries to the adults wasn't just for show.

When they neared the more open terrain that surrounded the near-beaver dam. Moriah, who'd been leading a bingo game built around collecting images of the various plants listed on a card, frowned thoughtfully as she surveyed the surrounding forest from a van window.

I wonder if there are any treecats nearby? This looks like their sort of landscape—well-watered, with both picketwood and crown oak. She made a note to alert Stephanie and Karl. She was pretty sure they hadn't done any survey work in this area yet.

"All right, Explorers," she said. "We'll be at the dam soon. What's the drill?"

"Lunch!" Archie Pheriss shouted.

"Not right off." Moriah shook her head. "Melanie-Anne?"

"First"—Archie's twin snuck a quick glance at her

datapad—"we survey the area from the van. Then, if it looks safe, we go out. We each have a partner, and we stay in our squads. My partner is *not* my brother. It's J.C. And we're in Natalie's squad."

"Excellent. How about the rest of you?"

There was a quick review. Wade's partner was Staysa, and Takumi Hiroyuki was partnered with Natalie. The adult rangers would supervise the group as a whole, but the plan was for Moriah to prioritize Staysa's group (in part to rein in Wade, if needed), while Rozie would be with Natalie's group.

The procedure review filled the time it took the van to reach the dam, and Rozie went into hover fifty meters above the lake to give everyone a good look.

Although near-beavers were clearly not as intelligent as treecats, they were currently on the "possibly to be viewed as tool users" list, a distinction they shared—as Moriah had learned when Natalie did a presentation comparing the two creatures in preparation for this outing—with their Old Earth namesakes. Near-beavers lacked the wide, flat tails of their terrestrial counterparts, but they shared the large tree-gnawing incisors. That difference in dentition was one of the ways near-beavers differed from near-otters, with which they shared other similarities of build.

"Who can tell me what two types of trees near-beavers don't like?" Moriah asked, and Larisa Zivonik's hand shot up.

"Picketwood and rock trees," she said.

"Very good. Are near-beavers herbivores, carnivores, or omnivores?"

Cameron Alba, a serious young fellow of eleven, got to answer that one.

"Omnivores, though they like plants best. Near-otters have carnivore teeth, and they mostly eat fish and little animals. They probably eat some plants, too, just like treecats."

"Good! Now that we've reached the area where the near-beavers built their dam, Takumi, why do you think the near-beavers aren't here anymore?"

Takumi wiggled shyly, but she managed, "Because they cut down all the trees and they went to find a new place with more to cut down."

"Good. Katarzyna, how far away from their dam do near-beavers go to get trees?"

Katarzyna Brooks was one of the older Explorers, very conscious of her thirteen T-years. She locked gazes with Moriah to show she wasn't "cheating" by consulting her datapad.

"They can carry smaller pieces of wood, but they drag the bigger ones on muddy slides. They even dig canals, but when the canals get too long and keeping them clear gets to be too much work, they quit. So how far has to do with lots of things, like the water table and how hard it is to dig canals but..." Katarzyna drew a deep breath. "But near-beavers usually don't dig canals longer than about half a kilometer, so I guess that's their limit."

"Great detail! Now, Explorers, if you look out the windows, you can see that the near-beavers created a really big clearing here, a half-kilometer to either side of the stream. We guess they'd been living here for quite a while. And you can see how they left picketwood and the bigger trees, like the crown oaks, in place. But even with those to provide leaf cover, the area's evolved into a meadow habitat."

"Since it's open and there's grass," Rysard Brooks, Katarzyna's twelve-year-old brother said, eager to show his sister wasn't the only one who'd prepared for the outing, "the range bunnies and wood rats and even the prong bucks will come here, and they'll eat the grass and leaves, so the near-beavers don't just create a home for themselves, they create homes for other animals, as well."

"Excellent! And that makes near-beavers a keystone species," Moriah said, "which is one of the reasons we're here to look at their work today. Now, before we get out, I want you to remember that the dam may look solid, but since the near-beavers moved out sometime before last winter, there's been nobody to make repairs for a full T-year, and it's almost certainly starting to break down. No going out onto the dam. And keep back from the edges of the canals, too."

She looked pointedly at Archie Pheriss, who'd been whispering to his buddy Rysard. Rysard's hand flew into the air.

"But we're allowed to collect artifacts, right? To bring back and show the other Explorers who couldn't go on this trip?"

"That's right," Moriah replied. "Do you all have your flagging tape? If you find something that's too large to put into your collecting bag, mark it with that. We'll choose a few of the best marked-specimens to take back with us."

While they were talking, Rozie had brought the van down onto a grassy spot atop a bluff above the lake. The slope down was steep enough to promise good drainage and a firm—and dry—landing spot shaded by a towering crown oak.

"All right, Explorers," Natalie called out as the landing gear settled and Rozie powered down the turbines, "counter-grav units on."

The Silver Cloud's grav plates had maintained one standard gravity on the flight out, but before they exited, the Explorers shouldered into their personal counter-grav units. Those who hadn't been wearing their uniform hats (embellished, in some cases, with animal ears) put them on now, and Moriah put on her own near-beaver stocking cap in solidarity.

"Don't forget your collecting bags," Staysa reminded the younger kids, "but you don't need to worry about filling them now. This is a preliminary survey. In about half an hour, we'll have lunch."

The ritual of donning their gear had created an aura of subdued (or in the case of Wade and Archie, not so subdued) excitement. The two team leaders went out first, followed by the others in their assigned pairs. Moriah and Rozie brought up the rear, each with the slung rifle prudence required in the bush, and exchanged smiles as the Explorers dispersed over the meadow. Everything was going great.

When it became clear the two-legs wouldn't be departing immediately, the chance to view them up close, especially the two-leg young, attracted more members of Sparkling Rocks to the region of the lake-builders' abandoned dam. Some of the more cautious clan members tried to keep them back.

<Surely one or two scouts are enough,> Ardent Claw, an elderly hunter, argued. <They will share their impressions with the rest of us. I have not lived so long without learning to think twice and twice again before inviting danger.>

<Someone else's memories are well and good,> Sharp Sniffer, a talented—and much younger—hunter replied. <But I am sure that if any of us were given a chance to taste clusterstalk for ourselves, we would not settle for a memory song of, say, Climbs Quickly's many meals. Some things are best experienced for oneself. And as Deep Memory already said, many eyes watching see different things and

note different aspects. We can compare all our impressions and learn more.>

It was a well-chosen retort, since Ardent Claw had often said how much he would like to try clusterstalk.

The People took full advantage of the spreading, new green-time foliage to hide themselves. The lake-builders never took down net-wood, so there were plenty of limbs to hold the watchers even where they had cleared away all but the largest trees.

Deep Memory kept to custom and stayed close to the clan's central nesting place, but she shared the curiosity about the two-legs to the full and she had a very strong mind-voice. Despite the distance between them, she tossed questions at the watchers as a burrow runner tossed nuts into its store.

<It is established that two-legs' coloring has nothing to do with whether they are male or female, as it does with the People. However, I have often wondered why they come in so many colors and with so many differing textures to their fur. At first, some speculated that the different colors might be an indication of age, as our older males have more rings about their tails. That belief is losing support as we see more of the two-legs, though. Still, it would be good to collect more information about that. Then there are the false furs. This group seems to have attempted to match one another. Does that mean they are a clan? Do two-legs use their false furs not only for protection, but as a way to show what families or clans they belong to?>

The two-leg visitors' actions were very interesting. They moved about in pairs and seemed fascinated by the strangest things. One youngling did a dance that would have done a courting horn blade proud while holding a chewed-upon piece of wood over its head. Another pair went methodically from plant to plant with one of the handheld things that, according to the memory songs, did something to make images. This fascination seemed especially peculiar, since the plants they were so carefully examining grew where the clan knew the two-legs lived, as well. And another group, a young hunter who had been in the meadow the day before reported, was collecting samples of animal dung.

As the People shared images with each other, Half-Tail was uncertain how much they were actually learning about the two-legs, since most of what they saw was more confusing than not. However, he liked the taste of this little flock or herd or whatever they were. There were only two adults among the group, but they managed their herd without much effort, with the help of some of the older younglings. Younglings of most species seemed to delight in loud noises when excited—whether kittens or fawns or round-bellied squeakers—but these two-legs settled for laughter, with only a few over-stimulated shrieks. Dirt Grubber of the Damp Ground Clan and his two-leg lived in a nest with many younglings, and he had shared memory songs that demonstrated the difference.

<Some of these younglings,> Half-Tail said to Sensitive Whiskers, <seem familiar from the memory songs. That lively one might be the same as one of Windswept's siblings. And now that I have watched them longer, I think the two almost-adults are the siblings of Shining Sunlight and Awakening Joy.>

Sensitive Whiskers must have shared his conjecture with Deep Memory, for the memory singer mind-spoke to him herself.

<It is hard to tell for certain from this distance, but I think you are correct.>

All in all, the People of Sparkling Rock were rather disappointed when the two-leg elders began shooing their charges back toward the large flying thing in which they had arrived.

<Do you think they are leaving?> Belly Filler asked. <There is still much daylight, and I was wondering if we would see for ourselves the things they used to make light in the night.>

<Let us wait and see,> Half-Tail suggested. <At the very least, I want to go look at the meadow after they have departed. A see and a sniff will tell us a great deal more about what they were interested in.>

42

A STRENGTHENING BREEZE SENT RIPPLES ACROSS THE lake as Rozie and Moriah gave the signal for the Explorers to settle down for lunch. There were a few reluctant "Do we haftas," but Archie and Melanie-Anne had been dropping hints all day about the delights their dad had arranged for both lunch and dinner. Given that, there really wasn't much trouble getting the stragglers aboard.

The meadow had been damp, which wasn't unexpected this time of year, but the fabric of the Explorers' trousers shed the worst of the dirt. Not all of it, of course. *That* would have required magic.

"I think," Larisa reported solemnly, brushing at a persistent mud patch on her right knee, "that the near-beavers' slides are all over, under the grass. I fell down a bunch."

They settled for the promised lunch in a circle around the outdoor firepit the older Explorers had built beside the air van. It wasn't nearly cold enough to require a fire, but learning how to make (and extinguish) one—safely—was another entry on the Explorers' skillset. And it was also where they would toast the traditional after-lunch marshmallows.

The lunch itself was just as interesting as the Pheriss twins had predicted. Each kid received a meal packaged in a three-tray box modeled off that used for the traditional Japanese bento. Everything included was finger food, and the top trays featured items that used at least one ingredient native to Sphinx.

"That," Melanie-Anne explained with deep satisfaction, "makes each lunch educational, as well as nourishing. And dinner's even better!"

Even Isa Manning eschewed the lunch her mother had insisted her little darling pack along. She dove into her bento, instead, with no sign of the picky appetite her mother had warned Moriah and Rozie about in numerous messages. In fact, instead of requiring extra pampering, Isa was taking her cues from Staysa and Natalie, clearly coveting the opportunity to be promoted to assistant on some future trip.

After lunch, the mostly empty bento boxes were collected and packed away, and Moriah sat all the kids down to discuss their morning's discoveries. Natalie and Staysa actually led the discussion, and Moriah felt a fresh glow of pride in them as they made sure every kid, even shy Takumi, had the opportunity to extol their finds.

"All right!" Moriah said when everyone had finished. "We have to head back in about three hours, and I'm sure *none* of you will be so tuckered out that you fall asleep on the flight home...however restful that might be for me and Rozie." That got the chorus of giggles and laughter she'd expected. "Before we leave, though, there are a couple of things that came up in your reports—like that branching canal you found, Beacon—that I want all of us to take a closer look at. And then we have to go over the bigger specimens you all marked and decide which of them we're taking home with us. So, find your buddies and make sure you've got all your gear!"

The Explorers bustled about, and she watched them with a glow of pride as they headed back out of the van into the breezy afternoon.

<They are not leaving after all,> Sharp Sniffer remarked as the two-leg younglings moved out across the meadow once more.

<Not yet, at any rate,> Half-Tail acknowledged. <But see how they are all staying together this time?>

<Why do you think they are doing that?> Belly Filler asked.

<I have been thinking about that,> Half-Tail said. <I believe that the older two-legs are taking the younglings as a group to see what each of the pairs of younglings may have discovered earlier. They are sharing their finds with one another.>

<That may be true,> Belly Filler said, <yet it does not explain why they are doing it.>

<You think not?> Half-Tail said. <Does it not seem to you that what we have seen them do is much like the fashion in which the People teach their kittens to become scouts or hunters? They went about in smaller groups, when they first arrived, and it seems obvious they were seeking specific things. Things their elders already knew, but which they were teaching the younglings to find and to understand. And now their elders are seeing to it that they share their success. They are mind-blind, after all. They cannot simply show one another the memories of what they have done.>

<That is a very good thought,> Deep Memory said

approvingly. <*And it may be that they have come so very far in order to find a place that was undisturbed by others of their kind.*>

<*It seemed to me,*> Ardent Claw put in, <*that they spent a great deal of time examining the lake-builders' dam and the ditches they used to drag branches and trees along. Is it not possible that they chose to come here because their elders already knew the lake-builders were gone, which would allow their younglings to poke about and explore without injuring—or provoking—the lake-builders?*>

<*That is very possible,*> Half-Tail replied, and tasted Ardent Claw's amusement as the older hunter tasted his own surprise that Ardent Claw had chosen to share an observation. But then Ardent Claw's mind-glow turned more serious.

<*If that is indeed one reason they have come so far, on what must have been a long journey even for one of their flying things, I think it speaks well for them,*> he said. <*I have tasted their mind-glows, and all of them—especially the younglings, but the older two-legs, as well—are full of happiness. They are enjoying themselves as they explore, and it would seem they have been careful to avoid injuring or frightening any of the lesser creatures. Those are not the actions of evildoers.*>

<*Indeed they are not,*> Deep Memory said approvingly. <*I could wish that at least one of the People who have bonded to two-legs were among them. If we could mind-speak with them, we would learn even more, and might be able to invite Death Fang's Bane and Shining Sunlight to visit Sparkling Rocks.*>

"Okay," Rozie said, three and a half hours later, as Staysa stowed the last knapsack in the Silver Cloud's cargo compartment and closed the hatch. "That's everything, right, Explorers?"

"Yes, sir!" half a dozen voices replied, and he nodded approvingly.

Natalie and Staysa, assisted by Isa, had made certain that every bit of refuse was collected and that every Explorer had his or her personal gear. They'd even collected his and Moriah's packs and loaded them before he and Moriah conducted their own final sweep. There'd been the inevitable irritating moments—more on the flight out than after they'd arrived, he thought—but overall, the kids had done really, really well. He hoped they understood how proud of them he was.

"All right! Everybody—back on the bus!"

The Explorers trooped aboard, with Natalie and Staysa counting them off. No one really thought they were likely to leave anyone behind, but it was important for the kids to understand that there were procedures and protocols for a reason. Moriah stood back and kept a careful eye on them, but, again, Natalie and Staysa did a perfect job, and she nodded in satisfaction as the passenger hatch closed, then started around to the still open flight deck hatch.

While the Explorers settled back into their seats, Rozie stood beside the pilot's seat on the flight deck and punched up the current weather conditions on the HUD. The predicted gusty winds had arrived a little later than Meteorology had projected, but they'd started making their presence felt in the last ninety minutes or so. Conditions were far from dangerous, but crosswinds could be tricky, and he wanted the latest data from both Planetary Meteorology and the Silver Cloud's onboard sensors before he lifted off.

Not as bad as I'd half-expected, he thought. *Not down here at ground level, anyway. Looks like windspeed's peaking at about thirty-two kilometers per hour, so—*

A sudden, far stronger gust roared through the tree branches. And Rozie's head snapped up as he heard a loud "Crack!" followed by a shrill, tearing sound. An instant later, something hit the air van's roof so hard he lost his footing and slammed headfirst into the console.

Moriah had just reached up for the flight deck steps' handrail when she heard the wind roar redouble. Then she heard the cracking sound and her head, too, snapped up. That was all the warning she had, and she flung herself frantically backward as an enormous crown oak branch—larger than many full-grown trees—came plummeting from above. It swung as it came and slammed into the Silver Cloud's nose like a hammer in the 1.35 G gravity. The van heaved as the blow drove it backward, landing skids digging deep trenches in the grass, and Moriah cried out as its rear end slid over the edge of the bluff. It careened down the slope, the enormous limb bouncing and then smashing down across its roof, until the last five meters of the van's fuselage slid into the lake.

She ran to the edge of the slope, then slithered down the bank, shouting Rozie's name. There was no answer, and her stomach knotted as she realized just how badly the limb had damaged the van's *front* end. The flight deck windscreen had been smashed in, and the Silver Cloud's crumpled nose was jammed in the angle of a fork in the massive crown oak limb. Stubby branches, each thicker than Moriah's torso, had driven into the ground on either side of it, and one of them blocked the flight deck hatch completely. She heaved desperately at the limb—not because she thought for a moment she could move it but because she had to try, anyway—but it refused to budge.

Natalie heard the same sound and just had time to grab the back of Beacon Drystan's seat before the limb struck. Then the entire world bucked impossibly and she went to her knees, just barely hanging onto the seat, as the van drove backward and sideways in a crashing, terrifying burst of sound. The internal grav plates went down, and she felt Sphinx's heavy gravity pulling at her, but she managed to stay upright until the rocking, heaving, *slithering* motion stopped.

She found herself kneeling in the central aisle, and realized the entire van was now angled sharply upward. It was also tipped at an angle of at least twenty-five degrees to starboard. All she could see through the windows on that side was grass and dirt, and she swallowed a gasp of surprise as she looked out through the portside windows.

For some weird reason, they were covered with green leaves.

Moriah made herself stop heaving uselessly at the tree trunk-thick limb blocking her out of the flight deck. She called Rozie's name again and fought through the tangle of whip-thin new spring branches until she could peer in through the flight deck's side window.

Her heart froze. Rozie lay on the deck, forehead bloody, and he wasn't moving. She called him again, louder, but he didn't stir.

The important thing, a preposterously level voice said in the back of her brain, *is to stay calm. If Rozie's . . . incapacitated, it's all on you to get the kids out of this.*

She drew a deep breath and raised her uni-link.

"Contact Ranger HQ," she ordered it.

"No satellite uplink," the uni-link replied calmly. "Next window in fifty-seven minutes."

Moriah's jaw clenched. Their uni-links had been tied into the van's com systems on the flight out. Satellite coverage this far out in the bush was sometimes sketchy, but the Silver Cloud's transmitter was more than powerful enough to reach Twin Forks or even Yawata Crossing, at least as long as they were in the air. But if the uni-link was reporting no satellite link, then it was trying to establish a transmission path of its own. And that meant the van's com had been disabled by the impact.

She tried not to think about what *other* systems might be down.

On the other hand, it was also Forestry Service issue, more capable and flexible than most civilian uni-links, so—

"Ping Rozie's stats," she told it.

"Pinging," it replied.

The two-second wait seemed an eternity, but then the display lit with Rozie's vital signs, and the breath she hadn't realized she was holding exhaled in a gush. His pulse was slow but steady; his respiration was fourteen breaths per minute; and his blood pressure was normal. That didn't guarantee he wasn't seriously injured, but...

She squared her shoulders and started feeling her way through the tangle of leaves and branches enshrouding the van.

No, that level voice said, *through the leaves and twigs. Boughs are the large branches growing out from the trunk; twigs are the smaller branches spreading out from the boughs.*

She paused and made herself draw a deep breath.

I wonder if I'm in shock? Thinking about proper terminology at a moment like this? What's wrong with me?

She shook her head and started squirming through the obstacle course once more. The thick limbs of the main bough were bad enough, but the interwoven, compacted-together thicket of smaller branches and leaves—many of them snapped and broken—were even worse.

Natalie pulled herself back to her feet.

A wild babble, half-excited and half-terrified, crashed over her. Most of the kids had been thrown from their seats by the impact, and at least one of the little girls was screaming again and again, her staccato gulps rising in near hysteria.

Natalie looked for the source, and her eyes widened as she realized the screamer was Larisa Zivonik. Larisa huddled against the forward bulkhead, as far forward as she could possibly get, crouching on her knees, arms folded across her head, and Natalie had never heard such terror in her life.

She started toward the younger girl, but Staysa was closer, and she used the seatbacks along the port side of the passenger compartment to haul herself up the steeply angled central aisle to Larisa. She reached her quickly and went to her own knees beside her, wrapping her arms around her. She hugged her little sister tightly, and Natalia heard her saying, "It's okay. This isn't like when Sumiko got killed. We've got a roof between us and the tree. You'll be all right, Larisa. It's going to be *all right*."

For a moment, Natalie's mind was blank, but then she remembered. Her family hadn't known the Zivoniks then, but Staysa had told her about Karl's girlfriend. His foster sister, raised with the family, and killed—

Killed saving Larisa's life. Crushed by the falling limb she'd just pushed Larisa out from under. Natalie closed her eyes. *No wonder the kid's losing it. It's a wonder she ever leaves the house, much less wants to be a ranger.*

Larisa's sobs softened, and Natalie shook herself.

"Explorers, get into the nearest seats!" she shouted in a pretty good imitation of Rozie's "command voice." She waved at the seats with her left hand, still gripping the one she'd used to pull herself upright with the other. "It doesn't need to be yours. Settle down. This isn't a drill. Settle down! I can't hear myself think."

Miraculously, the kids listened. Even Larisa scrubbed her forearm over her eyes, sat up straight, and then hauled herself back into her seat and gently shoved Staysa back toward the aisle.

Staysa started toward Natalie, but Natalie shook her head and pointed at the control box for the sliding bulkhead between the passenger compartment and the flight deck. She didn't say a word, but she didn't have to, and Staysa turned back toward it.

Moriah finally squirmed her way to one of the van windows. The Silver Cloud was tilted sharply enough she had to climb up on the port turbine air intake to reach it, but she managed and peered through the crystoplast.

The emergency lighting had switched on, which was a good thing. No light at all came in through the starboard windows, and the tangle through which she'd just fought covered the portside and blocked most of the light that should have come in through those windows, as well.

The emergency lighting wasn't what anyone would have called bright, but at least it let her see, and she exhaled in sharp relief as she saw Natalie standing in the aisle, obviously sorting out the smaller kids. Moriah couldn't get a hard count through the window, but it looked like all of them were in their seats or climbing back into them. From Natalie's body language, she doubted any of them were badly hurt, yet she felt an even sharper stab of relief as she saw Wade and J.C. sitting side-by-side.

She pressed closer to the crystoplast, trying to see out through the windows on the far side of the compartment, then muttered one of Rozie's drill sergeant words as she realized why no light was coming through them. The falling branch had hit at a sharp enough angle to roll the van sideways even as it drove it backward. It probably would have turned completely over if a solid slope hadn't stopped it. Instead of rolling all the way over, it was up on its side, leaning against the supporting hillside. And since both of the passenger compartment's hatches were on that side, they were blocked.

Well, if there's not a door, we'll just have to make *one,* she told herself, and reached for the SFS-issue bush knife on her equipment belt.

It wasn't there.

She turned her head, looking down in shock. Then she remembered. Staysa had borrowed it to trim out some of the tree specimens Archie Pheriss and Wade had marked. When she'd finished with it, she'd tucked it in her knapsack for safekeeping until she could get it back to Moriah.

And like the conscientious kid she is, she packed her knapsack in the cargo compartment with everybody else's gear.

Where I can't possibly get at it.

She bit her lip, trying not to swear out loud. Rozie had his bush knife on his belt, right where it belonged, and she couldn't get to *it,* either.

Not even the air van's tough composites could have stood up to the bush knife's fifty-centimeter blade. With it, she could have cut her way in—and the kids' way out—easily. *Without it . . .*

✦   ✦   ✦

"Okay," Natalie continued in the same firm tone. "Anyone hurt?"

Several murmurs reported bruises, bumps, and a couple of bloody noses. Then—

"I landed on my arm," Beacon Drystan said in a carefully controlled voice. "It doesn't look right. And it's starting to hurt. A lot."

Isa Manning climbed back out of her seat, crossed the aisle, and knelt beside him, clinging to his seat arm for balance. She looked at his arm carefully, then at Natalie.

"I just got my First Aid badge, so I'm not sure. But I think his arm's broken. Or maybe his shoulder's dislocated."

"Jessica's studying to be a doctor." There was no hint of his usual playfulness in Archie Pheriss's voice. "She's been teaching Melanie-Anne and me first aid. We know how to set bones."

Natalie bit her lip, then nodded.

"Okay," she said. "Pheriss twins on Beacon's arm. Isa, let's put that First Aid badge to work. Can you take a look at the other bumps and bruises?"

"Sure!" Isa said in a deliberately cheerful voice. "Who's first?"

Moriah suppressed an urge to punch the side of the van in frustration. The last thing she needed to do was break a hand! So instead of that, she inhaled deeply and keyed her uni-link again.

Natalie looked down as her uni-link pinged. The ID flashed, and a huge spasm of relief ripped through her. All she could see looking through the crystoplast bulkhead into the flight deck was Rozie, lying terrifyingly still. There'd been no sign of Moriah at all.

Now she tapped an acceptance.

"Natalie!" Moriah's voice said.

"Moriah! Where are you?"

"Look through the third window, portside."

Natalie's head snapped around, and her eyes went wide as she saw Moriah peering in through it.

"Hi, kiddo," Moriah said. "Looks like you're doing great in there!"

"I'm trying, anyway." Natalie heard the slight quaver in her own voice. The one she'd managed to keep out of it when she hadn't known if either Moriah or Rozie were even still alive. She cleared her throat. "Staysa's been a big help, and the other kids are being just super."

"I figured that," Moriah said, then paused. "Can you tell me how Rozie's doing?"

"No," Natalie turned toward the window, hiding her face from the other kids, and spoke softly. "The bulkhead was closed when whatever it was hit us. We can't get it open. Staysa tried. I think all the power's down except the emergency lighting, and the manual override's on the other side of the wall."

"Okay. Understood." Moriah kept her own voice calm and level. It was one of the hardest things she'd ever done in her life. "What about the other kids. Injuries?"

"We think Beacon may have a broken arm. Archie and Melanie-Anne say Jessica's taught them how to set bones. They're working on that now. I don't think we've got anything else that bad. Lots of bruises, a few bloody noses, that kind of stuff."

"Good! Put me on speaker."

Natalie tapped the uni-link. Its speaker was tiny compared to a handheld or console com, but it was big enough everyone could hear Moriah's voice.

"Okay, Explorers," she said, smiling at them through the window, "we're in a bit of a mess, but we're Explorers, and Explorers know how to handle things, right?"

"Right!" several of the kids replied, and she smiled more broadly at them.

"You guys probably can't see it from in there, but what happened is that we got a sudden wind gust, a lot stronger than any of the others, and it blew a crown oak branch loose. It's a big one, at least forty meters long and with a bunch of side branches, and it landed on the van. That's what knocked it all sideways and backward. Unfortunately, it also rolled the van up on its side, so the normal exits are blocked. I can't tell from here whether the roof hatch is blocked. If it isn't, we can get all of you out that way. But Natalie says the power's down. That means you'll have to open it manually, so I need somebody to check and see whether or not you can. Daire, you're a nimble one. Think you could check it out for us?"

Daire Yazzie was as agile as her older sister, Eldora, who'd burst onto the scene as an inter-planetary dance sensation last year. But Daire's chosen sport was gymnastics, and she gave Moriah a brisk nod that didn't quite hide how scared she was, then turned to Cameron Alba, who was seated across the aisle.

"Spot me."

Cameron had been very proud that the excursion van had been his mother's contribution to the day's outing. When they'd taken turns using the hatch for outside observation, he'd even been a bit bossy. Now he just looked tightlipped and pale, but he nodded and leaned back against the starboard bulkhead, reaching up to steady Daire as she climbed onto his seat back. Without the van's power systems, the only way to open the hatch was with the manual crank in the van's roof.

She balanced on the back of his seat and tugged at the release.

"I've got it," she said, and pulled harder.

The crank turned and the hatch began to move. A spontaneous cheer filled the compartment, but stilled instantly when she stopped cranking.

"What is it?" Moriah asked over Natalie's uni-link.

"It's moving...sort of," Daire said. "But there's a bunch of branches on top of it. And one really big one that crosses at an angle."

"Do you think it'll open all the way?" Moriah asked in a deliberately calm voice.

"It might—probably," Daire replied. "But there's already branches and leaves and stuff poking in through as far as I've already opened it. If I open it the rest of the way, I think they'll all push into the van. And even if they don't, there's no way we could squeeze out of it through all that stuff."

"Okay. At least we know," Moriah said. "Climb down now, okay?"

Daire climbed down, and Moriah drew a deep breath.

"That's not so good, guys," she told the kids calmly. The temptation to tell them everything was fine was almost overwhelming, but the last thing they needed was for the Explorers to think she was fibbing to them. "But, worst-case, we're just stuck here until somebody comes to get us out. I'm sure the van's crash beacon triggered when the limb hit us, so Chief Shelton and the other rangers know we're down and where we are. Their cruisers are a lot faster than the van, so they'll be here soon. Okay?"

A chorus of "yes ma'ams" answered her, but then Rysard Brooks waved a hand from his seat near the rear of the van.

"Yes, Rysard?" Natalie said.

"There's water seeping in back here."

Moriah's stomach tightened.

"Rysard," she said, keeping her voice as level as if this were just another routine quiz, "can you tell where the water's coming from? Did the van's water tank get ruptured, or the sewage line?"

"No, ma'am," Rysard replied promptly, reassured by her tone. "I'm pretty sure the water's from outside the van. It's *really* cold. And there's a chunk of wood poking through the side back here. It's pointy, like when the near-beavers gnaw a tree to cut it down. The water's coming from there. It's almost over the tops of my boots now."

"Put your feet up on your seat," Natalie said. Then, "How far has the water spread?"

Wade, whose seat was near the front, where his parents could have reined him in if needed, waved his hand.

"It's wet up here. Like one of the dogs peed."

"More like one of the horses," J.C. said from a few rows back. "*All* the horses."

Natalie was wise enough to recognize tasteless humor as bravado, and only nodded, then looked at Moriah.

"Okay," Moriah said, "let's get everybody moved toward the front of the compartment and out of the water."

"You heard her, Explorers!" Natalie said. "Come on— we don't want any wet feet, do we?"

More than one of the kids laughed. They were a bit nervous, those laughs, and Moriah smiled encouragingly through the window even as her heart turned into a lump of ice.

It was spring, but the lowest water temperatures occurred in early spring, not winter, and this was Sphinx. They might be far enough into spring that the water in the lake they'd come to visit wasn't frozen, but its temperature was no more than five or six degrees *above* freezing, and that made hypothermia a real and deadly threat. The kids' uniforms would offer some thermal protection, but not enough. If the compartment flooded badly enough to put them all in the water, even an adult would begin losing consciousness in as little as thirty to sixty minutes. Their survival time would be no more than one to three hours, and they were fifteen hundred kilometers from the nearest SFS base. Distances like that were almost routine on a planet with so few human inhabitants and a tech base that included counter-grav. But that meant minimum flight time for Search and Rescue was over ninety minutes. Probably closer to two hours.

And she couldn't be *positive* the crash beacon really had activated when the branch hit. It would be another—she checked the time—thirty-one minutes before she could confirm that with her uni-link, which could mean adding another half hour to her worst-case time estimate.

Worse yet, the slope under the van was steep, and a third of it of its fuselage was already submerged, and she found herself praying that the wreckage on top of it was massive enough to pin it firmly in place. Because if it wasn't, if enough water flowed into it, if it got heavy enough to start slipping even deeper when she couldn't get the kids—*her* kids, *all* of her kids, not just Wade and J.C.—out...

Fear hammered through her, and she wondered how long it would really take the SFS rescue teams to reach them.

43

STEPHANIE'S HEAD POPPED UP AS THE URGENT ATTEN-
tion signal warbled. It was the first time she'd ever heard
it outside a training exercise, and her eyes snapped to
the HUD as the lurid emergency message icon pulsed.

"Karl!" she shouted through the cruiser's open window even as her fingers stabbed to accept the message.

He was already turning, and she realized her uni-link
had vibrated perhaps half a second after the cruiser's
audible signal. His must have done the same, but that
meant—

"All units, all units. Orbital Surveillance reports
emergency crash beacon."

GPS coordinates—40° 56' 9.2988" N and 74° 9' 54.7992"
W—flashed in the HUD as the dispatcher's voice rolled
out of the speaker with flat, calm, clearly enunciated
discipline. "Beacon ID Foxtrot-William-Zero-Three-Niner.
No—repeat, no—further contact with the vehicle. Search
and Rescue is outbound. ETA ninety-seven minutes. Any

unit in range, respond immediately. Repeat. All units, all units. Orbital Surveillance reports—"

Stephanie's face went white as the GPS coordinates came up in the HUD's navigation window and she recognized the beacon ID.

Lionheart and Survivor flashed ahead of Karl, leaping into the cruiser before he could fling himself into the pilot's seat. Stephanie hit the button to close the canopy while he brought the counter-grav and turbines online.

"That's—" she started.

"I know," Karl replied, never looking away from his instruments as the turbines spun up and the LEDs turned green. "Rozie and Moriah."

"And the kids." Stephanie's voice was soft, her eyes dark with worry.

"We're almost two hours out, even at max," Karl said. "But it sounds like they need all the help they can get."

He pulled back on the control column, and the cruiser shot upward like a homesick meteor.

❖   ❖   ❖

<*Are the two-legs all right?*> Belly Filler's mind-voice was taut.

<*I do not know,*> Half-Tail replied, and knew Belly Filler tasted the worry in his own mind-glow.

Neither he nor any of the other watching People had been concerned when the day became increasingly windy. That was not at all uncommon at this season, and all of the watchers were perched in the net-wood, safely across the lake builders' lake from any of the taller trees. None of them had anticipated that sudden, much stronger burst of wind, however, and they had been as surprised as the two-legs must have been when it ripped away the enormous golden-leaf branch and dropped it directly onto the flying thing.

Despite that, Half-Tail hadn't been immediately concerned. Hadn't they all seen the wonders of the two-leg made things in the memory songs? Some of their flying things were powerful enough to push their way right up into and through the sky! He would not have believed that was possible, but memory songs did not lie. Both Climbs Quickly and Keen Eyes had shared the memory of flight aboard those huge flying things, as well as of the places where they nested in the blackness beyond the sky.

Although all of the watching People were startled when the golden-leaf broke, they were far enough away that only a few leaves sprinkled across them.

<The fires last fire season and the weight of snow and ice must have weakened that golden-leaf,> Sharp Sniffer commented, gazing down at the broad tangle of limbs, branches, and budding leaves. <The lake builders will be sorry to have missed such a feast!>

<I am more concerned about the two-legs,> Belly Filler said. <I hope the younglings were not too frightened.>

<As do I,> Half-Tail agreed, crouching on the net-wood branch as he stared at the flying thing, waiting for it to shake off the branch and rise into the sky.

But it did not. It simply sat there, partly buried in the lake, and worry flowed through him as it failed to burst upward.

<Come,> he invited Belly Filler and Sharp Sniffer. <The flying thing is too far away for us to taste their mind-glows from here. Let us get closer!>

He raced along the net-wood to the brink of the stream that fed the lake, then launched himself across the water to the nearest net-wood on the opposite bank. Probably, he told himself, Sparkling Rocks Clan would simply be treated to a closer view of the flying thing as it pulled itself out of the mud and water and pushed aloft, but—

<*The two-legs' flying things do not always deal well with wet and mud,*> he reminded the others. <*Remember how the marsh where Damp Ground Clan lives swallowed a flying thing that came to roost there? Perhaps some of their breed do not know how to swim.*>

<*There is something wrong about how that flying thing is sitting.*> Sharp Sniffer's mind-glow shared Half-Tail's concern. <*I think it was injured by the falling branch.*>

<*I think the two-legs agree with you,*> Half-Tail said grimly as they came within reach of the two-legs' mind-glows and he tasted the fear within them.

Moriah pressed against the window, keeping her expression and her tone calm even as she cursed the crystoplast that separated her from her kids. The only good news was that her uni-link had acquired one of the com sats and she knew the crash beacon had, indeed, triggered when the branch hit. The bad news was that SAR was still an hour out and almost half the passenger compartment was already flooded with icy water. The kids had climbed onto the seat backs, and if the water got higher, the seat cushion floats would at least keep their heads above water. But that wouldn't do anything about the hypothermia, and little kids had very little body mass. They'd feel the effect much more quickly than adults would. They'd grow drowsy, slip silently beneath the waters...and drown.

Her mind filled with the image of Wade tumbling off his perch, J.C. leaping to save him. Both her boys floundering as the cold slowed their movements. As the water turned their clothing to lead and dragged them under....

Half-Tail paused on the net-wood branch, no more
than three or four hands of a Person's length from the
broken golden-leaf, and the single adult two-leg's despair
flowed through him. He could not hear her mind-voice
as he could have heard the mind-voice of another Person,
but he recognized the mind-glow of a mother and tasted
her terror—not for herself, but for the younglings trapped
inside the flying thing—only too clearly.

And then he realized that the flying thing was filling with water. The openings in its side were pressed
against the slope, blocked by solid earth and stone, and
the opening at its top was blocked where the golden-leaf
branch lay tangled across it.

<*The two-leg younglings cannot get out. They will
drown like grass runners in a flooded burrow!*> he said.
<*We must help them!*>

<*Can we?*> Belly Filler asked anxiously. <*The branch is
very large. I fear not even our entire clan could move it!*>

<*Perhaps we need not move it,*> Sharp Sniffer replied
with what might be more confidence than was mer-
ited. <*Let us look more closely. If the large branch is
not holding the opening shut, perhaps we could clear
away enough of the smaller branches for a youngling to
squeeze through.*>

More of the watching People raced to join the front-
runners as they heard Half-Tail, Belly Filler, and Sharp
Sniffer. And Sensitive Whiskers' mind-voice flowed into
Half-Tail's mind. It was full of fear, but this time not
for him.

<*Save the little ones!*> she urged, and the passion of
her mind-glow made him somehow stronger. <*Even Ardent
Claw is running to join you. Hurry! Water is no kinder
than fire, only its opposite. Hurry, Half-Tail!*>

✧   ✧   ✧

Something thumped softly on the Silver Cloud's roof.

That was all she needed, Moriah thought bitterly—more stray bits of tree limb falling onto the van. Hadn't the tree done damage enough already? Why—

"It's a treecat!"

It was J.C.'s voice, over her uni-link, and Moriah's eyes widened.

"It's more treecats!" her son continued. "They're jumping onto the roof!"

Moriah looked up in an agony of disbelief and hope she dared not embrace. She could see very little through the dense tangle of branches and leaves, but then something wove its way through that tangle with incredible speed.

And then she heard more thumps. Dozens of them, and heard the treecats racing through the broken foliage.

"I don't believe this!" Natalie said over the uni-link.

"What?" Moriah asked tautly.

"The 'cats are cutting away the branches—the branches over the roof hatch!"

"What?" Moriah repeated.

"They're using their teeth and their claws to cut away the branches." Natalie spoke each word carefully as if to make sure Moriah understood them. "It's like they understand why we can't get out!"

"Spot me, Cameron!" Daire said, climbing back onto a seatback and reaching for the crank. "I can't open it yet, but—"

Someone squealed in excitement, the last sound in the world Moriah would have expected to hear.

"I got an image of one of the treecats!" Vernon Simpson called out. "Natalie's right. It's using its claws to cut the littler branches!"

His excitement was infectious. Moriah doubted any of the kids had forgotten the rising water, but for now they were far more interested in seeing who could record the best images of the treecat rescue operation. She leaned her face against the window, tears stinging her eyes, as she realized that kids really were far more resilient than adults gave credit for.

Or maybe, she thought, *they're just more trusting.*

The tangle of branches and leaves was a massive barrier, but the People knew that even the biggest death fang could be cut down to size by many claws. Their claws might not be as perfectly adapted for cutting wood as a lake builder's teeth, but they had ample experience trimming branches to make their nests. The task they faced now was much more dangerous than any nest building, of course. Many of the branches blocking the opening were bent—compressed under pressure, not broken—and when they were cut, when the pressure was released, they could strike a Person with bone-breaking force.

But this was no time to worry about that, and they worked hard, all too aware of the two-leg younglings huddled atop the platforms within the flying thing, trying to keep clear of the rising water.

"I think I can open it now!" Daire announced.

Natalie looked through the window at Moriah, who nodded firmly to her.

"Hang on a minute," she said. Then, "All the rest of you, stay as far back against the bulkheads as you can in case stuff falls through. Cameron, you be sure to hang onto Daire. We don't want her knocked into the water if something falls on her!"

"Yes, ma'am!"

"Everybody ready?"

A chorus of "yes, ma'ams" came back to her, and she nodded.

"All right, Daire."

<It is opening!> Ardent Claw cried.

The elderly hunter had forgotten his reluctance, and his claws and true-hands were slick with sap from the branches he had slashed away. Now triumph filled his mind-glow, and he grabbed a severed branch in true-hands and hand-feet, dragging it back as it tried to fall through the opening onto the youngling below.

And then the transparent floor which had closed the opening slid aside and a slender two-leg youngling hooked its arms over the edge of the roof opening and pulled itself through the space where the People had cleared away the branches. Its eyes were wide as it stared down at them, and it made a loud sound while delight filled its mind-glow. But then it turned back, hooked its arms under the branch the People were too small to move, and strained to lift it.

It couldn't, but it went back to its knees in the cleared space and made mouth noises to the other two-legs.

"There's not enough room for the bigger kids to get through," Daire said. "I don't think the 'cats can cut away enough stuff to make it big enough, either. And I can't move this branch. It's longer than the van and almost as big around as *I* am!"

"That's okay," Moriah said over the uni-link. "Explorers, I want you to pass your counter-gravs up to Daire, one at a time. And Daire, I want you to strap them around the limb. Get as many of them onto it as you can, and spread them along as much of its length as you can reach. Larisa, you're about the same size as Daire.

Do you think you could climb up there to help her if Natalie and Staysa boost you?"

"Sure."

The one-word answer sounded a bit drawn out and dubious, but Larisa climbed up onto the same seatback. Daire squatted on the roof, reaching down to take both of the other girl's hands while Natalie, Staysa, and Archie Pheriss boosted her from below. She squirmed through the opening, and Natalie started passing up counter-grav backpacks.

Half-Tail and the other People jumped down from the flying thing as the two-leg younglings began attaching made things to the limb. The People had no idea what *these* made things were supposed to accomplish, but the two-leg mind-glows had changed enormously when the first youngling emerged from the flying thing. There was still worry, especially in the mind-glow of the single adult two-leg outside the flying thing, but there was also hope, a sense of purpose, and a rising confidence as more of the made things were attached.

"That's all we can reach to fasten, Moriah," Daire announced, and Moriah nodded. Thirteen personal counter-gravs were strapped around the branch. She only hoped it was enough.

"All right," she said. "Start turning them on, and set them on maximum lift."

"Yes, ma'am."

Nothing happened, at first, but then, as Daire and Larisa activated more and more of the counter-gravs, the limb twitched. Then, slowly—ever so slowly—it rose until it hovered a handful of centimeters above the van.

"Now see if you can push it out of the way. Be careful! Don't get caught in the branches!"

❖   ❖   ❖

<If I did not see it, I would not believe it!>

Ardent Claw's mind-glow was awed as the younglings, barely removed from kittenhood, did something, one by one, to the made things they had fastened to the limb. For several breaths, nothing had happened, but now the limb had risen into the air! Not very far, but enough for the People to see a clear space between it and the roof of the flying thing.

The younglings turned their backs to it, bracing their feet on the edge of the opening in the flying thing's roof, pushing as hard as they could. But too many other branches projected downward, dragging across the earth. The limb quivered, but it did not move aside.

<They are not strong enough to move it,> Ardent Claw said. <We must help!>

<We cannot move it any more than they can!> one of the clan's other hunters said.

<We cannot move it, and they cannot move it,> Ardent Claw replied. <Not alone. But sometimes many can do what one—or only a few—cannot.>

The old hunter leapt back up onto the flying thing's roof and scampered to the side of the first youngling. It—no, *she*, he decided—looked down at him, and he patted her leg, then squirmed through the branches until he could add his strength to hers.

Half-Tail glanced at Belly Filler, and they went leaping after him.

❖   ❖   ❖

Daire Yazzie panted as she pushed with all her strength against the limb. She had to move it—she *had* to! Yet push as hard as she could, it refused to budge.

Despair flickered, but then she saw a flicker of cream and gray. A treecat appeared beside her. She looked down at it in disbelief, and it sat up to pat her knee gently, then wiggled around until it could reach the limb, as well.

Tears stung her eyes as that single, tiny helper pushed against the massive branch. Still it refused to move, but then there was another flicker of gray fur. And another. A flicker that turned into a tide, flowing back up onto the van, lapping about her and Larisa. Treecats dug their claws into the luggage tiedowns on the van's sharply angled roof and into the channels designed to drain rainwater from it, and braced themselves, quivering as they heaved at the limb with all their strength. Dozens of them—scores! They were *everywhere*, bleeking, pushing, fighting....

"It's moving!" Larisa cried. *"It's moving!"*

Half-Tail and the other People flowed back up into the net-wood and watched as the two younglings atop the flying thing reached down to help other younglings climb up and out. They wiggled through the branches still wrapped around the flying thing, and the adult two-leg's mind-glow was a firestorm of joy as it wrapped its arms around them.

<*This is good,*> Half-Tail told Ardent Claw, twitching his truncated tail in satisfaction as some of the younglings turned away from the flying thing, and raised other made things in their hands. He thought they were making images.

<*Well,*> Ardent Claw said, pretending his grumpiness even though he knew Half-Tail tasted better from his mind-glow, <*perhaps this will at least bring Death Fang's Bane and Climbs Quickly for a visit and we can finally try clusterstalk for ourselves.*>

44

SEARCH AND RESCUE ARRIVED FORTY MINUTES LATER, and unlike Moriah, they came equipped with their bush knives, not to mention heavy-duty counter-grav lifts and presser jacks. It took them very little time to clear the fallen timber from the crushed van, then tow it up out of the lake.

They got Rozie out of the flight deck even before the debris was fully cleared and loaded him into an ambulance.

"I think he's going to be fine," the senior medic told Moriah. "There's a fine line skull fracture, and I expect he'll have a concussion, but there's no sign of any kind of serious brain bleed. All the same, I think we better get him back to the hospital as quickly as we can."

"I can't argue with that," Moriah said thankfully, bending to plant a kiss on her husband's forehead. "Any of the kids banged up badly?"

"I think we have one broken arm. A couple of my kids—Jessica Pheriss's sibs—splinted it. Aside from that, mostly bruises and a couple of bloody noses."

"We don't have lift for all of them, but we can take the broken arm."

"Tina Alba's on her way out with another van." Moriah smiled crookedly. "I'm pretty sure she's pushing it a lot faster than we did on the way out. Don't worry, we'll get all the kids home."

"Good. Let us take a look at them, make sure there isn't any serious damage you might've missed, and then we'll get out of here." He shook his head. "Quite an adventure your kids had!"

"Oh, yeah. You might say that." Moriah laughed. "So did I!"

Stephanie and Karl arrived fifteen minutes after the ambulance had departed with Rozie and Beacon Drystan to find the Explorers full of their adventure and eager to describe exactly what had happened.

The treecats had melted away when the SFS team arrived, but the Explorers had captured ample images to show they'd been there, and Lionheart and Survivor headed for the picketwood with a purposeful air. Stephanie watched them go, then turned back to Moriah.

"—and then they all got together and *pushed*," Daire Yazzie said. "It was the most *amazing* thing, Stephanie! It was like they understood exactly what we were trying to do, and they *helped* us!"

"I don't doubt that for a moment," Stephanie said, looking across at Karl. He was busy hugging both of his sisters, but he looked up, met her eyes, and shrugged wryly. "It's like I've been telling people ever since Lionheart saved my skin. Treecats are good people."

"Yes, they are," Moriah agreed. "And a lot smarter than idiots like Jordan Franchitti have been saying they are."

Stephanie nodded. It was the only thing she could do, and the 'cats *deserved* the credit for what they'd done. But she already knew where this had to lead.

<You are Climbs Quickly of Bright Water?>

<Yes, and this is my friend and clan-brother, Keen Eyes,> Climbs Quickly replied as a pair of hunters greeted them in the net-wood.

<I am Half-Tail of Sparkling Rocks Clan, and this is Ardent Claw. We did not expect any of this.>

Climbs Quickly bleeked a soft laugh at the wry amusement in Half-Tail's mind-glow.

<Interesting things happen when two-legs are involved,> he replied. *<But tell me, am I correct in believing you rescued the two-leg kittens?>*

<That is probably fair,> Ardent Claw said judiciously. *<They were very brave, though, the younglings. And they never stopped trying to rescue themselves.>*

<That, too, is very like the two-legs, especially those like my own Death Fang's Bane. I think you will find they are most grateful for your aid.>

<We could not simply stand by and watch them drown,> Half-Tail said. *<My mate, Sensitive Whiskers, would never have forgiven me!>*

<And we would not have forgiven ourselves,> Ardent Claw said. He met Climbs Quickly's and Keen Eyes' eyes steadily. *<I am one who has had many reservations about the two-legs. But these two-legs have done much to change my mind.>*

<Indeed,> a distant mind-voice said. *<I am Deep Memory, and I have met with the elders while all of this was happening. Climbs Quickly, we would be most honored if you can convince Death Fang's Bane and Shining Sunlight to visit us at Sparkling Rock.>*

<*I think you may be sure they will do so in the very near future,*> Climbs Quickly assured her.

<*Good!*> Deep Memory said. <*We will look forward to meeting them.*>

<*And—*> Ardent Claw added slyly <*to sampling cluster-stalk, as well!*>

❖   ❖   ❖

"Your mom's about five minutes out, Cameron," Moriah announced. "Let's start getting our gear out."

The Explorers headed back to the crushed and crumpled Silver Cloud. Miraculously, the cargo compartment hadn't leaked a drop, and they unloaded their knapsacks and the specimens they'd already collected. While the other Explorers did that, Isa Manning and Katarzyna Brooks teamed up to collect samples of the smaller branches the treecats had cut away. They found a carry net one of the rescuers had lost in the confusion, as well, but instead of adding it to their collection, they carefully left it hanging from a picketwood branch where its owner could find it.

By the time Cameron's mother landed the larger, faster StratoCruiser van, the Explorers were more than ready to head homeward. The original plan had been for a leisurely flight back, but given how the day had gone, everyone was happy to take a more direct route. Especially when they were promised ice cream at the Red Letter Café when they got home. Moriah and Tina took turns riding with the passengers just in case, but the kids were even more resilient than Moriah had thought. Natalie and Staysa organized a word game for the older littles; Archie, Melanie-Anne, Larisa, and Daire went into a huddle around their hand-helds, studying the imagery they'd captured; and the only indication Wade gave that the day had been anything but a grand adventure was his agreement to sit in his mom's lap . . . where he promptly fell asleep.

We survived, she thought, still a bit shocky with relief. *I don't think we could have managed on our own. Not this time. The treecats saved us, complete strangers who they would've had every reason to view as invaders. Or as idiots getting what we deserved.*

"That was awesome, wasn't it, Mom?" J.C. said, looking up from a review of his own collection of images. "Do we still get our trip badge even if we didn't come home exactly the way we planned?"

Moriah laughed.

"Oh, I think so. I definitely think you *all* earned your badges."

The StratoCruiser was faster than the Silver Cloud had been, but it was still slower than an SFS cruiser, and Stephanie and Karl beat the Explorers back to Twin Forks quite handily.

By the time they landed at the Forestry Service headquarters, everyone knew the Explorers were all right. Despite that, a rather large group had assembled, anxiously awaiting the expedition's return. There were parents and siblings, family friends, and quite a lot of people who'd simply heard that something was up and come to find out what.

Nosey and Trudy were there, although Dulcinea had stayed home with the kittens, and Nosey was working directly with Chief Shelton to quell the rumors. But there was one rumor, soon confirmed as fact, that had everyone present murmuring. Treecats—wild treecats, who'd never had any contact with humans before—had come out of the forest and been instrumental in saving the trapped children.

Twin Forks was about the most treecat-sophisticated community on Sphinx, given that just about all the adoptees lived in the vicinity, but this news stunned even the Twin Forkers. As it happened, most of the treecat adoptees—and, of course, their treecats, aside from Dulcinea—were present. In addition to Nosey, standing up on a raised platform, answering questions, Jessica, Karl, and Cordelia all had siblings on the trip, and Stephanie was with Karl.

And then there was Duncan, standing beside Stephanie, Karl, and Stephanie's parents.

Down in front, Nosey was manipulating a holo projection from the SFS's preliminary report on the accident.

"The accident seems to have been due to a mixture of circumstances," he said, flipping through the imagery as he spoke. "As you can see, the crown oak limb walloped the van hard enough for it to slide down the bluff into the lake. That's partly because the near-beavers had left several slides and one silted-up canal on the slope. The slides helped carry the van down into an area where a bunch of sharp logs from the dam were wedged in the mud. You can see them here."

He flipped to another holo, and there were murmurs of horrified fascination.

"This hole"—he zoomed in on a hole punched through the side of the crumpled fuselage—"is from the crown oak. Apparently, part of a branch snapped off, and then the van came down on top of it. But *these* holes"—he shifted to a different view, looking up the slope at the rear of the van—"are from the logs in the lake. The one in the side was only the most visible. It looks like most of the water actually came in here. And—"

"Look!" someone shouted. "There in the background—in the picketwood. If you look close, you can see the treecats still watching! I bet they're waiting to see if the humans need any more rescuing."

Stephanie felt Karl's arm around her and looked up at Duncan.

"Well, Peanut," her cousin said with a crooked smile, "looks like we've got our work cut out for us. But I have to say, this is going to make real problems for the 'treecats are only dumb animals' crowd."

"I know," Stephanie said, thrilled and yet vaguely terrified, wondering what this would mean for the tree-cats. One thing was certain—the secret she'd guarded so carefully since she was eleven was out now. "And that worries me."

"That's because you're smart," Duncan told her, ruffling her curly hair the way he'd done when she was much younger. "But no one can deny they're sapient. Not now. Or that you Sphinxians share your world with another intelligent species."

"Maybe we'd better think of it the other way around," Stephanie said. "The treecats share their world with us."

"Yes, they do," Duncan said, and Stephanie reached up to where Lionheart perched on her back, with his single true-hand on her shoulder. She touched his ears, and he pressed his head against her.

"Bleek," he commented.

"Bleek yourself," she said.